TAKAHASHI

TOMLIN TAKAHASHI DUET BOOK #2

THE CAÑON SERIES BOOK #2

GIGI MEIER

Cover Design by Just write. Creations

Editing by Robyne Hunt

Author Photograph by Tara L. Grundemeier

ISBN: 979-8-9877336-2-2 (e)

ISBN: 979-8-9877336-3-9 (pb)

GiGi Meier Media LLC

DEDICATION

And to those who tear down the fortress and heal it.

TAKAHASHI

1

LOS ANGELES

"Get off your knees, Dani."

"Shut up and enjoy the view."

He should. This will be the last time I ever do this. And easy for him to say. He didn't almost die in that tin tube floating in the air over here. If I want to take a moment to thank God that we arrived on the concrete floor in LAX, then I will.

He wasn't the one being jostled around, vomiting his guts out in that coffin-sized bathroom. No, Mr. I-travel-the-world was lounging, reading a book in first class like it was no big deal through the turbulence.

That smug bastard acted like it didn't even bother him, while I was white-knuckling my seat. And the nausea, well, I never sweated so much trying to hold it in since they kept that damn seatbelt sign on the whole fucking time.

I twist my tongue. The piercing clacks against the top of my teeth, desperately needing mouthwash. So much for giving up cussing. That fucking plane ride ruined it.

"That's enough. Now come on so we can collect our baggage and meet the driver."

His calloused palm cups my elbow. If it weren't for needing to pee and hoping I don't shit myself, I would sit here longer. Not to mention, I'll need to burn my shorts from sitting on this disease-infected airport floor.

"You're either going to have to slip my ass a sedative for that return flight home or we're renting a car and you're driving me all the way back to Colorado," I complain, clutching the chrome handle of the row of adjoined seats where a teenager has been watching me the whole time.

"What are you looking at, huh?"

Tomlin shakes his head at the kid and flashes me an annoyed look.

"That's what humbles you? A little turbulence?"

Standing beside him, I sway a little. I don't know if it's my stomach still doing flips or losing its insides for the last half hour.

"A little? That plane was about to fall out of the sky, and you know it."

He chuckles, and it's the worst sound in the world.

"I've experienced worse. Now let's go. It's a walk to baggage claim where we are meeting him."

"I don't feel so good."

His hand slides down my clammy skin to hold my hand. The warmth of his rough fingers seeps into mine. I drop my head and lean it into his chest to peer at his dress shoes. Normally I'd never do this, but the dizziness makes me feel like shit. I know we are in a hurry, but I need a few more seconds for the wave of bile collecting in my throat to go down.

"Did you get up too fast?"

His deep voice rumbles against my head and his muscular arm sits atop my shoulders to comfort me. His clean, woodsy fragrance wraps around me and it's one of many reasons I freaking love this guy.

"Is this a new cologne?" I mumble against the crisply pressed dress shirt digging into my forehead.

Even on vacation, he's all dolled up. I swear he makes all his clothes look good. Especially those damn gray sweatpants he taunted me with last night when he lent me a suitcase.

"I don't think so. I have dozens."

Of course, he does.

This scent differs from the one he wore the night he held me and sat in my pain. He said he pulled a Dani, and I needed to pull a Tomlin. That sealed the deal. He captured my heart without even knowing it.

The last forty-eight hours have been a blur. He helped me drop off Anna at Eli's house and waited while Eli made the dog introductions. Apparently, you can't just throw them all together and hope for the best.

We visited Isla, who made me promise to buy her a California shirt to go with the Colorado shirt Hamilton bought her at the truck stop. I'm beginning to think she's starting a collection of state-themed T-shirts.

Tomlin even ran me by Hamilton's station and lingered in the lobby while they sized each other up. Hamilton assured me that he'll continue checking on Isla while I'm gone and that things were progressing at that stupid snail's pace in her case.

Tomlin offered some fancy family law attorney in Denver, but Hamilton grumbled he had it covered. I feel like they know each other somehow, but neither will tell me.

"I need to pee."

I lift my head, leaning against his arm to gaze into his warm chocolate eyes. His face softens, a half-smile hanging to one side of his lips when he suddenly tugs on my low ponytail.

"How do you have anything left in there? You were in the bathroom for over thirty minutes. Didn't you hear the attendant knocking?"

"Yeah, but I wasn't going to vomit or have the shits sitting next to you, so fuck them."

"Charming."

He squeezes my hand, conveying his words in touch. Our proximity to each other changed that night. We're standing closer, instigating small touches, and talking entirely too close for business partners.

Whatever happens on this trip happens. I won't initiate. I don't want to be rejected again. But if he leans in and starts something, I'm not stopping, no matter what he says.

"There's a bathroom further ahead on the right."

"Okay."

His arm slides off my shoulder to reposition his carry-on strapped across his body before leading us into the stream of people. His fingers tighten over mine as we weave through the crowd of wayward travelers.

This place is insane. The sheer amount of people is giving me anxiety. Combined with my nausea, I want to throw up or lie down, neither of which I can do right now. I breathe through my mouth when we pass a food court with its rancid smells.

Tomlin, like the proficient traveler he is, sails through the crowd, garnering curious looks and whispered words behind hand-covered mouths. Yeah, some people know him here, and that makes me more apprehensive.

I never thought about getting all gussied up for him, nor did I think about the photographers that could be here waiting for celebrities like him. It's common on Instagram and I hope we don't get caught in one.

With the way I'm feeling, I'll photograph horribly. Maybe he should pick me up around the corner. That way they can get the perfect picture of him and all his handsomeness, and I won't tarnish his image.

"I'll wait outside."

Tomlin releases my hand and reaches for his phone as I

glance up and see the women's restroom ahead. I don't bother replying because there's already a line forming.

I take my spot in line and keep an eye on him as his fingers fly across the surface of his phone in a texting war with someone. Probably his dad, judging from the look on his face.

As the line creeps forward, a family stops to talk to him. Two boys stand to the side while Tomlin shakes hands with the parents. The older boy suddenly steps forward to bow to him. Tomlin immediately straightens and bows back. The respect is really cool to see. The smaller, younger boy shyly steps forward and Tomlin squats to give him some knuckles. It's the most endearing thing I've ever seen. If I liked kids, I'd want to have boys with that fine-ass man.

Damn, that came out of nowhere. First things first, Dani. Land the guy and never think about kids again.

They disappear out of sight as I round the corner to an open stall. I hurry to pee, wash my hands, and get out of there because spying on Tomlin with his fans is fascinating. Something I never really thought about, even in his trophy room. By the time I get done, the family is gone, and he is back to angry typing on his phone. Wordlessly, I slide to his side.

"All set?"

He immediately locks his phone and shoves it into his pocket.

"Yep," I say then ask, "You okay?"

"Yes, why?"

He looks puzzled.

"I thought you were angry texting your dad."

A chuckle bursts from him.

"Angry texting is about right. But no, my agent this time."

Agent?

I never thought about that either. But every elite athlete has one. Why would Tomlin be any different? I don't know as much about him as I thought. He interlaces our fingers, completely unnecessary, as the crowd has thinned. But I vowed not to turn away any advances he initiates since I'm all chips in now.

We're late by the fast pace his long legs are setting, getting across the concourse. I look like a show pony prancing beside him to keep up. After walking a bazillion miles in my cute wedges, taking an escalator downstairs, and hunting for our suitcases in baggage claim, he finds the man in an all-black suit holding a sign with his name on it. My feet are killing me, my stomach threatens to wage war again, and I'm breathless from jogging.

"Mr. Takahashi, welcome to Los Angeles."

They shake hands and I nod when Tomlin introduces me. I'm not feeling well, and the newness of this place is a little overwhelming.

"I'll collect the luggage."

He whistles to another uniformed guy, who speed walks over with a dolly cart to load our luggage.

"Sir, I must warn you that there are buzzards outside," the driver mutters, leaning toward Tomlin while looking at me.

"I understand. Thank you," Tomlin says before reaching into his crossbody and pulling out those aviator glasses I've stared into countless times. "Dani put these on."

I'm confused about why I need glasses inside and even more confused about the buzzards outside. How are sunglasses supposed to protect me from birds that prey on roadkill?

"Why?"

Tomlin takes my hand again to follow the chauffeur.

"Just trust me," he utters, moving in front of me and tucking my hand behind his back to ensure I follow.

"This is weird," I grumble to myself before sliding them on.

The overpowering stench of exhaust fumes from the idling cars lined up at the curb blows through the double doors. My stomach protests. It doesn't need anything else to upset it.

Tomlin's hand is a vice grip over mine as he walks into a

flood of flashing lights. It's chaos. The flash and clicking of cameras, yelling his name and screaming to know who I am.

Coupled with the speed at which Tomlin pushes through the paparazzi to the car makes my dizziness return. My pulse quickens while adrenaline and heat surge through my body. Sweat prickles at the back of my neck and into our joined hands. This is nerve-racking as hell.

The sunglasses cut through the blinding lights, and I touch the edge to keep them from sliding down. How Tomlin can see through the flashes to the open car door is a wonder. He steps aside, helping me into the back of the car, before blocking my view for a quick photo op.

Ah, buzzards are the paparazzi.

The photographers are eating it up, calling for him to turn left or right. He indulges them for a few seconds longer while I duck my head between my knees to combat the fumes overtaking the cab of the car. It's entirely too much.

Tomlin slides in next to me, closing the door loudly while the guys load the luggage in the trunk. His hand swirls circles across my back. The leather seat groans when he shifts toward me.

"Try some water."

The crack of the cap is next to my ear. I sit up long enough to press the cold bottle to my forehead and pull his sunglasses from my face. The flashes continue through the blacked-out windows for a few tense moments until the driver and his helper get in the front and roll forward.

"That was—"

"Not too bad."

His hand moves my ponytail over my shoulder, allowing cool air to hit the nape of my neck. The exhaust fumes dissipate with the fresh-smelling air conditioning plowing into the car.

"That's insanity."

I sit up, forcing his hand off my back and drinking almost half the bottle before handing him his glasses.

"Thank you for those."

"Ah, you get used to it."

He tucks them in the open collar of his shirt, looking as relaxed as can be. Of course, calm, cool, and collected over here would say that, after participating in the three Olympics, and who knows how many other judo competitions.

"How are you feeling?" he asks when the car emerges into the sun and the city opens around us.

With that awful airport experience behind me, I can focus on the real fun of this unexpected vacation. Time off near the beach in LA. Yeah, I can easily lie in the surf for a day or two.

"Getting better."

I down the rest of the water, setting it in a cupholder, before relaxing into the black leather seat. Tomlin's long body sprawls across the back, looking casually relaxed as his finger drums the armrest of the car door.

"Good, since today is a travel day. I figured we'd take it easy and didn't book anything. I wasn't sure how you would do since this is your first time." Those thick black eyebrows pinch in worry. "And it's a good thing I didn't because you look a little pallid."

"I don't even know what that word means," I say, looking out the window at swaying palm trees, a cloudless blue sky, and the cluster of skyscrapers off in the distance. "But I haven't come all this way to park my ass in a hotel room. I'll give you that."

I don't bother looking at him for fear of missing something cool out my window.

"I want to eat corn dogs on the beach, see the car collection at the Petersen, and see the Hollywood sign. Although they better not make me hike that shit because I can hike back home."

He is already watching me when I turn my head.

"Do you hike back home?" His inquiry is soft and relaxed, not the usual aloof or arrogant Tomlin. It's very likable.

"Hell no, all I do is work and . . . well work. You know that."

That's a problem now that I think about it. I'm terrible at work-life balance. Having worked like a dog for Carl and then again for Tomlin. Not that I minded the latter. Getting that Gran Torino show quality ready with Lars was probably the funniest, most grueling, and most rewarding job I've ever done.

"Anyway, I want to go clubbing, drink too much, maybe dance up on some hot NBA players and get propositioned for a threesome."

His eyes widen at that last statement and thank fuck, he stops drumming on the door. When he opens his mouth to speak, I shut it down.

"Not that I would. Been there, done that, and will never do it again."

His mouth snaps shut. A weird look passes over his face before settling into displeasure.

"Don't look at me like that. Hell, with all your fame and good looks, you know your ass has woken up in a hotel room not remembering what happened with two hot bodies next to you."

He stares at me for the longest time before slowly answering.

"No, it hasn't. But it sounds like that has happened to you." Not displeasure, concern. "Were *you* roofied and you don't remember, because if that were the case, you could—"

"I don't want to talk about this anymore."

I revert to looking out the window again. He shuffles in his seat beside me, maybe trying to get my attention, but I was wrong for saying that.

What I meant to say is I want to have a great time while I am here. Who knows if I'll ever come back?

2

"This is amazing."

The penthouse suite is right up Tomlin's alley, with creams, gold, and marble everywhere. A mix of his modern museum in Denver and the mountain resort in Cañon City.

The ceilings soar two stories with a humongous chandelier in the middle of the room and breathtaking views of the Atlantic Ocean. I stride straight to the balcony doors, throwing them open to the muggy sea air.

The breeze whips a strand out of my ponytail to blow across my face while the seagulls caw overhead. The boardwalk is dotted with food vendors and skateboarders whizzing by. The beach beyond is crowded with umbrellas and families as surfers tackle the rough waves.

"Do you like it?" Tomlin asks, sliding up to my right.

I already have the biggest smile possible.

"Who wouldn't?"

That stupid bumpy plane ride is worth it if I get to live here for a week. The balcony is a wall of thick glass to keep us from plunging to our deaths without obstructing the view. I lean on the railing, taking it all in.

"It's exactly how I pictured LA to look. All beautiful beaches and beautiful people. This place definitely has its own vibe."

The swaying palm trees, the bright sun, and the roar of the ocean are everything I thought they'd be when scrolling through photos online. He hunches, resting his forearms on the glass and casually glancing around when our eyes meet.

"Thank you for this. I don't know if I could ever afford a trip like this."

His smile is both soft and sudden, reaching all the way into his dark brown eyes that crinkle in the corners.

"I would not be here with anyone else."

It warms my heart the way he says it. The attraction is undeniable the longer we gaze into each other's eyes. When his drops to my lips, I chant for him to lean in and connect them. If he could read my mind, he'd see I want him to take me against this glass balcony right now.

A ragged sigh loosens from his chest as if fighting the attraction is difficult for him. Good.

"I should head downstairs to check in with the event's organizers. Did you want to come? Or would you prefer to stay here?"

It's nice of him to offer. Since he won't be banging me, then I'd prefer to get down to the beach and stick my toes in the sand. It's my first time seeing the ocean and a beach, and a thrill runs through me.

"Nah, I'm going down there." I point to the beach, unable to hide my excitement while someone is flying a huge dragon kite that dips and dives toward the water. "I want to hit the water."

The breeze picks up his hair while he looks down at his watch. Since I'm on vacation, time has no meaning but for him, it does.

"Okay, I'm not sure how long I will be. I'll call you when I'm done, and we can figure out what we want to do tonight."

"You could meet me on the beach."

Show off that hot body. It's completely drool-worthy the last time I saw it nearly seven weeks ago. His gaze flickers to the beachgoers below and his lips press together.

"Not a fan, but by all means, don't let me stop you."

Like I'd let him stop me.

"Why not?" I ask as he straightens and motions for us to go inside. "It's because you're pale, huh? Do you burn easily? I'm sure this fancy place has sunscreen at the gift shop that you can get."

"Ah, Dani, only you can be offensive when you're caring," he mocks, walking inside and crossing the luxurious living room to answer the door. I didn't even hear anyone knocking.

The bellman is quietly wheeling in our luggage. I didn't know rich people didn't carry their own luggage until the guy wrestled it out of the chauffeur's trunk while Tomlin was passing out tips like free samples at the grocery store.

The guy separates our bags into the bedrooms on the opposite side of the living room before getting another tip and leaving. A completely unnecessary service.

"To answer your question, I'm not a fan of crowds or sand."

This dude is picky as hell.

"How are you not a fan of crowds when you're famous? Aren't people always following you to get your autograph?"

I run a hand over my hair, trying to soothe the flyaways when I really need to redo my ponytail.

His smile is coy as if keeping a secret, and I don't like it.

"You'll see. Do you need money or—"

He reaches for his wallet. I hold up my hand to stop him because his charity has gone far enough with this extravagant vacation. Plus, it feels a little like I'm a kept woman and I don't like that at all. Taking handouts isn't my thing. I enjoy making my own money.

"I'm good."

"And your stomach? How are you feeling?"

I had forgotten about it hurting. The humid sea breeze seems to do the trick of fixing my stomach while making me want to go swimming.

"A lot better."

A few seconds pass with us staring at each other, until he says, "All right, well make yourself at home. If you get hungry, there's a restaurant on the first floor, or you can order room service."

He pats his pockets until he finds the room keys and hands me one of them.

"No way, Jose. I'm eating hot dogs and street corn on the beach. Got to experience Los Angeles in all its glory."

I flick the card in between my hands, expelling some energy because I'm ready to hit the ground running on this vacation. He casts me a wary look while walking toward the door.

"Do you think that's a wise idea? You could get sick, especially after emptying the contents of your body on the plane."

"That's a dumb thing to say. No one plans to get sick. They just do. But I won't because lucky for me, I have an iron stomach, except when it comes to turbulence. Now go. You're killing my vibe."

He's not really killing it. I'm just eager to lay my ass on the sand and bake in the sun until I'm crispy.

"I am. If you need anything, charge it to the room if you are on the hotel property."

I shoo him away.

"Bye, T."

All his warnings and precautions are unnecessary because greasy food has never made me sick. He flashes that gorgeous smile before finally leaving me alone in this stunning penthouse.

I grab my phone from my purse to snap a ton of pictures of the two-story living room as sunshine streams through the gigantic windows and across the baby grand piano sitting in the corner. If I knew how to play, I'd be lost there all day.

Once I'm done getting pics from all angles of the living area, dining room, kitchen, and bedrooms, Tomlin's included, which looks the same as mine, I head out to the balcony. With the number of pictures I'm taking, I should stamp tourist across my forehead to warn people that they may or may not be in my shots. I take a selfie with the sun and ocean behind me to send to Eli, instead of Kylie.

She's upset about this trip, even though she's dating Ryan. When I told her, she was pissed and asked me a million questions. All of which I answered and kept on a professional level since that's all Tomlin and I are, business partners.

I haven't confided in her about my feelings for him. At first, I wasn't sure myself and was still trying to figure it out. The more time passed, the more confused I got about my feelings for him. I tried to keep it to business partners only, but I was struggling and didn't want to turn to her about it. It felt like a betrayal of her trust, even though working and living with him was her idea in the first place.

I turned to Eli as a fresh set of ears. He's never met Kylie and already sort of knows Tomlin, so he was more objective about the situation. At least that's how I justified it. I feared if I told Kylie outright, she'd ban me from liking him and that ship has sailed. Sailed so far, and fast, that it was on the other side of the world by now.

Eli helped me make sense of it all. His exact words yesterday were, "She shouldn't stand in the way of true love."

Not that I know if Tomlin and I are true love or not, but I want to see where it goes. If it goes anywhere at all. Eli's encouragement makes me feel better about the situation. More open to going with the flow and seeing where it takes me. Which is very un-Dani-like of me.

Turning around, I lean on the glass railing, the breeze caressing my skin while watching the crowds. I couldn't ever live here, far too many people for me, but watching them from way up here is intriguing.

After several minutes of taking it all in and getting a feel for the layout of the vendors and beach below, I venture inside to change into my swimsuit and coverup. Checking that I have everything I need, I position my sunglasses on the bridge of my nose and toss my backpack over one shoulder, then beeline to the elevator.

An elderly couple joins me when the doors slide open, and it creeps to the first floor. I debate about getting sunscreen from the lobby gift shop, but with the long line at the register, I forgo it. I rarely burn when I pound out the twisted steel of cars in the Colorado sun. I'm sure I'll be fine.

The boardwalk is more populated than I thought on the balcony, which kind of sucks. Like Tomlin, I'm not a fan of people, but seeing some super-hot guys in tiny speedos is the eye candy I need to make the crowds worth it.

Deciding to eat first, I wait through two lines to get what I told Tomlin I wanted and add a heavenly-smelling funnel cake to the mix. Balancing my chili cheese dog, corn, cake, and soft drink is no small feat when I find a spot near some people playing volleyball.

Once I spread my towel out, get situated, and strip down to my bathing suit, I dive into my food. If I wasn't busy stuffing my face, I'd ask to get in on the game. For now, I'm content to watch the fit, sweaty guys dive for the ball.

One game turns into two and then three before I finish my food and venture into the water. Damn, it's freezing. I don't even make it past my thighs before I'm rubbing the goosebumps on my arms. I expected it to be balmy warm considering the hot sun and warm breeze. Visions of me diving under the water to look at the ocean floor evaporate as I trudge out of the water, holding myself.

Sand coats my feet as I amble toward my belongings. I kind of get what Tomlin says about not liking the sand as it clumps to my wet skin. Oh well, when in Rome.

Once I get to my belongings, I lie down and wrap the towel over my legs to warm up. Closing my eyes, the seagulls squawk overhead, the sun dries my body, and the crash of the waves lulls me into a peaceful slumber.

The ship lurches in the melting sun. The side dips into the sea, and a wave tosses the vessel to the right, careening me across the deck and into the railing. My fingers clutch the dried-out wood for dear life until it snaps and tosses me into the dark water. The waves tumble over each other until I'm vomiting, spewing chunks of funnel cake and hot dogs into the black current.

"Lady, are you okay?"

The ocean isn't throwing me around. It's one of the volleyball players shaking my shoulder violently. I sit up with a start, covered in my own vomit. The smell is repulsive, forcing another gag from my throat and she jumps back. The game stopped, with all eyes on me. This is embarrassing as hell.

"Are you all right?"

I gaze up. The girl's long hair blocks the sun, and concern is all over her face. I want to burrow into the sand like a crab to hide how mortifying this is.

"Yeah, uh. I . . . drank too much."

A believable lie that gets her to back off. People have sympathy for sick people, not drunks.

"Oh, okay."

She backs away, then jogs to her friends, whispering what I said. Yup, no sympathy and a few disgusted looks. Perfect. My stomach cramps as I push to my feet, and speed walk to the water. I don't want to do it, but it's either take a cold plunge in the ice bath of the Atlantic or walk into the fancy hotel covered in vomit.

I almost feel sorry for the people around me as I plop down in the water and use the ocean as my bathtub. Hell, how many people use it as their toilet? Probably another reason Tomlin isn't a fan of the beach. His germaphobe ways couldn't tolerate swimming in someone's pee. Hell, it's grossing me out just thinking about it.

The cold water takes my breath away as I splash it over the front of my body, washing away chunks of undigested food. It's disgusting and makes me more nauseated. Ugh, stupid stomach for betraying me. First on the plane and now here.

"Oh shit."

Literally.

A sharp, shooting pain fires across my abdomen and I clench my butt cheeks to not shit right here in the surf. This crosses a line, even for me. I can't use the ocean like this.

"Fuck, fuck, fuck."

I pant, trying not to shit myself and have it slide down my leg as I speed walk to my towel to collect my things. Another stolen breath as pain spasms through my midsection again.

"Hold it together, Dani."

I pep talk myself as I squat to grab the trash. It takes everything in me to not crap right here in this squat.

"You got this. Just make it to the hotel."

I can't remember a time being in such misery, except for the flu a few years ago. This is much worse than that. I gag, and the sounds of my stomach rumbling and popping grow louder. It's a careful balance of hurrying everything into my arms, but not rushing enough to jar the diarrhea threatening to shoot out of my ass at any moment.

Easing back to my feet, I pause, clench my butt cheeks, and

shove my elbows into the pain radiating from one side of my stomach to the other. It's miserable.

I clench every part of my body to shuffle back to the hotel. Maneuvering around these damn tourists isn't fun as they walk like slow-ass cattle, forcing me to trek around them and risk losing my bowels.

My entire body flushes with heat, causing me to blink against the lightheadedness surging before my eyes. The clothes in my arms stick to my skin and sweat rolls down my sweaty back. My backpack swings from my elbow, hitting my legs as I shuffle toward the sliding doors.

Make it to the hotel.

It's my mantra as I scoot my tight ass cheeks through the lobby, hating all the cheerful staff welcoming me back. I'm practically crying in relief when I reach the elevator bank, so close yet so far away.

I lean heavily against the wall to push the button with my pointy elbow. I can't risk moving any other part of my body as I clenched everything as tight as possible to hold in the vomit and shit threatening to spew everywhere.

Make it upstairs.

Then I can slowly die on the toilet in my room. The pinging elevator is the best sound in the world. I dive in, praying no one else gets on to delay my ride up to the penthouse. Dammit for being high up. I love the view and hate the elevator crawling to the top floor. Thank God, I'm the only one in here and don't have to stop at other floors.

Please don't break down.

If it does, I'll shit everywhere. Rescuers will think someone died in here by the time they pry open the doors. Two more floors. I gag two more times. The burp is loud, and I vomit into the trash can by the elevator as soon as the doors open. I'll call the hotel later to confess my sins so they can clean it up.

Get to the door.

I speed shuffle to our door, then drop all my crap on the floor. It takes all my strength not to shit myself when I bend over to get the key card out.

"Oh no."

I lose the battle. Warm sludge squishes between my cheeks. More sweat pours out of my skin as I brace myself against the door to swipe the card and pray the card isn't demagnetized from my wallet.

I pant. My breath is harsh and fast, like I'm holding back delivering a baby and maybe I am. A poop baby. When the beautiful green light pops up on the door, I shuffle through it, leaving my crap in the hallway and hoping these tiny bikini bottoms can hold back the pending flood.

"Dani, you're ba—"

"Don't look at me."

I hold my hands up to block my face when I should hold them over my ass cheeks because it's rolling down the back of my thighs.

"Fuck it."

I slam my hands against my butt and run to my bathroom, unable to close the door behind me.

Please don't come in.

I gag repeatedly as I wiggle my bottoms down to plop my butt on the toilet and have explosive diarrhea. It's so loud, bubbly, and smelly that I vomit on the floor between my legs. I want to hang my head in my hands, but I have poop on my fingers. My whole body is cramping and shaking, as I purge and shit in succession.

"Dani?"

There's no way to hide what is happening. The sound of my retching, the stench, and the shit make it unbreathable, and it's all coming from me. It's awful. I grab reams of toilet paper, trying to clean my fingers to at least get my hair out of my vomit strings.

"What can I do?" Tomlin calls from my bedroom, respecting my visual privacy but not my overall privacy as he hears the horrific sounds coming from my body.

No guy, no friend, no business partner, and no love interest should ever hear these sounds. I'd die from embarrassment if I weren't already dying from my insides liquifying themselves out of both ends. Throwing the toilet paper from my hands behind me, I hope it reaches the bowl as I lean against the wall in between waves of throw-up.

"Go away."

"I'm going to see if my doctor has arrived yet." His voice is soft, worried and I am too. I don't know what is wrong with me.

Wave after wave comes until I have tears streaming down my face from vomiting so much. My throat and my butthole are on fire. This is about as miserable as I can remember being. Way worse than the flu.

3

When everything finally subsides, I clean up as best I can and waddle into the shower, bringing my bikini bottoms with me. Thankfully, there's a bench in here. Like an old lady, I sit and clean every inch of my body twice to ensure I don't miss anything.

The pain across my stomach isn't shooting anymore, having moved into a deep penetrating ache that keeps me nauseated but not vomiting. Probably because I have nothing left to throw up. The yellow bile attests to it.

The sweats I can't shake even after showering. The lightheadedness starts when I stand. As much effort as it's going to take to get out of this shower and clean up the bathroom, I linger on the shower bench to gather strength.

After a few more minutes of resting against the wall, I stand up and shut off the shower, steadying myself with the handle. From there, I reach for the robe on the hook, brush my teeth, and tiptoe past the mess I made all over the floor to collapse onto my bed.

The drapes are open to the blue sky. This traitorous day turned on me. This is not how my vacation is supposed to start.

"Dani?" Tomlin calls from the living room, but my throat is raw as hell, and I don't reply.

"She's in here."

I hear another voice with him, which I assume is the doctor he went to find. Tomlin appears at the side of the bed, squatting to be eye level with me.

"Wow, you're really sunburned. I'm going to take you to my room. Dr. Harris from my team was downstairs."

He brushes a wet strand of hair from my eyes, and it's the sweetest, smallest gesture anyone has ever done besides Dad.

"I'm sorry."

"Don't be. It's not your fault." His head tilts. The concern in his eyes is too much. I close mine. "Are you going to be sick again? I can get the waste basket."

My eyes open with Tomlin walking around looking for it. I attempt to sit up, to stop him but collapse to the mattress when the room starts spinning. It's not a second later when he's scooping me into his arms, leaving that shit-smelling room behind.

"I got you."

My head falls against his chest, taking in his expensive cologne still clinging to his body. It's one thing to feel like complete shit. It's another to feel this way and have someone I love take care of me. If only he loved me back.

He gently lays me on one side of the bed before moving to the other to drag the covers down, tossing the extra pillows on the couch across the room.

"Get comfortable. I'll send Dr. Harris in."

I crawl to the other side and face plant. The coolness of the sheets against my cheek feels divine. Laying on my stomach puts pressure on the pain, making me feel a smidge better.

"You can come in, Craig."

I stare blankly at the wood of the bedside table, too worn

out to even flip over. Tomlin explains what he saw and heard before leaving us to chat about my condition.

"Dani, I guess, Tomlin told you who I am and what I'm here for."

"Yes," I mumble against the bedsheets.

"Can you tell me what happened?"

I peel my eyes off the nightstand to switch to lying on my back. An older gentleman with salt and pepper hair wearing athletic gear stands over me, looking more like a contender than an actual doctor.

"I don't know. One minute, I'm lying on the beach, and the next, I'm vomiting in my sleep. It was weird." The dream of the ship felt very real. "Then it started to come out both ends. I tried to make it here and well . . ." They can probably smell what happened.

There's no expression on his face as if waiting for me to say more. He sets a red duffle on the bed beside me and starts digging through it.

"Did you eat food from the street vendors on the strand? Could it be food poisoning?" Tomlin asks as he lingers by the open door, his eyebrows pulled together in serious concentration. The doctor pulls out a thermometer to place under my tongue and then holds my wrist while staring at his watch.

"Very well could be. They are not regulated vendors like restaurants. Could also be heat exposure judging from the severity of her sunburn."

The thermometer makes me gag. When I duck over the side of the bed to vomit, Tomlin dashes into the bathroom to grab the steel trash can. Luckily, nothing comes out, and I wipe my mouth against the sleeve of the robe before falling against the pillows. My stomach aches, my head is spinning and all I want is to rewind this day.

"I didn't mean to fall asleep on the beach, it sort of happened," I murmur to the doctor.

Perspiration collects against the neck of the robe. If the guys weren't standing over the bed with worried expressions, I'd strip naked and soak in the cool dryness of the sheets.

"Vomiting, diarrhea, running a low-grade fever. What else, Dani? Tell me where it hurts." Craig holds the thermometer in his hand, and I point to my head and my stomach at the same time. "Your head? Are you dizzy? Lightheaded?"

"Yes, very. The room feels like I'm on a ship. It's making my stomach hurt and my head throb," I whisper, throwing my arm over my eyes because the bright light from the gigantic windows is making it worse.

"Okay, rest here for a minute." Craig touches my arm, but I don't move it. "Tomlin, can I talk to you in the other room?"

Normally, I'd hate to be talked about behind my back, but I couldn't care less. With vomiting my guts out and my butthole raw from explosive diarrhea, they can chat it up. I want to be left for dead at this point.

I wish this place has the fancy tablet that Tomlin has at his mountain resort, so I can press a button and close the drapes. Unfortunately, they don't. I use the few remaining pillows to block the light and put my back to the window to stare into his dark bathroom.

This blows.

The first day of my vacation and my iron stomach betrays me. Hell, I don't even care about my sunburn right now. If the pain in my head and stomach would stop, then I could worry about the stinging skin on my chest and shoulders.

Tomlin jinxed me. He warned me about eating the food. Challenge accepted because I ate it. The moment I saw it, I knew I had to have it. Dang him for being right.

"Dani?" His soft voice has my eyeballs moving in his direction, but even that hurts my head.

"Don't say I told you so," I mutter. My throat is burning

from all the bile and stomach acid that's not supposed to pass through.

"I wouldn't dare. I brought you some water. Do you want something else to drink?" He places a couple of bottled waters on the nightstand and squats beside the bed. I love him for that because then my eyeballs don't have to strain to look up.

"No. What did he say?"

I bunch the sheets over my mouth. Even though I brushed my teeth, I probably have vomit breath. There's no way I'm breathing that on him. It would make him gag too.

"That you need to stay in bed. Rest and get plenty of fluids to replenish what you lost."

"I'm sorry."

I really am.

This isn't how I wanted this trip to go. I have a bucket list of things to do. Lying in bed after the most embarrassing mistake of my life in front of the guy I'm pining after isn't one of them. A faint smile appears as he brushes the back of his hand against my forehead.

"You're warm. I'll get a cold washcloth."

My heart aches at how caring he is. My crush turned into falling for him, but now I'm in love with him. It's stupid how much I want to be with him. I stare at the nightstand, tampering my feelings back down because he doesn't want to be with me. Although, I'm here, and I still don't understand why besides standing on a mat in awe later this week.

"Thank you."

"Of course." His palm brushes against my hair. "I'm going to run downstairs to get a few things. The housekeeper is still working, stay here. Don't get up. I'll be back."

I mumble a plausible response before pressing my hot face into the clean-smelling sheets. My breath does smell awful. If I weren't dizzy, I'd brush my teeth again or hunt around the housekeeper's cart for mouthwash to get rid of the stench.

He stands and strides into the bathroom. The faucet runs for a bit, and I shift to stare at the ceiling, keeping the sheet over my mouth. Worry cuts his expression, with that square jaw muscle pulsing as he places the damn cloth over my forehead. The cold goodness brings a relieved sigh from me.

"We'll figure it out tonight when I get back. Do you need anything?"

His hands plant on his hips, pulling his shirt tight across his chest, and even now, sick as a dog, I want to jump his bones. He's both hot and caring, which is killing me slowly.

"I wish they had electronic drapes like your house."

He chuckles.

"I'll close them. Get some rest."

When I close my eyes, the room stops spinning, and the cold towel feels amazing. I wait for the drapes to scrape closed and his footsteps to recede into the living room before I untie my robe to let the cool air conditioning soothe my burning skin.

4

I don't know how long I was out, but when I wake up, the room is dark with a sliver of light cascading in from the cracked door. I'm mummified in my bed sheets. Even if I was twisting and turning in my sleep, there's no way I could've cocooned myself like this. Tomlin must have done it.

I unwind my arms from the soft linens to push the covers down, and my robe is open. Ah, I probably flashed him my boobs, and he covered me up. Oh well, treat for him.

With the dim light cascading into the room, I ease up and reach for the unopened bottle of water to take a sip. The coldness is long gone but the relief to my sore throat is instant.

Aside from the water tasting good, I still feel like shit. The sunburned skin on my chest and stomach must have tightened while I slept because it hurts when scratching my collarbone. My lips are chapped, and my robe is damp with sweat. I need another shower in the worst way. It's disgusting.

"Tomlin?"

I don't know why I'm calling him. I don't know what I need or how he can fix this. I remain silent as I can be, listening for him and only hearing faint piano music drifting in. He can't babysit me, I know that. This trip is about him, not me, but I don't want to sit here being miserable by myself.

Slowly, getting out of bed, I close my robe and tie the belt, to avoid flashing him again. This dude has seen my naked boobs twice now without me even intending to. Damn shame on my part.

I grasp hold of the furniture to steady myself while waiting for the room to spin again. When it doesn't, I tiptoe into the bathroom to splash water on my face and swish some mouthwash around before heading out to the living room. The music gets louder and when I round the corner, he's sitting on the bench playing.

It's classical.

Very sad or heavy.

I don't know what the right word is, but with only a lamp on and the night sky behind him, he's almost lost in the shadows of the room.

His expression is pinched with tension across his shoulders as he leans slightly forward and concentrates on the notes. A piece of his black hair has fallen across his forehead unnoticed by him while his long fingers strum the black and white keys.

Haunting.

That's what I'd call it. If I had my phone, I record him because everything about this moment is beautiful. An accomplished man, chasing demons in the dark and lost in a world that only he can see.

As if he senses my presence, his head snaps up to stare straight into my eyes and he immediately stops playing. He sits straight, his back cracking, and angles his body toward me.

"Did my playing wake you?"

I smile. This rich and famous dude could be out partying it up in LA, and instead, he's here playing the piano in the dark.

"That was beautiful."

I step into the room, as he fixes that fallen hair, sweeping it back with the rest.

"I'm rusty. I've been away from it for too long," he says as a sort of apology and goes to cover the keys with the lid.

"Can you play something else? Something haunting like that again?" I choose the couch closest to him, curling up in the corner as Anna does. "What was that one called?"

"Moonlight Sonata. Probably one of the most overplayed pieces ever."

What I thought was concentration on his face, now looks like stress. I feel terrible for adding to his already heavy load.

"Haunting, you say? I know of something."

He knocks back the rest of his tan liquor, setting the highball glass on the black lacquer and not caring about leaving a water ring on the expensive piano. Very un-Tomlin-like.

I rest my head on the arm of the couch, dragging a couch blanket over my legs as he starts slowly. The cords carry a distinct sadness to them and if I wasn't already feeling like crap, this sound would make me cry. It's fascinating watching him lose himself in the piece. His body sways, his dress shoes lightly tap against the foot pedals, and his fingers fly over the keys. He loves this.

I know he's good at judo. His entire room can attest to that, but this . . . this is something special. I almost feel guilty infringing on his private moment, yet he doesn't send me away and continues playing.

"What is that one?" I whisper when his fingers hit the last note.

"Chopin's Prelude in E Minor."

I won't ever remember that. His eyes flicker to mine for a second before they dart back the keys and shadow over them as if playing something else without touching the piano.

"Play another one if you want. You're very talented."

Seriously, is there anything this guy can't do?

He snorts at my comment, but begins another song and then another. I don't know how many he plays. He's completely enthralled with the music, and I'm enthralled with him playing it. Then he stops short, mid-song, and exhales.

When our eyes meet, beads of perspiration dot his hairline, and fatigue lines his cheeks, making them look hollow.

"Why did you stop?"

"I've been playing for over an hour. I figured you were bored when you kept closing your eyes."

He drapes a wrist over the top of the piano where his empty glass lies and rolls his shoulders back, eliciting more pops.

"Nope, soaking it all in. You play beautifully. I wish I could play like that."

I drag my head off the couch and rub my cheek, feeling the ridge of the fabric's indention against my skin.

"I could teach you when we get home. I have a music room."

When we get home.

How can four little words strung together mean so much? It makes my insides warm. I love it because it plants a seed of hope within. I hate it for the very same reason.

"You and all your rooms," I jest and he half smiles at me.

"How are you feeling?" This time, he pulls the lid over the keys and my private concert is over. "Do you feel up to eating something? Soup or crackers?"

The thought of food makes my stomach cramp all over again.

"Ugh."

I clutch my stomach. The music made the pain reside into a low ache, but I don't want to risk going through that all over again.

"If you're hungry, go get something."

He flips his wrist to look at the time on his watch.

"It's after 8 pm and I don't want to go out. Not without you. I'll order room service."

He stands, crossing the room in long strides, and comes back holding a thick maroon book. I adjust my blanket, bringing it closer to me, and then pat the seat next to mine. He's already flipping through the pages when he sits on the edge of the cushion.

"See anything good?"

"Yes, several. I'm behind on my protein for the day, well, really all my macros."

The intense way he's studying the menu as if it holds life secrets is hilarious. My default order is a burger most everywhere I go. It's interesting to watch him. I know he's calculated about everything, but I didn't realize it's food choices as well.

"Are you sure you don't want anything? Fruit perhaps?"

I shake my head, then change my mind.

"Can I have a ginger ale? Dad used to always give me that when I was sick."

He smiles for a moment, then says, "Of course. How about some toast? Something to get you back on the mend."

I've refused food a few times now but I decide to throw a dog a bone and let him order me toast.

"Sure."

More flipping of the pages occurs in the otherwise quiet room. I can see why he was playing. It seems a little gloomy and lonely here. If the roles were reversed, I'd have flipped on a movie, ordered a bunch of junk food, and had a mini sleepover out here while he slept.

After more minutes of studying the book, he whips out his phone and places our order. Once that is done, he tosses the thing on the coffee table in front of us and reaches for the remote.

"What do you want to watch?" he quizzes, his eyebrow

popping up. "And don't tell me porn and Netflix like you did last time."

I chuckle, remembering what I told him my first night at his cabin when he held me back by my shoulders when I tipsy kissed him.

"I don't care. I think I have watched more television at your house than in my whole life. In fact, I know I have."

A much broader selection than Netflix and porn since he has cable and hundreds more channels. An immediate frown appears, and he sets the remote back on the table.

"That's terrible."

"No, it's not. It means I'm relaxing a little more than I ever have before. In the years after my father died, I used work and partying as an excuse to avoid myself. It wasn't pretty. So, sitting here with you, watching TV is a step above where I've been."

He must like that answer because he pats my blanket-covered leg before clicking it on and flipping through the channels.

"Do you have a preference for what we watch?"

"I don't. I'm content to not be vomiting or shitting myself, so it's all good."

He doesn't smile, instead shoots me a worried look before turning his attention to finding something of interest. Thank fuck, we can laugh about it now because it's mortifying to know he heard it all.

Nights like this, where it's him and I cozy on the couch, have me fantasizing about being with him. I swear, I'm trying to shove these thoughts away as soon as I have them, but it's not working. There are too many all the time that have me wishing for a life together.

When he finds the sports channels, he flips between two of them before settling on one. The volume is low enough for him to hear and for us to talk. I don't really have anything to say, as I'm content to lie here and rest.

He grabs a pillow and props it by my blanket, leaning his elbow into it when putting his feet on the table. I adjust too, trying to get closer while technically not touching. I don't think he even notices my ploy because he moves the pillow against my legs and lays his head against it.

We're basically snuggling, and I'm trying not to freak out and read anything into this. Friends snuggle, I'm sure of it. Kylie does it with me occasionally, but then I usually shove her away because it gets annoying.

There's no way I'm shoving him away. I'll sweat my ass off in this robe if I have to. Won't be the first time today and for a much better reason than having the shits.

The blue light from the television flickers across his shiny black hair and I reach out to touch it. His hair is thicker than I thought and soft. It must be that expensive shampoo in his shower because I've noticed it working wonders on my hair too.

Crap.

What am I doing?

I pull my hand back because rubbing his hair definitely crosses the friend line.

"Keep doing that. It feels good."

His deep voice rumbles against the pillow and his eyes remain on the screen.

I hesitate. Do I, or don't I?

I mean, if this is making a move on him, and he doesn't reject me, could it lead to more? Not that I can hump it out feeling as bad as I do. Maybe this is a start if he's asking for more. I swear, I've never been so indecisive.

He cranes his neck to look at me before dragging my hand off my hip and planting it on his head. Okay. Decision made. This is unexpected. I'm not sure I'm even doing it right. Do I scratch his scalp? Or run my fingers through his hair?

I thought I made it clear that I didn't date. I don't know how to do all the cute stuff I see in movies. Well, I hope he likes what he gets because I'm pretty sure I'm the worst hair rubber or scalp scratcher he's ever had. I continue doing it until his breathing stretches out into long exhalations. Not quite snoring, but definitely asleep.

Is this what it would've been like with other guys? A closeness that's not about sex. Is this the fulfillment of the loneliness he talked about on the back deck nearly two months ago?

If it is, I want it too. I want to lie against someone and have them rub my hair on a quiet night in front of the TV. I understand his loneliness and wanting someone to fill it. I want the same thing, only with him.

The doorbell chimes. He jumps to his feet, looking startled, and his hair shoots straight up. He glimpses himself in the long mirror behind the wet bar and runs his fingers through it, trying to fix it.

"Sorry for dozing off."

He barely has the words out before he's walking around the couch and striding for the door. A room service gentleman nods at me in acknowledgment as he rolls a large cart in with various covered platters. Either Tomlin ordered more food than I realized, or they gave us the wrong order. I turn my attention back to the sports show while he handles everything.

"Do you mind if we eat here and not at the table?"

I glance at the glass and marble dining room table between us and the wet bar beyond it. It's formal and nice but I want casual and intimate.

"Nope. Go for it."

He wheels the cart further into the penthouse and carries two trays over before collecting the condiments and silverware. Setting everything up on the coffee table, he takes off the lids, and the aroma rises with it. My stomach growls. That damn traitor. After today, it can't be trusted.

"I ordered a little extra so you can see what agrees with your stomach," he says, cracking the top on my ginger ale and pouring it over ice. I sit up, moving the blanket over and stuffing my lapels together to not give him a free show. A smile ghosts across his face when he sees me do it.

"You realize I had to cover you up again. I'm beginning to think those beautiful things have a mind of their own."

"They're big enough."

I scoot toward my tray, putting my leg flush against his. He doesn't move away. Perfect.

"You shouldn't have a reduction. If you were mine . . ." He stops, his eyes dropping to my lips. I won't lean in. I refuse to lean in again. If this ever happens between us, it's going to be him initiating all the way to the very end.

"You what?"

The blue light plays across his face, but the desire pooling in his chocolate eyes is unmistakable. His shirt collar is open, revealing the dip of muscles below his collarbone. A perfect spot for my tongue to explore.

Don't lean in.

"If I were yours, what?" My voice catches in anticipation, holding my breath as he shifts a fraction of an inch closer.

"I'd worship them."

I swallow hard. My gaze drops away from the molten lava in his eyes to those full pink lips perfectly outlined by his trimmed beard. I want that mouth to worship them. Worship every inch of me as I'd him.

"Don't look at me that way."

The rasp in his voice is unmistakable. That chest I want to explore badly is rising and falling heavier than before. As if restraining himself when it's completely unnecessary. He can have me. Any way he wants.

He's struggling. His square jaw tightens, his shoulders flex, and the tent in his pants is clear.

We'd be combustion.

He said that. I agreed. And here we are again.

"What way?"

I lean in, the same fraction he did. It doesn't count as me initiating. I'm matching his actions. He has to come to the rest of the way. If he doesn't, I won't either. If he does, I'm all in.

"You know, Dani."

I watch the way his lips form each word. Taunting me to feel them against mine. To lick their softness and pull that bottom one into my mouth. I want to nip them, tease him, and devour his face as I ride him.

"Fuck," he groans.

His hand dives into my hair, pulling me to him. He doesn't close the distance. He forces me to, and it's the hottest damn thing ever.

Our mouths clash, a feverous desire to feel each other, move against each other and remember what it was like the first time we did this in his gym. I want to eat him alive, throwing that damn caution to the wind because this is what I want, business partners or whatnot.

I ram my tongue into his mouth, seeking his, and I'm rewarded when it twists with mine. He groans as he feels my piercing against his tongue. The rush from the barbell clicking against his teeth as he captures it is hot as fuck and sends a bolt of lust straight to my core. I'm throbbing for him.

I've imagined this a hundred different ways. Imagined how he'd react to my piercing and how it feels slithering against his tongue. Never did I imagine it being a hot bolt of lust straight to my pussy. It's far better than I imagined.

My arm locks around his neck, unwilling to let him refuse me again. It causes him to release my piercing from his teeth to pull me onto his lap.

Fuck yeah.

He slides to the back of the couch, the cushion pressing against my knees as I straddle him. His tongue never leaves my mouth as his hand splays across my back, the other kneads my ass. I drink him in, sucking on his tongue, and moaning for more.

My feet tuck under my butt, pushing my ass cheeks further into his hand as I grind against his dress pants. It's divine and torturous at the same time. Both needing and wanting more from this fine-ass specimen.

Then it's over. His hands curl over the tops of my shoulders, holding me back. His lips are swollen, his eyes are piercingly dark, and his dick is deliciously hard beneath me. I bite my lip, waiting for the words I hate to hear.

"We shouldn't."

It wasn't can't.

"We should."

I brace my hands against his chest, those hard muscles flexing under my fingertips. But I won't initiate, he has to. It's been too many rejections for me to attack those plump lips even if my body craves to do so.

His gaze drops past my lips to the hollow of my cleavage on display from the robe gaping open. His hands move toward the lapels, pushing them to the outside of my breasts, when he licks his lips. I can scarcely breathe, waiting for him to touch, kiss and suck the skin off them.

"Fucking gorgeous."

The fast and frantic pace from a moment ago is gone as he admires my rack. Goosebumps sweep over my skin when his rough hands stroke my naked ribcage.

"Touch them already."

It's a command that comes out as a plea. I arch my back, pushing them closer to his hands when that intense stare penetrates mine.

"It would never work, Dani."

His fingers splay, caressing up my side boobs and down to my waist. Never fully touching my breast and always avoiding my nipples. My fingernails dig into his shirt, trying to claw past the fabric to his skin. How lovely would ten little dents from my nails look on his skin when he's fighting this week?

"I like to be in charge. As do you," he murmurs, his eyes flickering to mine before returning to my body.

Fuck this. I'm breaking my own rule by leaning in, attempting to capture his swollen lips when he uses his grip on my waist to hold me back.

"Stop babbling and kiss me or touch me or fuck me already."

Desperation and frustration mix within my words, and he smirks.

"One of us has to relinquish control." Once he has me back to where I am, he caresses my sides again and drives me into horny madness.

"Who's it going to be?"

"You."

Two can play this game.

I lick my lips, then click my piercing against my teeth as I slowly rub against his cock. His eyes close for a moment. The pleasure ripples across his face and when he opens his chocolate eyes, triumph shines in them.

"I'm not letting this happen," he rasps.

His warm hands leave my skin to push the edges of the robe off my legs to grip my thighs, sending shivers over my skin. The only thing holding it on my body and not showing my pussy is the loose belt still tied at my hips. Excitement surges through me. His action is the opposite of his words.

Thank fuck.

Our bodies are saying yes, while he says no. I'm dripping onto his lap. I feel it coming out of me as I rub against his cock. His hands tighten, locking me in place on top of it.

Damn him and his disciplined life. He rules his perfect body like the iron fist he rules his life. He probably has never unexpectedly orgasmed in his life.

"I'm not letting this happen, T."

I'm not. I won't.

My resolve is wearing thin, but I can't keep throwing myself at him. He has to meet me halfway. His hands slowly ascend my thighs, the callouses scraping my soft skin as his thumbs get dangerously close to touching my wet lips.

"But you already are, little D. Those big tits are in my face, begging to be kissed, and your little pussy is right here."

When his thumb touches my clit, it sends a shock through my system and immediately floods his hand.

"You're very wet already."

I'm transfixed by the depth of his eyes, the brown going on forever. The way his chin rises in victory and the rhythmic stroking of his thumb against the very source of all my pleasure.

"Put your hands on my knees," he whispers.

One hand strokes my thigh, and the other strokes my clit. I do it. I stick my hands behind my butt, gripping his knees as he slips a finger into the knot and tugs at the belt. I'm completely bare to him. He sees all of me and the adoration on his face is clear.

If I didn't already love this guy to pieces, this look would send me over the edge. From the smoldering heat coming from his gaze, the way he licks his lips, and the slow rise and fall of his chest. Damn. I could orgasm off the tension between us.

"Fucking perfect."

His finger feels so damn good that I close my eyes. My body is on fire. My skin is ablaze with goosebumps and I slowly rub against his thumb. He slides the robe off my shoulders, letting it pool at my wrists and I don't care that I'm on display so long as he keeps rubbing.

"You're gorgeous, Dani." My eyes slit open, wanting to kiss him. When I lean forward, his hand leaves my thigh to push against my stomach. "No, this is for you. Only you."

I don't know or care why. When he plunges his mouth onto my breast, aggressively sucking the skin, I ride his thumb even faster. The time for teasing is over because the fire that he's stoking in me is building and intensifying. My breath quickens as I arch my back to get more of me in his sexy mouth.

His face shines in the blue light from the television. Mine from the warm glow of the lamp across the room. Mixed, they create a club-like ambiance, making it sexier and more reckless to sit on his lap, while he rubs one out of me. I'm giving both of us the best lap dance I've ever had.

If he didn't have hard liquor. If he wasn't playing sad songs on the piano. If I hadn't played in his hair. Several ifs should have prevented this from happening. Yet here we are. I'm making the most of it because it'll probably never happen again.

He keeps my nipple between his teeth, tickling the tip with his tongue. Then he releases it, blowing gently on the wet skin, and it hardens even more. My poor nipple is painfully erect and so sensitive that it needs relief in his warm, soft mouth.

Traitorously, his head dips to do the same to my other breast. Gone is his thumb from my clit. Replaced with three fingers, two inside, one outside. It couldn't be more perfect unless he wants me to sit on that cock straining to be free underneath me.

My nails claw at his knees, and my thighs burn with constriction. When the edge of my orgasm comes closer, my head falls back in a low moan. He continues kissing my breasts, licking the column in between, and kissing up to my throat.

"Come for me."

His words are a muffled demand into the base of my neck, heard in the pulsing of my ears and I fucking love his command. I'm panting as I ride his fingers and grind into his hand until I fall over the edge and ride it all the way out.

His lips nibble away at my skin, sucking, teasing, and

nipping anywhere he can until I stop moving. The slow dance between us is over and he holds me as the last embers of desire ebb away. When I raise my head and open my eyes, he stops kissing my collarbone and his fingers slide away. Awkwardness creeps into my mind as I unclench my fingers from his knees and reach for my robe.

I'm not good at romance. It's awkward and makes me uncomfortable. His getting me off is all for me. Selfless of him. I've never had a guy not want to get his. This isn't fuck buddy stuff, it's more. More sensual, more caring, and not what business partners do.

"Don't do that." He stops me and I'm confused. He's fully dressed and I'm naked. "Don't go putting that wall back up. What we did just now, we did because we wanted to, all right?"

Damn him for reading me easily. I bit my lip and want to look anywhere but at him when he captures my chin.

"Okay," I whisper, biting my lower lip, and not in a sexy way. I don't know where this puts us.

Once again, his hands caress the sides of my waist. He lifts his chin, drawing nearer as if asking for a kiss. When he closes the distance this time, I know it's really going to happen.

His lips brush mine, soft and inviting, not forceful and demanding from before. His tongue pushes against my lips, wanting but not taking. It's the kiss of familiar lovers. A perfect wrap-up to what he did to me. I pull away, my hands resting against his crumpled dress shirt caused by my fists.

"I guess I won. I'm in control." I wink.

He throws back his head and laughs. That carefree one that wipes away all my doubts and brings back my boldness.

"Only you," he says, returning my wink with one of his own.

"What? I mean it."

He collects my robe from behind me and slides it onto my shoulders, intentionally keeping it open down the center to admire my body.

"Control, it is merely foreplay, Dani. Meant to tease and entice. But now that I know you like it, I'll continue with it."

His index finger brushes a line from the top of my throat down to my core, leaving me squirming all over the place.

Foreplay for my ears. I've had way too much sex in my short life after losing Dad, but never sensual like this. Another thing he's good at. Verbal foreplay.

"Damn."

"Agree. Now go get cleaned up. I'm hungry and this." He licks the fingers that were inside me and the embers of my desire are roaring back to life. "Isn't enough."

I wrap my robe around myself and slowly climb off his lap with his help. "I fucking love it when you lick my cum."

"Me too."

He slaps my ass, catching me off guard until I notice the huge wet spot on the front of his pants, still a tent over his dick.

"What about you? Don't you need to, uh, clean up too?"

"I haven't decided yet. You smell as delicious as you taste." His voice is still husky.

Damn if he didn't say he's enjoying the smell of my cum. That's about as hot as him licking it from his fingers. I fidget wanting another go at him because suddenly what he did isn't enough.

"Go, Dani."

5

The rest of the night went normally as if he didn't just see me naked and get me off. After I got cleaned up and put on some undergarments, he changed too. I expected it to get awkward but true to his word, it wasn't.

He ensured it wasn't, and I thought that was the classiest thing ever. I get why girls want to be with him. Aside from his wealth, great looks, and fame, he's the right mix of a nice guy and an arrogant elitist. A combination I find very attractive.

Then I made the crucial mistake of thinking I could inhale my toast, soup, and part of his dinner, then guzzle down ginger ale as an elixir to soothe my stomach. Wrong.

I ended up throwing it all back up with Tomlin holding my hair. It was a mess. I apologized to him another bazillion times. He shook it off then handed me water to clean out my mouth and tucked me into bed with the trusty wastepaper basket on the floor beside me.

He offered to stay with me until I fell asleep, but that was imposing too much on him and his time. Plus, I wanted time alone to process everything that happened between us. The music, the making out, the little sex session and then eating dinner in front of the television like an old married couple. It was a lot to take in.

I didn't hear him leave the next morning, as I slept well into the afternoon. If it wasn't for my protesting bladder, I think I would've stayed asleep. After showering, putting hotel lotion on my sunburn, and getting somewhat ready for the day, I find the scribbled note he left on the bar. He's meeting with the organizers and getting some practice in with the team. He also said to take it easy and not overdo it.

I swear, he knows me well. Normally, I'd say fuck it and get all bent out of shape at him for telling me what to do. But after yesterday's double round of vomiting, I agree. I'm taking it easy in the penthouse since I can't tell if my stomach aches from cramping or if it's hunger pains.

It's Tuesday. I lost a whole day being sick, really two if I count today. There are still some things I need to do to prepare for Pebble Beach. My phone is long since dead from failing to charge it yesterday.

Not only do I need to call Lars about the transports, but I also need to call Eli and dissect what happened last night with him. He told me to stop overanalyzing the business versus life partners stuff and see where it goes with Tomlin. According to Eli, men don't always know what they want or realize what they want is right in front of them.

I find both hard to believe with Tomlin. His life has been planned out for him or by him since he was a child. Like seriously, who's been to three Olympics by the age of twenty-seven? That means he had to compete in his first one at sixteen, which makes him a child prodigy or whatnot.

This blows.

I've never been this insecure about a situation with a guy in my life. This unknown and go-with-the-flow is a bunch of crap that I'm growing to hate. Absolutes are what I need. Yes, we are together and dating. Or no, we're fucking around here in a higher quality situation than Zach. I hope it's the former and not the latter.

Hunting for my phone charger in my luggage, I plug it in and swipe the dining book and hotel phone from the table to go out to the terrace. It's another bright and beautiful day out as I drop into a chair partially in the shade to enjoy the view. The salt in the air is heavy enough for me to taste. It makes me hungrier as I flip through the pages.

Tomlin's right, the beach is overrated. Too crowded, sand in my crevices and the water is stupidly cold. Not to mention my vomit in the sand and the ocean as my toilet. Yeah, I'm not going down there again. One thing off my bucket list.

After debating between a couple of items in the book, I decide to play it safe with a grilled cheese sandwich and fries. The pictures of the salad looks surprisingly good, but I figure it might be rough on my stomach and the cheese is binding. Once I order that, I tap the side of the cordless phone, trying to remember Lars's number.

I guess. After a couple of rings, I think I might have the wrong number when he answers.

"Hello?"

"Hey Lars, it's me, Dani."

"What's up? I didn't recognize the number."

He sounds tired, which is odd because he has the same downtime as I do.

"Yeah, I had to use the hotel phone since mine is dead."

I shuffle the phone to my other ear so I can pull my legs up to my chest to avoid getting any sun on them. My burnt upper body is enough. I don't need the lower burnt too.

"How's LA?"

"Sucks. I got food poisoning and sunburned because my dumb ass ate from a street vendor and then fell asleep on the beach."

His big laugh has me pulling the receiver away from my ear.

"You have the worst luck. I'm surprised you didn't get stung by a jellyfish too."

"Hell no, man, the water is freezing. Even the jellyfish don't like it. Now I know why all the surfers here wear wet suits."

I spot two coming in when I squint toward the ocean.

"How did you know you had food poisoning?" Something crashes on his end, he curses, and suddenly stops himself. I wait until he's done talking to one of his sisters before telling him the whole story.

He laughs hard at my misery. It sounds as if he's crying. Yeah, I get how it's funny when it happens to someone else. It takes another minute for him to settle down long enough for me to get down to business.

"That brings me to why I'm calling. How did the paint job go? Have you seen her? Is everything ready to go? Is she on her way?"

I hold my breath because this timeline has been tight. We've had no room for error, and this is the final piece.

"She's a beauty. I really like the red he picked out. It matches the seats perfectly."

"Are you complimenting yourself since that's your red?" I jest, knowing his rosacea is probably beet red.

"No, ah. What the hell? Maybe I am. Anyway, her clear coat is on and she's in the dryer. She'll be ready. I'm going to drive her and load her myself. I know you trust these guys, but I'd like to do it from start to finish if you don't mind." He raises his voice over the chatter of his siblings in the background. "We need another job soon. I forgot what it's like to be home with them day and night."

I chuckle. I don't know how he does it. Working with me and working at home. He's like an exhausted mom, which makes me chuckle harder.

"I don't mind, but I doubt they'll let you load her. Liability reasons and stuff. And don't worry, that car will get us jobs."

"You figure out a garage yet?"

I frown and try not to sigh into the phone. This should've been done well before we landed, but I've procrastinated. I'm waiting for the right time to discuss it. However, that right time never seems to come up.

Not to mention that things haven't gone as planned here and last night, well, that took a different turn in the right direction. Plus, going with the flow and keeping my feelings to myself is consuming all my brain power outside of being sick.

Lars isn't wrong. I need to woman up and do it. Sick or not, and lovesick or not.

"I haven't, but I'll talk to him when he comes back."

He hums his acknowledgment, then asks, "He's not there with you?"

I stand to scoot my chair further out of the sun and sit again.

"Yes, but he's busy doing stuff with the charity. I suspect he'll be back this evening."

"Gotcha. What else?" I can't tell if it's aimed at me or his siblings that seem to stand next to him, yelling into the phone. "Hold on a sec."

A cramp hits my hamstring, and I straighten my leg to prop it on the railing. I hate the sun on my burn, but I need to stretch the muscle as I rub it with my hand. The yelling gets lower and then a door slams on his end.

"Okay, I can hear you now."

"Did you get all the flight and hotel stuff I forwarded from Tomlin?"

I flex and point my toes, trying to get the cramp to ease while waiting for his answer. The night he asked me to go to LA, I fell into bed with fantasies about us. By morning, I awoke to a spry Tomlin that already had my coffee cooling on the counter and a few more ideas to share with me.

One being that Lars should come to Pebble Beach. I loved

the idea. I was too preoccupied with what happened between us the night before to have thought about asking about Lars. Or at least, that's what I tell myself in retrospect.

Tomlin, in his quiet way, likes Lars although they are polar opposites. The tribute Lars did on his seats sealed the deal. Not that there was an issue between them. They were more strangers and, with Tomlin's aloof nature, he probably would've let it remain that way. But the respect Tomlin has for Lars is obvious. Lars definitely hit it out of the ballpark with that one.

Tomlin's not only paying for Lars's trip but also paying a family friend to cover Lars's babysitting duties while gone. To say it's generous is an understatement. When I told Lars the news, my cheeks hurt from smiling so much. Being that we both come from poverty, it was like winning the lottery.

"I did. I still can't believe I'm going. It's unreal, ya know?" His voice still rings with surprise and I'm glad.

"Yeah, he's a good guy underneath all that arrogance." The best guy and hell, I freaking love that arrogance.

"He's not that bad, Dani. I don't know why you're always giving him a hard time. If I was that accomplished, I'd have a way bigger ego."

I know Lars's smoothing things over as he always does to ensure there's no conflict between any of us related to business. I think if we ever had real drama, Lars would lock the doors and make me work through it. He handles everything head-on, whereas I avoid things at all costs.

And it's nearly impossible for Lars to have an ego. He's too nice of a guy. I'm not sure if those little sisters wouldn't let him be egotistical. I met them once when his mom had to work a day shift and he brought them to the cabin.

They kept his ass humble to the core with all their demands and made me sweat over someone possibly spilling something on that damn white carpet. I essentially banned them from being inside Tomlin's house for fear they would ruin something expensive that I couldn't fix or replace.

Speaking of said sisters, they must have found him again because I can barely make out what he's saying over their raised voices.

"I gotta go. See ya in a few days."

"All right, text me pics of her," I yell into the phone and quickly end the call.

I don't know how he keeps his sanity in all the noise. It grates on my nerves. I tap the side of my phone, needing to call the transport company to double-check they are ready for the car tomorrow when my phone rings from my bedroom. I dash into the penthouse and snatch the charger out of the wall to answer it, before going back to my spot on the terrace and plugging it in out there.

"Hey, bitch." She's super chipper, and I wonder if that's because of Ryan. "How's LA? Did you go out to a club last night?"

Tomlin's smolder as I sat on his lap while he got me off flashes through my mind. "I got food poisoning and a bad sunburn. I didn't go out last night. I was vomiting and shitting my guts out."

"No way! How did that happen?" Her voice lowers a notch with concern.

"I ate some stuff from a food cart vendor on the beach," I say, watching a group of volleyball players take over the sandpit.

"The crap you eat." I can hear her eyes rolling. Said the girl that orders a salad at a bar and then smothers it with ranch dressing. "It's no wonder you got sick, that food bakes in the sun all day. Was Tomlin there?"

Getting into dicey territory on how much I say here. Flashes of the hot make out session, the hand job I got, the intimate piano concert, holding my hair while I vomit, and tucking me into bed run through my mind.

"Yeah, he got housekeeping to clean up after me, and his team doctor checked me out."

"Wait, you shit right in front of him? How embarrassing. The smell must have made him gag." Good, let her only know the embarrassing parts.

"Yep, yep, and yep."

"Oh my God, and here I was jealous of you and this trip. But there's no way he'd be interested in you now. Not that I thought he was before, but certainly not after you shit in front of him."

My eyebrows pinch together. I can't decide if I'm angry or offended. Equally both.

"Why wouldn't he be interested?"

I try to keep the edge out of my voice, but I don't think it's working. Her words speak to my fears of this being more of a fling than the start of a relationship.

"Because you're you. And he's him."

She's on the run, evading my question, and that statement doesn't hold.

"What does that mean?"

This time I let the edge fly across my words and she nervously giggles. The giggle she uses when I bust her saying crap that hurts my feelings or is an outright lie.

"Nothing. I'm saying he's worldly and cultured and you work in a hot garage, smell like sweat, and have motor oil lining your fingernails."

That's the second time she's made that comment. I glance at my nails. Granted, sometimes they do, but I scrubbed it all out for this trip.

"I'm not putting you down. It's just you two are in totally different worlds. It would never work. And he doesn't want kids." She's definitely putting me down.

"I don't want kids."

"You don't want kids?" she says, aghast. I'm pretty sure she already knows that about me. Or should've figured it out by now.

"No, I don't." My mood is souring from this conversation. "Look, I got to go. Room service is here."

"Room service? I thought you said—"

"Bye Kyles."

It's both true and a lie. The second I cut her off, the doorbell rings and I venture inside to answer it. The bellman rolls it into the middle of the foyer. After I sign and tip, I carry the tray to the coffee table and hunt for the remote to watch television while I eat.

My mind picks over what Kylie said. Worldly and cultured. I know exactly what she's talking about. It's not my fault we were born into two different lives. But I hardly think they couldn't merge, and we'd be happy together.

Last night was unexpected yet it felt right. Even when it got embarrassing at the end, he read my awkwardness and smoothed it over.

From the piano to sex to the dinner after, it all felt very couple-ish. Very much our own way. Last night didn't seem like we were worlds away, a rich guy slumming it with a poor girl.

It felt like us. T and little D.

I don't want to think about what Kylie said. For this week and however long it continues, I want to think of Tomlin and me as being together and seeing where it goes. It could end in disaster, or it could end up being great.

But I refuse to let her words haunt me these days that I get him all to myself. For now, I push Kylie and her mean girl words from my mind.

6

I text Hamilton. I have nothing in particular to say. I know I should check in, even though Eli would've texted me if there was a problem. After all, he's more of a friend than an acquaintance even if he still grumbles about me calling him Officer Hamilton when he's on duty.

My stomach growls in response to the aroma when I lift the lid from the plate. I gingerly take a bite of the grilled cheese. Even though I want to devour it, I take my time so I don't end up in the bathroom for the third time.

There's a car restoration show I find on when flipping through the channels. One episode turns into another and then another until the sun is setting, my food is gone, and I'm snuggling in the comforter I dragged from my bed.

Tomlin walks through the door, drenched in sweat. His sculpted muscles pop out from his shorts and tank as he tosses his gym bag on the dining room table and walks toward my room.

"Dani?"

"In here."

I hold up my hand, peering over the back of the couch

when he strides over. His straight hair is glistening wet, looking bed tossed and my fingers itch to run through it like I did last night.

He walks around the couch, glancing from me to the tray. A large sweat ring circles his neck as he pulls the buds from his ears to hold in his hand.

"How are you feeling? Did you vomit today?" His voice drops into worry when he sees me all bundled up. "Are you running a fever?"

His hand is already pressed to my forehead, not giving me a chance to answer. It's stinking sweet as I lie here and watch as concern turns to relief before he straightens up and looks at the tray.

"You finished?"

"Yep."

His eyes cut to mine before picking it up and striding away to place it in the hallway. I wonder how his practice went because he seems very intense right now, not warm and open like last night.

I push the comforter away and wait for him to come back. When it's quiet in the room, I peer over the couch again to watch him putting his earbuds away. He catches my glance and I scoot up to drape my arm against the back frame to talk to him.

"Are you going to answer my questions?" he clips, grabbing the hem of his shirt to wipe the sweat from his face. It gives me a superb view of his ridiculous eight-pack abs. "Stop ogling and start talking."

I don't know whether to be turned on by demanding Tomlin or pissed off that he's being bossy and abrupt. Maybe both, more the former since I'm horny as hell, and last night was an appetizer to my desire.

"I'm good, T. I've kept down everything I've eaten and slept a ton. More than I have in months." I can't remember the last time I was this relaxed. My answer brings visible relief to his stance across the room. "And you can't blame me for ogling. Look at you."

He snorts, sauntering to the back of the couch and running a teasing finger down my arm, leaving goosebumps in his wake. I swear, this man can get the fire burning in me with one touch. It's stupid and ridiculous.

"And look at you."

That finger teases up my shoulder, across my collarbone, and over the tops of my tits stuffed into my camisole. My lips part, barely breathing when he caresses my cleavage and wiggles his finger between them. With it smashed in between my generous tits, I envision his dick being there, and I gaze up at him.

His eyes are smolderingly dark, bouncing from mine to his finger pumping in and out of my flesh, confirming he's thinking the same thing. It's the hottest damn thing ever.

"Do you feel up to going out? Nothing big, just a ride around town to see the lights and such?" he asks, but my mind isn't processing words. It's trying to hold myself back from jumping over this couch and attacking him in the best possible way. "Or do you want to stay in?"

Does staying in mean a repeat of last night? If yes, then hell yeah, let's stay in, make out, ride his beard, blow him, and fuck him until his practice tomorrow. I can't hide the excitement on my face at the thought of staying in.

"I don't mean like last night." Dammit, if he didn't take the wind out of my sails. "Don't get me wrong, I very much enjoyed what we did. However, you came here on vacation to see the sights and I feel bad that you have been cooped up in here ever since we arrived."

Yeah, well. If he puts it like that, then we should go out. That doesn't mean we can't come back here and do it afterward.

"I'd love that," I murmur against his finger, trailing up my throat to rest under my chin. If he could lean over and put his lips to mine, it would relieve some of the ache pooling between my legs. "Um, casual clothes, I guess?"

"That will work. I'm going to hop in the shower. Can you be ready in thirty minutes?"

I stare at him. He stares at me. That finger still resting under my chin, and I close my mouth to push my lips out. A half smile, half smirk plays at his lips, knowing exactly what I want and denying me.

"I'll take that as a yes."

Excitement courses through me, waiting and wanting those pillowy lips against mine again. When his finger drops, I pout. Like for the first time in my life.

Okay, Dani, get ahold of yourself. This crosses a line even for you. You're not Kylie after all. Naturally, I do what is most quintessentially me. I shoot him double birds and stick my tongue out, knowing he likes my piercing. But after teasing me like that, he will not feel it for a long time.

Two can play this game.

"Yep, I'll be ready."

I shift away from him, grab the comforter with as much attitude as possible, and stand to an amused look on his handsome face.

"You're definitely feeling better," he says, the curt aloofness evaporating into his easy humor.

I ignore him, dragging my comforter with me on the way to my room to get ready. I rush through my shower, dry my hair, and slip on different clothes before sitting on my bed to call the transportation company to ensure Tomlin's car will ship on time.

There's a light knock on my door before Tomlin pushes it open. He's dressed in a white linen shirt, pressed navy shorts, and boat shoes. I swear if his judo career ends, he could model rich people's brands with how gorgeous he is.

"You look nice." I compliment him, and his eyebrows go up for a moment. I know it's the first one I've given him outside of telling him how hot he is all the time. "Hang on."

I hold up my finger when his mouth opens to say something.

"Hello, hello? Yeah, I'm here. This is Dani Winters. I'm calling to confirm my reservation for tomorrow?"

I stand up to walk over to the window, hoping to get better reception, and Tomlin joins me, leaning his shoulder against the glass.

His expression is stony and intense, listening to my side of the conversation as I relay the reservation number. The guy confirms we are still a go for transport. I also let them know about Lars delivering the car and wanting to load it up, but the guy declines the loading, as I figured. Not once through the brief conversation does Tomlin's eyes leave mine until it gets awkward. I look at the dusk sky painted gold and orange.

Once I'm off the phone, I ask, "Why were you watching me like that?"

He doesn't answer for a minute, just brushes a stray strand of hair away from my face and says, "No reason. You ready to go?"

I want to demand a reason. Demand to know what he's thinking and what's happening between us. But if I push, he'll back away, or worse, reject me. I don't want either. I hate this go-with-the-flow, but I can't risk ending this before it even starts by being pushy.

"Yup, let me get my purse."

I cross the room, duck into the closet to get my purse, and then stop to look in the mirror. What's he looking at? Same old Dani is looking at me in the reflection, nothing new, other than my sunburn. I shrug, chalking it up to who knows what.

"Lead the way," I say, dropping my phone inside and throwing the strap over my shoulder.

He doesn't say a word. Not down the hallway, in the elevator, or as we walk out of the hotel. I'm dying at this unexpected silent treatment until he strides over to a metallic green Lamborghini Roadster. When the chirp of the alarm sounds and the lights flash, I stop in my tracks.

"You're shitting me."

His smile is as broad and happy as my face. This is why he's quiet. He wants it to be a surprise. It certainly is. The best of surprises, aside from him asking me to come on this trip.

"Do you like it?"

I close my mouth because I can't believe it. "This . . . this is a million-dollar car."

I don't know whether to look at him or the car. With the colorful sky behind him, and the setting sun reflecting off the metallic paint of the car beside him, I'll remember this moment forever.

"I didn't buy it, Dani. I rented it. Now come on," he says every word but duh. Something he would never say but implies just as easily.

He walks to the passenger door and opens it, waiting as I take it all in. Buying and renting a million-dollar vehicle is in a world that I'm not a part of. This is literally a once in my lifetime opportunity.

I run to him and throw my arms around his neck to give him the tightest hug possible. He immediately hugs me back, a hand splayed between my shoulder blades to hold me in place as his mouth dips to my ear.

"I'm glad I made you happy."

If he only knew. And it wouldn't take a million-dollar car to make me happy. It would only take him. I move my head back to look into those soft brown eyes gazing down at me.

"I don't know how to thank you. I could never . . ."

I bite my lip to stop them from pressing against his. He has to take the lead. Every time. It's the promise I made to myself. I sort of broke it last night, but my resolve renews when I offered him a kiss upstairs and he denied me. I tilt my chin up, silently daring him to kiss me, and when his face descends to mine, I close my eyes.

His cologne fills my sense as his lips brush mine, gentle and imploring. Different from the lust-filled frenzy last night. I slide my hand into his hair, wanting more when he smiles against my lips and breaks our kiss.

"Demanding Dani. That's what I should call you," he murmurs, teasing those sweet things against mine long enough for me to chase them for a deeper kiss.

"Kiss me, T. For real."

His hands slide over my back, one into my hair to grip my neck, the other a hard band around my waist, trapping me against his very hard erection. I'd jump up and wrap my thighs around his waist if I could, but he's holding me too tight to allow that.

"I'll kiss you." His tongue licks up the side of my neck, nibbling at the sensitive skin and sweeping chills into my hair. "When I'm good and ready."

Ah, he wants to play control. I'm beginning to love this game. I loosen a hand from around his neck to slide past his collarbone until I find his nipple. My fingers rest on his ribs as my thumb strokes back and forth across the fabric until he groans.

"Naughty girl."

He traps my hand under his. His breath fanning my heated flesh.

"I was going to let you drive." His teeth graze my ear lobe, holding it in place to lick the ticklish area and I squirm against him. "But I don't think you can handle it."

My hand courses up and down the back of his head, encouraging him to keep those lovely lips against my skin as his playful words make me wet.

"Joke's on you. I'm very skilled at handling shafts. Big ones even."

His breath rushes into the shell of my ear when he smiles.

"You're an expert, are you?"

I move my face to press against his, whispering in his ear, the same as he whispers in mine.

"Yes, T. You'll be in excellent hands."

With that, he backs me against the car, the front panel hitting my butt as he plunges his tongue into my mouth. The swiftness and urgency of his kiss match his roaming hands. Gripping and squeezing different parts of my body until one settles on my breast and the other on my ass.

My senses are going haywire with his tongue twisting with my piercing, his thumb strumming my nipple, and his palm kneading my ass cheek, all in desperation. It floods my panties. I'd lay myself naked on the hood of this million-dollar car if it meant he'd finally fuck me.

I moan. My hands are in his hair, pushing him into me as he edges me with his cock pressed right against the source of all my lust. Smashed between him and this fancy ass car has never turned me on more.

I want him.

I need him.

My tongue twists with his until he captures my piercing in his teeth, holding me in place. Fuck. Another moan rolls out of me and into him, and when he shoves his knee between my legs, I vigorously grind against it.

It's obscene to make out like this in a back parking lot, especially if there are buzzards around. But if he doesn't care, neither do I. This is lewd. They probably couldn't put it on TMZ. Not that I give a shit because this fucking perfect man feels amazing all over me and in my mouth. If only he were in another hole. Hot damn.

He's manhandling my breast, alternating between stroking

my nipple and squeezing the shit out of it. The way he grips my ass, smashing me against his leg, encourages me to ride it harder.

My clit is painfully tender against the rough fabric, and it causes my legs to tremble. My core aches, my thighs clench and he's unrelenting in holding my piercing in his teeth.

It's all him. All in control. Other than my hands clutching his neck and shoulder. I'm powerless against his advances and loving every fucking second of this. I moan nonstop, encouraging him to continue with everything he's doing.

When he finally releases my piercing, I'm breathless and panting. His lips suck the burning flesh of my neck. A deep groan rumbles at the back of his throat. My orgasm is close as I rock faster against his taut thigh. My eyes squeeze shut, and my body is as rigid as possible, waiting for that sweet release to overtake me.

"I'm close," I mumble.

His mouth covers mine, taking my breath away and plundering with reckless abandonment. It's everything I need to fall over the edge and when I moan out my release, my head falls back forcing his lips to my throat. He cradles my head and hums against my skin.

"I'd love to lay you out on this hood and have my way with you."

I open my eyes. The sky darkens behind him, and his brown eyes are full of lust.

"I was thinking the same thing."

Good thing the parking lot is virtually empty. Although I'm sure we put on quite a show for the hotel rooms with views of this parking lot.

His lips lift to mine. Dusting them once, twice, three times as if saying goodbye for now before loosening his arms and straightening both of us. When he removes his leg from between mine, there's a huge wet spot on the edge of the fabric and glistening on his leg. My shorts are stuck to me like a second skin and it's kind of grossing me out.

"That's a lot."

I mash my lips together, not knowing what else to say.

"Agree."

His thumb captures my chin, quickly kissing my lips before stepping back to straighten his rumpled shirt. He looks down, a huge grin spreading across his face.

"I think you need to change."

I look down and am surprised.

"It looks like I peed my pants."

Damn, the thin fabric of these cute cotton shorts. If I wore my denim cut-offs, I could've concealed it better. He laughs, then finds my hand to hold in his and gives it a little squeeze.

"It does."

"You know this is all your fault."

I shove my index finger in his face, and he covers it like he always does.

"I'll gladly take the blame for pleasuring you. Proudly." The smirk is too big to wipe off his face and his chest seems to swell. "Now go change and I'll meet you out front."

"What about you? Don't you need to change?"

His smile is wicked. I already know the answer before he says it.

"Not a chance, Dani. Now go."

He releases my hand and steps back, making a sweeping motion toward the hotel entrance. Normally, I'm not embarrassed by anything because I don't give a damn, but this fancy hotel with all these rich people is different.

"Fine, but you owe me one hell of a ride after this."

His expression changes to serious and his stare intensifies. "Soon, very, very soon, you'll get that ride."

I meant the car. He meant him and my mouth curls into a silent oh. For once, I'm speechless. I turn away, not believing what he said or how he said it. One thousand percent serious. That's what he is. Not pushing me away. Not rejecting me. Just a promise to ride him in the very near future. And just like that, I'm running back into the hotel, purse smashed to my crotch and smiling as if I won the lottery.

7

"Let's go up the coastline. I know of a spot where we can open her up," he says, over the throaty rumble of the engine under the hotel's porte-cochère.

Excitement rushes through me and giddily I reach for my seatbelt.

"Can I drive? When we get there?"

"If you're feeling up to it, of course. Do you want any music or —"

"Whatever you decide. I just want to listen to her purr."

I twist my hair into a knot at the base of my neck, knowing it will hold for a scenic drive. He selects some local station that is playing 1960s music, which couldn't be more perfect.

I'm lucky in that my side of the car runs alongside the beach so I have the best view of the coastline. I lean my head against the seat rest. The gentle breeze brushes against my cheeks as my hand dips in and out of the car, the warm air cutting through my fingers.

If I could bottle this feeling forever, I would because it's one of peace and tranquility. When I gaze at Tomlin, he's already watching me and I smile, saying, "Thank you for this."

He moves his arm across the console and offers his hand to me. I glance at it for a moment, a flicker of questions popping into my mind and I quickly dismiss them. Go with the flow and see where this goes.

I slide my palm into his, both calloused from hard work, albeit different kinds. The view of the water draws me back. We ride like this for a long while. His warm fingers curled around mine with an occasional swipe from his thumb. It's the smallest of gestures but feels romantically connected to him.

Sex, I can do. No problem. Romance kills me. I'm terrible at it and it sends my brain into overdrive, picking apart every little thing. Somehow with him like this, I'm calm.

He saw me at my absolute worst yesterday and still wants to be around me. Took care of me when I was sick and then selflessly got me off. It's a weird mix. Something I could dwell on way too much if I wanted to. But I don't. I want to live, feel, and enjoy this for however long he wants this to last.

When the beach thins out into a rocky coast and the crowds disappear, he releases my hand to accelerate. The throttle roars under us and throws me back into my seat. The car glides down the road with fluidity and grace. When I glance at the speedometer, we're hitting over a hundred miles per hour.

This ride differs greatly from his mom's car. That one was sobering, and I worried for our safety. This one is carefree and exhilarating. One was chasing away old nightmares. This is creating lasting memories.

The wind sucks the moisture from my eyes. My hair flies out of the knot to rage all over my head. I grasp at it to gather it in one hand while the other clutches the hand-rest tucked into the door frame.

His arms lock. His hands are white-knuckling the steering wheel while his thighs strain under the machine gripping the road. His face is tight in concentration, with his hair blown straight back and his teeth clenched.

Man and machine, interlocked and interdependent, bringing me this experience. It's the hottest fucking thing ever. I'd more than bang it out with him on the hood of this car. Damn, I might beg him to do it when we stop.

This visual combined with the threat of danger makes my heart race in my chest. If he wanted to, he could kill us in an instant. Sending the car over the edge of the road would ensure instant death. I never believed I'd trust another man aside from Dad. Yet here I am, trusting Tomlin with my life and his. It rips something anew within me.

Acceptance.

It's as if barreling down the coast with the wind harshly whipping at my face gives me the acceptance I have always yearned for. Accepting that Mom left Dad. She left me. That Dad did his best. Gave me all he had. And that it was good enough. I was good enough. No matter what Kylie or anyone else says. I'm good enough to be a business owner and life partner.

I lose myself to the exhilarating feeling of being free and untethered by life, with my newfound acceptance of the past and myself. Who knew this feeling would come as the needle pushes close to one hundred and fifty miles per hour?

Maintaining the speed is an endurance challenge for him. When his foot lifts from the gas pedal causing the roadster to coast down the road, I'm relieved. Not that I'm worried about my safety. More that I don't want to lose this euphoric feeling and its enlightening perspective. If I could bottle it and keep it in my purse, I easily would.

The sleekness of the body's design, the way it cuts through the elements, and the aerodynamics sending the wind around us is an impressive feat that garners mad respect from me to their engineers. It's no wonder this is a million-dollar car. It's worth every penny.

He pulls to the side of the road, his chest heaving from the experience. His hair is an absolute mess, sweat beads against his forehead, and the happiness on his face matches how I feel.

"That was amazing," I say, shifting in my seat to face him. He unbuckles his belt and dumps his phone in the holder before looking at me.

"It's pretty cool. Maybe I should get one."

His fingertips brush across the dashboard, admiring the instrument panel.

"For the cabin. All those open roads around there, it would be fun." He nods, talking mostly to himself.

But those open roads around the Cañon remind me of the trance he was in when driving his mom's car and if I hadn't stopped him, would he have stopped at all? How much is too much when it comes to speed?

"You don't need this."

I sound like a mother, and I instantly hate that.

"I don't need any of the things I have, but they do make life more enjoyable."

He pushes something to turn off the music, long drowned out by the road and wind.

"Why do you like cars so much?"

This is probably not the best time or place to bring this up, but I want to know. I need to know because of what he did back in Colorado, especially after finding out about his mom. I'd assume he'd hate them, not collect them. The smile falls from his face when he looks at me.

"It's the only place I'm in control."

I'm stunned. I stare at him. My mouth opens and closes a few times, trying to come up with a response, but I've got nothing.

"It's hard to believe, I know," he says, pushing against his seat, and stretching his long legs to relieve them of the pressure it took to floor this exquisitely crafted machine.

"I don't. I don't believe it. You are your own boss. You make your own money. You decide everything about your life. You're in complete control."

I can't even begin to understand what he's saying. I look at the starry sky above to make sense of what he's talking about, and when I can't, my gaze returns to his.

"No, Dani. That's where you are wrong. I have several bosses. Companies, sponsors, endorsement deals, you name it. Like this charity event, it was not my idea. It's for a good cause and it brings the sport to the underserved in this city. If I'm involved in the sport, then I need to be a good ambassador for it. But by no means am I in control of my life."

He picks at something on the dash while I process everything. Here I thought he had everything. Living a charmed life that everyone wants.

"Do you remember when I asked you about loneliness that one time?"

"Yes."

Little does he know how much that conversation haunts me.

"And you said I don't know. But you do know, Dani. I get we were not in the best place to talk about it back then, but now, tell me the truth. Are you lonely?"

I blow out a long breath, knowing what he's getting at and already hating myself for how long I have dwelled on this feeling.

I release my hair, letting it fall down my back as I gather my words before answering. His finger brushes against my temple to tuck a strand behind my ear and my gaze lifts to his.

"I've always been lonely."

Four little words bearing the weight of my confession. Whispered into the night air with an innocence that only comes with losing someone and not knowing how to move on.

"I hate it," he quietly admits.

I press my lips together, trying to stop the lump swelling in my throat.

"Tell me, Dani. Tell me what has you looking like that. I feel as if there's so much more about you. Far more than this tough exterior and ambivalent attitude."

I lay the side of my head against the seat and sigh.

"What do you want me to say that I haven't already told you the other night by the fire?"

With the desolate landscape and not a car in sight, the only light to illuminate his face is coming from the instrument panel. When his hand reaches for mine, I easily give it to him.

"Tell me why you are always lonely."

His thumb toys with mine, stroking it and then stopping. Wanting a connection and running from it at the same time. I know how that feels.

"I'm scared."

I shrug, my mouth twists trying not to let too much emotion out as I divulge my greatest fear.

"I'm alone in this world. Sure, I have Kylie and I relied on her for a long time, but even now, she's kind of gone with her new boyfriend. People don't stay in my life, Tomlin. I don't date and I don't have real relationships because they won't last, and I can't feel that pain again. Being alone is very lonely, but I think it's easier than falling in love."

Even now, admitting this to him has me terrified because I love him, and I fear he'll go away.

"I know I'm a lot to handle. I get told that all the time, but if I push people away first, then they can't hurt me when they leave. I watch it happen to Kylie all the time. I don't want to be her."

I raise my chin, swallowing past the burn sitting at the back of my throat and willing the tears to not well up like they did the night he held me in his living room.

He looks down at our joined hands, as do I.

"You have me."

I barely hear him, almost imagining it when he looks at me.

"Do I?"

I take in every feature I can make out on his handsome face. The near frown pulling at his lips. The tightness of his jaw clenching and unclenching, and the heaviness of his brow line.

"You push me away too. All the time. We're supposed to be business partners. You made that clear many times over, and then yesterday, last night . . . what was that?" I ask, leaning into the question burning in my mind and the opposite of going with the flow.

His gaze falls to my lips as if recalling it too.

"Me giving in."

I pull my hand from his. A barb of rejection coming. I know it.

"Giving in?"

I shake my head, trying to make sense of what he's saying and fending off the drop my stomach does at his words.

"Giving in to me? Don't. I don't need your pity or sympathy or whatever this is. Just don't."

He leans over the console, trying to pluck me from the door I'm leaning against to get as far away from him as possible. If it wasn't so dark and desolate, I might walk back to the hotel.

"No, Dani. Not giving in to you. Giving in to myself. To what I feel."

I need him to spell it out. I want him to because I can't be a fool again, thinking something is happening between us. I can't be the only one feeling this.

"What do you feel?" I whisper. "What are you saying?"

He nervously licks his lip, his chest rising and falling under his white linen shirt. This is hard for him too. I uncross my arms and lean toward him, aligning my lips with his, keeping them inches apart.

"I don't know. I don't know what this is." He runs a hand

through his hair, squeezing the back of his neck, but his eyes never leave mine. "But I think about you more than you know. And not just the things I said about your mouth."

Confused, I ask, "What did you say about my mouth?"

"That sailor's mouth begs to be kissed, sucked, and fucked. Although not a sailor anymore. I can't believe I'm going to say this, but I miss your cussing. The rest still holds."

Little does he know that I still cuss a steady stream in my mind. But the rest, yes, I understand. He's kissed and sucked, yet to fuck because he's been giving and not receiving at all. That's been a mind fuck in and of itself. What guy doesn't want to receive a blowjob?

"So, you *do* want to have sex with me," I clarify, still not fully understanding where this is going.

"I've wanted that ever since you carved your initial in my door."

"That's been five or six months ago."

"I know."

"And now?"

"And now, I want to be near you, with you, because I can't get you out of my head. And it's not to fill the loneliness. It's because we're more alike than you think. I said that before, but I think we're good together. I want to enjoy my time here with you."

My heart leaps because he finally wants me. Finally, finally, finally. After all this time of hoping and wishing, he's finally saying the words I've wanted to hear.

"And then? After this week?"

"We figure it out. See where it goes."

He looks even more uncertain when his gaze passes me to the sea, quietly tickling the beach with its waves.

"You've been told you are too much, which I don't agree with. You're feisty, I'll give you that, but you don't falter and that's admirable," he says when his eyes return to mine. I flush because no one has ever said they don't agree with that label. His words are a balm over a lifelong gash. "I've been told that I'm not an easy person to be around. I'm too demanding and too intense because I expect the most out of people. I can't help it. It is demanded of me and I, in turn, demand it from others."

Demanding, I know this already. He's ridden my ass about his car before Carl fired me. Before he became my legit boss. As far as intense, yeah, he's not a barrel of laughs. Then again, I don't want to be with a clown.

"Combustion, you said. That's what we'll be," I offer as my acceptance of us.

He gives me a soft smile and captures my chin between his thumb and forefinger.

"Then it's decided. Combustion."

His lips descend to mine, teasing their way to the corner of my mouth and over my cheek as his fingers twist into the strands at my neck.

"One day I'll make good on that promise of taking you on a car hood."

"Or you could bend me over this one right now."

He groans, tugging my hair to mash our lips together before plunging his tongue into my mouth. I want to climb over the console and sit in his lap, ride the hell out of him when he pushes me away.

"I can't," he mutters against my lips.

Not this again. He's panting, his erection a tent in his shorts, and when I try to go after him, he holds me back by the shoulders. I grab at his arms, trying to push them off me to straddle this console to get to him.

"I only have so much restraint and you getting off on my leg was it."

His voice is a plea, tilting his head for me to believe him. I don't know what the hell is happening. This feels right. No one is around on this deserted stretch of highway. Why is he stopping it again?

"Why?" My tone is whiny to my ears, with a level of desperation to it.

His collar is open, and my tongue could trace the pumping of his vein up the side of his neck. I'm practically dying to attack him. Make our first time together be in the seat of a million-dollar car. That's both hot and memorable.

"No sex before my match."

His solemn words slap me back into reality. I sag in my seat, negating the need for his hands to hold back my shoulders. They slide down my arms to hold my hands instead.

"Why?"

"It takes the edge off. The only two times I have lost are because of it."

"Wait, Tokyo was not that long ago. Like a couple of months back."

Jealousy swirls into my brain and my heart thunders in my chest. He had sex with someone else while he wanted me. After I racked him for calling me a girl and then I called him an asshole.

"Three and yes. I'm not proud of it."

I look to the highway beyond him, the quiet field, and the crickets chirping in the distance.

"I was jealous. You wouldn't have me, and you were hooking up with that guy. It hurt my pride at the time, but if I'm being completely honest, it hurt my feelings now."

"Zach," I whisper, returning to look at him.

He's right. I was, and I didn't care that I racked him and left him in the stairwell. I thought good riddance.

"Yeah, it got in my head," he continues, dipping his head and I see how much it bothers him.

I assumed no one turns him down, and I did several times. I guess his rejecting me all those times before is the same stinging hurt as the times I rejected him. I didn't realize it until now. The way the corner of his mouth pulls in says it all. He's wanted me far longer than I wanted him.

"And who was she?" I sound jealous but I can't help it, because I want to beat her ass as much as I want to beat his. "Why are you telling me all this? Why not keep it a secret from me?"

"I want nothing coming between us. Fresh start or clean slate, whatever you want to call it, but no lies. And to answer your first question, she was a fellow contender. A one-night stand."

I hate that I know. But I respect his honesty.

"I don't like it. I wish you hadn't told me." It's half true. I wish he was a celibate monk until he discovered his feeling for me. "And since then? Another woman—"

"No, just Tokyo, and Kylie before that."

And Kylie. I can't get past that part because am I taking her sloppy seconds? What will she think when I finally tell her how I feel? How he feels? He said let's see how it goes. That buys me time because if we don't work out, then I won't tell her. But the thought of us not working out makes my stomach hurt. I want us to work more than anything in this world.

"Can I ask, are you still seeing him?" His voice is timid. Not a very gentlemanly thing to ask, but I get it. I dug all through his recent body count.

"No." He doesn't need to know about my confrontation at Zach's apartment while we chatted it up in his complex parking lot. "Not since the night before I broke Judd's nose and broke the window."

His shoulders sag in relief and a squeeze of my hands confirms it.

"The day that will live in infamy."

"Something like that." The door digs into my back. I move

my shoulders to relieve the discomfort, which loosens his hands from mine. "I don't like this conversation anymore."

"Neither do I."

I rub my arms, wanting to comfort myself against what I learned and how I came to learn it. His hand runs through his hair too many times to be fixing it. I think he's as uncomfortable with this conversation as I am and looking to distract himself from his pervasive thoughts.

"Remind me never to ask why we can't have sex before a match."

Because this conversation derailed into hellville.

"You got it."

He tries to smile but fails miserably.

Then I realize. "That's why your dad said no more women that day he saw us in your living room."

"I'd assume so."

"Ah, it makes sense now."

I scratch my head, putting it all together and how he thought I was just another woman there to mess up his son's winning record. That's why Tomlin went away. To not lose again. Everything is falling into place now and I see the full picture. I'm sure his dad will be here this week and so will I. This should be fun.

"Did you want to drive?" His question cuts through the fog of my thoughts, moving us past this awkward situation like he usually does.

"When does this go back?"

The joy of getting to drive it has dissipated. All I want to do is think and ponder everything that transpired tonight.

"Friday. If you're not feeling well or up to it, we can try again tomorrow."

I nod and roll my lips together. It's a passable lie.

"Okay, did you want to go for ice cream or head back?"

It's a sweet offer, normally one I wouldn't pass up. But there remains a weird vibe between us that I can't just bounce back from to eat fro-yo with him.

"Head back, please."

His frown is deep and instant. I understand he wants more time out, but I need time alone to work through all these feelings. Even though I'm not nauseated from food, my stomach isn't sitting right with all this new knowledge.

"All right."

We both buckle our seatbelts before he does a U-turn across the highway to head toward the city lights dotting the dark horizon.

8

I slept horribly last night. In the wee hours of the morning, he was at the piano playing more haunting songs. I can't say it woke me up, but it kept me up as I gazed out the window at the starlit sky.

When we had returned, he asked if I'd sit with him and talk through some things on his mind. I bailed and faked a stomachache, which he attributed to my sickness. Another half-truth.

My stomach did ache, turning sour from our conservation of discussing sex partners and clarifying past misunderstandings. It helps smooth over my bruised ego of realizing our rejection score is basically the same. But I can't keep carrying that around.

I flip to my back to stare at the blinking red light of the smoke detector and realize he laid himself bare. Said he liked me and wanted to see where this goes. Isn't that what I have wanted all along? I've been driving myself crazy wondering where I stood with him. Now I know.

Then why do I feel crappy about it?

The longer the thoughts roll one after another through my

mind, the more awake I am as I listen to him play for almost an hour. I know he can't hear me tossing and turning, but every time he ends a song and begins another, I hold my breath, hoping he wouldn't tap on my door.

Once the piano stops and his footsteps sound on the living room floor, I doze off, then startle awake and look at the dark sky, glad it isn't sunrise yet. I drift off again and when I finally wake up, my mouth feels as if I chewed and swallowed rocks in the night. The dry soreness of my throat wills me out of bed for water, which turns into a desperate need for coffee.

Throwing on a robe, I trudge out to the bar, make myself a cup, and then lie on the couch to enjoy the blue morning light from the terrace doors. I remain there for a long time, sipping the mediocre liquid, thinking about him and us and how this all plays out. I doze off again, startling awake to Tomlin, in only his tight briefs, coming to lie against me like he did the night I rubbed his hair.

His beard is coming in thicker as each day passes, making his square jaw and the accompanying clenching when he's deep in thought more pronounced. His hair juts in all directions and the dark rings under his eyes speak to the rough night he's had too.

"I slept like shit," he grumbles into the pillow pushed against my butt as I lie facing the terrace.

"Same."

My eyes drift closed again until he adjusts the pillow under his head and slides his hand under it to rest against my ankle. This is fast becoming my favorite snuggling position. Actually, the only snuggling position between us so far.

"You made coffee?" His morning voice is deeper and coarser. Kind of hot if my mind wasn't a scattered mess about us.

"Just a cup. I wish it was your machine."

He exhales in a rush as if finding humor in my statement

but is too tired to laugh. Then he shifts, flipping onto his back and groaning again. Little does he know, I'm getting a fantastic view of his carved chest and abdominals, not to mention his bulging package. My mouth waters at the sight of him.

"This thing is like a rock," he complains, stilling for a few moments before flouncing around again.

"I'm not forcing you to stay here. Go back to bed."

I push against his head because its weight is making my hip hurt, and I was rather content alone before he joined me. Muttering under his breath, he swings to his feet to hover over me.

He has the perfect amount of black hair covering his legs and if I weren't so tired, I'd make a sex joke about his package being in my face. But I'm too grumpy for that.

Those chocolate eyes travel from my feet to my face before squatting and scooping me into his arm. He smells stupid good, a mix of musk and faded cologne. He feels even better, carrying me as if I'm light as a feather. Okay, I get how chicks like this move in movies.

"Uh, what do you think you are doing?"

I barely have time to ask before he tosses me on his bed. I scramble to the middle, shove the lapels of my robe closed, and wait for my explanation.

"Sleep, Dani. You were snoring logs out there. That's what woke me up."

Oh.

If I weren't so busy eye-raping him, I'd have noticed him trying to nudge me toward the side of the bed. Impatient by my lack of movement, he yanks on the covers trapped under my butt and gives me a rather dull expression.

"Will you move?"

"Don't be grouchy with me," I huff.

He's definitely not a morning person, but he doesn't need to take it out on me that he stayed up half the night.

"Will you move, please?"

The attitude doesn't change but he adds the word "please" for effect. His head tilts and his hand continues to tug at the bedding waiting for me to move.

"Better," I say, scooting over and freeing the bedding for him to sweep under it. The bed groans as he flops in, arranging the covers at his waist and giving me a different angle of his gorgeous upper body.

"I'm not having sex with you," I blurt out.

Although I probably would if he wanted to break his rule of no sex before a competition. Imagining the way his muscles flex and contract while I'm buried underneath him lights a fire in my core.

"That makes two of us."

He punches his pillow twice, adjusting it under his head before sliding his arm under what would be my pillow. I'm left wondering what to do. I nibble at my bottom lip as those chocolate eyes watch me.

"Lie down already. You act as if you've never slept with a guy before," he grumbles. The exhaustion in his voice is clear and his eyes close for a few long seconds before they open again.

I gaze at him. How relaxed and comfy he looks against the white linens and how much I want to sleep in here with him. Having enough of my indecision, he winds his thick forearm around my waist, sliding me down the bed to fit into the curve of his body.

"Isn't this nice?"

The heat coming from him is stupid nice. It's like cuddling with a personal heater. But the safety I feel with him pressing into my back, his heavy arm over my waist, and the one under my head are indescribable. It's nothing I have ever felt before and it makes me both calm and uneasy.

The calmness I understand. Protection is primal, what

every girl wants. The uneasiness is a little tricker. I figure it's because I don't want to feel this and have it taken away.

"Relax, it's me and you, remember? What we do is between us."

I release a big breath and say, "I've never done this before."

"Done what?"

"Sleep with a guy. I mean, just sleep."

I tug the pillow further under my neck and collect my hair to get it out of his face. Although he didn't seem to mind his nose buried in it. This is all new and weird. I wish I could relax, but this is way outside my comfort zone.

"I'm your first?"

The irony. But yes, he's my first in a lot of things.

"Yeah," I whisper, rather overwhelmed at how intimate this simple act feels.

In response, his arm tightens around my ribcage as he tucks me under his chin.

"Good."

The finality in that word lets me know he's headed back to sleep. Something I should do but can't. What if I need to pee or cough or snore and it keeps him awake? Plus, my damn brain can't stop overanalyzing us.

I know what he said last night, and I almost can't believe it's happening. But I'm also waiting for the other shoe to drop because things don't work out for me. It's always one step forward and two steps back.

I can't think of one good thing that has happened without something bad following right behind it. That's what makes me uneasy about us. I want this so badly with him that I'm also preparing for it to end. I hate that.

After staring at the wall long enough, I will my eyes to close and snuggle deeper into the warm comfort he provides. The next time I wake, I'm on my back and he's propped up on an elbow watching me.

"Was I snoring again?"

I wipe my mouth against the sleeve of my robe, hoping I don't have completely disgusting morning breath. His finger dips into the edge of my robe, trailing into my cleavage and back up to my collarbones. It stokes the skin to life beneath his touch and leaves a trail of burning lust.

"Yes, you were."

That husky morning voice, along with his finger, is doing things to me. Things that make me want to flip him on his back and ride the hell out of him.

"We'll have to work on that when we get back home. Because once I have you in my bed, you're not getting your own anymore."

When we get back home.

He said it again. That means this isn't just a California fling. He sees longevity in us. That brings a sweet smile to my face because I'll most certainly share a bedroom with him.

His teasing finger dips closer to my underboob with each stroke. I'd love for that finger to go straight south as it did before.

"Lower," I whisper, tucking my hand behind my head to watch him.

"I'd love to go lower, but we need to get going if we're to make the Petersen Museum."

"We're going to the Petersen Museum today?"

Badass, it's totally on my bucket list and something I'm dying to see.

"I thought you might enjoy getting out for a bit. I hope you don't mind me making plans for us."

"Mind, heck no. Let's go."

Of course, he doesn't answer nor make a move to get out of bed, and neither do I. And the stroking continues, going lower but not quite low enough. After a few torturous seconds, I decide two can play this game and I reach for him. He captures my hand, kissing it on the palm before holding it across my body.

"Nice try."

"You're such a tease," I accuse, flipping to my side to face him, which smashes my boobs together. He releases my hand to push the lapel back, exposing me completely.

"Actually, you are the tease. I've delivered twice." I open my mouth and then close it.

Man doesn't lie. He's 0-2.

"But it's not your fault."

His fingertip strokes a circle around the nipple, never touching it, and damn him for that.

"I know it's not my fault. I was thinking of how much I want to pin you to this mattress and ride the hell out of you." I smash his hand to my boob, forcing him to squeeze it, and he smiles.

"You can try demanding Dani." In one fluid movement, I'm buried under him. His erection is painful against my pelvic bone and his eyes are hooded with want. "If I let you."

Oh, let's play this game.

I try to move my hips against his to create some friction, but he clenches his thigh muscles, essentially stopping me. His elbows rest on either side of me, waiting for my next move. I wind my arms around his neck, trying to pull him toward me to kiss, but he smirks and doesn't move.

"You're cheating. Using your strength against me."

I try again with my arms, the sleeves sliding down my skin toward my shoulders, and he drops a couple of kisses on my forearm. Humor cuts through his face, and his eyes glint with satisfaction. I love the way he's gazing into my eyes, lively and playful. Teasing Tomlin is a surprise and one I'm coming to like the most.

"I'm using my advantages on you. You have some over me too."

His head dips to nip the skin on my breast. That perfect

beard of his is tickling my flesh and causing me to flinch. He does it over and over again as I laugh and wiggle underneath him. Never once does he lose the smirk plastered on his face. When he stops, I bite my lip in thought because I can't think of one advantage I have over him.

"Like what?"

"Where's the fun in telling?" He swiftly dips his head to give me a few quick kisses on my lips before lifting off and getting out of bed. "It's for you to discover."

"Ugh, I hate you."

I launch a pillow at his head, hoping it'll knock some secrets loose, but he catches it and chuckles. His muscles flex and constrict in the best possible way, putting on a little show of how they might grip and grab me.

"Got to do better than that, Dani."

He tosses the pillow at me before turning to walk into the bathroom and starting the shower. I don't know if he's intending for me to shower with him, but I can't do that. That's another first that I'm not willing to give yet. This is a lot of intimacy in a short amount of time, and I need to maintain some boundaries to protect myself.

I roll out of his bed, fix my robe so I'm completely covered, and walk to my room to close the door. Granted, he's seen me naked. Maybe it wouldn't be a big deal to him, but it's still a big step for me to shower with someone. I know we'll eventually get there, but it doesn't need to be today.

Excitement builds within me, knowing that the museum awaits. I can't help but wonder about the exhibits, the ages of the cars, and what the basement vault contains. It's going to be cool to see what is there.

When he first asked me to go to LA, I looked up a bunch of cool things to do and the museum popped up. I drooled over the pictures in their gallery, but now I get to see them firsthand. Well, hell, I think I died and went to car heaven.

To be able to touch them, view the craftsmanship up close, and see cars I've never seen in my life, is going to be awesome. And honestly, this is a perfect surprise and possibly a gift from him to me. It makes my heart explode with how much I love that fine-ass man. It's like our first date, even if he didn't say so.

I rush to get ready. Hopefully, we can grab breakfast on the way. When I open my bedroom door, he's dressed in his usual uniform of a dress shirt and slacks and sitting on the couch reading the newspaper.

For a second it reminds me of Dad and a fleeting thought of whether he would read the paper to me passes through my mind. I'm quick to dismiss it because that's way down the relationship road and I'm getting too far ahead of myself for that.

The moment he sees me, he folds the paper and tosses it onto the coffee table to stand. His eyes sweep appreciatively over my dress, and I'm glad I packed it.

"You look nice."

I smile because I think this is actually the first non-sexual compliment he's ever given me. Not that I need them, but receiving one from him after what we talked about last night is nice. I think it's the same compliment I gave him yesterday that caught him by surprise. Look at us getting all relationship like. Not to mention, my wedges put me closer to his lips, making it easier for him to kiss me.

"Thank you. I'm pretty excited about going."

"I am too. Are you feeling okay? Your stomach?" Worry appears out of nowhere and I chuckle.

"You weren't concerned about it when you were smashing your dick on it this morning," I say, swinging my purse onto my shoulder and walking toward the penthouse door.

He chuckles behind me. "Touché."

I throw open the door, waiting in the hallway for him to collect his wallet and keys from the bar top. As we walk to the elevator bank, he asks, "Do you want to drive?"

“I don't, maybe after. I was hoping we could pick up some coffee and muffins on the way there.”

Standing next to him and going on a semi-date, is giving me all the feels. This is what Kylie blabbers on about with each guy she dates. There have been many, but if this is the feeling she’s trying to get, I understand her chasing men for it.

The elevator pings and when we step inside, he texts the valet to bring the car around. The valet’s eyes lit up last night when Tomlin tossed him the keys to park it. Lucky guy is like me in that the only time he gets to drive a car like that is when rich fat cats like Tomlin let us. It makes me smile. Tomlin’s benevolent in ways he doesn’t even know.

“Sure, that's a great idea. We'll look for something on the way because I doubt they'll allow us to have food around their exhibits.” He flicks his wrist to look at his watch, a frown appearing. “We’ll need to hurry, or we could forget breakfast and grab lunch afterward. That might be better if you can wait so we can take our time and not rush.”

“Let's do that.”

Once the elevator doors open, I’m practically skipping in excitement. Partly because this is the first activity since arriving here other than that debacle on the beach. And looking at classic cars and their craftsmanship is one of my favorite things in the entire world. Plus, I get to do it with my favorite person in the world.

The second I see the car, I dash over to it and throw open my door to get it. The valet is still getting out as I’m getting in. Tomlin chuckles while dropping in beside me to pull out his sunglasses, arrange his phone in the holder, and fiddle with the music.

“Someone’s excited.”

“Yup, I can’t wait.”

I reward him with a smile, drop my purse on the floorboard, and adjust the hem of my dress to block the sun from my legs.

Once our seatbelts are buckled, he pulls away from the hotel and starts driving.

The ride is scenic. Having been to LA many times before, Tomlin points out different attractions while relaying facts or stories of his experiences at each place. At some point, I take out my phone to snap some pictures, looking exactly like a tourist.

Listening to his adventures makes me feel worlds apart from him, even if he acts like we're not. He's lived this whole other life. No, several lives compared to me, and it whispers to my fear of not being good enough. It's what Kylie said. It's what I accused him of at the cabin. What I hide underneath all my bravado.

He saw right through it and called me out on it. Forcing me to confront it, the same as he's confronting his feeling for me and seeing where this goes. Maybe we are more alike than I care to admit.

If only we could fast forward time, so I know if we'll make it or not. I wouldn't have to worry about us ending because I'd know we wouldn't, and I could enjoy every minute I'm with him. I hate waiting for the other shoe to drop. It's miserable, but I can't recall a time it hasn't.

Doing what I do best, I shove these haunting thoughts out of my mind. I don't want it to dampen my exhilaration as we enter the museum district.

When he passes a humongous red building with chrome waves, I want to jump out of the car and run inside without him. To think he set this up with me knowing about it, well, it's a nice surprise. Another one and it's swaying my opinion of surprises.

The second he parks the car, I'm out of it and bolting to the glass doors to yank on them. If this is my version of Christmas, I can't imagine what Pebble Beach will be like. I'll probably pee my pants when we get there.

"Eager, huh?" he says, joining me at the locked door.

They must recognize him because an older man in a blue suit appears out of nowhere to unlock the door and make introductions. He offers to show us around, but I shake my head. I know what these cars are and what they can do. I want to enjoy taking it at my pace and lingering where I want to linger without a dude yakking at me the whole time.

Tomlin spends several minutes catching up with the guy. It appears they know each other from Tomlin's car searches, which leaves me wandering the museum alone. Perfect.

The place has it all. From horse and buggy to hot rods, vintage cars to movie production, and replica cars. Many I've never seen or heard of before. The displays are perfect and organized. One flows into the next and then the next. It isn't until I completed the first floor that I realize Tomlin is giving me time alone to take it all in.

I thought he is still with the guy until I turn the corner and he's wandering amongst the cars. It's nice having someone else that appreciates the craftsmanship as I do. Of course, Lars would love it here too, but he's not the one I'm interested in. Tomlin is lingering in the Andy Warhol exhibit when I approach him.

"This is amazing," I say, looking around at the colorful artwork hanging on the wall that matches the cars.

"It makes me want one of my own."

His eyes shift down to mine, then back at the 1954 Mercedes Grand Prix Car.

"Yeah, well, I don't know if it's for sale. I doubt they even have two that exist in the world." I point to the silver and black car with the racing number on the driver's side door.

"No, a museum of my own."

Did bro say a classic car museum?

"Uh, why? You can come here and admire them."

I can't fathom how much that would cost. The insurance

policy alone would be out of sight. I can't believe I'm going to say this, but I might side with his dad on this one when he said no more cars.

"I don't have any hobbies. I don't plan on having children, so what else am I going to spend my money on?" he says, walking deeper into the exhibit.

Wait, I thought he had rooms for his hobbies. The trophy room, gym, and music room. Ah, yeah, those aren't really hobbies. There's a sadness to that statement. One I can relate to in the hardest way because I don't have hobbies either. It's pure survival mode for me. Not having children? I'd be a terrible mother, although I kept Anna alive for nearly two months. To be honest, I miss that little bugger. She grew on me but I don't miss the extra responsibility. That's for sure.

"I don't know. Travel? Vacation like this?" I offer because I don't know what rich people do in their spare time. I'm not one of them.

"That's all paid for by the sponsors or hosts."

His footsteps clack on the concrete floors, an echo following as he leaves one exhibit and strolls down the aisle of the Ghostbusters and Back to the Future cars.

"Would you help me? If I wanted to expand my collection, would you source cars with me? Maybe restore them if necessary?"

I don't think this is a good idea. It's as if he's lost, filling a void, and reminds me of the loneliness conversation again.

"Are you sure about this?"

I don't want to dash his dream if it's truly what he wants. But he seems to be grasping at straws.

I'm proud of myself. This is very insightful of me. Normally I take everything at face value, but in turning over this new leaf, I'm trying to evaluate more and act less. Be more Tomlin-like.

"No, but would you?"

His face is earnest, and my heart clenches.

"Don't be dumb. Of course, I would. But you need to think about this. Where would you store them? It'd have to have max security. And don't even get me started on insurance costs, jeez. And when would you have time? I mean, you work almost as much as me, maybe more."

We walk past millions of dollars in cars, and he wants to start one of these himself. I can't even fathom how much money he has to start his own vintage car museum. Internally, I shake my head. Outwardly, I'll support him the best I can.

"I'm retiring."

I stop walking because I must not have heard him right. His face is deep in thought. His long body leans against a column, admiring another car as if he didn't just drop a major bomb on me.

"You're retiring? But why? You're freaking amazing. Your fans, your sponsor—"

"After the Olympics next year, I'm done." A smile plays on his lips, and I stare at his soft expression. "I've achieved everything I have set out to achieve. It's done. I'm done."

"Does your dad know? Your sponsors or endorsement people? Does anyone know?"

My eyebrows are glued to my hairline because he didn't just say he's done. Like all the people that count on him will be unemployed. He didn't tell me that here of all places.

"No. Only you." He reaches for my hand. "I wanted to tell you first."

"Why?" I'm still processing him not being a judo champion, traveling the world, and collecting medals, even crappy silver ones. "Why me?"

"Because it affects you the most, our partnership. The business we are starting. I'll be around more, able to help you with it, and grow it."

"I need to sit down."

I untangle my hand from his and speed walk to the bench in front of the Terminator truck to plop down.

"I thought you'd be happy for me. Happy about my decision and what this means for us."

He sits on the edge of the bench, pressing his fingertips together as his forearms rest on his thighs. All these changes are traveling at light speed. He's making plans so fast about our future that it's making my head spin.

"Why are you upset about this?" he implores, rubbing his chin and the whiskers scrap against his fingers.

I'm on uneven footing here. All these confessions are hitting one after another, and I'm not used to this. First, he has feelings for me, but now he's retiring, and it affects me too. Ever since he's come into my world, it's been one thing after another.

All these truth bombs he's dropping are more of the same chaos. I sigh, facing him, my knee brushing his thigh, and he instantly straightens.

"I'm not upset. You caught me way off guard. Like this is your livelihood, all you have ever known, and you want to walk away from it. That's a big deal."

"I realize that. It's why I have been planning it for the last two years."

My jaw drops.

"Two years and you haven't told anyone?"

I can't imagine holding a secret that long. Honestly, I can't hold secrets at all because then I act all different, and I out myself.

"It's no one's business. I almost regret telling you, by your reaction," he murmurs, running his hand through his hair and squeezing the back of his neck. I lean forward to look into his eyes, trying to show him my sincerity like he's done with me so many times.

"I'm sorry. If this makes you happy, then I'm happy for you. I really am."

"And you? Does this matter to you?" His voice lowers, and I look past him to the other exhibit. The seconds tick by, causing the tension to build.

"I don't know."

He stands abruptly, walking away and leaving me to stare after him. I honestly don't know. I'm not a planner like him. I don't have my life all mapped out. I'm trying to survive day to day. Well, less now that I work for him. But even then, I haven't thought about the future, other than to hope this show brings us more clients. If it doesn't, well, I'm screwed. Lars too.

When he disappears into another exhibit, I let him go. Doesn't he realize we've been idling for months? Then suddenly, he wants to go from zero to one hundred in two seconds. Granted, I'm used to living life by the seat of my pants, but even this is too fast for me.

It matters to me, and a part of me wants to believe all he saying. The plans he's making for the future sound as though they include me beyond business partner, but again, the damn old shoe-dropping mentality is getting likelier as this is too much goodness in the shit show that normally is my life.

There's usually a total collapse of my life, and then figuring out a new norm. It happened when Dad died. It happened when Carl fired me. It's bound to happen again.

And how would it work?

I know Lars asked me to talk to him about a garage, but would it be where my life is in Cañon City or his in Denver? Would I live with him or get my own place? Could we work and date and not kill each other?

Doing his car is one thing. He stayed away the whole time because of his dad. But if he's there every day and every night, would it be combustion in a bad way? He knows how independent I am, and he is too. How would that work?

9

Exhaling, I push off the bench with the weight of the world on my shoulders. Maybe this is why he's pinching his neck all the time. The stress of planning the last two years wearing on him as it has on me for the last five minutes.

I follow him, glancing around the various exhibits until I glimpse his back heading down to the vault. Jogging after him, I skid to a stop at the sheer number of classic cars before me. The collection is breathtaking. I'd love to take a bunch of pictures, but first, I have to right this wrong before he completely turns away from me.

He's lingering next to a Round Door Rolls Royce, his shoulders slumped forward with his hands stuffed in his pockets. I walk to him, my presence not registering until I lean into his side.

His hand slides out, folding me into his side and tucking his arm around my waist. It's the same way he held me by the El Camino the night Dad's belonging got soaked and I agreed to take on his project.

"I'm sorry, T."

I gaze up at him, his expression unreadable.

"If you're not happy, then you're not happy."

The resignation in his voice is completely wrong and very un-Tomlin-like.

"Don't. I'm happy, but I'm scared too. Like I said last night, this is all new to me so I had to take a minute. You've been planning this for two years but I just learned about it."

I need him to see things from my point of view because I want to be with him. I want to make this work, but I still don't have any idea what I'm doing. It's all new and he must understand that to understand me.

He closes his other arm around me, drawing me against the front of his hard body.

"You're right. I did sort of spring it on you."

I smile. I want to assure him it's okay.

"Yeah, you did. And I have a million questions, but I'm with you on this."

"That's all I wanted to hear," he murmurs before his lips descend to mine in the gentlest of kisses. I like the variety of which he kisses. Some demanding, some playful, and some sweet as can be. This is the last one, where my arms wind around his neck and his rest at my waist. His soft lips brush along my cheekbone and into my hair as he squeezes me.

"I don't think I can get you off against this car."

I burst out laughing, the seriousness of his bombshell announcement fading away when I lean back and catch his wicked expression. In true Tomlin fashion, his wit clears the tension and changes it back to us being us. I marvel at his ability to do it.

"Definitely not the Round Door Rolls Royce," I say, sliding my palms down his shirt to rest them on his hard pectoral muscles that flex for a second and then relax. "But if you want to do it again outside, I'm game."

He groans, looking up at the ceiling before gripping my

waist.

"You have no idea how much restraint it has taken not to bend you over every surface I see. It's all I think about. That and this damn mouth."

His palm slides up my ribcage, grazing my side boob to cup my chin and press his thumb against my lower lip. I lick it with my tongue, and he slides it into my mouth where I suck it as enthusiastically as I'd like to do to another part of his body.

"Christ."

The hand at my waist yanks me to the right and aligns with his erection. It's as painfully hard as it was this morning. Mad respect for him holding all this in because if someone told me I couldn't have sex, I'd go on a murderous rampage.

"Mmm," I moan, sucking even harder and grinding against his dick because I'm horny as hell right now.

"Mr. Takahashi?"

A male voice calls from behind him. We both freeze, guilty as hell. Tomlin's eyes widen, matching mine, and he slowly slides his thumb out of my mouth. Luckily, his body is blocking my view so the man couldn't see what I was doing, but if this place has cameras, then damn.

No way can Tomlin turn around with that hard cock. It would be embarrassing for him personally and professionally. Something we should've thought about. I drop my hands, his fall away a second later, and I step to the side.

"Yes?" I ask the man that greeted him at the door. "Did you need us?"

I'm stalling to buy Tomlin time to calm himself down.

He clears his throat, trying to be discreet. "Er, well, yes, I was coming to tell you that your reservation is ready. At the café on the second floor."

"Great. Can you take me there while Mr. Takahashi makes an important phone call?" My eyes slide to his momentarily where he mouths thank you. "I'll see you upstairs."

I pat the side of his arm and walk over to the curator, who is staring at Tomlin's back. The guy hesitates for a moment, but his manners kick in. He leads me out of the vault, into the elevator, and to the restaurant booth overlooking the corner of Wilshire Boulevard and Fairfax Avenue.

The server is over in a nanosecond, making introductions and getting my drink order. I'd order for Tomlin, but I have no idea what he wants. It's probably a good ten minutes before he appears, calm and confident, striding through the quiet restaurant to me.

"All good?" I ask when he slips into the booth across from me.

"Yes, thank you." His cheeks are pink, and the embarrassment is clear.

"I forget you're famous and stuff. We probably need to cool it on the PDA. Or at least keep it rated PG."

I pick up the menu to peruse the options while he sets his phone and keys on the table.

"Agree. This is new to me too, Dani. I've never brought someone to travel with me, especially not someone I'm interested in."

His confession is sweet, and I chuckle.

"Well, look at us and all of our firsts. I guess there's still some virgin left in both of us."

I don't bother looking up from the menu. But when I don't get a response, I move it out of my face to an awkward-looking server, and Tomlin's stare boring into me. All I can do is shrug and order fried cheese and a firebrick pizza before handing the menu over. I'm probably going to need to rein in my mouth. I don't want to embarrass him.

He quietly orders while I look at the activity on the street. A couple strolls down the sidewalk, pointing up at the building while cars zoom by. The pace is much faster and glitzier here. I couldn't take it. There are other museums in the area that I'd love to see, but I don't know how much time Tomlin has today.

"Hey, are you training today or doing anything with your sponsors?"

When I look at him, he's frowning at his phone, which seems to be a more common occurrence than I realize.

"What's up?"

His eyes level with mine and then back to his phone to finish typing a message. Once he's finished, he locks it and sets it face up on the table again. Something that Kylie warned me about in all her relationship drama. Face up is good. Face down is a red flag for the crap they are hiding.

"Dear old dad, wanting to know my whereabouts. And to answer your first question, yes, I need to head back to train tonight. Unfortunately, I'll have to train all day tomorrow, but maybe we can grab a late dinner if you don't mind waiting for me."

I have a day to myself to run around LA.

"Of course, I'll wait for you or have a second dinner. That's not the issue. What's the plan for Friday?"

The server brings his drink order while I tap the straw against the table to remove the wrapper.

When the server leaves, Tomlin says, "Simple. Prepping for the match with the team, the charity event, and the fan meet and greet. I'd like you to be with me throughout the event if you wouldn't mind."

"Um, like in front of people?"

His eyes crinkle in the corners when he gazes at me. Then realization when he sees in my expression that I don't know what he's talking about. His forearms rest on the table as he leans in, as if apologizing and asking at the same time.

"Yes, the event is sold out."

Me with him in public, being watched and photographed. Like we're barely even an us and now he wants me to stand beside him in front of other people, play the part of dotting girlfriend? I mean, how do I not freak out and tell him that's really not my type of thing? I mean, you can take the girl out of the garage, but you can't take the garage out of the girl.

I'm not fancy like Kylie. I don't have fake nails, fake eyelashes, or extensions down my back. Hell, I only brought two dresses and these wedges are the only nice shoes I have. And he wants me to get all dolled up, stand beside him, and be charming.

I'm not like that. What if I say the wrong thing to the wrong person? Knowing me, I'll do that several times. And what of my piercing? What will they think of him being with a girl like me? Maybe Kylie is right, we are culturally and worldly too far apart.

"I'm not sure."

It's the only words I settle on. This is the wrong time and place to bring up all these fears. He grimaces as if my answer physically hurts him. We are barely over the misunderstanding from downstairs, only to head into a new one. His hand flips to rest open on the table, an invitation for mine, and I drag it out of my lap to place it in his.

"Why?"

I release a huge breath. Looking at the cars outside, the billboard beyond it, and finally back to those deep brown eyes.

"Dani, why?" he repeats, squeezing my hand at the same time.

What does he always say? It's him and me. What happens between us stays between us. I know it's his way of saying I can be open and vulnerable with him. Sexually, I get it. Emotionally is even harder, especially in the middle of a public place and in the middle of the day.

"T."

"Dani."

"It's not you."

"Don't even start with that cliché stuff. It's not like you. Tell me what is bothering you and we can talk it out."

I pause, squeezing his hand this time before releasing it and sitting back.

"I don't fit, T. Look at you and look at me. I don't match you. Kylie said it, and it's true. The more I'm pulled into your life, the more I don't understand it. I'm not trying to start a fight with you, but I'm not all fancy and from that world like you are. I'm as opposite as can be. What if I say something embarrassing? Do something that embarrasses you in front of all those people? I'd hate myself and you'd hate me too."

It's not the best words I could've used, but I guess it gets close to what I'm trying to say.

"First of all, you can never embarrass me. For that to happen, means I care about others' opinions over mine. To further that point, the only opinion that matters aside from mine is yours."

He closes his hand and rolls his wrist to press his palm against the table.

"But what about the airport? What if it lands in the papers or online or wherever the hell they post that crap? This event is that but ten times worse because I'll have to talk to people, and you know my mouth. I thought I could sit in the back, watch from afar, not be plastered to your side. Plus, I'm blunt as hell and—"

"And it's one of the things I find attractive about you. You're not a yes person. Everyone tells me what I want to hear. You tell me how it is. I value that. And don't worry about the pictures or the papers. If you are in them, then who cares? My agent can deal with it. He can spin it as more press for our new garage."

Our again. I love when he says that. He pushes his index finger into the table as he speaks to drill home his point.

"I don't want you to be like me. It's one of the things I love most about us. We're different in all the right ways. It brings variety and differing viewpoints. I have an opinion and method for every part of my life, and you don't. It's refreshing to have someone carefree and bold in my curated life."

He sorts through my points, making a convincing argument for each one of them. It makes me warm inside and I sit forward, wanting to hear more.

"Dani, I don't know what Kylie said to you, but from the sounds of it, it's not good for you or us. I know she's your best friend and my ex, but at the end of the day, we didn't work out because she wasn't her own person. She molded herself to what she thought I wanted. You'd never do that. You'd tell me to fuck off or get out if I tried. Actually, you've already done both." I burst out laughing because he's right. "Exactly. You know it's true, and that's what I want. I want to be with you for exactly how you are. Not for how you think you should be around me, my fans, or my sponsors. Be yourself and everything will turn out fine."

Dammit, if this man didn't just say he accepted me once again with all my flaws. My heart swells with so much love that I scoot out of my booth and join him in his. I grab both sides of his face and plant the most obscene kiss on his face.

I know we shouldn't make out in here as we did downstairs, but damn if I don't want to reward him for all his pretty words to me. He breaks the kiss and maintains some decency in this place. Our lips are inches apart, eyes boring into each other's, and smiling like lovesick teenagers at each other. If I could get a copy of the security footage of how we are looking at each other right now, I would, and I'd carry it on my phone forever.

"Then I'll go."

He rewards me with that panty-dropping smile and a quick kiss to follow.

"Thank you."

I pucker up for one more kiss, which he grants before I return to my side of the table.

"It sounds like a long day for you."

I plunk the straw in my soda and take a long drink.

"It's exhilarating. The excitement of walking into that place feeds my adrenaline for the match and the high I feel from the win carries into meeting fans that are as excited as I am. My description doesn't do it justice."

The smile on his face is genuine. When his gaze flickers out the window for a moment as if lost in thought, I wonder how's he going to replace this feeling when he's retired.

"If you feel this way, why retire at all?"

That draws those soft brown eyes back to me and the smile clears from his face.

"It's not one thing per se, but a combination. Probably the most glaring is to get away from my father. Although I could fire him, it would send a shock wave through the sport if I did."

"Why? You seem to hate each other. That would be understandable."

He shakes his head. "No, not understandable as we hide our hatred well."

I don't understand that. I'm pretty clear on whom I like and hate, and those people know as well. Judd and Carl come to mind.

"Okay, what're the other reasons?"

"Ego. I don't want to decline. I want to go out on top. I've seen too many athletes stick around and try to compete when they should've retired. It's almost an embarrassment to themselves. It ruins their record by adding many losses as they age to a record achieved when they were younger, faster, stronger, and overall better."

That one I get. Go out in a blaze of glory and not a decrepit skeleton trying to hold on to their former glory.

"Yeah, I agree."

The server slides the fried cheese sticks into the middle of the tables and hands out little plates.

"Want one?" I ask, knowing he'll decline.

"Are you sure that your stomach can handle that?"

His eyes narrow at the delicious gooeyness that is seeping out of the breading when I move it to my plate and pour some marinara over it.

"Nope, but we'll see."

I bite off a piece, sucking in air to cool it off, and he shakes his head.

"If I get sick again, I'll be fine, since you'll be busy doing your judo stuff."

"It wouldn't please me if you were sick again." Yeah, it wouldn't *please* me either. "I thought you wanted to do touristy things?"

He pats the side of his cheek, indicating I have something on my face.

"I do and I will." I wipe the sauce and continue eating the best damn fried cheese I've ever had. Must be the crispy breading. "Now, what are these other reasons?"

"A general restlessness. I love the sport and I love the fans, but I don't think I want to be a coach. Coach Dad killed that for me. The endorsement deals are nice. Working with the organizers can be a hassle at times, but overall, I think I'm done. It's been a part of my life longer than it has not. Although the sport has been good to me, I want to try something else."

He arranges his silverware, lining it up, so it's all even, and looks at me.

"And starting a car restoration garage, is that something else? Don't answer that, I already know what you said. But why don't you stay in the sport? I mean, I don't know anything about it. But those football guys retire, and they become sportscasters. Is there some sort of sportscasting for judo?"

I polish off another cheese stick before slurping down more soda. So far, so good on my belly.

"There are opportunities to stay in the sport, and I have

been mulling those over. Some organizations are better than others that I could work for, but in general, I don't know. Focusing on getting our business going is intriguing, like a new challenge, something I could learn."

I stop mid-chew because I want to set things straight before this goes any further.

"The garage is mine. I'm not having you skulking around as you did at Carl's place and driving me crazy. If you're in for the day, then you're working. If you're not working, then don't be there."

Before he can answer, our food is being delivered. Mine is a bubbling and gooey pizza and his is boring fish surrounded by vegetables. One day, I'll get him to eat as badly as I do.

"I want to be part of the process, Dani. I missed out on my mom's car, and I want to be there for the next. Even if it doesn't belong to me. Can you see why?" He leans forward, putting his elbows on the table, which he never does to convey his point.

"I thought you said I was gonna be running it? I distinctly remember you saying I was going to be the new Carl, but it sounds as though you're going to be the new Carl."

I learned my lesson with the fried cheese and am waiting for the pizza to cool down before I eat. Tomlin isn't eating his either, but I doubt it's for the same reason.

"I don't want to fight with you. The garage is yours to run. I only want to be included. I thought you, of all people, would understand that."

I pat the top of his hand to assure him I won't cut him out. Because his request has little to do with the actual garage itself, and everything to do with the loneliness statement we've talked about before.

"Look, T. I don't know how this will all work until we start, but I'm just trying to say I need space to work. Boundaries and all that crap. Plus, we don't even have a garage, which is something I was discussing with Lars."

I take a bite of my pizza, still piping hot, but not enough to scald my mouth.

"There's this place I know not too far from the house. That would be ideal." He collects his silverware to eat. "I could get a broker on it when we return."

"On the west side of the mountain?"

He stops cutting into his fish to look at me.

"In Denver."

If my mouth wasn't already full of pizza, it would've fallen open. I shove it to one side and say, "I'm not moving to Denver. You agreed to Cañon City."

His head tilts.

"Are you sure? I don't think I ever said I'd start a business in that town."

The certainty with which he says it fills me with doubt. When he eats, it's as if the conversation is over, making my stomach hurt.

"But you know I hate Denver. I told you that. About my father and . . ." I sigh and look across the restaurant. Did I imagine him agreeing or did I assume? Did I really set up my whole life around him and now I have to move away?

"What about Lars? He can't move either. Not with his family situation and all."

His eyes shift to mine for a second before eating a fork full of veggies. I scratch my head, knowing he knows. But his flippant attitude about it is pissing me off.

I'd have to move away from everything I have ever known. Kylie, Lars, Eli and Ronnie, Isla, and Anne. And what would Lars do? He'd have to find another job since I wasted his time with my pipe dream that Tomlin's dashing.

"Why can't you move, T? Why uproot everything just so you can stay in Denver? You'll be retiring. That gives you the flexibility to live anywhere."

I push my plate away. My appetite is gone due to this conversation.

"So can you. You don't have anything tying you to that dusty little town other than your memories, and Carl destroyed some of those already. Staying there puts you in direct competition with him. If you moved to Denver, you don't have to worry about him possibly suing if clients leave him and come to you since you have no wait list whereas he does. It would be a fresh start, maybe rewrite Denver in a positive light, separate from the loss of your dad."

He's doing it again. Molding things his way. Didn't he do this before, back in my apartment? Before I got fired and when I wanted to talk this out with Carl. It's not the same but it feels similar.

"I don't know what to say. I've already uprooted my life two months ago and now you want me to move from the only town I have ever known?"

"Dani." His hand slides across the table, seeking mine, but I shake my head. "It's a new beginning for both of us, personally and professionally."

"Wait. To be with you, as in being with you, I have to move?"

I slide to the edge of the booth. Confusion wrinkles across his face as his open palm still rests on the table waiting for mine.

"I assumed you wanted to be with me. Live with me as you have been."

"But we really haven't. You're in Denver. I'm in Cañon City. I figured it would continue like that. You said it yourself, we're both extremely independent people. I thought the long distance was what it was going to be. Hell, I hadn't told you this because I didn't want to think about it myself, but I was going to move out and find my own place when we got back."

I can't believe I blurted that out. But since we're putting all the cards on the table, might as well.

"You're moving out? How long have you been planning this?"

His temper flares. The open collar gives way to his chest, rising and falling. His palm curls into a fist, sliding back to rest beside his plate.

"You weren't even going to discuss this with me? You were just going to spring it on me in your usual Dani fashion?"

Now my temper is flaring, causing me to plant my elbows on the table.

"What does that mean? Usual Dani fashion?"

His eyes narrow, a ferociousness in them that I don't like. I ready myself for what he's going to say next.

"You fly by the seat of your pants. You act first and think second. It's a lack of impulse control, which is fine for small things, but not everything in your life can be that way."

Sucker punch, right to the gut.

"Well, if I'm such a horrible person, then why be with me? Both personally and professionally," I sneer, not caring how nasty I sound. "I'm sure you can find a nice, polite robot of a girl that doesn't swear and doesn't work on cars, that will love to play house in your modern museum."

I'm panting, fire burning through me at his haughty attitude. Didn't he just say he doesn't want a yes girl? But damn if he didn't describe the perfect version of one. What he says and what he wants seems to be two different things. If he wants a yes girl, then he can go find her. Over my dead body will I be a yes girl.

I need some air.

"I can't even with you right now."

He tries to reach for me, but luckily the booth is too wide.

"That's not what I'm saying. Don't run away. Stay here and talk to me. Let's work through this."

I grab my purse and shuffle out of the booth to stand. He attempts to do the same.

"Don't get up. And don't follow me. I'll make my way back to the hotel when I'm good and ready."

Rage burns through me and the last thing I want is to sit here with him. He'll talk it out, manipulate me to his will, and I'll hate myself for doing it. Yeah, walking away and taking some time to myself to cool off is exactly what I need. He's out of the booth, standing before me, with an anxious look on his face.

"But Dani, you don't know this city, and what if—"

"I can take care of myself, Tomlin. Don't worry about me."

"I do worry about you."

His dark eyes are filled with the same sincerity as in his voice, and it's too much. This is how he wins, and I lose.

I step back and shake my head, saying, "No, I need time."

Time to think, clear my head, and not cave to his will for the umpteenth time. With that, I cross the restaurant, not giving a backward glance before walking past the hostess stand and out the door. I'm fuming, stomping down the stairs and pushing out the front door of the museum.

Once I'm on the street, I gulp in the warm air and try to calm down. The sky is impossibly blue and the palm trees sway in the wind, but I can't enjoy how nice the day is.

This is a complete shit show. For someone who thinks he communicates a lot, he doesn't say anything at all and then vomits a year's worth of thoughts on me.

The traffic is loud, and the exhaust fumes are too much as I stand in the doorway. My phone is vibrating non-stop. I know it is him trying to convince me to go back inside and talk this out. Maybe it's immature of me to run off, opposite of my new leaf. But not this time. I need a break to process all this.

I hook a right and walk toward the museum I saw from the restaurant windows. Hopefully, he'll listen to me and not follow. Knowing him, he will, and I need to get out of here. I jog down the street, looking back once as I round the corner. Sure enough, he's running out of the building looking to the left. The traffic light is green, but I don't care as I dodge the cars to race across the street.

An enormous cluster of old fashion white and silver streetlights catch my eye. I speed toward them. There's a plaque explaining what it is and the date of the installation. People are taking turns posing and snapping pictures and the thought of taking a selfie is sour to me.

This trip isn't turning out as I had thought. When Tomlin finally gives me the attention I want and I think we are going somewhere, he snatches it away by wanting me to move. I'm not wrong, he is. He's making no concessions and I'm having to make all of them. He's used to getting his way. I get that, but not this time.

The conversation about how his life isn't his own and his lack of control comes to mind. Maybe that's why he thinks I'll move. The areas he has control over are wielded and held tightly, suffocatingly so. If that's the case, I don't know how we will ever work.

I don't like being controlled. He knows that. Hell, it's been an ongoing feud between us for the last six months. When I think back, he's ended up getting his way every time. And I am the one that caved. The same with Carl. Me bending to everyone's will. Well, that shit won't fly.

No.

Not at all.

As I stroll through the lights, I duck behind one when the metallic roadster streaks by. He has his glasses on, but from what I could see, he's scowling. Good, let him be mad. I'm mad too. And I'm not compromising. I've lost enough. He can lose this time. He'll have to bend, or he can find that robot girl that will do as he commands. At least my phone has stopped vibrating.

I sigh, leaning against the pole when a spaceship of a

building in the distance catches my eye. Where windows should be are fan-folded white panels with a cylindrical rock wall in the middle and a winding stone staircase hugging the structure. I've never seen anything like it.

As I walk toward the building, a cluster of bushes surrounds the monument sign that says it's the Pavilion for Japanese Art. Of course. I'm mad at that hot and sexy part Japanese guy and the universe plants my ass in front of this museum. Of all the places in LA, I'm here.

"Hilarious," I say to the sky above and then proceed to the front doors.

The moment I step inside, my eyes adjust to the soft lighting and the serene setting. Naturally, museums are quiet, but this seems calming by the way the attendant whispers the exhibit is free and no flash photography. She hands me a pamphlet of the featured exhibits and then points through the doors for me to wander at my pace.

The place is all curving pathways with chrome railing, glass panels, and sand-colored walls. It reminds me of the clean lines of both his modern museum house and the mountain resort. Simple and peaceful.

The air even smells clean and fresh. It's definitely rising up to greet me. I stroll past a bright-colored canvas with classic symbols of Japanese culture, a massive oil painting with the country's flag, and a collection of stunning samurai warrior uniforms.

The longer I amble from room to room, the faster my anger dissipates as I lose myself in a culture that isn't my own. The long and fascinating history, the plaques detailing the famous leaders, and the retelling of tales from long ago have me spending hours reading everything in this place.

By the time I hit the exit door, I'm so enriched and impressed by his culture that all I want to do is ask him about it. Once outside, I find a concrete bench over by the park and sit to pull out my phone. The smog of the city compared to that exhibit has me wrinkling my nose. This place stinks.

The sun darts behind a cloud, making it easier to see the dozen missed calls and text messages for Tomlin, begging me to come back and talk to him. Maybe I overreacted. But he has to understand that this is one thing I can't compromise on.

Why do I have to uproot my life for him? I want this to go somewhere. I want to be with him, but I can't walk away from my life. What if it doesn't work out? What if I'm the one asking Kylie to deliver a box of his things and a sappy card that she rips up?

I already put all my eggs in one basket with Carl and look where that got me. I knew it was a risk doing the same with Tomlin professionally, but now he's asking to do it personally as well. It seems to be too much too fast. Jeez, it's only Wednesday, and he's dropped more truth bombs than I can handle. Surely, he's got to understand that. Not that I wanted to fight with him but with the intensity of his stare and how quickly he shut me down, I had to get out of there.

I'm not used to having this many major decisions to make. His applying pressure to make them all at once with no further discussion or consideration for my feelings is bullshit. My life has remained relatively unchanged in the years following Dad's death, so fast-tracking all these milestones is overwhelming.

Although he called and texted that many times, he only left a couple of voicemails. As I listened to them, neither are angry or upset, just a quiet desperation for us to work through this, that there will be many discussions we'll need to have, and running off solves nothing.

He's right. Running off solves nothing, but it brings clarity. I know I should call an Uber, but I want to walk around the museum district a little longer before I have to go back and face the music. Tell him that I'm not moving to Denver, and that's final. I hope it's not the end of us.

10

The penthouse is dark, other than the same light he left on when he played the piano for me. I figured he'd be gone by now, seeing as how he told me about tonight, but a part of me is still disappointed I didn't get a chance to tell him my decision.

The door swooshes closed behind me, and I cross the room to drop my purse on the wet bar where he's left a note. It says he had them package up the pizza and it's in the fridge if I want it. He hopes we can talk later tonight if it's not too late.

I drop the note back on the marble countertop and walk over to the fridge to dig it out. I didn't intend to stay as long as I did at the museum area, but it was nice to walk the streets and see the sights, taking a few more pictures on my phone. With the pizza box in one hand and a soft drink in the other, I collapse on the couch and eat in front of the TV.

Halfway through eating, my phone vibrates, and I dash to get it, hoping that it's Tomlin calling. When I pull the phone from my purse, it's Eli and I immediately answer it.

"Hey, Eli."

"Hi, Dani."

"Why are you out of breath?"

I walk back to the couch and flop on it, putting my feet on the coffee table like Tomlin does to sink into the cushions.

"I was jogging with the pups."

I grab a clump of my hair to look for split ends creeping up the strands. A haircut before coming would've been good, seeing that I'll be meeting important people later in a couple of days. If Tomlin still wants me to go after today. I swear, things are such a mess now.

"Ah, I didn't realize you were a runner," I say, propping the phone against my shoulder to hold it in place while I break off a split end. "I can let you go if it's a bad time."

"Don't you dare hang up. I called you. Of course, I run. How do you think I maintain this slender physique?" he jokes, and I honestly have never wondered that. "How Los Angeles? What have you seen? Did you tour celebrities' houses? See the Hollywood Walk of Fame?"

I love how he asks four questions at once in his endless supply of enthusiasm.

"I got food poisoning and have been down for the count until today."

"Sweetie, no. Don't you have the worst luck? Here I thought you were living it up over there and you've been barfing your guts out instead?"

"Basically, but I went to a car museum today, which was pretty cool, and a Japanese art one too."

And got into a fight with Tomlin about upheaving my entire life. I debate about telling him about that, but he didn't call to hear my drama. I drop my strand to hunt for more split ends.

"That sounds fun," he says sarcastically, and I chuckle. "Are you feeling better now?"

"Yeah, mostly."

"Okay, what's going on? I hear it in your tone." There's a

bunch of racket on his end, dogs barking and a door shutting. "Sorry, had to shove them inside. I can hear you better."

"Nothing." I intentionally spike my voice to sound more cheerful, to take his focus off me. "How's Anna doing with the dogs and Isla? And don't worry, I haven't forgotten her t-shirt request."

He hums, not believing the 'nothing' part.

"Anna, that little peanut, apparently rules the roost now. She's a feisty little thing, but seriously. Who in their right mind would have five dogs and add another one to the mix?" He chuckles at himself, which has me smiling too. "She even wants to sleep with us. Ronald isn't happy about that. He doesn't like dogs in the bed and wondered if she picked up that bad habit at your house."

I remember when Tomlin looked at Anna with disdain. He'd die walking into a house with six of them. I don't want to admit that I did break down and let her sleep with me in the bed. It came after one extreme thunderstorm that shook the house, scaring her and me. She was whimpering and I placed her in bed with me, which turned into an apparent 'bad habit'. He doesn't need to know all that though. I'm sure they will fix or cure her of it.

"Only good-hearted people like you and Ronnie would have that many animals, not to mention the ones at the shop."

"But Dani, I have to tell you something, and it's not good."

I drop my hair, dread swimming with the pizza crust in my stomach.

"What's wrong?"

A sigh loosens from him and then his throat clears. It's bad. I drag my feet from the table to sit up.

"A group of girls attacked Isla earlier today. Apparently, they've been bullying her for some time now, but Isla said nothing to anyone."

Fury burns through my body and I'm up pacing in front of

the terrace doors. My reflection follows me as the sea and sky beyond are pitch black.

"Why the hell not?"

My accusation is hot and fast at Eli, even if he's not at fault here.

"Because she didn't want it to interfere with the foster approval process."

Of course, she wouldn't. That girl is a victim of abuse. She wouldn't do anything to jeopardize getting out of there and away from those little bitches. My hand rolls into a fist as if I can punch their lights out right now. Hell, I would if I could. Be damn justified too.

"Yeah, well. Is she okay?"

"She's at the hospital."

"What?! The hospital?! Holy crap, Eli. Lead with that, not telling me about Anna."

I can't pace any faster. Being thousands of miles away and unable to charge up to that facility and kick whoever's ass is responsible for this makes me feel helpless as fuck.

"I'm sorry, sweetie. I was trying to ease into telling you since you're on your trip and supposed to be having a wonderful time." His voice drops, the reality of the situation taking the chipperness right out of it. I appreciate his reasoning and consideration to not ruin my vacation but, still, this is major bullshit.

"What did they do to her? I swear I want to break their faces."

"She has a broken arm and a black eye. One girl punched her, and she hit her head on the concrete floor when she went down. They scanned her for a brain bleed, which she doesn't have, but they are keeping her for observation to be cautious."

A restrained sob loosens from him, and I don't blame him. Where I rage, he cries. His is a better response than mine, wanting to kick kids' asses.

Needing to punch someone right now, I settle for punching the pillow on the couch. My chest heaves as I'm blinded by rage. Those little fuckers picking on that tiny girl who'd never harm a fucking mouse.

"When I get back, I'm going to burn that fucking place to the ground over this. I'll get Hamilton to report them to the . . . wait. Does Hamilton know?"

His crying settles into soft sobs on the other end of the phone.

"Eli, I'm sorry. I didn't mean—"

He lets out a ragged breath, then says, "Officer Hamilton . . . sorry, this just breaks my heart and I'm a little emotional."

This guy who has a menagerie of animals and has a bazillion more at the pet store to take care of doesn't need to apologize for being emotional. He's everything that's right in this shitty world.

"Don't apologize. I get it. That's why you'll be a great dad to her. You'll hug and do all that mushy stuff that she needs, whereas I'll scorch the Earth and live amongst the ashes."

He chuckles. We couldn't be more different in how we show we care.

"That's what makes you great, sweetie." He sniffs again, clears his throat, and continues, "Officer Hamilton was the one that called us. He met us at the hospital and has been an absolute doll all day."

Good, Hamilton's doing his job. As he should. If he wasn't, I'd kick his ass too.

"He thinks this might be favorable for us to get her into our custody faster. Our attorney is exploring that as we speak. Isn't that ridiculous that her getting attacked might fast-track some processes?"

"That's fucked up."

I click my piercing against my teeth, walking over to the

terrace doors to throw them open. The warm air brushes my skin and if I wasn't already burning up, it would be nice.

"What started all this? Like why today?"

I hunch over the railing, propping my elbows on the glass edge as the waves lazily roll out.

"Apparently, it started when Ronald and I bought her some new clothes because, as you know, she didn't have any. And girl, you saw her drowning in those sweats they gave her."

Yeah. They hung off Isla to the point she had to carry the waistband in her hand to keep them up since they didn't have a drawstring.

"Well, one girl got jealous and told her friends. They have been taking whatever we give her that could fit one of them. When she asked us to stop buying her new stuff, we assumed it was because she was out of space to store things, which makes sense. After all, she basically gets a bed and a small dresser at the end of it."

"Like a prison," I say, never seeing her room because that's not allowed but envisioning it being as sad and cinder block as the rest of the place. Hamilton chided me for calling it a kid prison, but it looks and sounds like one.

"It's not a prison, Dani."

I roll my eyes because Eli's always putting a happy spin on everything, which I mostly like.

"But she told Hamilton and me about the toiletries and pencils in the very beginning. Hamilton said he was going to do something about it, and I even followed up with the ass to make sure he did. He reported it to somebody important over there because he said it had stopped."

"That stopped. They moved on to bigger things, like her clothing. Anyway, it escalated today when we gave her a charm bracelet. She was unwilling to part with it when they saw her wearing it."

That girl has nothing to her name. After all she's been

through, she deserves every little charm and trinket, clothes, and whatnot the guys want to buy her. I grip the railing, wondering if this place has a gym because I need some way to expel this murderous energy. I haven't gotten into a fistfight in nearly two months. It's basically a record for me.

"Isla cried when we gave it to her. It had five little charms on it, something meaningful to her that she didn't want to give it up. This was the first time she fought back and then they piled on her. It was brutal . . ." His voice trails off with emotion.

I look to the sky, wondering how many more hits this poor girl can take to her already shitty life.

"That fucking kid prison pisses me off. Whose ass can I beat over this? You know I have been itching for a good fight."

"To start, you won't be beating anyone's butt. These are teenage girls," he says calmly, after taking in a few deep breaths. "And they'll lose privileges over this."

"Like what? Not being able to watch TV for a day or two?" My fingers are going numb with how hard I'm clutching the metal and I release it to get the feeling back. "As if that's even enough punishment for landing this girl in the hospital. Or some lame ass bullshit like that?"

"No, it's more severe than that, but we don't know all the details yet. Officer Hamilton had to leave, but he's going to let us know."

"He better. In fact, I'll ride his ass like a fucking donkey so he doesn't forget, and then you guys can focus on her. What happens now?"

The dog barking in the background gets louder, and he mumbles to someone else. I wait a few long seconds.

"Sorry, Ronald is home and was wondering why I was outside on the phone. Well, she'll get released in a day or two. The attorney is working on it and then Hamilton's part. Otherwise, that's all for now."

I go back to pacing the terrace, the wind pulling my hair in different directions.

"Good. I hate that I'm not there for you and her." I exhale my disappointment into the phone.

"Sweetie, don't. Nothing can be done that hasn't already been done. Enjoy your vacation." He chuckles. "Oh, yeah, I forgot that it's been awful. Now what is going on with you? I feel like there's something you're not telling me."

Dang, his intuition. I lean against the glass railing, admiring the crystal chandelier dangling from the middle of the living room.

"I don't want to get into it. I don't want to take away from what you're already dealing with."

"Dani, don't take this the wrong way, but nothing you can say will take away from my worries about her. Her becoming part of our family is all I think about, and I have you to thank."

I appreciate him saying that, but my part is small potatoes compared to his commitment to being a parent to a teenager.

"Does this have anything to do with that handsome man you're traveling with?"

He takes my delay as an immediate front to Tomlin, and he couldn't be more right.

"Yeah." I sigh into the phone. "Everything is going too fast between us. I didn't really know where I stood with him before and ever since we got here, he's been all affectionate and open with me. It's weird."

I start at the beginning, with Tomlin's sudden change and admitting to caving to his feelings for me.

"Really?" His surprise matches mine. "What did he say?"

I'm scratching my head and staring at the dark ocean as if the answers are floating in there.

"What has he not said? It's such a long story and I don't even know what to think."

The wind picks up, echoing into the phone and making it

harder to hear Eli. I walk inside, close the terrace doors, and lean my head against the glass.

"Ronald's making dinner and feeding the dogs. I've got time," he says softly, walking the line between being supportive and not intrusive. Typical Eli fashion.

He's been a good friend, helping with both Anna and Isla. I launch into everything that has happened, leaving out the sex parts because that's private, but he gets the gist.

It's a few seconds of silence before he says, "What are you going to do?"

"I'm not moving, Eli. It's not fair for him to ask me. Why can't he move?"

Anger builds in me again. I pull myself from the door and wipe away the grease print from my face. My pizza is laying cold in the box, beckoning me to finish it but my stomach is full of worry and angst.

"But isn't that months away or wait a year from now if he's going to the next Olympics? Wow, to say I know a famous athlete is really neat. And I know I can't tell anyone about his retirement. Don't start threatening me over it."

He knows me well.

"Stop fangirling over him. He shits like everyone else. But seriously. I can't move away. My whole life is there. You guys, Lars, Kylie, hell, even Hamilton is sort of my friend."

I set the phone on speaker, click off the television, and collect my pizza box and soda to put in the hallway.

"That's sweet honey, but don't worry about us. We'd visit you anywhere you go."

Of course he would. He'd figure out a way to load up all those dogs in a van and make a road trip of it, snapping photos of their adventures to post on Instagram. Would probably set up a family website too. He really is something else in the best way.

"I appreciate that, but you're not listening—" I say, shutting off the living room lights to get ready for bed.

"Sweetie, I don't mean to interrupt, but I'm listening. I agree that this is all very fast now, but haven't you two been dancing around each other for months? It's like the slowest slow burn possible, which would kill me but apparently is still too fast for you, which I understand. I'm not criticizing, but you said he decided to go for it. Why shouldn't you? Free fall into the abyss. It could turn out great and not the disaster you claim it will be."

I think about what he says while brushing my teeth, stopping long enough to spit and rinse before responding.

"I'm confused. You want me to open shop in Denver? That's the opposite of what I want."

I mute the phone to pee while waiting for his explanation.

"No, I'm saying separate the two. Just because he joined them together, doesn't mean they need to stay together. I get why he wants to have you with him in Denver. He has another year before he can move out of that city. He doesn't see any tie for you, such as a job, kids, or family. From his perspective, you can easily join him. However, from your side, you have a lifelong friend and amazing new friends." He coughs his name, which makes me smile.

"And obligations to your new employee. I know you said that to him already, but since he doesn't have those things, he doesn't understand. He only has himself to be responsible for and from the sounds of it, he doesn't have many friends or any, if you can't name one."

I can't. He's never even mentioned one. I should ask.

"Get him to see the importance of those things to you as being equal to him being tied to the Olympic training center."

I finish in the bathroom, washing my hands and closing my bedroom door before undressing.

"Ugh, this is why I bang it out with fuck boys. Relationships are too damn complicated."

I groan and slip under the cool sheets. They feel delicious against my sunburned skin when I flip to lie on my stomach.

"We can always fill up on a bag of Cheetos because they are cheap and convenient when what we really want is the slowly grilled juiciness of a filet mignon."

Tomlin is the juiciest steak dinner a girl could ever want.

The stars sparkle in the dark sky outside my window. If I'm dumb enough to think it worked, I'd wish upon one to resolve all this my way.

"Can you fly here and work this out for me?"

"Where is that tough chick I first met? The one that walked into my shop with him following her around like a puppy and paying for everything," he says, and I smile against the soft sheets. "You got this. Figure out what you want and tell him. I'm sure the two of you can meet in the middle. If you can't, then maybe it's not meant to be. Relationships are compromises, not dictatorships. They are hard work and worth every second. If it falls apart this early, then it was never meant to be."

I don't like what he's saying, even though it makes sense. I want it to work out, but he's right in that it can't always be me making the sacrifices. If relationships are full of compromises then Tomlin has to do it too.

"You've given me a lot to think about. Even more than what was stirring around my old brain."

"Good. Now I have to go. But call me whenever you need me, or I'll check on you in a couple of days. You know I'm on your side. Team Dani," he chants. He must have opened a door or something because the dogs' barking overpowers his words.

"Thanks, Eli. And let me know when Isla is out."

The call ends while I wait for him to say goodbye. It doesn't bother me because that racket on the other end is too much. One more thing, Hamilton.

I hammer out a text to him, demanding the details of what happened and what his ass is doing about that place. Naturally,

I threaten to report them to the State if he doesn't handle it before mashing the send button.

Hamilton's a good guy, but I have to ride his ass way too much. It's annoying. When I get back home, he and I are going to have a little chat about that place and how he needs to be pushier.

Reaching over, I plug my phone into the charger and silence my alarm. Sleeping in sounds divine as I bury myself under the covers.

Tomlin himself is worth the hassle of a relationship. The other requirements surrounding him are not, and I still don't know what to do. Where Tomlin's wrapped it all together like a nice present, Eli says to break it apart in two, but how?

I'm conflicted. He asked me to stay up to talk this out but I'm not sure I'm ready. Things need to be clearer in my head in order for me to communicate my needs without botching it all up. And right now, they are a jumbled mess.

11

The knock on my door eludes me at first. In the haze of sleep, I'm sure it came from my dream. When I hear it a second time, with Tomlin calling my name, I know he's on the other side of the door. I reach for my phone and it's well past one in the morning. Far too late to be coming in from practice and instant anger clears away my sleepiness.

Nothing good happens after midnight. Something Dad always said. It's true. My worst decisions were always made after midnight when the bar closed, and I didn't want to be alone after Dad died. I don't want this to be another one.

If I walk out there and smell alcohol on his breath or worse, perfume, it will be over before it even starts. I refuse to date a guy that finds his solution at the bottom of a bottle. I learned that lesson myself when I mourned Dad, and I can't go back to those dark times. If Tomlin is trying to talk to me now, then no good will come of it. He can wait till the morning.

With that, I flip onto my stomach and stare at the nightstand, listening for his footsteps. It takes a few seconds and then the quiet click-clack of his dress shoes on the penthouse floor echoes back to me. It validates my decision not to talk to him because if he was really at practice tonight, he would've been in his athletic shoes, and those squeaks, not clack.

What is he playing me for? A fool? Now that he decided to give me a shot, I'm supposed to just fall at his feet and agree to everything? And if he thinks he can corral other women at the same time, well, I haven't resorted to violence in a long time, but I will. He won't have to worry about his opponent blackening his eyes. I'll do it.

The longer I lay here, the more frustrated I get about the situation until I hear the low cords of the piano. More somber music. A different song from the other night. I flip to my back, staring at the ceiling, and listen until I can't take it anymore.

I climb out of bed, wrap the comforter around me and open the door to him hunched over. His forehead rests on his arm as it lies along the top of the piano while his right hand plays the keys. He's indeed wearing dress pants, and a shirt pulled open at the collar with the suit coat draped over the couch.

If I wasn't so mad at him, I'd actually feel sorry for the guy because he looks exhausted. When he glimpses me, he raises his head, and that's when I see his slightly swollen eyebrow and eye socket. I tilt my head, a silent question, and he puts his forehead back down to continue playing. Tonight is different between us. He's not chasing after me demanding answers. It's odd. I move toward him, pausing by the couch, which seems as many miles away from the piano as is the space between us now.

"I was worried about you," he whispers, still drumming the keys in an agonizingly slow manner that doesn't resemble a song anymore.

"I needed time to think."

Silence. Not even the waves of the ocean outside can be heard.

"And?"

And? What do I say? I still haven't decided myself, let alone separated the two, as Eli said.

"I don't know."

I press my lips together for saying the traitorous but true words. I want to be with him, but I can't move to Denver. Lars can't move to Denver, and I can't abandon what I have.

"That's what I surmised when you didn't call or text."

The defeat in his voice matches that of his posture and I close the distance to sit on the bench with him. He sits up and slides over to allow space for my big comforter. I don't smell alcohol or perfume on him, just a faint lingering of his own clean scent. And that makes me feel better.

"Why is what I'm asking so bad? I've racked my brain and I know you are leaving your hometown, but wouldn't it be a good thing?"

Half of his face is drowning in the shadow of the dimly light room, but his solemn expression is still clear.

"I don't know. This is all very fast, T."

"It's not though. I already explained that I wanted to be with you many months ago."

"Sure, but then you rejected me. Told me business partners only and went away for six weeks. I don't get it. You run hot, then cold, and now scalding hot. I'm having a hard time keeping up."

He reaches out to touch the edge of the bedding that is pressed against my neck to run a finger up my skin to tuck my hair behind my ear. His eyes follow the path of his finger until those dark orbs connect with mine again.

"Why do I feel like I'm begging you to be with me?"

The angst in his voice stabs at my heart, and it takes everything in me to not cave and move to Denver. My gut has to be stronger than my heart because I can't give in here too. He has to compromise.

"Why can't you move to Cañon City? You already have a

home there. You said you use it to hide out from your dad. That can only be a good thing. Heck, you even know Margaret, because you're there so much. That's got to mean you like the town, right? Like it's sort of your hometown too?" I search his face, hoping for a glimmer of understanding.

"I have another year, Dani."

He sighs, his open palm dropping into my lap in search of mine. I untuck my hand from deep within the covers and lean against him to rest my head on his shoulder. We interlock fingers as his head rests on mine, letting the silence in the room consume us. We stay like this for a long time. Neither talking, just lost in our own thoughts, until he kisses my head.

"What happened to your eye?" I ask, breaking the silence with something not life-altering.

"I was distracted, didn't have it protected."

His deep voice vibrates into my body, and I snuggle closer. He releases my hand to wrap his arm around my shoulders for a tighter embrace.

"Because of me?"

A pause.

"Because of you," he whispers, hitting some sad notes with his left hand.

Guilt.

It's a terrible emotion and one that hits hard. I didn't mean to make him worry, but running off in a new city, and not answering his calls or texts. Yeah, I can see where that made him worried and distracted. The last thing he needs before his match in a couple of days.

"Can we?" I stop, trying to figure out what I'm asking, and he stops playing.

"Can we what?"

His inquiry is soft, without a hint of the arrogance that's quintessentially him. I love seeing this side of him, where he's patient and vulnerable. But tonight, I hate the reason for it.

"Wait. Do we have to decide now? Or can we go a few more days without deciding?" I'm kicking the can down the road because this distraction caused him to take an unnecessary blow. "Wait until after the competition when you're not distracted, and you don't lose."

His spine straightens, his chest sticks out, and he says, "I won't lose."

The arrogance I was searching for a moment ago flares from the depths of his despair. It makes me smile.

"Of course, you won't."

His hands move to cup my face, with his thumb stroking the skin on the side of my mouth, and the smoldering look on his face says everything.

"Okay. We'll wait until Pebble Beach to decide. In the meantime, we'll enjoy each other, starting now."

The urgency with which his mouth descends to mine makes me flush with heat and I stop clutching the comforter tightly against my body. His tongue shoves into my mouth, a frantic exchange of desire and apologies for today, what happened between us, and all the decisions left unmade.

My hand slides up the side of his neck, pushing his collar aside to feel the ropey cords of his muscular traps. I continue my ascent until my fingertips are in his hair, pulling him forcibly into my mouth where our teeth clash.

His calloused palm pushes away the comforter as it caresses down my back to grab my flesh. I shiver as the cool air hits my warm skin. His other hand grazes my waist, gathering me up to place on his lap.

"Christ."

He breathes against my lips before nipping at them repeatedly. I arch into him, wrapping my arm around his shoulders while my lips dust kisses over his coarse beard and jawline to whisper in his ear.

"Fuck me, T."

I trace the shell of his ear with my tongue, taking his lobe in my teeth for a little bite while his erection grows underneath me. It's warm and inviting. I grind into him, teasing both of us.

His response is sudden, standing abruptly for the bench to topple over with a loud clatter that ricochets across the penthouse. It goes unacknowledged as those powerful strides carry me to his bedroom. The brown irises are gone, eclipsed by black desire so strong that I can't help but stare when my bare back hits his bed.

"You're so damn beautiful."

His body is heavy on mine, solid muscle sinking me further into the mattress, and it sends a thrill of excitement through my core. I kiss the side of his face, noticing a light abrasion on his cheek. My fingertips reach up to touch it when he captures my hand to kiss each finger.

"It's nothing."

"But—"

His mouth plunders mine, taking what I'm offering as he moves his hips to press his hard shaft into my soft flesh. It's deliciously painful to feel him and I'm eager to get him naked. I wrap my legs around him, trying to flip him when he interrupts our kiss with a smile.

"You want to be in charge?" He dusts his lips to mine. "I don't think so."

Damn.

Heat burns between my thighs and I rub against his pants even more. I try to flip him once more and he tightens his hold on me until I'm immobilized.

"Take off your clothes, T." I want to see him, feel him, and taste every inch of him. This is what I have been waiting for. So long I have wanted this, ever since he teased me at the cabin. Maybe even before, if I'm being honest with myself. "I want to fuck you."

"This mouth."

His head lifts, his eyes boring into mine as his lip pulls into a half smile.

"I miss the foul words that fall from here."

He kisses me only long enough for my lips to chase his back and come up empty.

"I miss these beautiful tits and the way you flaunt them in my face."

He quickly nips at my collarbone.

"But I think you're going to miss the control you think you have. Because in this room, demanding Dani, I'm in charge."

Holy shit.

I think he gave me a mini orgasm. I tighten my arms around his neck, trying to force him to kiss me, and the dark eyes glisten with naughtiness. In one smooth move, he unwinds my legs from the sides of his waist to shove them straight under his, further trapping me. It's the hottest fucking ever.

"What are you going to do now?"

His tone is teasing, his body is a vice over mine and the only defense I have is my arms straining against him to pull his mouth to my lips. Slowly, I slide one down the side of his neck until he captures it, kisses the palm, and holds it at the side of my neck. When he reaches for the other, he does the same and pins it to the mattress, I'm completely at his mercy and dripping all over my thighs.

"Answer me."

I can't.

This is such a mind fuck in the sexiest fucking way.

"I'll help you find the words. Repeat after me."

When his face descends, I'm silently cheering until his lips slide by mine to linger on my right cheek.

"I surrender," he murmurs against my skin, setting it ablaze underneath his grazing lips.

Oh fuck. Surrender to this slow torture? No. Surrender to fucking like rabbits? Hell, yeah.

"No."

His body tightens a fraction, showing his power, and when I rub my hips to create friction, he increases the pressure to stop them. Damn, this is fun.

"You know you can't win."

His whispered words are a breath against the goosebumps sweeping over my skin. If this is his version of foreplay, I can't imagine what fucking him will be like.

"I'll win. I'll fuck the shit out of you in a second."

I strain my arms against his hands, and they don't move a fraction. He has the upper hand in every way and I fucking love it. I see a lot of wrestling matches in our future if he continues to challenge me like this.

"That's where you're wrong. The only person fucking is me to you, and that's not happening tonight. I told you that."

His lips brush over my temple, down my cheek, and rest on my lips. I go limp because I don't want to play this game if we aren't going to have sex.

"Let me up," I demand, the playfulness dissipating between us. Once again, his head lifts, his eyes level with mine, and he doesn't move an inch.

"No, Dani. You're going to surrender and I'm going to eat out that nicely shaved pussy of yours."

Well, damn. That will work too.

His devious eyebrow twists up and I'm back to engaging. I'll take oral sex if it's on the table. Hell, I'll take anything he's willing to give because this is far better than my fingers alone in my bedroom.

"Ah, you like that?"

"Fuck yeah, I do."

That damn panty-dropping smile of his spreads across his face.

"There's that foul-mouth girl of mine. Now, who's in charge? Say it."

My body tenses under his, the anticipation bursting all over my skin making me tingly and hot. If this is how it will be with him, I'll say whatever he wants. I bit my lip, wanting to draw this out. Wanting to see what else he'll do. And I slowly shake my head.

"Such a defiant one."

He wipes the smile from his face and flips us. Me on top, naked, and exposed to the cold air. Him on the bottom, with his arms tucked behind his head, watching me, and daring me to leave or lead. My choice. With his hands off, I'm left to clutch at his shirt, still straddling the wet spot, and drenching his pants. I feel too vulnerable, and I hate it.

"I don't like this," I admit mostly to myself. I've always taken what I could get from a guy. A wrestling match of getting what I want and getting off.

But with Tomlin, it's different. He's willing to give what I need, taking the burden off me so I can receive, and I don't know how to process the switch. I thought I knew everything about myself sexually, but he's telling me that's not true. He's opening me up sexually, as he has done emotionally. Always challenges me but in the best ways.

"Don't like what?"

"I don't know."

My fingertips curl into his shirt, gripping it even tighter. Then his reassuring smile and soft hands come out to rub up and down my thighs.

"Take off my shirt."

His command takes me out of my weird head space to get back in the game. As I race to unbutton his shirt, a hand slides over my thigh to graze my lower stomach before finding my clit. His thumb rubs against it and I jolt at the goodness before grinding with him.

My eyes fall closed as I lean back, allowing him more access to play with my core. We find a rhythm that gets me wetter and hornier until he suddenly stops. My eyes fly open, about to object, when he brings his thumb to his mouth to lick. Those dark orbs drill into mine and I'm entranced.

"Damn, that's hot, T."

I spread his shirt wide. Those brown nipples are hard pebbles on his round pectoral muscles. He has a faint bruise along his right ribcage that my fingertips pass as I explore the dips and valleys of his abdominal muscles. His eye wasn't the only hit he took from the looks of it.

"Can I?"

My fingers play at the H of his belt, wanting to unbuckle and get rid of all this fabric between us. If he's not outright fucking me, will he let me blow him?

A cocky smile toys at his lips while his thumb returns to caressing my clit and setting me on fire. It's mesmerizing. The pure lust on his face, the passion in his eyes, and the rhythmical stroking of that thick pad against me. It takes everything in me to stay on task and not surrender like I did the other night.

"Asking gets you everything. Demanding gets you nothing."

Oh, challenge accepted.

He moves my hand to the buckle when I fail to do it. It's hard to concentrate when his hand moves to my breast to stroke the nipple opposite of the one stroking my clit.

"You look hot right now. The pink in your cheeks, your hips grinding into my hand."

My fingers fumble with his belt, unhook his pants, and right as I'm about to dip my hand inside his waistband, he catches my wrist.

"What did I say?"

"Come on. A hand job isn't sex," I practically whine.

Even though he's touching all the right places, I want more. A hand job leads to a blow job, and that leads to sex. I'm two tiny steps away from getting what I want. It's driving me crazy.

He slides two of my fingers into his mouth and tickles the pads with his tongue before removing his thumb from my swollen mound and placing my wet fingers there.

"Show me."

Watching guys jack is hot as hell and a major turn on. I get why he wants to watch, and the little wickedness in me swells with power again. First, he needs to lose the shirt. When I tug on the sleeve, he leans up long enough for me to get it off him. Once that's done, I ball it up and toss it on the floor.

I greedily devour the sight of him under me, his broad shoulders crushing the pile of pillows supporting him and the hollowness of his collarbones buried under muscle. The way they flex and tense as my fingers trace the smooth expanse of skin.

His hand reaches for my breast, but I catch it and slam it into the pillow above his head. I do the same with the other. He grabs the pillow and adjusts it under his head for a better show.

"No touching," I tease, sliding up his body to sit on his abdomen, letting my wetness saturate him as I poke his hips to lift. He complies. His narrow waist pushes into my mound, and I try my hardest not to grind against him as I help push his pants down his thighs. "Now, what do I get if I show you?"

"What do you want?"

His question is swift. A breath after mine and his jaw muscles pulse in and out. The amount of restraint he's showing is remarkable. It's why he's excellent at what he does.

I squat over him, wetness glistening around his belly button, from where I just sat. I run a finger through it and dip it in his mouth. He makes an obscene display of sucking it and I swear I need his mouth on me like that right now.

"I believe you said you'd eat me out."

His cock is a long outline in his boxer, dangerously close to popping out of the waistband. I sit right on top of it and slowly sway my hips into him. His grunt is primal, nearly a growl as he flips me onto my back, catches the back of my knees in his hands, and shoves them up to my shoulders. I'm laid out like a feast, and he doesn't hesitate to give in. It's the hottest fucking thing ever.

His mouth latches onto my mound, sucking my clit through his teeth. I moan and clutch the back of his head to rub vigorously against his face. The short hairs of his beard prickle my delicate flesh, making it that much more divine.

My orgasm builds, and if he keeps this pace, I'll explode in seconds. Suddenly, he shakes my hand out of his hair, captures it, and plants it behind my knee to hold it in place while his long fingers find my entrance and push inside.

"Fuck yeah."

I chant. My eyes slit to his, visible over my mound, and a tautly little eyebrow flashes up before he closes his eyes and sucks even harder. His fingers are hard and fast, whereas his tongue and mouth are soft and luscious.

"Right there, T. Right there."

He hums into my wet mound and it's the greatest fucking feeling. Those chocolate eyes flash open to watch me. It's hot as fuck to see the intense lust in them and know he feels the same as I do. His hand pushing against the back of my knee tickles down my ankle and pulls it to rest my foot against his shoulder. He gives my inner thigh a quick nip before blowing on my pussy.

"You do not know how much I've wanted to taste you. Next time, you'll ride my face."

Fuck.

That blows my mind and nearly blows my load all over his face now. His beard glistens with my wetness. His skin collects with perspiration, matching the heat rising in me. His words echo how much I want him. Having rubbed my clit raw after getting off those nightly calls.

"Deal," I mumble when his mouth returns to suck even harder than before.

This new position, one leg up and the other one down gives me leverage to push against his hard shoulder and make my body taut as I rub harder.

We're working in opposite parallels. I'm pushing, he's pulling and everything about this is so, so right. My orgasm is close. My body is tight, raising off the bed to better align with his mouth and plunging fingers. I'm a moaning mess, clutching at him, and right when I'm about to explode, he shoves his face away to blow across my clit. I burst while his fingers keep pumping in and out, my cum covering my thighs. When I look at his face, the lower half is drenched.

The tension collapses as my body does, the pleasure and release overwhelming as I pant in his hands. His fingers are buried deep within me as he crawls up my body and makes out with me, the same as he did my stuff. I taste myself all over him. It's hot as fuck.

His grunts are deep and feral. His sculpted body is hard and crushing over mine as he grinds against me, devouring my mouth. Then he stops, pulling his lips from mine to look down between us and I don't understand what is happening until I hear a long moan. His fingers slide out of me because he's close to coming. I'm making him blow his load. I'm damn proud that I latch on his neck and suck the sensitive skin under his ear. His groan is sexy and raw as he grabs my hand, shoves it down the waistline of his briefs to wrap around his thick cock, and shows me what speed he likes.

He moves his head, his eyes glued to my hand as mine are glued to his face, watching how fucking hot he looks, relinquishing his control to me. It's the hottest damn thing, and it makes me even hornier than before.

Combustion.

It's my new favorite word. I'm about to make him burst

when I swipe my thumb across the crown and stroke right under the back of the head. As if on command, he pumps into my hand and releases long and hard. His load is an endless hot stream shooting through my fingers and I fucking love it. I bite my lip, trying to hold back my smile, but it's too late when he looks from his dick in my hand to my face. His expression is one of surprise and relief, seeming to wipe away the day of worry between us.

"It's your fault I'm going to lose," he murmurs against my temple, kissing the side before falling onto his back, and forcing my hand from his warm, hard dick.

"A hand job isn't sex."

I move to my side to look at him, and he rolls his arm around my shoulder to pull me to him. My head rests on his chest and when he reaches for my leg to drape over his thigh, I realize he wants me to snuggle him. The cuddling yesterday and now tonight, it's new but nice. Something I didn't think he would do. That aloof, cocky exterior is what the world gets. The playful and cuddly Tomlin is what I get and my smile couldn't be wider.

"I can't believe I did that. I usually have better self control."

He scrubs a hand down the side of his face, side glancing at me and I realize he rubbed my cum on his skin. Then again, his lower face is plastered in it. I don't know why I thought he'd be a neat freak lover. Apparently, I'm wrong because this guy eats cum, feeds it to me, and doesn't care. It's liberating.

"You haven't jacked this whole week? Not once?" I can't keep the surprise out of my voice.

"Nope, you know my rule. Well, you broke my rule." He flexes his arm, wanting to kiss me, and I comply. "I should punish you for it."

"You wish," I say, as my fingertips explore his chest and ribs. His breath catches with my hand at his waist and I'm about to tickle him when he stops me.

"Another first, T. Not only is this our first time at you doing that to me, but it will be the first time you get a hand job and don't lose. We should test that by having full-on sex. Really obliterate your rule."

He chuckles, interlacing our fingers and laying them on his stomach.

"Let's not. But I do like the idea of more firsts with you."

I snuggle into him, moving my head to rest in the crook of his shoulder as I contemplate the firsts we have already experienced and the firsts yet to come. I exhale at how good this feels and close my eyes, wanting to commit every detail to memory in case we don't agree on Denver and this ends in a matter of days.

I hope it doesn't, but if my life has taught me anything, there's always a shoe waiting to drop when things are too good to be true. And dread nips at the edges of my happiness.

12

He claimed another first last night. My sleepover virginity. That's what I called it. He kissed me hard, obviously happy he took my first and our first. I still didn't shower with him. I don't know why, but that's still too intimate, even after he sucked my soul through my pussy.

Showering is different. There's nowhere to hide. It's like being stripped bare, literally, for him to judge me. Not that he hasn't had the chance to judge me this entire time when he can, and he sort of has. But being wet and naked with him washing me, and taking care of me, brings a different vulnerability that I'm not willing to share yet.

It sort of represents someone taking care of me in a way that I can already take care of myself. It means surrender. This type of surrender is slow and caring, asking someone to perform a selfless act and letting myself receive in return. I have no experience with this. In having sex with Zach or the guys from my past, I took what I wanted and didn't care. This doesn't even compare. Sex and intimacy are two different things to me.

After showering and climbing into bed with him, I laid my

head on his chest and told him all about the Japanese museum and beautiful exhibits.

He told me about his dad's side of the family. Being a first-generation American was difficult, bridging the gap between two cultures with more to prove and his dad forced him to take advantage of opportunities he never had. The way Tomlin justified his dad's behavior after what Kylie told me about his mom doesn't sit right. He didn't say a word about his mom, how his parents met, or what events lead to her death. Obviously, it wasn't the right time. I chalked it up to a conversation for another night, as Tomlin always says.

He took me through the next two days, the schedule of the events, what to expect and the people on his team. I tried to remember as much as possible, but when my eyes got heavy and his sexy voice got monotone, sleep prevailed.

My phone rings across the penthouse, awakening me from a deep sleep. At first, I'm taken aback by my surroundings until I remember everything that happened last night. A happy grin slides onto my face as I stretch, throw back the covers, and dash for the phone. Hamilton. Good, I have a bone to pick with him. My anger fires up from yesterday's conversation with Eli.

"Hamilton, what the fuck is wrong with that kid prison?" I swear my vow to stop cussing is getting ruined by what happened to Isla.

"I know you're mad, Dani. I am too, for that matter."

He sounds tired or frustrated, I can't tell which. I can tell that this bothers him too. Good, it should.

"What are you going to do about it?"

I need to know because I don't want to fly back there just to blow that place up. Well, I'd have to make Tomlin drive me because there's no way I'm getting back into that floating tin tube.

"They are opening an investigation, which I won't have

jurisdiction over since it's a state-run facility. Meaning the state police will look into it."

Hmm, that's decent, I guess.

"That sounds like a bunch of red tape. What happens to the pack of bitches that did this to her? You know, Isla would never stand up for herself. Hell, I wish Tomlin could teach her some self-defense moves. He did this crazy judo stuff back in Denver to these—" I stop, realizing that Tomlin basically assaulted them while protecting me. Blabbering about it to an officer of the law is a terrible idea. "I mean, what's going to happen now?"

"You've spoken to Eli. You know we're trying to get her released to their custody with the court's approval." More red tape. "Otherwise, she's safe for right now."

"I hardly considered being hospitalized safe for now. How traumatic for her, especially with all the other stuff she's dealing with. Damn, man. What will it take for them to let the guys have her already? I swear, this system is fucked up."

I sit on the edge of my bed.

"It's the only system we have, so you need to trust the process."

I'm going to beat his ass if he makes one more excuse for that lousy system.

"Hamilton—"

"Dani, I know you're frustrated, and the kid appreciates you going to bat for her, but we're doing everything we can. All of us, so relax a bit. Aren't you supposed to be on vacation with what's his name?" His voice gets all low and accusatory. He knows his name. There's something between them that I keep forgetting to ask Tomlin about.

"Yeah, I got sick, but I'm doing better. Probably will go out, do tourist crap and whatnot today."

I don't know why I blabber on about it to him. It's not like we swap secrets like old drinking buddies. More like I bitch at him, and he tells me to calm down.

"Why do you ask? You checking up on me?" My hackles are still up, wanting him to do more than gloss over the situation with red tape excuses. "I'll have you know that I've been minding my own business out here. I didn't even hit this kid that was giving me all sorts of looks at the airport and I easily could have."

"Wow, your patience is almost unrecognizable." Sarcasm. Apparently, the same way as Tomlin's interior designer. "You deserve to have a nice trip. You were looking pretty ragged these last couple of weeks. Isla even commented on it. You had us a little worried."

I pull the phone from my ear to stare at it. Hamilton and Isla were worried about me. I mean, that's kind of cool, but why? I smash the speaker button as I walk into the bathroom.

"Why?"

Staring at my bare chest, I press a finger to the sunburned skin. It doesn't sting anymore and will turn into a killer tan by the time I get to Pebble Beach.

"Why wouldn't we worry? You're working yourself to the bone. It was showing on your face." His voice rumbles through at the same time his radio goes off about some crime in progress. "I got to go, but I'll keep you posted on things as I know them. In the meantime, have a great time out there."

I stare at my phone screen, wishing he had FaceTime because something gives. Hamilton seems way friendlier than normal. Saying he's worried and telling me to have a good time isn't like him. Another thing for us to discuss when I get home and have a word with him.

"Uh, thanks."

I linger on the phone, wondering if he'll say more, but he doesn't and the call ends. It's not one thing or another that bothers me about the call. He confirms what Eli said, but the well wishes don't sit right, leaving me scratching my head on the way to order room service.

Whatever. I can't dwell on Hamilton when I have enough to think about with Isla and Eli, and, of course, my situation with Tomlin.

I take my time getting ready and when the doorbell rings almost an hour later, the timing couldn't have been more perfect. I handle room service and carry the tray out to the terrace to eat. The salty air is thick and muggy. The beach is barren. No volleyball players and surfers, only a few moms and their kids playing in the surf.

I reach for my phone to look up another bucket list place when the red bubble catches my eye. My phone is loaded with red bubbles. My inbox has over a thousand of them, which doesn't bother me. If people need me, they can call. End of story.

But this one, the one hovering in the corner of the phone icon, one of the dozens, is Carl's. His unanswered voicemail loiters there ever since the day my life changed. Another can I've been kicking down the road. I've been avoiding all the feelings it stirs up in me when thinking back to how everything went down with Carl and Judd.

I should've listened to it long ago. Gotten the guts up to do it, maybe after a good day with Lars or when I had gotten off the phone with Tomlin during one of our nightly talks. Now it's too late. I can't listen to it because it could be the other shoe dropping. If I listen to it now, it might change everything. That's been my fear all along.

At first, I was angry and didn't want to hear his excuses or justification for firing me. I figured that's why he called me. But the longer that bubble remains, the more it has morphed into different things. Him regretting firing me. Apologizing for putting Dad's stuff by the dumpster. Begging me to come back. Any or all those things. That bubble taunts me to the point where I still can't listen to it. The length tells me that it's long. Way too long to be good.

It's like a reminder of the shitty life I left behind working in that hostile environment with a pack of sexist assholes. Them trying to pull me down to their snake in the grass level. But I won't. My new life is going places they can only dream about. And when I get to the top, I might shit all over them or I might refuse to acknowledge that they exist in this world. I haven't decided yet.

The instant dread it brings up every time I think about it is enough to shut me down. Here it sits on my phone, two months later, unanswered and not deleted. A deep exhalation escapes my lungs as I drop into my chair, staring at the red bubble. I lick my lips and shake my head. No. Not today. I won't sabotage my happiness and this vacation today.

The food is covered with silver domes and when I lift them off, the aroma of buttery pancakes and greasy bacon makes my stomach growl. The all-natural maple syrup tastes like candy when I dip my finger in it and I can't wait to dig in. I munch on a strip of bacon while looking up things to do in LA. A bunch of sightseeing and movie star stuff comes up, which is even lamer than the theme park. The page is loaded with options and I'm almost indifferent until I see it.

The Nethercutt Collection features cars from the early 1900s. I instantly smile. It's a little north of the city, too far for an Uber, but maybe Tomlin would let me drive that fine-ass machine parked downstairs. Excitement surges through me as I stuff a stack of gooey pancakes into my mouth and moan at the deliciousness. If I hurry and finish eating, I can be there before noon. Maybe hit the Petersen Museum again for a do over since running away yesterday ruined it.

That is something that I have got to stop doing. He's said it many times and yet it's my default to bail when things don't go my way or when I need to think about things. If I'm going to make us work, then I need to change that.

I need to be the adult I claim to be and stay in the situation until it's resolved. Sounds grueling, but I'm going to try it. The next conflict I have, I'm going to stay and work it out, even if my insides curl in on themselves while doing it.

With my day planned, I polish off breakfast, take the tray to the hallway and grab my purse to find Tomlin downstairs. When I step off the elevator, it's chaos. People are lounging in the lobby couches, others are streaming in and out, and I almost get run over by the bellman toting the racks of luggage toward the bank of elevators. I dart around screaming kids, arguing couples, and a couple of tourists to get to the front desk to ask where the competition is. Ballroom, second floor.

I fight my way back to the elevators and slip into the corner right as the doors are closing. The ride is short and, when the doors open, it's a different kind of chaos, with athletes, coaches, and trainers clumped together down the hallway leading into a line of vendor booths that wrap around the corner.

Different conversations strike me as I pass. A young female athlete in tears is scolded by her coach for not making her weight category. An older teen discusses strikes and strategies against a known competitor with his team. A trainer discusses calories and macros, whatever the hell those are, with a skinny kid who looks like he needs to eat a few hamburgers, so he doesn't pass out.

It's no wonder Tomlin is disciplined and regimented. The mental toughness it takes to survive and thrive in this sport, not to mention the pressure to stay at the top, has got to be unreal. Something I couldn't do as I'd end up throat punching those that pissed me off.

As I pass a doorway, there are tan square mats surrounded by green ones set up in an obscenely long ballroom, surrounding a very large mat smack dab in the middle. I assume that's the one that Tomlin will be on tomorrow. The place smells of sweat and antiseptic spray, with fresh oxygen pumped in so loud I can hear it coming through the vents. The temperature is set to subarctic, and I shiver as I walk into the ballroom.

Chairs surround each square with athletes and their gear spilling into the aisles. A small white tent sits in the far corner with First Aid emblazoned on it and next to it are more tables with officials sitting behind them. It's fascinating to get a glimpse into his world. And I wonder if he would mind me staying to watch.

I walk along the outer rim of the room, looking across the sea of people and wishing I wasn't so short to get a better view when he suddenly appears from a doorway opposite of me. My timing couldn't be more perfect.

He doesn't have a shirt on, those gorgeous muscles are glistening with sweat and the faint bruise on his ribcage is even lighter today. His swollen eye looks better, almost unnoticeable as does the slight abrasion on his cheek. His head bows, listening to a short guy with hair fringing a half circle around his head and sporting a windbreaker.

His dad isn't far behind, wearing a scowl and frown lines that cut deep grooves into the skin between his eyes. He's turned away, surveying the place when our eyes connect, and I make a ridiculous show of waving at dear old Dad like a crazy fan. I know it burns his ass to see me when his eyes narrow, and not for having poor vision. He turns his head a fraction toward Tomlin and barks something at him because then those beautiful brown eyes fall on me. His expression immediately softens when a smile pushes away the concentration from a second ago and gives me a wink.

I swear, I'd mount him right here and now with how sexy he looks. Hell, I might even do it in front of his dad to show him that he can go fuck himself. Okay, that's taking it too far, even for me. I toy with my tongue piercing to remind myself why I got it.

"New leaf." I breathe and cross the room to Tomlin.

I sidestep bags strewn everywhere and guys wrapping their wrists until I'm near him. His long legs close the distance before mine to kiss me hard and fast. And I wish Tomlin wasn't so tall, so I could see his dad's face with this very public display of affection.

"What are you doing here?"

He hugs me tightly, my cheek pressed against his sweaty chest. Normally, that would gross me out, but it must be love if I'm not shoving his ass away.

"Am I in trouble for being here?" I lean out of his arms. "I can leave."

I throw a thumb over my shoulder to the door and his head shakes.

"No, no, I didn't mean that. I just—"

"Tomlin, why is she here?" his dad barks when he joins us. "She shouldn't be here. It's not proper."

"Nice to see you too, Mr. Takahashi," I say sarcastically and then give him my brightest smile ever. "I was asking Tomlin if his oh-so-charming sperm donor was going to be here."

I have to hand it to myself. I think that's a pretty funny comeback on the fly.

"Dad, Dani, not here."

Tomlin purses his lips while scolding both of us, and I don't like that one bit.

"He started it," I defend, hearing how childish that sounds to me, but seriously, he did. "Fine. I'll be good."

I close my lips, twist my fingers like locking them with a key and throw it over my shoulder. Tomlin smirks in amusement, and I know we're cool again. On the other hand, his dad yells in Japanese and then storms off, kicking an athletic bag that he passes.

"Lovely guy," I mutter, gazing up at him. "You look hot as hell. I was thinking we could go at it right here on the mat if you wanted."

He chuckles. His eye droops from the hit he took yesterday, but still looks better.

"You want to take me on, huh? How do you think that will work out?"

His knuckles caress my cheekbone before capturing my chin between his fingers to give me another couple of kisses.

"Hell yeah! I'll horizontally wrestle with you," I say, garnering a couple of glances from some female athletes standing a few feet away. I might have said that too loudly. "It's not for lack of trying on my part."

"Why do I get the feeling, once you have me pinned, you'd never let me up?"

"Because I won't. Be warned," I tease, clasping my hands around his narrow waist and trying not to grab his ass in front of everyone.

His hand slides up my spine, drawing me close to whisper in my ear, "It's been driving me mad wondering how that piercing will feel on my cock."

The wickedness in me shoves my tongue out, playing with it against my teeth to give him a preview. It's completely inappropriate and I've wondered about it too.

He'll be the first.

Another first for us.

I love it.

"Me too." The bulge from his black shorts presses against my stomach and I raise my eyebrow in victory. "You seem to have a problem, T."

He stacks his forearms across my shoulders, and I rest the back of my head against them to gaze at him.

"Why do you always do this to me in public?"

His chin slides down, sending a lock of black hair over his forehead.

"You do it to yourself. But I'm more than happy to obliterate that rule tonight. Whenever you get out of here."

I try to glance around, but with me locked in place, it's impossible.

"Tomorrow, demanding Dani." I open my mouth to say when tomorrow and as if he reads my mind, he finishes with, "After the match."

"Dammit, T. I hate your rules."

"Ironically, you follow them really well. Except for last night. But enough talking about that or else I'll never go down," he says, playfully pulling my hair. "Now tell me what I owe this visit to?"

"I want to borrow the roadster to drive to the San Fernando Valley."

A strange look slides over his face.

"Why?"

"There's this collection of cars from the 1900s, like another museum but smaller. I can show you on my phone, but it's too far for an Uber." I unhook my arms from his waist to reach for my phone.

"You don't need to prove it to me. I worry because you are not familiar with the area." His arms loosen from my shoulders, and I roll them back, realizing they were getting heavy.

"I'll be fine. I can defend myself. Remember, I broke two noses in one day once."

"You threatened to break mine that day. Although we both know I would not let that happen." A low laugh ripples out. "But I would have loved to see you try."

"I could do it right here, right now." I'll accept his challenge. "Let's fucking g—"

The words aren't even out of my mouth before I'm spun around with my back smashed against his chest. I don't mind though. His hard dick presses into my low back, but the speed at which he's done it is remarkable.

"You were saying, my foul-mouthed girl?"

His breath tickles against my ear, and the rise and fall of his chest against my back are hot as hell. It takes everything in me not to rub my ass into his cock.

"Keep it up, Dani. I love how challenging you are. It only makes this . . ." He thrusts it into me. ". . . harder."

"Ugh, stop already. I'm going to need to go find a bathroom and handle myself before I leave," I groan, feeling a stream of wetness coat my panties. "I swear, T. Tomorrow night, I'm fucking the skin of that cock of yours."

He leans over, crunching me to him, to whisper, "You can try demanding Dani, but first you'll be on your knees with those gorgeous baby blues looking up at me while that barbell swirls around it."

Holy shit.

His words are fucking my ears.

My knees buckle at the visual he's placed in my head. More wetness flows out of me, sticking my panties to my skin. I fan my face with my hand. The low rumble vibrating from his body and into mine is hot as hell too.

"Christ. I'm even harder than before."

He doesn't have to tell me. I feel it digging into my flesh, wanting to fuck as much as I do. Damn practical Tomlin and his stupid rules. He puts a fraction of space between us, trying to calm himself down as I continue fanning my warm skin. I could've sworn this place was freezing when I first walked in. Now it's an inferno.

"The keys are by the phone on the wet bar. And be careful, please."

I turn in his arms, avoiding his dick.

"I will. I know how much it costs."

His eyes bore into mine with a serious intensity that I don't see often.

"I don't care about the cost of the car. I finally have you and I don't want anything bad to happen to you."

I bite my lip. He finally has me. And I finally have him. It makes my heart want to explode with all the love I feel for him. Then his chin drops and understanding washes over me.

I get what he's saying. It goes beyond that car, the road up to the Valley, and that museum. It has everything to do with losing the ones we loved most in this world to car accidents. His mom and my dad. His greatest fear is mine. A shared fear that only people who have loved and lost know and understand its power to wield cautious words.

"I understand, and I'll be fine." The words sound hollow in the weight of the grief that still surrounds our parents. "I'll have my phone on me the whole time."

"Is it too much to ask that you are back before dark? I don't want to invade your freedom but in a new city and a car like that. You could get the wrong attention and . . ."

He doesn't have to say the rest. Normally, I'd get all bent out of shape thinking he's trying to control me, but I understand the place where all this is coming from. Not just the safety to avoid a car crash, but my personal safety. As if he doesn't want anything to happen to me, period. I honor and respect it.

"Don't worry, I'll be home well before you walk in the door."

He frowns. "I won't be upstairs until very late. Promise me you'll be careful."

The noise volume increases with a match starting to my right. I lean in, angling my mouth toward his ear and he dips his head. His hands hold me loosely.

"Only if you promise to find me in bed." I give him a peck on his cheek, the stubble of that sexy beard scarping my lips.

His smolder says everything and my body flushes with heat. "One more day, Dani. One."

He holds up his index finger for emphasis and I cover it with my own, doing what he usually does to me.

"I. Can't. Fucking. Wait. I'm going to eat you alive," I reply, gazing from under my eyelashes at him and attempting to match his smolder. He runs a hand through his hair to squeeze the back of his neck.

"Go."

His eyes look down at his problem that's not going away and back up to me. My smile is wicked when he plants his hands on my shoulders and turns me around to push me forward.

"Bye, T," I tease over my shoulder, grinning at him and then at his dick.

I would've never guessed how playful and charming he is. His aloof and conceited side makes so much sense now that I know what he does for a living. This side, he keeps very much hidden.

It adds to the allure and mystic of him. He's calculating with everything planned out that waiting to have sex with him has been both fun and torturous. I wind through the room, the contenders meandering in to watch the match already underway and another that is starting on the other side of the room. I pause at the ballroom doors and look for Tomlin to see if he has a practice match I can watch. When I don't see him, I head out.

13

The roadster is amazing. The power in my hands is indescribable as I speed down the highway to the museum. The collection is stunning. True artistry to innovation for the era in which these cars were produced. If I didn't already love preservation work, I'd have fallen in love.

I spend nearly four hours combing over every detail, taking a million pictures, and sending some to both Tomlin and Lars. My pictures don't do it justice. I know both would enjoy seeing these fine machines in person. If he's serious about starting his own collection, then he's got to see this place. It makes me wonder how many other museums and collections exist like this.

It also makes me realize how small my existence is, being holed up in Cañon City my whole life. Maybe Tomlin is right in that Denver would broaden my horizons and bring in new opportunities I didn't even know existed.

Walking past all the turn-of-the-century cars makes me curious about the former owners, what they did for a living, and what were their hopes and dreams for themselves and their families.

If I have to be honest with myself, it makes me think beyond myself and dream about a life I've never thought of. A life of Tomlin and I traveling the world looking for cars to rebuild for himself or others, making a name for our company to compete with East Coast Paul.

I know Tomlin's fame could bring leads, but I don't want jobs that way. I want them on my own. He said my reputation preceded me, which I didn't believe at the time. Maybe he's right. Maybe my staunch stance on remaining in that small town is holding me back, even if it's justifiable in a way.

If I flip the model and look at it from Tomlin's point of view, all that he has experienced, all the places he's gone, is Denver too small for him?

I figure the Olympic training center keeps him in that city, but is he as stuck in Denver as I'm in Cañon City? Are both of us anchoring to the past, as a stabilizer to the uncertainty of the future?

Once he retires, once the endorsement deals dry up, would he become an average Joe like me? I wonder if he's thought of that, and maybe that's another thing to consider when we finally make that decision.

What about Lars? He needs this job and I honestly need him too. He's not only my first employee, but he's also my friend. I can't abandon him for my own happiness. That would never sit right with me. He's a great guy with a big heart. He deserves better.

I sigh, rub my temples, and continue into the next exhibit, content to push this out of my mind again.

The curator catches me drooling in the grand salon by the marble columns. The crystal chandeliers, the art deco décor, and the rare collection of Duesenberg's, Maybach's, and other exquisite machines were once owned by Hollywood royalty. Some are going to be featured at the Concours d'Elegance along with Tomlin's car.

My chest swells with pride to be in the same show. I eagerly exchange information, hoping to connect with him while there to introduce him to Lars, who would equally die over this collection.

As we walk the floor together, he explains each car, the maker, the origin, and how they came to be in possession of it. I feel like I've won the lottery with what ends up being a private tour. I could stay here all night if it isn't for a private party closing the museum early and my commitment to Tomlin to be back before dark.

I'm on cloud nine when I leave. With a little more time left before dark, I drive the magnificent metallic green roadster with a new appreciation for its engineering. Driving back to town, it garners as many looks as it deserves.

It is a work of art, with technology as innovative for this time as those old ones were for theirs. I pull into the Petersen Museum, check the time on my phone, and see I've got less than an hour before they close.

It's enough time for me to get down to the vault and study those stunning cars in greater detail. I send more pics to the guys. Lars and I trade texts as I send them. He's blowing up my phone with question after question and demanding to see more. He's such a car nerd that I wish he was here with me right now. It lets me know that we're going to have a killer time at Pebble Beach, drooling over those cars as well.

After closing down both museums, my mind is overflowing with ideas for the business, and I sit in the roadster, jotting them in my notes app, when Kylie calls.

"Hey Kyles, I'm glad you called because—"

"Why are there pictures of you on Instagram?" Her tone is curt and angry, the opposite of my happy one for once.

"Uh, I don't know." I'm going to need a lot more to go on than that. "Am I standing in front of a car or something? Possibly one I restored?"

"No, you're holding hands with Tomlin, wearing his glasses, and pressing them to your face. It looks like you're dating."

The airport.

Oh shit.

She's super pissed. My high from the car museums is fading with each accusatory word she spews. I brush the hair out of my face trying to buy time to think of what to say. It must've been taken by the buzzards as we were leaving. I was feeling sick after the flight. We weren't even together together that day, he simply held my hand to get me to the car through the swarms of them. Surely, it doesn't look like we're dating.

"Dani?"

"What are you talking about?"

Deflect. That's what I do to Tomlin. I'll do it here too. My phone pings in my hand.

"I just sent it to you."

I mash the speaker button on my phone and then open my messages to click on the picture. The caption is asking what they were shouting. Who is Tomlin's new girl? It looks every bit as bad as Kylie's making it sound. What do they say? A picture's worth a thousand words. Well, this one speaks a million.

"Dani?"

Tomlin looks happy, almost carefree with his open-collar shirt, rolled-up sleeves, and easy smile. His eyes are warm, the edges crinkled in amusement as he looks directly into the camera.

Our fingers are tightly intertwined with my head down and his sunglasses blocking a large portion of my face. My hair caresses my shoulders, my shirt slipped forward showing too much cleavage and my legs look stupid long in the wedges and shorts.

I stare at how good we look together. Our opposite features complimenting each other. His dark hair, my light. He's tall, I'm short. He's pale, I'm tan, thanks to spending two months working in the sunshine on the mountainside.

Granted, he and I are never in mirrors together except for that one time in the gym at his house. And I wasn't looking at any of those at the time, that's for damn sure. Seeing this picture of us brings a huge smile to my face and I wanna make it the home screen on my phone.

"Dani!" she repeats, snapping me out of my admiration for us.

"Yeah?"

I don't know what to say. I love how we look, and I like the direction we are going. But this is the conversation I have both dreaded and avoided. Do I face the music now or later? Can I kick this can down the road like the decision Tomlin and I are making in Pebble Beach or the unanswered voice mail from Carl? I'm getting good at kicking cans. What's one more?

"Are you guys dating?"

If I say yes, it's going to be a bloodbath from the sounds of her fury-filled words. If I say no, I'm lying, and I hate doing that to her. But didn't Tomlin lie by omission to me about his mom's car and I got over it? Sort of after spilling my guts to Lars and him changing my perspective.

"Why Kylie? You have Ryan. Aren't you happy with him?"

Avoidance. Let's go with that. Ask a question with a question so I can talk this out with her in person when I get back and not over the phone. Yes, I can metaphorically hear myself launching this can off the tip of the shoe to land down the road.

"Don't make this about me. Answer the question, Dani."

I squeeze my eyes shut and grit my teeth, counting the seconds as I debate.

Lie. Don't lie.

Lie. Don't lie.

Damn me.

"Yeah." I breathe into the phone and peek my eyes open to

gaze out the windshield at the passing cars. I wait for her wrath, knowing it's coming judging from the negative and angry tone of this whole call.

"How could you? We agreed to never date each other's exes and the second we break up, you throw yourself at him. Was that your plan all along? Like all this bitching about him was a cover until I moved on and then you swooped in to get him."

Wow.

I take a few deep breaths to calm down.

"I know you didn't say that to me, Kyles. I was the one that came to you and said I didn't think it was a good idea. You were practically jumping up and down and patting yourself on the back, saying that this was an opportunity I should take. I didn't exactly throw myself at Tomlin. You know me better than that. And it's not like I waited for you to move on. You're happy with Ryan, so why can't you be happy for me now?"

My patience is wearing thin and I'm trying not to burn down my best friend, especially when she's crazy about a different guy. It's like she wants to run for second base while keeping her hand on first in case she gets picked off. Doesn't work like that. And I don't ever recall agreeing to not date exes. Hell, I don't have any for her to date.

"You're unbelievable if you think this has anything to do with Ryan."

"Then what does it have to do with? Why does it matter? You moved on. I thought you'd joke with me about sloppy seconds, but never in a million years would I think you'd be pissed at me for dating him." Anger edges my words and if it were anyone else, I'd tell them to go fuck themselves. But this is Kyles, my best friend, my confidant, my sister from another mister.

"Come on Kyles. You know this isn't like me." To date guys, I want to say.

"Yeah, it's not like you to stab me in the back. But I

should've seen it coming because eventually, you put yourself before everyone else. It's always been like that and maybe I'm tired of it. I'm done, Dani. I can't with you."

The call drops, leaving me staring at the phone screen. My hand is shaking, proof of the restraint I have in trying to stay calm and talk this out. Hell, I took a page out of Tomlin's calm book, and it still blew up in my face.

What a fucking mess.

I shouldn't have to choose between my best friend and the man I love. I'd never make Kylie do that, so I can't believe she's asking me to do it now.

I gazed out the window, shaking my head in disbelief. I stare at the museum across the street and the crowd waiting to get in, trying to make sense of what just happened. It's not my fault that Tomlin held my hand when I was feeling sick when they snapped the picture and posted it on social media.

It's not my fault that I fell in love with him after fighting it for so long. It's not my fault that Tomlin's finally giving me a chance and acknowledging he has feelings for me. It's not my fault that Kylie can't see all this, but it is my fault for not telling her in the very beginning that I was developing feelings for him.

I did it on purpose. A small part of me knew, or maybe expected, that this would be her reaction. And I wanted nothing else or anyone else telling me no. I was already fighting my own feelings for him, coupled with Tomlin's rejection. There's no way I could've handled her opinion too.

"Well, this fucking sucks," I mutter over the rumble of the engine.

It's dusk. The sun setting in the West paints the sky pinkish purple with deep streaks of blue. Even the sunsets are different here. More vibrant, like the people. It's the opposite of my foul mood.

14

When I finally arrive at the dark penthouse, my feet are killing me, my stomach is growling, and my head is hurting. Another round of room service comes and goes as I plant my ass in front of the television yet again.

The only difference tonight is that I have my notes app open, jotting down ideas for the name of the garage, the logo, colors, design, and the layout of the garage for maximum efficiency. I even start an account on Instagram to post Tomlin's car. I tag him as the owner. Look at me getting all business partner-ish.

Planning gets you this.

That's what he said the first night up on the mountain and I was in awe. Look at me now, sitting in his penthouse on vacation in LA and planning. Not throwing a rager. Not grinding on some NBA players, as I had joked in the car. No, my ass is sitting on the floor, planning like that huge, hot nerd.

What he forgot to tell me or didn't count on is how good it feels. It fills me with deep satisfaction and accomplishment that I stayed here and worked instead of going out partying.

I'm proud of myself for making strides toward this new dream and for leaving my normally complacent ass behind. As Eli said, separate the two. I finally get what he means. Even though my personal decision is on hold, I feel invigorated to move forward on the business side, bound to make it work.

By the time I fall into bed, I'm freshly showered and shaved with a new vigor for the days ahead. All I had to do is wait for Tomlin to crawl in next to me and cuddle out our last night of celibacy.

I gaze at the crescent moon slicing through the overcast sky and think about Kylie. That's another thing I want to push out of my mind. I hate how things went down between us. At the same time, I don't want to deal with it either. I want to stay in this bubble where only Tomlin and I matter. Kylie will have to take a back seat until I get done with Pebble Beach. I'll add her to my Colorado list, where confronting Hamilton is at because both friendships need straightening out.

I lie mulling over everything that's happened on this trip and how some things have turned out better than I could've imagined, while other things have turned out worse. The longer I lay there staring at the stars through the window, the heavier my eyelids get until they droop closed. My body is cloaked in warmth, a heater at my back. When I squirm away, a hard band wraps around my waist.

"Dani."

The haze of sleepiness fogs my brain. But when his clean scent hits my nose and soft lips touch my temple, I relax into his arms.

"Tomlin?" I breathe into the dark room. The shuttered drapes block the moon's glow.

"I'm here. Go back to sleep," he murmurs against my ear as his arm slides under my pillow.

"What time is it?"

I shift in his arms, wanting to face him, to gently kiss him goodnight.

"Late, after midnight." The coarseness in his voice hints at his exhaustion.

"You were training all this time?"

The thought of him being somewhere else wakes me up. I never asked him why he was dressed in a suit last night and coming in late tonight.

"Did you go out tonight? Like out on the town?"

The arm at my waist squeezes me closer, his hand pressing against my low back as his leg drapes over my hip.

"Yes. Can we talk about this in the morning? I'm beat," he murmurs, his breath elongating as I make out his closed eyes in the shadow of the dark room.

"Is there someone else? Someone here that you are seeing." I'm too tired and it's too late to hide the fear that has crept into my mind. "Be honest. Dinner last night, another tonight."

He groans, his leg pulling away from mine as he reaches for the bedside lamp that blinds us both.

"Damn, T, warn a girl."

His beard gets fuller with every passing day. I can't decide if it makes him look more rugged and sexy or if I hate it because it's not the smooth face I'm used to. One thing that's for sure is he looks beat from the constant training and relentless schedule he's keeping. He catches his breath as he slides up to lean against the pillows. I flip to my stomach, planting my chin on my palm because it sounds serious by his tone and my worry rackets up a notch.

"I want to see your face when I tell you this. Last night was another endorsement deal, mid-seven figures to be the face of the sport for the next three years. Which means no retiring after the Olympics." He pinches the bridge of his nose as redness rims his pale eyelids. "Or at least not immediately."

"Mid-seven figures?" I shake my head in utter disbelief.

"What does that mean?"

"Twenty million."

My breath catches while my brain fails to comprehend that kind of money. It's life changing. Well, many, many people's lives changing. I stare at him in astonishment.

"Yeah. Tonight, was a meeting with my agent, bringing me three opportunities. Coach for the national team after I retire—"

"Wait, I thought you said you only told me about retiring." I squint at him, knowing he never lies. Why start now?

"I've only told you, but I'm aging, and you see . . ." He waves a hand at his lightly bruised side. "I'm taking more hits than I used to. My agent knows and is looking into the future already."

My mouth feels suddenly dry at all this added pressure on him. The last thing we need to decide is our relationship if he has all these life-changing plans happening.

"And the other two?"

"Write a book and go on a speaking junket."

I scrunch my nose because that sounds least like him. Tomlin likes his privacy and becoming a motivational speaker doesn't match.

"Or?"

"Or go into politics. To quote my agent, everyone loves a national hero." His head falls to the pillows behind him while his palm strokes my arm.

"That sounds worse than writing a book." His lips flatten to a line. "I'm sorry, that was out of line for me to judge."

"No Dani, it's not. If we're going to make this work, all this affects you too."

Oh jeez, no pressure.

I slide to my hands and knees and then shift to sitting with my legs crossed. Thankfully, I wore the hotel robe to bed, I'm not completely flashing him my naked body.

"Don't do that. Take me and us out of the equation. What

do *you* want to do? What would make *you* happy?"

I point at him each time because I don't want another man to give up on his dream to be with me. Dad did it to raise me and it took a toll. I don't want that for Tomlin.

"How can you say that? Of course, you're a part of this. You're what I want, not a book deal. Come here." His hand catches mine, pulling me into his bare chest and disregarding my body lying against his hurt side. "I want to do the garage with you. All those cars you sent today solidified that for me."

"I want you too. I want us, but I already watched another man's dream die. I won't let you do it, too."

My chest burns as I say it and a lump forms in my throat. If I need to let him go to pursue his dreams, I will. I'll swallow mine and let him go, even if it might kill me. His response is instant, grabbing me forcefully to pull me onto his lap and bear hug me into him.

"Don't ever say that again. I know exactly what you are talking about and you're wrong about your dad and you're wrong about me. I would've liked to have known him, but he had to have been some kind of man to raise a woman like you. There's no way, and I mean no way, I'm letting any of this come between what we are starting."

His chest rises and falls quickly. The panic in his voice matches my own when I think about walking away from him. My arms wrap tight around his neck. It probably hurts, but I don't care. I want him to know I feel the exact same way because I scared the hell out of myself thinking of walking away. His breath evens out as I bury my hot face into his warm neck, trying to crawl into his skin.

"I'm loaded, Dani. I don't need any more money. But this." He squeezes me and I'm dying. "Money can't buy. I've been looking for this for a long time and I'm not giving up that easily."

There it is. Someone to fight for me. Someone to have my

back and go to bat for me like I had wished all those weeks ago on the back porch.

My arms tighten while fighting off the tears trying to crawl into my eyes as I take calming breaths of his scent into my lungs. He squeezes me as hard as I squeeze him. The side of his beard grazes my skin when he lies his head against mine.

I didn't know he's been looking for this for a long time. I hadn't been looking at all. We couldn't be more opposite. I told him that back at the cabin and he countered with how alike we are. I didn't see it then, but I'm seeing it now. The past haunts us equally. Our trauma brings us together in ways that are both similar and healing. I never knew it could be like this with another person. Certainly not the guy I called an asshole for several months. But now I know for certain I'm fucked. I love every last ounce of this man.

He lets out a ragged breath before saying, "Nothing will be decided tonight. Let's get some sleep."

His lips press to my head and when I lean back to stare lovingly into those warm brown eyes, he cups my face and gives me the sweetest, prolonged kiss I've ever had.

"Okay," I whisper against his lips and uncurling my arms from his body. He reaches for the lamp, clicking it off and enveloping us in darkness. I scoot off his lap, onto the bed, and get settled facing away from him.

"Drag that ass back over here. I want to sleep with my dick in your crack," he demands from behind me, and just like that, he brings the playfulness back, letting the seriousness fall away.

I laugh.

"So demanding, T." I move into the curve of his body, and his hand splays across my stomach to push me closer.

"I took a page out of your book, demanding Dani."

With a kiss on the back of my hair, we get comfortable together and settle into the cocooned warmth of us.

15

Tickling fingertips down my spine awakens me and I shift away, needing more sleep. The mattress dips behind me and, as much as I wanted this last night, it's a terrible idea. My eyeballs need rest.

"Good morning, Dani."

His deep voice rumbles behind me. His warm lips and hot breath press into my neck, sweeping kisses from the back of my ear to my shoulder. Goosebumps spread over my skin, and I lift my shoulder to block his face from doing it again.

"Leave me alone," I grumble into my pillow, squeezing my eyes closed against the sunlight streaming across the bed. "And make me some coffee."

"Ah, someone is grumpy this morning," he teases, sending those wretched fingers down the curve of my spine a second time, and I squirm.

"Do it again and you lose your finger."

Of course, he does it again, and when I flip over to attack him. He catches my fist and drops his lips to my exposed breast.

"Lucky for me, you took off your robe in the middle of the night, complaining about being hot."

His tone is as teasing as that damn finger, and I hate both right now. His teeth scrape across my soft flesh, dragging up the mound to my nipple and his tongue circles the areola. They are too sensitive in the morning and it tickles more than his fingers on my spine.

Where I'm barely awake, trying to peel open my eyes, he's fully awake and very playful. Normally, I'd love this, but I feel like shit for not getting enough sleep.

"It feels like I just closed my eyes," I whine, sucking in a breath when his mouth latches on my nipple and vacuum sucks it. Heat fills my body and the ache between my legs starts. "I'm so tired."

"I bet. You tossed and turned most of the night," he says, releasing my tit with a pop. His brown eyes are dancing with playfulness. His coarse beard grazes the tip of my nipple and I shrink inward to avoid it.

"I'm going to need a nap before tonight."

I adjust my body, lying flat on my back with him hovering over my other breast. When his head dips and his tongue swirls around the nipple, I hiss from the sensation. Being sleep drunk and foggy in the morning, I'd be more agreeable and probably jump his ass.

Hell, if he woke me up in the middle of the night for sex, I'd let him do whatever he wants. Now, all I want is to go back to sleep. Screw having sex, especially when I remember his rule.

"Yes, you will, because I'm not letting you get any sleep tonight. You've been teasing me with these beautiful breasts for months and taunting me with those sheer underwear you like to wear," he says, with his bed hair sticking up in all directions. "I almost busted a nut when you were bent over in your apartment digging for that god-awful cottage cheese. When Hamilton came in and you were still wearing them, I was livid."

"That's why you acted all blow hard like you were in charge.

I wondered what was up. I kicked you out and you wouldn't leave." I smile at him, surprised he remembers.

"Of course, I was not leaving. He was looking at you like a kid in a candy shop. My candy shop, for that matter, so no, I was not leaving."

He moves to the hollow of my breasts, planting his face in between them. If he would lie on top of me, I'd dry hump the hell out of him and get some release from this torturous pleasure.

"You were jealous," I say with surprise because he's always in control. Always does the exact right thing at the exact right time. His jealousy is unexpected and very un-Tomlin-like.

His face raises enough to kiss the inside of each breast before answering.

"Of course I was. I still am because I will not stand by and watch another guy shoot his shot in front of me."

"Hamilton's not interested in me."

I raise my hand to cup the side of his face, stroking his soft beard outlining those perfect lips.

"Trust me, he is. You say the word and he'll be there. But lucky for me, you're all mine."

His hand slips under my back to slide me underneath him. It's everything to be cloaked in his warmth with his hard dick stabbing me in the stomach. My body hums with desire. I slowly grind my hips into his as I lean forward seeking his lip.

"Lucky for me, you have a thing for big tits and sailor's mouths."

I click my barbell against my teeth, knowing he's eager to have it against his dick. He growls, clenching his body over mine, and covering my mouth with his.

He's relentless and aggressive. It's a clash of his tongue with mine until he victoriously captures my piercing in between his teeth. It's only for a couple of moments, then he releases it to dive back in while slowly thrusting against my stomach. My arms curl around his neck to stuff more of my tongue into his mouth as I grind into him.

The friction is delicious. His body rubs achingly slow, in contradiction to the frenzy of his mouth on mine, sucking until I'm out of breath and pushing against his chest for air. He doesn't break the kiss immediately. He rolls onto his back, taking me with him and letting the force of the movement break us apart.

"Sit back. Let me see you."

His words float over my panting and when I don't respond, he pushes against my shoulder, making his intentions clear.

Using his chest for leverage, I slowly straddle him, aligning my wet mound to sit atop the outline of his dick in his briefs. It's ridiculous how hard he is and with me on top, it's taking all my will not to slide down and pop it into my mouth.

"You're exquisite," he says, desire blackening his eyes while his calloused hands stroke the sides of my rib cage, grazing my boobs.

He's seen me like this before in the dimly lit room, but in the direct sunlight coming in from the gigantic windows that he opened while I slept is something else. I flush at his compliment. I know I'm pretty and use it to my advantage, but hearing the words fall from his lips is another feeling altogether.

"Thank you," I whisper, leaning forward to kiss him when he stops me with a hand on my clavicle.

"No, sit back up."

His voice is low and commanding. He's taking charge and I fucking love it. I can feel my wetness pool underneath me. When his thumb skims over my clit, I jump at how divinely sensitive it is.

"Put your hand on my thighs."

Damn, if he's going to get me off again, well, then hell yeah. I immediately comply with a coy smile.

"Like this?" I ask, biting my lip and gazing at him with all the desire surging throughout my body. I shiver in anticipation. My skin prickles with goosebumps as I grind against his shaft. It won't take me long, not long at all.

"Arch your back."

His fingers tickle around to my back, encouraging me and when I do, he gives me a rewarding smile. My nipples are hard and pink, pointing directly at him and begging for his mouth to return to them. My thighs are clenching against his, while his thumb works its magic on my clit. My breath comes out in quiet pants, faltering now and again from the pleasure of wanting more. Much more than being on display while he strokes me.

"Damn. I want a picture of this."

With his broad shoulders and chiseled muscles shoved against the pile of pillows, the shadow of his swollen eyebrow drooping over his eyelid, and that fine-ass beard enhancing his jawline, I want a picture too.

"Same."

His thumb strums me carefully, calculatingly slowly as his fingers caress from my back, down my ribcage, and under my breasts. Like the other night with the opposite timing.

It's a mind fuck where my brain can't decide to focus on my tit or my clit. Both demand his attention. It's why he's good at this. My thighs clamp tighter as I grind harder and harder into his dick, forcing more pressure on his thumb.

That perfectly thick pad rubs aggressively against me and stokes the flame of an already burning fire waiting to explode. I close my eyes, both parts of my body stinging with pleasure.

"Play with your other breast. Show me how," he commands.

It breaks my concentration, and my eyes open to him, licking his lips in anticipation. I want to lick them too, but there will be a time for that later.

I lean my weight to my right hand, keeping my back arched, steadily grinding to reach for my breast. My nipple is painfully hard. I twist it between my thumb and fingers, and he groans, which brings a mischievous smile to my face. Then I pluck it, elongating the pink bud to stick between my fingers and I'm rewarded with his thumb increasing.

The more I play with my tit, the sloppier his hand gets and the more wetness seeps out of me until I'm breathless and on the edge of coming. My eyes squeeze shut. My body tightens. My nails dig into his hard thighs, and I feel it slide over me in one continuous stream of pleasure. I moan. My hand falters, dropping to his stomach as I pump against him and ride my orgasm out.

"Christ."

With a wicked grin, he sucks the juice from his thumb as his other hand skims over my skin to rest on my thigh.

"I could get used to this."

How he doesn't blow his load right now, I have no idea. I can't last at all around him. I feel like a cat in heat with her ass in the air the moment he touches me.

"Me too. I can't wait for tonight."

I rake my nails over his strained thigh muscle, feeling how taut he is and holding himself back. His thigh flexes, lifting his hips slightly, and he begins groaning when I start grinding again.

"Don't, Dani."

His voice is a deep plea coming from the back of his throat. I tease my fingertips up his ripple stomach to strum his pebbled nipple, and he captures my wrist, pulling it toward him for my body to follow.

My cum squishes between us when he rolls me onto my back, giving me several quick kisses before lifting off me completely. The cold air makes me shiver and I reach for the sheet to cover up. Cum is stuck to my legs and rolling down my butt crack. If this is a preview, I can't imagine how much we'll ruin these sheets.

There's a huge wet spot on his brief covering the entire

front panel as he stands at the end of the bed, bold and proud. His body is magnificent, sculpted with pale skin that reminds me of the statue of David with his jet black hair in sharp contrast.

"I can't stay in that bed with you any longer or else. . ." his voice trails off and his straining dick says it all.

"Do you shave your chest?"

I tilt my head, realizing he has no hair, not even stubble. His hand immediately brushes over his pectorals as if surprised by the question.

"You don't have any hair."

"Not that I grow much, but I get waxed," he answers, sweeping his palm over his arms and I noticed there is no hair there either. I lean over the side of the bed to look at his legs. "What are you looking at?"

I scratch my head and straighten up. "Trying to see where you have hair."

"Legs and head." My eyes explore every inch of his skin. "How is it you are now noticing?"

"You're always dressed nice. Dress shirts and slacks."

"And yesterday?"

"You ate me out. I wasn't noticing anything but the back of my eyelids and the swirling yellow in them when I came," I blurt out because yesterday was a quick and satisfying release that only makes me crave more and more of him.

"Fair enough."

"Even your stuff is waxed?"

I make hand motions of pulling and stretching his junk in different directions, laughing at my joke. That would be painful though.

"You'll see."

He winks, planting his hands on his hips. I love that only I get to see him like this. Playful, content, and almost naked.

"Now, we need to get dressed and downstairs. Can you be ready in thirty minutes?"

"Holy shit, T." I throw back the covers and scurry out of bed to his chuckling behind me as I dash toward my room to start showering. "Why didn't you tell me sooner?"

He's in the doorway when I turn around, hand clutching the door frame.

"I didn't mean for that to happen this morning, but you flaunted those breasts in my face and now you have half an hour."

"Fine but still." A great reason to be late, but a girl still needs some time to pull it together for an important event such as today. "And make me coffee."

"Demanding Dani is back." He pats the frame with a twinkle in his chocolate eyes. "Thank you for the enjoyable show you put on for me."

16

Three things I have to do to get out the door on time. Get ready, check. Drink the instant coffee that Tomlin made, kind of check. He's turning me into a coffee snob with that espresso machine back home. I barely choke down half the cup. Check on Lars since we're both flying to Pebble Beach tomorrow. Almost check. I'll text him on the way down.

I beat him getting ready if I count his phone call. He's outside on the terrace. His usual frown is marring his handsome face, but seeing him in his uniform, or whatever they call the white pajamas they fight in, makes me want to attack him. I see some judo role-playing in our future.

He flicks his wrist to look at his sports watch and opens the door, motioning for me to get off the couch, when he strides over to his huge duffle bag. I don't care that he's on the phone while we walk toward the elevator.

I hope the person yelling on the other end doesn't affect his match today. Then again, this is Tomlin we're talking about. If he's too disciplined to ruin his match with an orgasm, I'm pretty sure yelling isn't going to do it either.

I send a quick text to Lars to make sure he's good for tomorrow. He sends me an immediate thumbs up and I smile. This is going to be great. Heck, this whole trip is great aside from getting sick. As the elevator descends, I find myself getting nervous for Tomlin. I know he's got this, but still, it's important that he does well.

"You look pretty," he whispers away from the receiver, and I reward him by holding his hand as we descend to the second floor.

I know I look good. I thought so in the dressing room yesterday and the saleslady in the hotel shop downstairs confirmed it when I stopped in to see what they had. And I should look pretty. This sucker cost me nearly two hundred dollars. That didn't include the straw wedge sandals she paired with it called espadrilles or something fancy like that.

The elevator chimes on the second floor and the doors open to a sea of chaos. More than yesterday. It's packed tight in the hallway leading to the ballroom and I hesitate. Only when Tomlin releases my hand to touch the small of my back am I propelled forward.

Two security guys immediately step forward, bracketing us, when a swarm of flashbulbs and fans push through the crowd. Tomlin ends his call, rolls his shoulders back, and seems to grow taller beside me. When he seizes my hand and steps forward to use his body as a shield through the people, I feel a smidge better.

He's taking control of the situation, something he always does with me, but seeing him like this is different. He's different. The playfulness from earlier is wiped away by the daunting intensity that is his elite competitive world. It's both awe-inspiring and overwhelming.

The pressure he lives under is something I never thought about, and he makes it seem too easy. As if he's comfortable with this three-ring circus. Mad respect.

People are shouting his name, shouting at me, and shouting about his opponent. Anxiety sweeps into my body, my heart pounds against my windpipe and I clutch the back of Tomlin's white jacket to hide from everyone. It takes us forever to get through, even with another two security guys jumping in to create a pathway.

Sweat collects at the back of my neck, causing my curled hair to stick uncomfortably to my skin. His hand clutches mine like a vice grip with an occasional squeeze to ensure we don't get separated when the crowd pushes in toward us. Security attempts to coral them back and Tomlin walks past as if this is normal. It's anything but normal.

Seconds feel like minutes when we finally clear a set of double doors where trainers and coaches are working with their athletes. Security falls away, disappearing out the door while Tomlin pushes through a smaller door to join his team in a separate room.

A couple of guys stand when he enters. Tomlin greets them, dumps his bag on the floor, and then guides me into an adjoining bathroom to lock the door behind us.

"Are you okay?"

His eyebrows hang low over his piercing stare. He said it would be like this. Tried to prepare me for what to expect when we lay in bed, but hearing the words of warning and experiencing it are two different things. His knuckles caress my cheek, sweeping into my hair to cup the back of my neck.

"Am I being selfish wanting you here?"

The fact that he's worried about me instead of himself or his match is astonishing because all his focus should be on this and not on me.

"No. I want to be here, T," I murmur, yanking on his belt to bring him closer. His hand glides down my back to join the one gripping my waist. I'm careful not to get make-up on his white uniform.

"You told me it would be like this, so don't worry about me. I'm still the girl that racked you in the stairwell."

My joke erases the tension in me. The corner of his mouth twists down into a slight frown, making me wonder if my joke is the wrong thing to say.

"Yeah, you are, but I always worry about you, Dani. This is different. I'm used to all this. It's my world for the next year, and I want to share it with you. Once the garage is up and going, I'd like for you to travel with me."

The bombs keep on dropping. First asking me to move to Denver, then retirement, the endorsement deal, and other options this morning, and now this. Bro, if it's not making my head spin.

"Kiss me, T."

I slide my palms over the rough white fabric, fighting the urge to kiss his exposed chest, but I'm wearing lipstick. It wouldn't be very respectful if the star of the show is covered in bright pink lipstick.

He obliges, gently kissing me as if I'm the most precious thing to him. This is what I want. I don't know about all the other stuff, and all these decisions looming over us. I'm kicking all those cans down the road as long as I can to stay in the cocoon of us. I melt into his lips, slow and sensual as they move with mine. One of his hands moves down to my butt, pushing me against him, and I smile against his mouth when I feel his hard dick between our layers.

"Better be careful," I murmur before flicking my tongue into his mouth in search of his. He captures my piercing between his teeth for a moment, releasing it almost instantly while his palm moves up my ribs, over my breast, and into my hair to tilt my head for deeper access.

It would be so damn easy for him to bend me over this count and take me. Simply flip the hem of my skirt and pull down my panties. I'm so wet. He could slide in with one thrust and fuck the shit out of me. A loud knock startles me and my eyes fly open. He doesn't care, continuing to kiss me until his dad hollers his name.

"Remind me to fire him," he groans, reluctant to untangle himself from me. I fully agree. Fire him for hitting his mom. Fire him for being a sucky dad to Tomlin. And fire him for being an ass to me.

"Definitely fire him for interrupting," I whisper, leaning forward to tug on his belt for a couple of quick parting kisses. "And T, I'm here for you. Through thick and thin."

That gets me two more kisses before he shakes his head, a sexy smile on his face when he lets go entirely.

"I need to stop to calm myself."

I glance down, see his boner, and laugh as I turn to the mirror to fix my hair. He's content to watch me with his dick planted against my ass when I lean over the counter to reapply my lipstick. He uses a couple of tissues to wipe away the lipstick smeared on his lips, but part of it is stained on. It accentuates his already swollen lips against his dark beard, causing me to stare at him.

"Don't look at me like that."

He groans, his hands fisting the back of my skirt as if contemplating what I thought a moment ago. I playfully bend over, rubbing my ass into his crotch, and he groans while looking at the ceiling.

"This isn't going to help your problem, T."

"Tomlin, now," his dad hollers again, nearly caving in the hollow door with all his banging.

Fury sweeps over Tomlin's face and he steps back so fast that I straighten up in surprise. When he whips open the door, his dad steps back, momentarily startled. For a split second, fear flashes through his eyes, knowing Tomlin could take him down. Kylie said Tomlin put a stop to the abuse, but seeing the instant change in his dad is strangely fascinating.

"You!" He scowls, unfortunately getting over his flash of fear to bark at me.

"Hi Mr. Takahashi," I say sweetly and thank the karma gods for blessing me with that second of insight that his dad is still scared of Tomlin. Good. "I hoped I'd see you again."

Old Đani would've racked him by now. New Dani is sarcastic as hell. Something I'm learning is effective, but not as satisfying.

"Get her out of here!" he yells at the other guys in the room.

Tomlin blocks my view to bark out something in Japanese. It's the first time I've ever heard him speak it. I watch his reflection in the mirror, his body leaning toward his dad to intimidate him as the speed of his words picks up. Damn if it doesn't sound as rough and harsh as he probably intends it to be.

Their exchange is heated. As much as his dad probably deserves whatever Tomlin's saying, I don't think this is the best head space for him to be in before his match. I lay my hand in the middle of his back, and it's rising and falling rapidly.

I don't know what else to do when their arguing continues, so I lean my chest to his back as he has done to me before. It made me calm down when he did it. Maybe it will work on him too. It's the only thing I can do for him.

Tomlin's word is the last one.

His dad storms off when I peek around Tomlin's broad shoulder to look. Realizing that I broke contact with him, Tomlin leans back, trying to reestablish that connection as he runs a hand through his black hair to squeeze the back of his neck.

Without him asking, I shift to place my hands on his shoulders and try to rub the coarse knots that have collected at his trap muscles. They are tight as hell, and now I understand why he rubs them all the time. It's got to be uncomfortable. He groans as my thumb works on a knot at the base of his neck.

"Damn, these are tight."

Good thing I have finger strength from the work I do, or else I couldn't break up the knotted muscle.

"Trust me, I know," he says, moving his ear to his shoulder to elongate the muscle.

"Mr. Takahashi, they are ready for you," A lady says somewhere in front of him, and I immediately stop rubbing.

"Do the other side."

He tilts his head the other way, ignoring the lady. I use both hands to work from the top of his neck all the way to the tip of his shoulder to make sure it's nice and loose for his match.

"That's good."

He rolls his shoulders several times, his back popping in response before stretching his neck from ear to ear a few more times. He turns to face me while he works the rough fabric of his uniform and adjusts the belt before cupping my shoulders.

"Hey, that was kind of hot hearing you speak Japanese. Maybe you can speak it tonight when we celebrate upstairs." I raise a knowing eyebrow at him when he says something in Japanese. "What does that mean?"

"It means, behave. Now go with my team. They'll take care of you. As you know, my match is last. If you want to mix and mingle, go right ahead, but I'd prefer you be there when I compete."

The fact that he's still worried about me more than his match says everything I need to know. I won't mix or mingle. I'll be in my chair the whole time, in case he needs me. I want him to know exactly where I'm at all times, so he doesn't have to worry about me, and he can focus on himself.

"I'll be fine. Now plant one on me for good luck and go kick some ass."

His shoulders slouch as if my rubbing them relieved some tension before he leans over and brushes his lips to mine.

"I can't wait to kiss your ass," he murmurs against my lips. I rest my hands against his chest to push him away.

"You behave, T."

My smile is as big as his and I'd be lying if I said I can't wait for tonight. A thrill goes through me, causing me to cross my arms and rub the goosebumps away. He turns to leave and an older blond pops out from the side of the door to lead him out of the room. His entourage follows and I wait as they pass until one dude, almost my height in a super nice suit, pauses to hold out his hand.

"Rex Matthews. I represent Tomlin."

He's older, wearing a pinstripe suit and pocket square. His head is shaved bald with rimless glasses over dazzling white teeth and a cocktail ring on his pinkie finger. This is his sports agent? The dude looks like a mobster.

"You're the agent," I say, sliding my hand into his warm palm where he grips it firmly and nods. "Nice to meet you, I'm Dani Winters."

"The girlfriend."

The finality of what he says has me narrowing my eyes at him.

"Careful with that term," I warn, the word making me uneasy as I toy with my tongue piercing.

His hands fly up as if I'm holding him at gunpoint.

"What Tomlin said. Here's your badge. You'll need to wear it to get around back here."

He hands me a lanyard with my name and a picture on it. The picture from that car magazine I did with Carl and the owner a year ago. I smile, proof that Tomlin trolled me online.

"If you'll come with me."

He's holding the door for me, and I hang the lanyard around my neck, dwelling on 'girlfriend'. Did Tomlin really say I'm his girlfriend? Or did Rex make it up to make me feel better? I know Tomlin doesn't lie, but I'm not sure Rex wouldn't. Aren't sports agents paid to tell you what you want to hear, which may not always be the truth?

Girlfriend.

It's such a heavy word. It means a serious and committed relationship. If I'm being honest with myself, I don't want to label it yet. It feels like all those decisions he wants to make that I'm not ready for.

The entourage snakes to the left as Tomlin, his dad, coaches, and the training team walk to the right. Security follows them, leaving one guy with us as we're led into the ballroom.

The noise is deafening. Different reporters are spread throughout the venue, giving updates as to the status of the events, and a couple are doing interviews with other athletes.

It's fascinating being this close to the action and not necessarily understanding what's going on. If I were a fan, like some of those we already passed, I would be star-struck. But that's not me. In a way, I'm thankful for that so I can enjoy this experience and be more objective about it.

Granted, it's extremely overwhelming and a lot nerve racking. How many people want to get to him and touch him as if he's God or a healer that cures people is weird. I don't know how he handles that part. For sure, there's no way this world would go to my head.

Maybe that's what the problem was with the other girls he's dated in the past. Maybe they wanted to make the cameras and the fans all about them, or an opportunity to promote themselves to fame. I doubt Kylie would do that, but he said she got lost in him. Something I'd never do. Tomlin knows he has nothing to worry about with me. Fame is the last thing I want.

"Have you ever been to something like this?" Rex asks as we line up at our seats before the first match starts.

"Nope, can't say that I have. It's chaotic, though."

I glance around, wondering how everyone outside the ballroom is going to fit into this already packed room.

"Ah, this is nothing. You should see Worlds or the

Olympics. This is a little exhibition to support the local clubs." Rex waves a dismissive hand while talking. "When he was in Tokyo a few months back, fans rushed our car, and we couldn't get out to dinner. Tomlin ended up getting out of the car and signing autographs and taking pictures for almost two hours. Now that was chaos."

"Wow, that's crazy," I murmur, gazing at him.

Tokyo, where he slept with a competitor and lost. Where he said he was upset with me for having Zach and rejecting him. Also, where he came directly from the day, I busted Judd's nose and saved Isla. Yeah, Tokyo seems to be a milestone for more reasons than a two hour autographing session.

"It was, Tomlin was supposed to host a party at a nightclub, but he refused, saying he was catching an earlier flight to take care of some things back home," Rex continues, his eyes bouncing all around the room as he leans in close to me to share this. "He fought like shit. Practice rounds were sloppy. He even took a shot to the eye. I asked what was up, he wouldn't tell me. I think it was his old man. The guy's on his ass twenty-four-seven."

Little does Rex know that I know exactly what was up. Me, or rather us, was bothering Tomlin.

"I've noticed."

"You've met the guy? Before this?"

Rex seems nice enough, but he's a little too fast and loose with his tongue for my preference. Maybe all agents are like this, but I'm not comfortable talking about Tomlin's business so openly.

"Yes, we go way back." That's all I'll give him because I don't want to talk about his dad either. Then I wonder about what Rex said. "Why do you think it was his dad?"

"Because he wants him to go into coaching with him. Open their own training facility."

Rex leans across the aisle to shake the hand of some man.

This would be a fifth opportunity, different from coaching for the national team, I assume. Two coaching gigs, a twenty million endorsement deal, a public speaker, or a politician. It makes my head spin thinking about his many offers. And then there's mine or ours. Open a garage and build his museum. More surprises from his side and more cans to kick.

"It's nice to have a face with the name, though. A pretty one at that," Rex says, startling me. I figured Tomlin told him about me over dinner last night, but this sounds like he's known me, or my name, longer than that.

"You knew about me before last night?" I ask, gazing into his blue eyes, and noticing a green ring around his irises. I assume he knew me in order to get my badge, but there seems like a back story here.

"Yes, Tomlin never travels with anyone. When he asked me to arrange flight information for you and gave me your name, I looked you up. You'd be surprised at how many women latch on to elite athletes like him."

I don't know whether I'm offended that he's looking me up to make sure I'm not a gold digger, or happy that he's protective over Tomlin. A little of both.

"Well, what did you find?" It's really none of my business, but he's the one that brought it up. Asking can't really be that bad. "Did you figure out that I'm not after him for his money?"

"I'll tell you this, you have a very little presence online. I couldn't find any social media accounts for you."

"True, I'm too busy working to mess with that stuff." Although I won't tell him about the one I started last night for our garage. It sounds as though Tomlin hasn't told him about that and I'm not spilling the beans. That's for sure.

"Good, stay off it. Only causes trouble for me. I found out that you're into cars, as is Tomlin. I figured that's what brought you together."

Rex shrugs, as the announcer makes his way over to the raised platform, forcing the crowd to quiet down.

"More or less," I say.

That's not at all how I came to know Tomlin, but unlike Rex, it's no one business but our own. I hope he doesn't chat up Tomlin's business to just anyone.

And what does he mean it only causes trouble? Has he had to cover up social media scandals for Tomlin before? Well, damn. I need to show Tomlin that picture Kylie sent and talk to him about her reaction before Rex finds it and has a situation to address.

Uneasiness settles in my gut, and I squirm in my chair as the announcers start.

17

The first two contenders are young. Probably early teens bowing at the edge of the green mat and patting their chest and legs before entering the square. Rex explains each competitor has a pre-match ritual that they can do at the mat. If this were a ranked match, they'd have to do it before coming out.

Tomlin didn't do one in the bathroom so I'm curious what his is. I strain my neck to look for him, but he's not in sight. Maybe doing his ritual with his team backstage or whatnot.

They meet in the middle, bowing to their competitor while their names are announced, and then it starts. No sign from the referee dressed in a blazer and dress pants, just them bouncing around each other.

I don't know what to expect, but I'm surprised when it's not as many kicks as I thought it would be. Maybe that's karate. I'm really not sure. I probably should've watched some of Tomlin's matches before, but the thought never occurred to me. If I'm going to be his girlfriend, that word making me uneasy, then I need to study up on this sport and Tomlin's role in it.

Rex whispers in my ear, explaining different things

happening and the strategy each opponent takes. I appreciate it. It builds my understanding, something else I should've Googled before I got here.

The sport is fascinating. When one kid flips the other over his shoulder and holds him there, a piercing sound rings out, with the referee holding up his hand. They immediately stop, allowing for the opponent to pop up from the mat and adjust his judogi, as Rex tells me that's what it's called.

Then they are back at the center of the mat, squaring off. One kid is a statue staring down his opponent, the other is swaying side to side with nervous energy. They're generally the same height and build, but attack in very different ways.

When they start again, the same guy is pinned, even faster this time. Rex explains his foot hit the green mat and not the tan. Another couple of rounds and then the match is over. How fast they cycle through a mat is surprising compared to baseball and football, which drag on for hours.

With my short attention span, I could definitely get into judo. Maybe have Tomlin teach me some badass moves, so the next time I get into a fistfight I can cut a dude down faster. Although that's the opposite of the new leaf I've turned over and been working on. Either way, probably good to know some moves to protect me for safety purposes.

There's a brief wait in between until the next age group starts. It reminds me of boxing and the different weight classes, ages, and skill levels. With each age, the speed increases, as does the aggression and strategy.

Rex continues whispering in my ear and after a while, I'm getting the gist of it. I move when one takes a bad hit or duck as if I'm on the mat. Rex touches my elbow for me to stop, but it's hard not to get into it.

The interlude before Tomlin's match is brief, allowing the younger competitors and their families to crowd into the ballroom and line the walls. The temperature seems to rise with the added body heat and even though Rex hands me a bottled water. It isn't enough to cool me down or calm my nerves.

My knee bounces as I straighten the hem of my dress and wipe my sweaty palms against the fabric. Anything to calm myself from the anticipation building in the room to see the three-time Olympian.

When Tomlin appears at the back of the room, everyone stands, cheering, clapping, and chanting his name. Goosebumps sweep over my skin and into my hair. My stomach tightens into knots, and I clasp my hands together in front of me.

It's only a charity match, nothing like the Olympics, but I'm suddenly nervous for him. Wanting him to do well so he's happy with his performance and proud of himself. I'm proud of him, win or lose. Competing or retired.

His dad and two other coaches stand in front to keep the aisle clear. Tomlin is smiling and waving in the middle and a couple of trainers bring up the rear. His entrance definitely reminds me of wrestles and boxers without the loud music.

"There's our boy," Rex shouts near beside me.

He's wrong.

Tomlin is no one's boy.

He's a legend.

Something both his agent and his dad would do well to remember because, without him, I suspect they'd be nowhere. I keep my back to Rex, focusing on how much the people love him and how good Tomlin is at being the face of the sport. The endorsement deals make sense. Bringing the sport to inner city youth makes sense too. Why couldn't he marry those two together to start a gym here? Or in any inner city area?

He could start his own competition, like the Arnold Classic.

A sixth option.

The ballroom is electric, buzzing with a ton of energy from the deafening chanting of his fans that sparks my adrenaline.

When the coaches shuffle into the front row on the opposite edge of the mat, Tomlin bows deeply before stepping on it. The roar of the crowd rises as he walks to the center and bows in each direction of the room.

The sport, the tradition, the respect from him to his fans, and vice versa, clogs my throat with emotion. Tears fill my eyes and it's unexpected. I realize I'm emotional because I'm proud of the excellence he's built and honored that he's including me in this.

My heart quickens and I duck my head to wipe my eyes before Rex notices. When he stands from his bow, our eyes meet. The smile on his face is for them. The wink is for me. I cover my mouth with my hand, trying to choke back a sob at how humbling Tomlin is to his stature as one of the greatest in his sport. The greatest, according to Rex, whispering it to me.

An official steps onto the mat with him, bringing a microphone for Tomlin to thank his fans, thank the organizers, and the sport that has been good to him. He tells about how the sport has changed since he first started over two decades ago and how he sees it continuing to change and grow in the future.

I can't help those damn tears that fill up my eyes and spill over the edges. It's literally watching greatness be great. My throat burns with happiness, my heart aches with respect, and my stare blazes with love.

How he can imagine stepping away from all this is blowing my mind. How do you retire when you're so loved? How do you leave something that has been good to and for you to sit in an old garage watching cars being fixed up?

I can't fathom stepping down at the peak of my career to start at the bottom of the mountain with something else. It's simply beyond belief. I get the ego check that he doesn't want to get old and achy and tarnish his record, but damn, doesn't he have several more years versus one?

Tomlin hands the microphone to the organizer of the event,

allowing him to speak about the organization, how they're helping the youth, and how it's their aim to keep them in a productive after-school activity such as this sport and off the streets and its challenges.

The longer the guy talks, the more I think this is the direction for Tomlin. Opening inner city gyms may be what he and they need. They shake hands again when discussing the partnership that they formed, and Tomlin's competitor bows at the edge of the mat to join them in the middle of it.

They clasp hands and then clap each other on the back. The smiles they wear are both friendly and familiar. The announcer explains that they're both competitors in the sport and colleagues on the US national team.

After a few more announcements about meeting the competitors and the fan meet and greet, they take several official pictures before the organizer wishes both men good luck and exits the mat. We take our seats, and my knee bobs again.

Tomlin nods. His face changes into a mask of stone and concentration. His jaw muscle pulses in and out as he takes several steps back to roll his shoulders and get into his stance. It's fascinating to watch this elite athlete, the intensity of his stare at his competitor, and the fierceness that overtakes him when he takes the final bow to start the match.

Where Tomlin's long and lean, his opponent is shorter and stockier. I'd think he'd have the advantage, but Rex explains it is much more than that when I ask him. Tomlin has speed and agility, is light on his feet, and is quick to attack. The other guy deflects his attacks and dances around the mat more. Their approaches and techniques are completely different.

Tomlin wraps around him, his long arms and legs holding him from the back of the belt while gripping the front of his judogi. Attacking on both sides puts the bulkier man on the defense and is at a great disadvantage when Tomlin swipes a leg through his to roll him over for his first takedown. The speed and fluidity with which he does are remarkable, and I'm shaking my head in disbelief.

They start again, squaring up in the middle of the mat before Tomlin lunges at him. This round is longer, and more equally matched in effort and strength. I dodge and deflect with each move as if I'm in the match. It's hard not to.

It reminds me of the days when I used to fight first and think second in school. Not that I'm dumb enough to compare my stupid street fighting to the likes of these elite athletes. It's that I can't sit still knowing how it feels to have punches to your body and hands gripping your flesh, trying to take you down.

Something about watching these two beasts battle for physical superiority while grunting at the exertion from it is primal and turns me on. Probably not the best thought right now, but if tonight wasn't the night, I'd force it to be after watching the sheer masculinity, power, and strength of them fighting to win.

I drowned out the crowd, and Rex's running commentary in my ear to focus solely on Tomlin and his judo. His opponent looks to have the advantage, crouching under Tomlin and forcing him to elongate over the man's body and balance on one foot. I slide to the edge of my seat, my hands twisting together in my lap that this dude might take Tomlin down.

But in one seamless move, Tomlin interlocks his arm under his opponent's arm, squats deeply to grab the back of his belt, and once again rolls the dude head over heels to land flat on his back while Tomlin restrains him in an armhole. The referee calls it, and the two men separate once again to meet at the center of the mat.

The third round is faster. Tomlin attacks instantly, grabbing the opponent's sleeves to control his hands. The guy lunges into Tomlin, causing him to stumble back long enough for his opponent to throw a strike to his face.

However, Tomlin uses his backward movement to drop to

his knees and roll the guy over his back to pin him to the mat again. He takes less than five seconds to do it.

They start again, and this time I notice Tomlin's dad sitting quietly in a chair with his arms crossed and a deep scowl on his face. The other two coaches are standing, screaming, and pacing between the chairs. It's an odd contrast and pretty intriguing. Something I need to ask Tomlin about as I try my best to stay seated and not block those behind me. As the two men rage on, it's hard not to and I pop to my feet.

With each takedown, the fans yell, cheering him on and screaming his name. I almost feel sorry for his opponent, but I suspect it's got to be like this most everywhere Tomlin goes.

During one particular takedown, I get a clear picture of Tomlin's face and the ferociousness on it is something I have never seen before. Sweat drips from his hair onto the guy's face as he kneels to hold him there.

Then it's over.

The abrupt ending surprises me and Rex says they competed for twice as long as a normal match since it was an exhibition. A match comprises six five-minute matches for a total of thirty minutes. They competed for almost an hour. It went by in a blink, and we all want more.

Tomlin and his opponent bow to each other and the room, then clap each other on the back and remain side hugging for everyone to take pictures. They separate to allow the organizer's people in for pictures too. Then the coaches and trainers, everyone except his crusty old dad, whose ass remains planted in his seat across the room. Good, he'd ruin all the pictures anyway with his nasty attitude.

"Ready to go back to the room?" Rex touches my elbow, and I shake my head.

"No, I'll remain here." Never taking my eyes off Tomlin.

"He will not come over to you. His team will take him back, so it's probably best if you come with us."

His insistence draws my eyes to him.

"No, I'll remain here," I repeat it with venom in my voice and a death stare to match, because no man tells me what to do. Certainly not his team of men.

He acts as if his shirt collar is suddenly too tight around his neck when he adjusts his suit jacket. Rex can do what he wants to do, and I'll do the same.

"Of course," he says with an awkward bow of his head. His little show of agreement doesn't last long when he spots someone across the aisle to blabber to.

The ballroom is clearing out, with athletes and their teams filing out the door, leaving the die-hard fans behind to take videos and selfies with Tomlin in the background. I'm content to stay here, observe everyone, and soak it all in.

18

It's probably about twenty more minutes of formalities for him, when his team of coaches and trainers collect at the corner of the mat, waiting for him. Tomlin holds up a finger to wait while he jogs over to me.

He's beaming, the same as I'm beaming at him. My body is buzzing with happiness for him and in awe of his mastery. He throws his arms around my body and lifts me off the ground for a hard kiss in front of everyone. My arms are around his neck in a flash, and I kiss him right back.

His face is glistening with sweat, some getting on me and when he shakes his head, droplets go flying. It's playful. His entire expression changes to boyish fun when he does it, causing me to laugh.

"How did I do?" he asks, putting me down and his fingers splayed around my waist. His brown eyes crinkle with delight, already knowing the answer, but wanting to hear it from me.

"You did amazing, but you already know that," I tease, gripping the front of his judogi for emphasis.

"I know. But did you like it? Did you enjoy yourself?"

He steals another kiss.

"It's remarkable. You're remarkable, T. Your intensity, speed, ferociousness. If I didn't know you better, I'd fear you."

I can't stop smiling at him. He's mastery in motion. He doesn't need me to tell him that. He has an entire room to tell him.

"You'd better fear what I'm going to do to you tonight." He flashes me a wicked smile.

"*You* better be fearful because I'm going to fuck the shit out of you after seeing you two beasts battle it out," I threaten right back because my underwear is sticking to me with how much I want him inside me right now.

"Beasts."

He throws back his head, releasing a loud, carefree laugh and looking absolutely happy doing it. I giggle along with him, happy that I'm making him feel this way. Out of the corner of my eye, a couple of fans snap pictures of him, and I wish they could text them to me because this is probably the happiest I have seen him ever.

"Beasts eat little girls," he counters with a slight growl, dipping his head to kiss me again.

"I know. You did. And I want you to do it again."

"I will trust me. You'll be riding my face."

Damn. I think I came in my panties.

"Is that a promise?"

"Definitely a promise."

He seals the deal with another quick kiss. I can't wait for tonight either. Little does he know I bought lingerie yesterday. The scrapes of lace from the demi underwire cup my breasts but don't cover them and the single triangle piece barely covers my lower lips. It will make him lose his mind. Who is going to be scared of who is up for grabs tonight.

"I need to head back and dry off a bit before the fan event. Will you come with me? There should be food to eat as well."

"Of course. I'll go anywhere with you."

That panty-dropping smile spreads quickly across his face as his fingers intertwine with mine. "That's exactly what I like to hear."

He leads the way over to his team, where Tomlin introduces me. Some share smiles, others make small talk and his dad scowls his hatred. Good thing we're on the same page with our feelings. I don't usually bother with hating people, but I've collected a list now. Judd, Carl, and now Tomlin's dad. For what he did to Tomlin's mom and how he treats Tomlin. Yeah, I'm fine with adding him to the list.

Like before, I'm tucked behind Tomlin, hands interlocked as his dad leads the way and the rest of the team follows. This path is shorter, taking us to a different room this time. Not the same one but more of a conference room, with frosted glass, sandwiches, fruit, and drinks in the middle of the table. Along the wall is a padded table with a cutout for a face and different tools in a bag below it.

Tomlin and a trainer quickly undo his belt to strip off his judogi, leaving him in his tight compression shorts. Another trainer is toweling off his back while Tomlin scrubs one over his face and hair. They work in a seamless motion, one in front, one in back, drying him off. Probably done this a thousand times before.

I crack open a bottled water and sink into a conference chair near them, while the coaches stack plates of food to sit on the other side of the table.

"Help yourself, Dani."

Tomlin motions to the food before hopping onto the table with a groan. He didn't take too many hits this time, but the physicality of his performance warrants more than one groan.

"I'm good, T. Do you want something?"

The room is too quiet, all ears on us, and I realize this is as new to them as it is to me. Tomlin seems to be the only one comfortable here. His dad grumbles something in Japanese, which Tomlin ignores, and leaves the room.

"In a minute, but please get something, because it's going to be a long time before we can have *dinner*."

His emphasis on that word is about eating, but not dinner. A thrill goes through me when we connect eyes. His naughty little eyebrow popping up before collapsing on his back with a smile and letting his trainers take over.

I love all this teasing. I hope we'll live up to the hype. It would be gravely disappointing if we didn't. Pushing that terrible thought from my mind, I maneuver to the food and pile it high before sitting back down. The coaching team talk amongst themselves, and I settle in to watch the trainers work on Tomlin.

He groans at various parts of them manipulating his muscles, smashing some, diving others for them to roll away from the pressure. Other than the murmur of the guys at the end of the table, and Tomlin muttering to his trainers, it's very quiet and peaceful. A nice transition from the fierceness of the match. I assume it's like this every time.

Half an hour passes, my plate is empty, and the coaches are gone before the trainers stack cold packs on his back and hamstrings while he lies face down. That lasts another little bit while they eat and eventually leave us alone. Tomlin's arm dangles over the edge of the table, to circle his fingers around my ankle and caress the bone with his thumb.

"What do you think? Could you get used to something like this?"

His voice is deeper with his face pressed into the cushioned table. Not sure if this is the best time to talk about it because I'd prefer to watch his expression to know if what I'm saying is right or wrong.

"It's definitely exciting. And you are impressive to watch."

"But?" His thumb stops moving.

"Not really a but for me. More a but for you. Are you sure you want to leave all this? It's amazing what you've built. The fans, your team, your agent, the intensity, and the level at which you compete. Won't you miss it?" I shake my head because I still can't imagine walking away at the top of my game, or the peak of my career. "I mean, you are the face of the sport from what I've seen here."

"Probably."

"See? If this is nothing, which to me, this is everything, why are you walking away at the top? I know you lost twice, and you're taking more hits than before, but you're still at the top. I overheard a guy behind me say no one can touch you and that you're on a whole other level."

"I hear that as well. However, I'm not as fast as I used to be. Even I can see and feel the difference."

I can't tell if it's the padding against his face, the exhaustion from the match, or how he really feels about the situation, but the disappointment in his voice rings loud.

His thumb starts up again and I scoot close to him.

"Can I run something by you? Another option to consider?"

He sits up, ice packs falling all over the floor. When I make a move to get up, he says, "Leave them."

Concentration hardens his face as he stands, twisting and turning with a few pops escaping before walking toward the food and picking grapes off the vine.

"Tell me."

"Granted, I don't know much about your sport, but do you know how they have the Arnold Classic for bodybuilding?"

He grabs a handful of fruit and a bottled water before falling into a chair next to mine.

"Why couldn't you do something similar for judo? Like opening your chain of gyms for inner city kids. You said yourself that you're loaded so they wouldn't need to make money, just break even. Then you could bring all these kids together to compete across the nation? Kind of like you did this charity match and each of the different age groups got to compete, or maybe it's like the Olympics of judo, but for kids that couldn't qualify for the Olympics, I don't know what I'm saying. Do you get the gist?"

His head nods slowly, taking it all in as he pops a strawberry in his mouth.

"They already have the ATJA Judo Nationals."

"Well, they have Miss America and Miss USA. Couldn't you have another one? I don't know what it takes to get in, but surely some of these at-risk youth can't afford to travel across the nation to compete. So, you pick the ones from your gyms to go to that competition or you can start one of your own. Heck, you could get sponsors for each gym even. That would help defer the cost and also bring awareness to the sport. It's an idea, T. Seeing how much the judo athletes look up to you and your fans, it makes better sense to me than what Rex's offering. By the way, he talks too much about your business, or at least he did to me."

"Rex is like that," Tomlin dismisses, and it irritates me because he lets his dad disrespect him and Rex gossip about him. "I like your idea, Dani."

He polishes off the few remaining berries in his hand, then leans forward, his muscles rippling as he grips my chair to slide toward him. My crossed legs fit in between his and his hands rest on my thighs, slowly pushing my dress over my knee. The sunburn from earlier faded into a nice tan and the coral of my dress makes it pop.

"This is the first time I've seen you in heels."

One palm is already under the hem, massaging my thigh muscle, and the other is running a finger under the spaghetti strap tied at my shoulder, attempting to undo it.

"It's not. You saw me in them the other day."

I bit my lip against his tickling fingers because the anticipation between us has been building all day. It's taking nothing for me to get wet, wanting more of him.

"No, I know for a fact I have not. Those were sandals, these are heels."

Sandals and wedges, who cares? When his finger can't untie the stitched spaghetti strap, he slides it down to my arm and tugs on the top. I chuckle when he frowns at my strapless bra impeding his view. "I don't like this."

"I can't have my boobs flopping all over the place," I say, his palm climbing higher to my core and caressing a finger at the top of my panties. With my legs crossed, he can't get to my cooter biscuit. Now's not the time or place for that.

"Later they'll be."

Little does he know, they will not.

The creak of the door startles me, and I fly away from Tomlin to adjust my clothes as he stands over me to block the view of whoever is coming in.

"Didn't mean to interrupt, but here's your clean judogi," says the lady from before. "And it's time."

I'm not usually one to get embarrassed, but having been caught multiple times by his staff is getting out of hand. If we're to get through this event respectfully, I need to stay as far away from Tomlin as possible.

"Give us a few minutes." Tomlin's voice is unaffected, whereas my heart is beating in my throat. The door softly clicks closed when he turns and looks down at me. "Sorry, I shouldn't have done that."

"I shouldn't have let you," I say, pushing my chair further back to stand up and straighten my dress. "But I know you can't keep your hands off this hot piece of ass."

His smile is wide when he winks at me and throws the hanger of clothing on the table to get dressed.

"Love the confidence, babe."

Babe.

That's new. It does something to me. Never one to be into pet names or even have one, I don't know why my thighs seize when he says it. It's cliché and rather juvenile, but I can't deny the warm feeling it gives me.

Demanding Dani is playful too, but sex games and role-playing are both fun and something I've done before. Babe is uncharted territory. It's a casual companion, implying we aren't just trading sexual chemistry, but we are together. I like it even though I shouldn't.

"If you continue to stand there and ogle me, I'm going to put this dick to work since it's technically past my competition," he says, stepping into his pants.

Snap.

It clicks in my head that he's right. I instantly step to him, my hands on his ribs, one traveling up his chest, the other trailing down to the waistband of his compression shorts.

He sucks in a quick breath, which feeds my wickedness, when my mouth clamps onto his nipple, dragging the pad of my tongue and barbell over his tight bud. In a flash, I'm in his shorts, seeking his long cock to grab in my hand and squeeze it.

A long groan rips from his throat as his hand tangles in my hair to force me up to his mouth for a deep kiss. I plunge my tongue into the sweet fruit-tasting cave, searching for his tongue with a tug up and down on his hard shaft. I'm drooling in his mouth at the thought of him in me in a matter of hours.

One tiny event stands between us and dinner time as he called it. Hell, I want a taste now. Why not? He's tasted me all week long. I cut off the kiss, surprising him to squat on my heels when a quick hand cups my elbow to stop me.

"No."

He pulls me to stand, which forces my hand out of his shorts and away from his hard shaft. Disappointment settles in as I search the hard lines of concentration on his face.

"Not here. Not like this. I've waited too long to have you.

And when I finally see you on your knees, I don't want it to be quick or clothed."

Damn.

That fucking statement causes a flood between my legs. His chocolate eyes burn with intensity, desire darkening his face, and the seriousness with which he instructs makes me flush with heat.

"Kiss me, T."

His gaze falls to my parted lips, while his hands slide over the goosebumps on my arms to cup my face. The tip of his thumb pushes my chin higher, and I step closer, pressing my body against his to feel that delicious bulge and promise for a great time later.

"So damn demanding," he whispers. His breath is my breath as he leans closer, his lips dusting mine once, twice, and after the third time, he continues, "But tonight, upstairs, no demanding, only pleasing."

Me pleasing him. Him pleasing me. I don't know and I don't care because I'll get mine. I always do. He's been pleasing me all week. If he wants to reverse the roles, then let's go. I'll please the hell out of him.

The ache in my core pulses, wanting him to kiss the hell out of me. This teasing stuff is driving me crazy. My hand glides up his broad back, dipping in and out of the muscles as they flex to hold me tightly in place. The other travels down to cup his ass, gripping it as I grind against him.

"Deal."

I seal my fate and am rewarded with a soul-sucking kiss that has him nipping at my tongue and twisting my barbell. My mouth molds to his, aiming to please and demand at the same time.

His dirty talk is the best mind fuck ever. At this point, I'll do whatever the hell he wants, asks, or demands. Anything to put an end to this torture and finally be his or him be mine. I don't know which, nor do I care. He can play all the games he wants tonight. Hell, let's fuck all night so I'm delirious, sore, and exhausted for the flight tomorrow. I'd love for him to put me in a fuck fest hangover.

Those beautiful swollen lips of his close around mine, lingering in a long goodbye kiss and ending our make-out session.

"Damn," is all I can say when I unclench his muscular ass and back.

I've never been so addicted and obsessed with having sex with someone as I have with him. Maybe this is the psychobabble Kylie spews about how loving someone makes sex better. I never believed her, but it could possibly be true if this is what I'm feeling. It's over the top between us and I never want it to end. I practically want to live in his skin at this rate.

"Now be good and help me get dressed," he jokes while pulling the drawstring on his waistband to fit snuggly against his trim waist.

"Shoot, tell yourself that. You started it," I toss back while squeezing by him to unhook the jacket from the hanger and separate the belt from the clip. He grabs my ass before digging around in the bag under the massage table to retrieve his deodorant, hair gel, and cologne.

It's a strange mix to watch him get ready with me in the room. Each day that passes brings down another barrier that previously resided between us. As if moving from two different individuals into a couple. Watching him get dressed, put on his deodorant, and mess with his hair brings an intimacy that I'm having a hard time putting it into words.

The only other man I ever watched get ready was Dad. This closeness shoves a lump in my throat that has me laying his jacket on the table and turning away. I duck my head and try to sniff as quietly as possible but damn this tiny ass room for outing me.

"Dani?"

Worry rims his words and I get it. I'm not one to be overcome so easily with emotion. It must be that time of the month or something because I don't know what my deal is.

"What's wrong?"

His body covers mine, cloaking me from behind to hug the life out of me. When his chin rests on the top of my head, I quickly wipe the tears from my eyes, the action not going unnoticed by him.

"Hey." His face slides across my hair until his lips are near my ear and he interlocks our fingers. "Why are you crying? Is something the matter?"

How do I tell him that everything is so perfect that I'm scared as hell? Like everything I have wanted since he escaped to Denver, that day is finally coming true, and I'm terrified something will end this.

Things never work out for me, and this is going so well, it makes my heart hurt. Because I love him, so damn much, too damn much, almost near Dad level. I vowed never again to feel that kind of pain, and yet I'm on the cusp of it. On the cusp of loving him, as I've only loved one other person this much in my life.

I inhale a ragged breath, sucking in enough air to stop the tears that are welling up again. He waits patiently while I get hold of myself. Not pushing or forcing me out of my comfort zone like he normally does. No, this version of Tomlin is patient and understanding, and it makes my chest ache with adoration.

"I-I'm happy, T," I stumble through the words. His arms tighten, his fingers squeeze mine until they are numb, and he dusts a gentle kiss to my temple.

"I am too."

I gaze down at our interlocking fingers, how much I love the feel of them and lean into the comfort of his body. Everything about this moment feels right, and it takes my breath away at how good this feels in my soul.

"I'm sorry. I don't know what's wrong with me. Aunt Flo must be coming or whatnot," I defend. I will not be a sissy about it, but I feel I need to say something, so he doesn't expect me to be all emotional and sensitive. That's not me.

"Dani."

He unwraps his fingers from mine, to place them on my waist and turns me around to face him.

"I know this is a lot. This whole situation is pretty overwhelming. It's okay to be vulnerable with me and it's okay if you need to cry. I'm not judging you. I'm done judging you. I know I have in the past, and that's a mistake I'm deeply sorry for. In the time apart, when I was in Denver, I thought a lot about you and me, and I love our banter, but I don't want it to come at the expense of us. I know we joke and have a good time, but I'd never intentionally hurt you. And I'm sorry if I judged you before. That was not fair of me to do that to you."

Those warm chocolate eyes are pools of sincerity and regret, and I know exactly what he's talking about. We went for each other's jugular frequently, but that's all in the past now. I know we have decisions hanging over us right now, but we're good. I know he would never intentionally hurt me as I wouldn't him. There's a fragility between us that I don't fully grasp yet, even if I know it's there.

"Don't apologize, T. We went at each other pretty hard. And honestly, I like that you don't put up with my bullshit. And I love our banter too."

I clutch the rough fabric of his pants to pull him toward me, smash my face into his chest and wait for him to squeeze the life out of me. He does exactly that, holding me for so long that there's a knock on the door again, reminding him of his commitments.

"We've got to go, Dani."

I breathe in his combination scent, deodorant, aftershave, and hair gel before pulling out of his embrace at the exact moment the lady enters and leans against the door. She doesn't say anything, even if we know we are very late.

With our privacy gone, Tomlin's face clears of emotion to return to his serious and intent mask of professionalism. He makes quick work of getting ready well under the lady's watchful eye as I step to the edge of the conference table to wait for him.

I look around the room at the ice packs still on the floor, his open duffel bag, and plates of half eaten food on the table. It looks like a bomb went off in here and the guys are leaving it that way. Something about it bothers me. I step toward the table to pick up everyone's empty plates, when Tomlin strides to the door, turns, and looks at me.

"Don't worry about cleaning up, Dani. We'll be back here after the fan meet and greet," he says with certainty in his voice, before extending his hand for me to accompany him to the event. I'm not exactly comfortable doing what he asks, but this is his event and not mine, so I grab my purse, put it on my shoulder, and cross the room to join him.

19

The fan meet up is loud, crazy, and way too chaotic. The fan line snakes through the ballroom with hundreds of people clustered against the wall and out the door. There are security guards everywhere to keep people in line while his coaches and trainers chat up the fans waiting behind the red ropes.

The organizers put up a backdrop with both their logo and Tomlin's logo and a dedicated spot for picture-taking. Next to that is a booth for fans to purchase merch, posters, and other stuff with his name or face on it. It makes me wonder how much he gets off these sales. Like he said last night, he doesn't need any more money, so I'm curious about who gets it.

Tomlin leads me to a chair to the side of the picture-taking backdrop where I can watch everything that is happening while being separate from the crowd and mayhem. I can't imagine how long it takes Tomlin to come down from a high like this. Maybe that's why he never sleeps, never having time to truly relax.

It's both exciting and fascinating to watch. Some fans bow before approaching, and Tomlin mirrors it. Others, usually females, are too exuberant and rush up at him, hoping to get a hug. And some people are star-struck, sort of frozen when they get to the front of the line. With all his years of experience, his finesse in interacting with people and handling their different emotional reactions is admirable.

Nothing phases him. His respect for the sport, respect for the fans, and their dedication to him are evident in how much time he takes talking with them, asking their name, and asking what they like most about the sport. He truly is a great ambassador and again I wonder how in the world he's going to leave all this.

The energy of his team working together to move fans from the merch booth to taking pictures and then exiting while leaving them shrilling over their excitement at meeting their hero is something else. There's a cohesiveness that shows they've been doing this for years and the transitions between the different functions are seamless.

Hours fly by as the line dwindles, the mats are gone, and the room empties. Athletes and their coaches have long gone. The hotel staff is bustling in and out, breaking down tables and stacking chairs, and the organizers are dismantling the last remaining booths in the room.

Through it all, Tomlin is on his feet, smiling and gracious with every single fan, and only has a few sips of water to keep going. No doubt I work hard at what I do but seeing his energy level and how giving he is to others is something I could never fathom doing.

It reminds me of the comment he made the other night about how he's not in control of anything, merely a puppet to a puppet master. I see it first-hand now. If he hadn't made that statement and if I hadn't seen it today, I would've never understood. It makes sense why he wants private time away to collect cars. Why he plays the piano in the middle of the night. Why he sleeps so little here and at the mountain resort. Those are all the things that he can control and are the inner part of him.

Rex flutters in and out, shaking hands, clapping people on the back, and schmoozing for the first hour or so, but then disappears like all the rest. Tomlin's dad sits stoically across the room watching all the interactions, the scowl never leaving his face until finally he left about half an hour ago.

Tomlin monitors me with a few winks and a couple of smiles but otherwise stays focused on his event. I remain the entire time, snapping pictures and taking a few videos of the event. When the last few fans are upon him, I nearly crater in relief because I need food, a nap and to pee. I can't imagine what Tomlin needs. The energy level it takes to keep up with this is insane.

Hell, if we need to postpone tonight for him to recover, I certainly understand. Wait, what am I saying? That's not happening. Hell, I'd fuck him asleep if he'd let me. But I'll be patient and not jump his dick the second we get to the penthouse. Let him take the lead on how it goes down tonight since this day has stretched on for hours.

When the last fan finishes taking pictures with Tomlin, he turns to his team of coaches, trainers, and staff running the booth to shake hands and thank them for their time and help today. I stand, stretching my back and releasing a stiff groan from my tight legs and numb butt. Tomlin's smile is fast and easy when he approaches me.

"That took longer than I thought. Are you okay?" He reaches for my hand to hold my fingers loosely in his.

"Of course. All I've done is sit on my ass all day. How hard is that? But what about you? You have got to be exhausted."

I wave my hand at the room behind him, still stirring with vendors and staff working to return it to a ballroom and not a judo match.

"I'm not tired, Dani. I'm hungry." That smolder bores into

me, and the panties that dried out long ago are getting wet again. "Are you ready?"

I reach for his arm, wanting to clutch him tighter than his fingers toying with mine.

"Hell, yeah. I've been ready for the last two months."

His smile is captivating and slightly naughty when he raises a knowing eyebrow. "I meant, are you ready to leave?"

That fool knows exactly what he's asking and leaving this room, isn't it? I know he's probably trying to keep it clean for any lingering ears, but I stopped giving a damn about an hour ago. The faster that line dwindled, the closer our night was coming, and anticipation had my knee bobbing for the last half hour.

"Oh yeah, I'm definitely ready. You have no idea." I yank on his jacket to kiss me, and he bops me on my nose. Keeping it clean is killing me slowly.

"I think I do. Let me say goodbye to my team and grab my things before we head upstairs."

His chin drops for a second, intensifying that smolder for a nanosecond before clearing it away and releasing me entirely.

"Okay, I'm going to pee."

Damn if it isn't both a promise and a warning. Good, let the best man or woman, in this case, win. He rejoins his training team, chatting with them for a few seconds while I make my way across the room and out the exit to go to the bathrooms.

Luckily, the lobby is mostly clear, with a few lingering vendors breaking down their booths and packing away their products. The bathroom is empty as well, which gives me plenty of time to do my business, fix my hair, smooth out my dress, and reapply my lipstick. After a few more seconds in the mirror to make sure I look my best, I throw open the door and walk like a woman on a mission to Tomlin, as eager to get upstairs as he is.

"Dani, do you have a quick second?"

I hear my name but don't recognize the voice until I turn around and Rex's charging toward me. Although he has been nothing but nice and a tad pushy at times, this tone is neither friendly nor kind. If I had to be honest, it's more in the tone of Tomlin's father, which instantly puts my guard up.

"Rex?" is all I can muster to say, because this short little man and his insistence on talking to me stand between fucking the shit out of that fine ass specimen one room over. I click my piercing against my teeth as a reminder to not let the curse words flowing through my brain fall out of my mouth.

"Have you seen this?"

He thrusts his phone screen so close to my face that I grab his wrist and force it away. If I'm not already irritated with his ass, I'm bordering on the level of homicide for both his rudeness and abruptness. He gets the point and steps back, moving his phone a respectable distance away from my face.

Now that the screen isn't all in my nose hairs, I see the picture that Kylie already sent to me. However, I don't know what the big deal is to Rex.

"Yeah, so?"

I shrug while he swipes through other pictures that I didn't see. Pictures of Tomlin helping me into the town car, me bent over with my head down, looking coincidentally close to Tomlin's lap and Tomlin's hand splayed on my back. It looks as bad as it seems and for once I'm at a loss for words.

"Yeah, so? This is disastrous. Why didn't you tell me that this had occurred when I sat beside you today? I could've done damage control if I knew these were out there."

Rex's accusations drop one after another and his face gets redder and redder with every word he spits out. The fact that he's making these as lewd as they seem pisses me off because this isn't at all what happened. And shouldn't Tomlin's agent get all the facts before jumping to conclusions?

"I wasn't blowing him. I know it looks like I was but I'm here to tell you I wasn't."

My hand tightens on my purse strap, a compromise for not choking him. Two vendors pass by right when I say it which makes it so much worse. This couldn't be a more inappropriate place to talk about it. If Rex wants to confront me, he should do it in private with both Tomlin and me.

"That's not what these pictures look like and it's all over social media now," Rex chides, lowering his voice to an angry whisper. "I shouldn't have let Tomlin bring you. When he called to add you to the list, I should've told him no."

I glare at him. One hand twists the fabric of my strap to keep from punching him, and the other grips the side of my dress. I click my piercing and count to ten, trying to take a page out of Tomlin's patience book before answering him.

"You know what, let's talk to him about this, shall we?"

I squint my eyes and intentionally slow my words to let him know I'm not putting up with this shit. If Tomlin's leaving the sport has anything to do with everyone trying to control him, then that I get. This is bullshit. Rex wouldn't even have a job if it weren't for Tomlin.

"He hasn't seen these either, I take it?" Rex asking me is absurd.

How the hell would I know what Tomlin knows and doesn't know? Bro needs to ask his client himself. Deciding I'm done with Rex, I turn on my heel and speed walk into that ballroom to where Tomlin is quietly talking to some guy.

Rex is on my heels like a freaking Chihuahua and when Tomlin glimpses both of us out of the corner of his eye m, he knows shit's about to go down. I don't know if it's the murderous expression on my face or the nervous one on Rex's, but Tomlin squares off, ready to address both of us.

"This doesn't look good."

Tomlin's stance widens as if reading himself for a match

with his competitor. He grabs the bottom of his jacket and tugs it straight, the fabric rustling as he crosses his arms over his chest. I can't recall a time he's ever taken this body position with me, and it throws me for a loop. I pop one of my eyebrows up, expecting an explanation when he simply mirrors my expression.

"Rex thinks I was giving you head in the town car at the airport," I blurt out.

No need to sugarcoat it to Tomlin after the way he treated me in the hallway. Rex nervously looks around the room while Tomlin's eyebrow joins the other to reach for his hairline.

"Go ahead, show him what you showed me."

Rex appearing uncomfortable shuffles the phone to Tomlin, without saying a word, and waits for him to draw his own conclusions. Tomlin's expression changes from one of surprise to fury and then that aloof mask I've seen so many times descends as he angrily swipes through the pictures. He hands the phone back to Rex when his eyes fall on mine and glances away to survey the room.

His face is unreadable, probably trying not to get mad about the situation. Not that I want to agree with Rex, but he's right in that this would've never happened if I hadn't come. It was a completely innocent thing that happened, and the media is painting it as something disgusting.

"Well?" Rex presses Tomlin and his eyes drift back to mine.

"Ignore it." Tomlin's voice is hard. The finality he tries to use with me is even harsher with Rex. I don't know the dynamic between these two, but I know enough that Tomlin's livid and so is Rex, for two very different reasons.

"Tomlin, you must—"

"What is our policy on things like this?"

He forms it like a question, but it's anything but. Suddenly, I feel nervous, as if I did something wrong. This isn't good for his image. Not exactly sure what his image is, but from the looks of it here today and this week, it seems to be squeaky clean. This picture could be seen as highly disrespectful to this crazy respectful sport.

"Fine," Rex quips, obviously not happy with Tomlin's stance. "If I'm asked, it'll be no comment, as usual."

He locks his phone and stuffs it inside his coat pocket before swiping the palm of his hand across his forehead.

"Good." He nods to Rex before uncurling his arms and extending a hand to me. "Dani, come with me to get my bag."

I glance at Rex, our eyes meeting and his narrow slightly. It's obvious he blames me, which is bullshit, but at the end of the day, I don't want anything wrecking Tomlin's reputation. I already know how hard it is to come back from a ruined reputation when you're the innocent party. It sucks.

My hot palm slides into his cold hand and he immediately tightens around it as we cross the quiet ballroom leading back to the conference room. He throws open the door to the room. The food and drinks are cleared away. The massage table and ice packs are gone, and only his bag remains at the end of the table. I feel bad for a moment that I didn't help clean up, but I guess this is expected for the treatment you get when you're famous.

"Um, Tomlin?"

I don't know really how to ask him without blurting it out. Being in delicate and sensitive situations isn't my specialty. He releases my hand to hold open the door, allowing me to walk through it, and I wait by his bag with my hand glued to my purse strap.

"Yes?"

Gone is the playful, vulnerable Tomlin that I enjoy when we are in private. The man that stands with the table dividing us is the same one that Rex got a moment ago. And I'm not too sure I like this version.

"You said to ignore it? But is that the right thing to do?" I ask, biting my bottom lip as his hard eyes stare into mine. Maybe I'm not right for questioning his decision, not knowing his world, but surely putting out a statement explaining the situation would be better for his reputation. And a sudden wave of panic fills the pit of my stomach when I think about what I need to ask him next. "Has this sort of thing happened before?"

Maybe it's none of my business, and maybe I don't need to know. Or maybe he won't tell me at all, but with the look, he's giving me now, I already know the answer.

He breaks my stare to reach for his bag and to toss it over his shoulder As I wait for him to respond. Long seconds tick by before he looks at me again and says, "Let's talk about this upstairs."

I definitely don't like that answer, and my stomach drops in response. I nod, the only thing to do when he starts for the door to open it again and waits to usher me out. I'd be lying if I said my heart isn't beating faster and my mind is going a hundred miles a minute trying to figure out why we have to go upstairs to have this conversation.

20

There's no one in the conference room and I'm pretty sure the place isn't bugged, so why not clear the air immediately? The longer he delays, the more nervous I'm getting as to what story he has to tell me. The silence growing between us as we walk to the elevator bank isn't helping. While we wait for it to come a few people approach to say their goodbyes to him.

Of course, Tomlin's manners are impeccable in making everyone feel acknowledged and welcome, even in the middle of these tense moments between us. When the elevator pings and the doors open, trepidation builds within me as I braced myself to hear more unfortunate news. Granted, I don't know much about Tomlin, and he said that he's never traveled with someone, which I believe, but if this isn't such a big deal, why not say that in the first place? Then we can put this all behind us and have a fun night.

I swear this damn elevator crawls to the penthouse with a stone-silent Tomlin beside me. He doesn't reach for me nor I him and I can't decide how that makes me feel. I don't know if I want him holding my hand when he breaks the bad news to me or if that'll make it worse since I don't like truth telling and hand holding at the same time. I didn't like it when Eli did it at the pet store, and I certainly won't like it now.

When we finally get to our floor and the doors slide open, my nerves are practically vibrating with anxiety, half wanting to scream at him right now to tell me and half wanting to go back to the bliss of the unknown where Rex never approached me about those pictures. I know I have to tell him about Kylie's picture and conversation, and I thought that was going to be difficult, but this seems so much worse now than it looks like I gave him a blowy in the car.

We walk in silence side by side to the penthouse. I wait as he digs out the key card, then practically bolt into the place to kick off my heels and throw my purse across the dining room table before turning to face him.

"Okay, we're here, so spill your guts," I demand, planting my hands on my hips, trying to be powerful looking when I really dread what he has to say.

He gently places his bag on the dining room table next to my purse, then walks away from me to stand by the couch. His eyes linger on mine, his expression changing from that aloof elite athlete downstairs to one of sadness up here. A sigh loosens from his chest as he sweeps a hand through his hair and squeezes the back of his neck.

I know those tightly corded muscles have to be bothering him from his match, but now isn't the time to feel sorry for him. He needs to tell me exactly what's going on before I lose my shit.

"Dani, please have a seat," he says woefully and motions to the couch.

I slowly comply, my eyes never leaving his face as I round the couch while he moves over by the piano. I don't understand why he doesn't want to sit with me, but picking up on all his body language, I don't press him on it. If he wants to stand, so be it.

"To answer your last question first, yes, something like this has happened before."

My stomach feels sick at the thought of him getting a blowjob from someone else. Naturally, he's had them. It's a completely normal thing to do, but assuming, knowing, and having camera proof are three different things that make me nauseated as hell.

"Okay."

I don't know what else to say. My hands clutch together in my lap, and I twist my piercing around, preparing myself to hear the rest. His eyes travel from mine out the window beyond the terrace to the coral evening sky. The faraway look that he had on the back deck in Colorado when he asked me about loneliness, and the same one he had when he was chasing demons in his mom's car on that vacant road, is the same as he's having now.

"I didn't want you to find out this way. I knew I'd have to tell you eventually, but I guess I wanted more time. Not more time to know you because I feel very close to you already. But it's something I'm not proud of. I handled the situation the best I knew how at the time, but I've replayed that night a million times in my mind."

He walks over to the lamp and clicks it on, still lost in another time. As if reporting the events that happened outside of experiencing them. There's a certain detachment, like the memory of it is too difficult to relay, and to protect himself, he's void of emotion.

"We had gotten back home from when I had won my first Olympic gold medal. It was a long flight, with turbulence and delays. My father was pacing the aisles of the plane and getting into arguments with the flight attendants. My mom was nervous, praying that we'd make it, that the flight wouldn't go down, and that my father would calm down. You name it, she was doing everything to stave off his fury. I didn't know it at the time, but that was the buildup. My father's anger kept building and building from the time we left the Olympic Village to when we finally arrived home."

My mind is racing. This sounds like what Kylie had mentioned, but it's not at all what I expected him to say. Like an idiot, I thought this was about another girl when this is about something much, much deeper and much more important. I scoot forward on the couch to stand up when Tomlin holds up a hand to stop me.

"Please stay where you are so I can tell you everything. I'm not too sure after this that you will want to." He moves back toward his spot at the piano, and I open my mouth to interrupt, to tell him that there's nothing that can make me walk away from him, but he says, "Please."

His expression is pained, as if physically hurting and pouring his anguish into that one word. I press my lips together and I slide back on the cushion to wait for him. He takes a few seconds to compose himself and lets out a ragged breath before continuing.

"I-I couldn't fathom what was happening. I won. All those years of training, hard work, sacrifices, and regimented eating, forgoing my childhood and I had done it. I thought it would be enough."

His head shakes, the lock of black hair falling forward as his voice catches. I don't know his pain, but I know this pain and it has everything to do with the grief that we carry with us.

"I was in my room, talking on the phone, when I heard my mom scream. Naïve me thought this win would be enough. My win would end what my mom was going through, living through, and damn it if I shouldn't have stood up to him before. But . . . I didn't, Dani. Here I had won the Olympics, I had beat other athletes at the highest level of competition and yet I had never thought to take on my father. What's wrong with me? Why didn't I do it sooner?"

He's absolutely gutting me. Taking my heart and ripping it from my chest and shredding it with the guilt that he has still to this day for actions that aren't even his. Actions that are solely the responsibility of that motherfucker that walks beside him, acting as if Tomlin's victories are his own.

My hatred for that man couldn't grow any more than it already is. I swear I'm gonna murder him the next time I see him for what he did to that sixteen-year-old boy, the man that stands here before me, and the mother that's in a graveyard somewhere.

I know men can be assholes and motherfuckers, but this is a whole other level. This is pure evil that walks beside him, bitching him out in Japanese and scowling at everyone every damn day.

"Tomlin—"

"No, no, no. Please, Dani."

His head shakes again, and I'm dying sitting here on the couch, not allowed to comfort him.

"That night I shouldn't have left her alone. I shouldn't have made that call to my friend. I should've done so many things differently, but I didn't and that's something I'll regret until the day I die. My bedroom was across the house when I heard her scream. I ran. I knew what was happening and yet a part of me didn't know. I didn't know where in the house exactly, but I knew it was coming. I knew by his behavior and his temper that it was building, and his release was imminent. She was alone when he cornered her, unloading the laundry from our trip. I followed her screams into the basement, where she was tucked in a fetal position between the wall and the washing machine. Her arms were protecting her head while he was kicking her in the side. He had already broken her nose and gave her a black eye."

I gasp, my hand covering my mouth and tears immediately fill my eyes at the horrific life his mom led behind closed doors. What that woman put up with I won't ever know, but hearing the traumatic words fall from Tomlin's grieve-stricken voice gives me an idea.

Tears rim his eyes as well. His thumb and index finger pinch into the bridge of his nose, trying to compose himself. I grasp the pillow on the couch, twisting it in my hands as we both cry. I'm trying to be brave for him as he was brave for me back in Colorado when he held me by the fire and let me tell him about Dad.

I'd give anything to hold him now, but respect that's not what he wants from me. He wants me to listen so he can get it all out and probably never have to tell me again. I understand that. I don't want to tell him my story again.

He wipes the tears from his eyes as mine cascade down my cheeks. My chest aches for him and her. I crave to touch, hold, and comfort him. It takes everything in me to stay planted on this damn couch.

"I don't even remember it, Dani. I think about that night, and I only remember pieces of it. But I will always remember my mom curled up on the floor with a black eye and a broken nose, bleeding because the man she loved and married was beating her to death. It was like my rage and fury blinded me, years of witnessing this abuse, years of guilt for not doing something sooner. It was pure vengeance to end one parent's life over the other. Only one other person knows this. But Dani, that night, if there was going to be a parent to die, it was gonna be him and not her. I was going to do it."

I can barely breathe. My heart seizes with sorrow for his pain, my throat burns, and I want to vomit. I'm sobbing uncontrollably for all the anguish and destruction that has taken place and those two innocent lives.

Tears run unabashedly down his face. His hands are on his

hips. His chest rises and falls rapidly, and his shoulders slump in defeat. He's gutted. The guilt he carries is unjustified and not his. It belongs to one smug bastard that deserves to burn in hell.

"My mom stopped me. She crawled across the basement floor and begged for his life."

He shakes his head and looks away, still trying to reconcile with the events of that fateful night. It's heartbreaking. His eyes remain glazed over, staring at the darkening night sky. The silence gets loud as if trying to remember and wanting to forget the worst night of his life.

"And we hid it. My mom said it would . . . it would, uh, ruin my career. I didn't care. She said I'd go to jail for assault, and I was fine with it. In that moment, in that blind rage, I was fine with that. I was fine with putting him where he deserved to be. Fine with spending the rest of my life suffering the consequences of that decision."

His gaze returns to mine, a dark and scary energy in them. His expression hardens as if making that decision again today, right now in this very room.

"But my mom . . . she begged me to stop. Tried to hold me back as best she could with her injuries and begged me not to ruin my life. Begged me not to put his life over mine. If there was a life to pick, I was the one she would pick, not him. And yet, four years later, she picked her life over mine. Why did she do that? Why did she pick me over him but then turn around and pick herself over me? Didn't I do the right thing by her? I know I was late. I know I should've taken action years earlier, but wasn't what I did good enough for her to be here on this journey with me, and not him? I can't reconcile that, even to this day. I-I can't . . ." His voice trails off into a whisper, and he's a complete wreck. I can't take it anymore.

I jump to my feet and rush to him, throwing my arms around his waist to press my face into his chest. I don't know if he's got it all out. I don't know if he wants me to still sit over on the couch, but I can't do it when he's ripping his fucking heart out and taking mine too. I need to comfort him.

I need him to know the love I have for him. Even if it's not the time to tell him that I love him with every fiber of my being. I need him to feel it in my embrace. In my body when I hold him. In my eyes when I gaze at him and in my hand when I wipe away his tears. I don't have the words to say to him. I don't have his eloquence.

Thankfully, he doesn't want them when his arms wrap around me, his palm cradling my head against his chest and his forearms locked around my waist. I'm sharing the grief he's carried all these years. Our grief becomes one, joined and shared. We're one. So far beyond business partners, so far beyond life partners, we're grief partners. And anyone who has lost a parent that they love more than life itself understands that.

His trauma and grief are at a greater level than mine, and yet his capacity to forgive and let that monster walk beside him is remarkable. Something I'll never understand. I don't know how long we end up holding each other until Tomlin's deep voice rumbles against my ear.

"The cops never did press charges. In fact, it was never even on my record as a minor. But somehow there was a police report buried somewhere in the system and when my mom committed suicide, it all came out. I didn't have Rex at the time. He had heard what was happening with me and reached out. I know you think he may talk too much about my business, but Dani, that man has been more supportive than my father. He helped me when I was at my lowest. Found me a therapist, who helped me get back on my feet after losing my mom. I owe him everything. If he wants to brag about the good times, I don't mind. I'm glad that there are good times to talk about."

I squeeze him as tight as I can. This beautiful man has

suffered so much and still has compassion and understanding in his heart. It all makes sense why he holds everything so close to the vest. This isn't everyone's business, it's his business. I can't fathom how he's survived all this heartbreak and devastation.

I'm utterly speechless, my body physically aching from the pain that he shared and my mind's a scrambled mess trying to process everything he's been through. He squeezes me right back, not nearly as hard, while his lips press against the crown of my head. His heart throbs in my ear, and he takes in a few deep breaths, trying to calm down while the tears still streamed down my face.

After a few seconds, his embrace slowly releases, his palms sliding down my arms to hold my hands and stare into my eyes. The tip of his nose is red, the edges of his eyelids are swollen, and tear tracks wet his angular cheeks. Those expressive eyes are windows to the pools of guilt and pain at the bottom of a long pit. Wordlessly, he guides me to the couch, sits beside me, and looks at our intertwined hands.

"The wins are for her, Dani. That house, that room, all the medals, everything I have is for her. She always wanted to move to the mountains. My father wouldn't hear of it. We could never move away from Denver. He'd never think of moving away from the training center. On the rare occasion that my father was away for work, and we had the day to ourselves, she'd take me out in the Grand Torino, and we would drive for hours. Her favorite place was the mountains. And we went to all of them."

"Come here," he says, pulling me onto his lap as if holding hands isn't enough.

I straddle his lap and lie against his chest. My face is in his neck, his pulse throbbing against my forehead, and I close my eyes. This is so much to share. Probably not what he wanted to do, but I feel honored he shared it with me. I couldn't possibly love him anymore.

"Did she ever get to see it? The cabin?" I murmur against his salty skin.

He clears his throat while his hand caresses my back.

"No. I only built that in the last few years. But the front post was there."

"The one with the antlers? That looks all cowboy-ish?"

I open my eyes when a rush of air leaves him that resembles a light chuckle.

"Yes. My mom always loved cowboy television shows and old westerns. What she saw in my father, I'll never know. One time, when I caught her watching a Clint Eastwood movie, she confided in me that she always wanted to be a rancher's wife." He pauses and when I'm about to ask, he says, "She drove by that place on one of our rides. When I tell you we rode all over Colorado, we sure did."

His voice lightens, a sliver of humor as if back in the memories of the good times that he shared with her. If I were to move out of the crook of his body to look at his face, I'm almost convinced that he would have that faraway look again.

"I don't know what year it was, or no, I take that back. It was when my father was in the hospital, recovering from what I did. My mother looked absolutely terrible and didn't want to go out in public, but she wanted to go for a long ride in the bright sunshine and that's when we found that place. The sky was endlessly blue, without a cloud in it. There was a chill in the air, and for once, we both felt free from his reign."

His hand stops circling my back and I push off his chest to look at him. The dreamy look I figured he has is on his face. The corner of his mouth moves upward into a half smile when he gazes at me.

"We stopped at a gas station, picked up snacks and drinks for the ride and as we ate them, she turned down that road, crawled up the side of the mountain, and stopped when she saw the antler fence. I don't know what it meant to her. She never did share. We idled by the side of the road for a long time while she stared at it. Now that I think about it, she was probably envisioning a different life. One where she was a rancher's wife living at the top of the mountain and bringing her closer to her dreams. That's really all I can come up with."

I lay my hand on the side of his face, stroking my thumb across his beard, and his jaw tightens.

"That's a beautiful memory."

He smiles for the briefest of moments before his lips settle into a deep frown.

"I wanted to buy that land for her, Dani. But I was a minor and all my earnings went to my father. Sure, he was earning a small salary as a coach, but nothing like what I made. I never saw a cent until I turned eighteen. And by then I was starting back at zero, supporting my mom. My father divorced her, kept my earnings and I hadn't made enough to buy it before she died."

Fresh tears flood my vision as my lips pressed together to hold back another sob. It's so fucking heartbreaking to hear about the love he had for his mother, trying to be an adult before he was even a man, and shouldering the responsibility solely for himself. I only had to raise myself one more year to adulthood, and that was with Carl's help. I can't imagine being a year younger and shouldering the responsibility of both me and the parent I love.

"How old were you when she passed?" My voice rasps at the words.

"Twenty. I never saw it coming. In the months following both my mom and dad's assaults, I knew she was battling depression, and I begged her to hold on. My father wouldn't pay for treatment and my mom desperately needed it. When he divorced her shortly thereafter, I knew it was going to be bad. Luckily, the judge saw what was happening and mandated treatment. She was away for several months, getting the help she needed while I trained and competed. I missed her an awful lot, but she sounded better on the phone. Happier, and chattier and it gave me hope. And when she returned, I thought everything would be fine since she was away from him. I don't know why she did it. Why she couldn't hang on? All I know is, I couldn't save her that last time, when had I saved her so many times before."

His chest falls, his breath exhales harshly, and his hands stroke up the sides of my body when his eyes level with mine.

Holy shit.

I don't know anything about suicide or what people go through when they're battling these tough times. Granted, I've had my own dark days. The pain of losing my dad was more than I could bear sometimes, but it never crossed my mind to end it all.

I coped with the loss in other destructive ways. Not that I'd be so ignorant to compare what I went through to what she went through, but I can't imagine how incredibly painful and horrific everything has been for him. If there was some way I could take it all away, save him from this devastating experience, and bring her back, I would in a heartbeat.

I know I don't have the right words to say to him, but he has to know that he's no longer alone and that whatever happens, I'll always be here for him.

"I don't know much about these things, T. But I know it's not your fault. It's a shitty thing for me to say that it's not your responsibility, but it isn't. Like you said, you saved her so many times before. She had to have been grateful. She had to have been lucky that you were there for her in all her dark moments. And I'm so very, very sorry that she didn't leave a note, or she didn't tell you why, or you had no clue what was going on with her. I can't make sense of a lot of things in life, T. But I know, as hard as it is to accept, she chose to do it. I think we get in trouble when we try to rationalize it ourselves. We're not in the place that they're in. We're not thinking the thoughts they are thinking. We don't have the same information or emotions or whatnot that leads up to these things happening."

I tilt my head, pouring so much love into the way I look at him that I hope he knows what I'm trying to say.

"I'm not saying your mom's situation is the same as my dad's because it's completely not. But I don't know why he went to visit her that day. It was his choice, something he felt he had to do. I always wondered if he knew that would be the end of his life. Would he have gone anyway? If he had left five minutes earlier, gotten stuck behind a train, been pulled over by a police officer, or a million other things that could've prevented that accident. I don't know. And now we're always trying to get the answers, trying to make sense of something that's senseless. As shitty as it is and as gut-wrenching as it is, I think sometimes we never get to know. And that not knowing is the hardest damn thing to live with."

His hands slide around my back to pull me back into his body. I adjust my legs on either side of his, tuck my arms against his chest, and lay my cheek against his collarbone to just be.

I don't know what else to say. Although our circumstances of how we lost our parents are different, some emotions are the same. And I've learned that sometimes you need to sit with them in silence for them to clear away on their own. And that's exactly what we do, my breathing syncs up with his as he cradles me in his arms.

21

I'm nearly asleep in the comfort of his embrace and the warmth of his body. The rapid rising and falling of his chest leveled out a long time ago when he slid us down the couch, stretched out on his back and I laid on top of him. The terrace doors catch our reflection and I take a mental picture of this intimate moment.

Tomlin's eyes are closed, with his muscular arms heavy at my waist and holding me in place. The harsh lines of heartbreak cutting into his handsome features ease as he relaxes into the soft leather couch. I can't tell if he's sleeping or meditating until I move my head and his body stiffens, holding me in place.

"Don't go," he murmurs into my hair. His deep voice vibrates in my chest.

I've never been one for snuggling in the past, but I'm getting used to this. Not that I can do this with just anybody. Of course, it has to be him. But him taking the time to simply lie with me and cuddle makes me feel worthy of being loved. This is the shit that no one tells you about when you're single. They keep it a secret how warm and cared a relationship can make a girl feel.

"I'm not."

"Good."

I twist my neck, seeking his lips to press a long kiss to them before setting my head down on the middle of his chest. That powerful heartbeat throbs slowly in my ear and I close my eyes, content to snooze when I remember Kylie. It might not be the best time to bring it up. With Rex talking about the same picture, Tomlin needs to know.

"Kylie called me today."

"Oh yeah? How is she?"

"She's mad. She saw the picture of you and me holding hands in the airport on the way out to the car and asked if we were together," I say, debating on telling him everything but then deciding I should since I need his help on what to do.

It's only fair that I talk with Tomlin, and not always run to Eli with everything. Not that Eli would gossip around about our business, but in all fairness, I should talk to the guy that I'm in love with first.

"What did you tell her?"

His hand slides from my waist down to my ass to give it a big squeeze. Clearly, he's not meditating or sleepy.

"Well, I didn't say much. She was pretty upset and kind of bitched me out. I know you told me why it wouldn't work between you guys, but Kylie kind of made it sound like it could have. I sort of feel guilty because I didn't mean for this to happen. I had no idea it would happen. And it's not fair of her to ask me not to see where this goes."

I lift my head to look into his eyes, waiting for his reaction. He cranes his neck forward to plant a couple of kisses before responding.

"I'm not here to talk bad about your friend, and I don't want you to think that you have to pick between me and her. I'd never ask that of you. But she should only want the best for you. If being with me makes you happy and you tell her that, that's all you can do."

His fingertips caress across my forehead and down my temple as he moves the hair that has fallen forward behind my ear. He makes it sound so simple. It's his usual way of cutting through the bullshit to get a resolution.

I bite my lip and then let out a long sigh before responding.

"I know, right? It makes me mad too. Like she's moved on with that Ryan dude, so why is she still trying to hold on to you? Or maybe it's not holding on to you, but it's blocking you from me. I don't understand it.

If I ever dated someone and we were over, and she wanted to date them, so be it. And trust me when I say, I'm not letting anything come between us."

And I'm not. It's unfair of Kylie to get mad and ask me not to be with him. I don't want to choose between her and Tomlin either. I shouldn't have to, and I don't want to lose either of them.

"Good, because I'm not letting anything come between us." He rewards me with a few more kisses before saying, "Do you think she's jealous?"

"I do."

I hate admitting that. I hate that it's even true. But there's no other justification I can come up with for her behavior. Honestly, this is the first good thing to happen to me in the shit-show my life has been. The first thing that she could be jealous of, and she is.

Of all the good things that have happened to her and her life over the years, I've never been jealous of her. Even when she has a super close relationship with her mom, and I never have, I wasn't jealous of that. She should give me this.

"Would it help if I talked to her? I'd be more than happy to, especially since I'm the reason coming between you two?"

His offer is considerate, and I look across the penthouse, trying to decide. I don't know if it would make it better or worse. Honestly, I don't want to even think about it. Maybe I kick this can like all the others and deal with it when I get back home.

My eyes return to his before answering.

"I honestly don't know, T. I'm not sure I even want to deal with it right now. No, that's a lie. I definitely don't want to deal with it right now. I want to enjoy this vacation, enjoy us, and go from there."

His hand continues to knead my ass, and I'd rip his judogi off right now to fuck the shit out of him if it were appropriate. I'm not sure where we are after that emotional conversation. My heart bleeds for him, and with both of us having puffy eyes from crying, it doesn't exactly elicit sexy feelings or horniness.

"Agree, it's smooth sailing the rest of the trip."

His hand cups the back of my head, encouraging me to kiss him. My lips descend to his. A gentle touch while keeping my eyes open to watch for his expression. I can go from zero to horny in about two seconds with this man, but I can't read what he wants. He breaks my teasing kisses by leaning back and torquing up a thick eyebrow.

"Why are you looking at me?"

I stack my hands on top of each other, lay them on his chest, and drop my chin on top of my knuckles.

"Well, for one, you're hot as hell, so you can't blame me for looking at you. And for two, I didn't know where we stand. I mean, I know tonight was supposed to be the night, but after everything we talked about, I'm not sure or . . . if you don't want to or if now isn't the right time . . ."

I don't know what I'm trying to say but it's getting awkward as fuck trying to say I want him, but I understand if he doesn't want to have sex tonight. Honestly, I didn't think tonight would end this way. I envisioned jumping his bones into my new lingerie, not bawling our eyes out.

"Hey, what did I say?" His hand slides off my butt and up my spine to rub my back. I don't know what he's talking about, so I sort of shrug. "You give me this look as if you want to escape or are trying to hide. It's alright to be uncomfortable, but it's me, Dani. I know you and you know me. Just us, remember."

I nod. I know, but if I had more experience with dating, I might not be uncomfortable in these awkward moments.

"How about we start this night over? Things got off track with Rex and the discussion of my mother." I mouth that I'm sorry and he smiles gently. "Don't be. It was necessary and something we should discuss. I wished it had occurred under different circumstances."

He sighs and I mirror the action. I don't want to go back there again, but if he needs to talk to me again about his mom, I'll more than listen and support him. And I'm glad he told me everything. I wonder if he told Kylie everything.

"Did you tell Kylie everything you told me?" The words aren't even out of my mouth before a very deep frown sits on his face.

"No. I told her a few details, but not what I shared with you. And I'd appreciate it if you didn't communicate what we shared here tonight." The sadness returns to his eyes and I'm shaking my head emphatically.

"I'll never tell anyone. It's not my news to tell. And as you said, what we do is between us."

That's probably one of my favorite things about Tomlin. It's his verbal agreement that we'll be the keeper of each other's secrets. Adding another layer of trust to this beautiful new relationship. That chases away the sadness in his eyes and suddenly his hands are underneath my armpits, dragging me up his body so our faces align. My hands cup the sides of his cheeks. His hand cradles my head again, a silent command for what to do, and I eagerly follow.

I kiss him aggressively, letting the worries from a moment ago fade as my desire mounts. He groans when his tongue finds my piercing and his hand twists my head to the side for deeper access. I hitch my leg up, trying to crawl up his body when his hard dick pushes into my pubic bone.

His fingers lazily stroke the outside of my exposed thigh and I moan with want. He captures my piercing, holding it between his teeth, and I smile against his lips. It's easily his favorite thing to do. As fast as he captures it, he releases it to devour my mouth while my fingers slide down his beard to curl around his neck.

My hips grind into his, desperate for friction as my body warms with lust. I want him, I want us, right here, right now. Damn, my new lingerie, our puffy eyes, and his sweaty judogi. I want him in me right now.

I break the kiss to push off his chest, eager to untie his belt, when his hands cover mine. He looks smoking hot with his swollen lips, messed-up hair, and lustful eyes. The way they watch me is hot as hell as I tug on the rough fabric, wanting to rid his hands from stopping mine.

"Not here. Not like this."

I throw my head back to stare at the ceiling. My breath comes out in pants as he steadies his breathing as well. Both of us calm down for two different reasons. Mine is because he turned me down, his is because I don't know why.

"Ugh, you're killing me, T."

My eyes return to his and I yank on his belt about ten more times while he chuckles. It's almost a temper tantrum with the way his grip tightens over mine.

"I'm not saying no. I only want to shower and possibly eat before, so I can take my time licking, sucking, and fucking you."

His words are a betrayal of the lust covering his face and the smolder of his eyes. Doesn't he know I don't care about him being sweaty? Hell, if we fuck the right way, we'll both get sweaty. It's the best kind of sex. But dammit if I don't get it. He only had a handful of fruit today and burned up a million calories competing and meeting his fans.

I release the longest, most frustrated groan possible before saying, "Fine."

He chuckles again, and I reluctantly climb off his lap. My panties are practically shoved up my pussy from how hard I was grinding on him. Not that I'm picking them out in front of him, but changing out of them would be nice. Hell, I'll go commando the rest of the night. Wait, then I might drip on the furniture with how much I want him. Whatever. I'll clean it up.

"Hey, I didn't say get off."

His long fingers capture my wrist to encourage me to sit back on him. I eagerly resume my position of straddling his pants while slowly grinding against him. If he's telling me to wait again, I'm going to torture him in the process.

His palms slide up my thighs, pushing the hem of my skirt all the way to where my panties are showing. No doubt, the light-colored fabric is translucent from the wetness flowing out of me and his eyes glisten when they spot it.

"I like this view a lot," he rasps and I fucking love that he's as affected by me as I am by him. His thumbs sit on each side of my panties, dragging them away from my lips to slip a digit inside.

"Now, tell me. Do you want to go out? I could get us a table somewhere, then we could find a club so you can dance up on those NBA players like you wanted."

Damn him for teasing me with my own good time. But double damn him for stroking my soft clit while doing it. My breath falters for a second and I can't think straight. I wanted the former. It's on my bucket list.

But being here with him, after this week, after everything

we have shared and experienced, I couldn't care less about hot athletes when I have my very own sitting underneath me, sloppily stroking my pussy.

"Damn you, T," I whisper, my eyes burning a hole in his as my hand grips the back of the couch to grind against his finger. It feels so fucking good, the right amount of pressure to drive me wild and so not enough to make me get off. I love him and hate him all at the same time.

"Damn me, huh? I'm offering, Dani. It's what you said you wanted," he teases, knowing full well it's not what I want. "Or if you changed your mind, we could stay in. Order room service, maybe a little champagne, some chocolate-covered strawberries, and other sweet things to go with this sweet thing."

His thumb sweeps faster over my clit, and I lean back, giving him more access to my sweet thing. His other hand pushes the fabric of my skirt behind my butt before pushing against my stomach to force me further back.

Oh, I know this position. I reach back to clutch his knee as his foot plants on the floor. It's enough room for him to angle two fingers inside me with my panties tucked to the side.

The fabric strains against my skin, cutting into my ass in the best way possible, and I wish he'd rip them from my body. It would be hot as hell and completely necessary to make it easier for his large hands to take me properly.

But he doesn't, leaving me to grind in the tight space and his fingers to work their magic like he's done twice before. I try to maintain eye contact. Try to stare into those deep chocolate orbs, but the pleasure mounting in me is too great. My eyes slip close to focus on my core and the amazing things he's doing to me.

"Tell me, Dani. What do you want?" That deep voice teases at my ears while his fingers slow down.

"No, no, no. Faster." My eyes fly open, my chin tilts down, and a smile plays on his lips. His pace slows, barely moving and

I'm barely breathing as my heartbeat thunders in my chest. "Tomlin."

"Tell me what you want," he says slyly, obviously enjoying torturing me. "NBA players or me?"

Both sets of fingers stop and it's horrible. I try to grind, but the angle is wrong, and it becomes painful when I do it.

"You, T. Only you. You know that."

I tilt my head, my hair dusting against my shoulder, and he gives me that panty-dropping grin. I try again to grind but can't, and his eyes sparkle in delight. Power play. It's heaven and hell all at the same time. Not enough to get off, but so damn close.

"I know that, demanding Dani. Now slip off that dress and let me see those beautiful breasts."

The thumb on my clit slowly starts back up and I'm eager to comply, by wrestling with the zipper at the back and then lifting the whole thing over my head to toss on the floor. I pause for a moment, wondering if this is enough when he answers.

"Take off the bra."

Question asked and answered. I unhook the front clasp and toss it onto the pile of my dress, waiting for his next instruction. He licks his lips and damn this position because I'd lick him too if I could reach him.

"Perfect. Now arch your back and I'll finish."

I almost throw out my back, arching it hard, and craning my neck to keep watching him. When his smile drops into a smolder and his gaze drops to my breast and clit, I close my eyes, let my head fall back, and ride his fingers. It's achingly slow and deep, not fast or feverish, both of us enjoying our part of this.

My core is tight, my breath is harsh, and my clit is hard. My skin is burning in the cool air conditioning and my body is on fire for him. His hips rock in time with mine. The fingers inside me set their own pace opposite of his thumb at my clit and everything about this is so right, it's almost perfect.

My orgasm builds as slowly as he's finger fucking. I want it to go on forever and I want to come already. I can't decide which. If this is a precursor to sex, I'll want everything all at once. He consumes me both body and mind now. It's making the anticipation of fucking his brains out that much better.

His thumb reverses direction and I shudder. I want more. I need more. I ease forward, changing the pressure on his fingers curling toward my G spot and it speeds up my orgasm until it's suddenly rushing through me as I moan and open my eyes to his intense stare.

"You're so damn beautiful," he murmurs, his eyes traveling from my face, lingering on my tits and my exposed pussy lips. If he could only see how hot he is watching me.

Damn. As I ride out the remanent of my orgasm, I lift off his fingers and lean forward to make out with him. It's wild and messy, with his thumb trapped against my clit and his wet fingers gripping my ass cheek.

His resolve is remarkable, and I almost feel selfish for getting off again. I'll make it up to him. I'm as eager to test out this tongue piercing on his dick as he is. He groans in my mouth, his fingers kneading my flesh, and I know it's unfair of me to continue like this. I end the kiss this time, hovering above his lips with a faint smile on mine.

"I think I owe you about ten orgasms by now."

I lift slightly off his hand to travel away from my sensitive clit for it to caress my side boob, popping out as my tits rest against his judogi.

"You don't owe me anything. I love watching you come."

I know he does. The way his hand pushes against my clavicle to lean back says it all. One day, I'm going to put on an obscene show for him. Look, but don't touch and watch him combust.

"But seriously, Dani. Do you want to go out? I know you have many things on your list that you haven't been able to do."

His short nails scrap against my delicate skin, teasing at another round of fire still burning within me. "I can get us dinner reservations, take the roadster out and find a bar or someplace afterward. I was, after all, kidding about making you choose between myself and the basketball players."

The fact that he's clarifying all this in the first place is sweet. But feeling bad about this penthouse, his event taking up so much of his time, and the joke about the players is a whole other level of consideration that I'm not used to from any guy. But Tomlin being Tomlin, he's always had proper manners and clear communication which I'm appreciating more and more.

I thought I wanted to go out and party it up when I first got here. But now, spending all this time with him alone, I want that to continue. I want to stay in this bubble we created in this penthouse for tonight, since it's our last night here and tomorrow's events will take away time from us.

"Honestly, I'd like to stay here. It's our last night, and I want to spend as much time with you as possible."

That brings the biggest smile to his face, and I beam right back. I don't want to be anywhere else but right here next to, under, and on him.

"I feel the same. How about I place our order while you do whatever it is you need to do?"

I laugh and a confused look passes over his face. Sometimes his phrases are so formal, and I remember back when I used to scoff at him being raised by the Queen herself.

"Shower, T. That's what I'll be doing." His eyebrows pop up and his mouth opens, but I cover it with my hand. "Separately. I need to shave parts and stuff." It's a believable half truth. I *want* to shower. I *need* to slip into my new lingerie.

His eyebrows wiggle for a second, and he gently bites the palm of my hand before releasing it. I move it out of the way and slowly ease off him to stand up. His hand slides up and down my leg, as I bend over to collect my clothes.

"What do you want to eat?"

I didn't hear it earlier, but there's a certain ring of exhaustion in his voice and I'm glad we're staying in. It makes sense that he's asking, even though he knows I basically eat junk food. Sitting down and going through that big book of room service options isn't what I want to do right now. Rather, I want to let the hot water reign over my body in anticipation of the droplets being replaced by his hands later.

"I don't care. Surprise me."

My panties are still shoved to the side, and I'm definitely not going to fix them while he's watching. My clothes act as a barrier to his eyes, leaving his favorite tits on display. His fingers lazily stroke up and down my skin, leaving goosebumps in their wake.

Long seconds pass. His hand tucks behind the pillow, content to watch me as I watch him, waiting for his response. His white jacket is open, a sliver of a brown nipple, and miles of gorgeous muscles are showing with a huge wet spot on the front of his pants.

A knowing smile plays at his lips and satisfaction glints in his eyes while I catch my bottom lip between my teeth. Other than the fatigue from the day on his face, he looks both relaxed and amused.

"I'll surprise you all right."

A threat and a promise.

One he's already delivered on with this trip and acknowledging his feelings for me. But he's not the only one with a few tricks up their sleeve. Stuffed in a bag in my room are some tiny scraps of fabric I'm dying to get on.

"Well, all right then, I'm going to go shower."

I swear I could stand here flirting with him all damn day, but that won't get me any closer to getting laid. Not to mention that he needs to shower as well. It's prudent for him to order food, I know that, but if I had my preference, my back will be up against the wall with his dick buried in my body.

When I round the couch, he winks at me and my body flushes with desire. He sticks his fingers into his mouth and it's still the hottest fucking thing ever.

22

Room service comes and goes. The squeaky wheels reverberate through my bedroom door as I sit on the edge of the bed to calm my nerves. My shower is exceptionally long, not from having to shave every part of my body. I already did that this morning.

No, it's from me standing in the stream of water, lost in my thought, or rather the sudden nervousness that has my heart hammering against my rib cage.

Never in my life can I recall a time when I was nervous to have sex. Too drunk? Definitely. Too desperate? Certainly. Too horny? Always. Too angry? Hell yeah, who didn't like rage fucking? But nervous? Never.

Yet here I am picking at a hangnail and anxious as hell because tonight is different. Something special. It's one thing to be in a horny haze and have him get me off. That's what he's been doing, but it's another to consummate the start of a relationship where feelings are involved.

With my hair and make-up done and my new lingerie on, my breath hitches. I look hot, like a stripper. But damn these butterflies in my belly right as I'm about to walk out there.

Not that I'm a virgin, far from it. But those feelings of it being my very first time aren't too far away when I think about this being *our* very first time. I guess what's tripping me up is that I'm a selfish partner.

I take what I want, knowing guys will get their own in the end. Tomlin's different from all that. I want to please him. I want him to have a hell of a good time with me as I'll have with him. As I have been with him. But it's not the way to be in a relationship. Kylie has told me as much.

Suddenly I'm insecure and freaking out. What if I'm broken by casual sex? Or watching porn that I can't get off to a deeper connection? What if I'm a lousy lay because I'm so caught up in my head and feelings? I don't know why I hadn't thought of this before. Now that I'm on the cusp of doing it, I can't help but worry that it will all go to shit.

The gentle knock on the door jars me from my ruminating thoughts. I jump to my feet and gather the edges of my robe to tie it closed.

"Dani? You okay?"

His voice floats past the wooden door, pausing for several seconds before pushing it open. He's not nearly as casual as me, but the light gray tee shirt stretched across his chiseled chest and the black shorts beneath are super casual for him.

An instant smile and a flash of relief cross his face when his eyes landed on me. And even though he crosses the room to cup my hands, the nervousness doesn't go away, it only heightens. I pressed my lips together and take a calming breath.

"What's wrong?"

I hate that I have the worst poker face ever. Or that he can read me like a book. In a way, I want to tell him how I feel, and, in a bigger way, I don't. This is so damn stupid, and the timing couldn't be worse, but I almost wish that we had casually fucked, so it's building on something we've already done and not something completely new. Damn these fucking feelings.

"Nothing, T."

I tug my hands away, trying to walk past him and out to the awaiting dinner when he catches my wrist.

"Your face doesn't say nothing. And you've been in here an exceptionally long time." His voice lowers, his chin drops, and his eyes are imploring. Too imploring, and I look away.

It reminds me of the time when I first kissed him, and he rejected me. I hid out in the bathroom then and he accused me of crying like a girl. Recalling that bad moment doesn't boost my confidence, it only makes my gut tighten.

"Dani, talk to me. Tell me what's wrong?"

This is stupid. I'm making this a bigger deal than it should be. I've had sex hundreds of times and never did I feel this. Guilt, sure. Regret, definitely. Shame, occasionally, but not this.

I bite my lip when my gaze returns to him. I've never been this big of a titty baby about anything and yet here I am, freaking him out as much as I'm freaking out.

"It's dumb. It's nothing."

I try to pull away again, but this time he doesn't let me. My gaze flickers down to the warm ring of his fingers circling my wrist and the way his thumb swipes sporadically across my skin.

"It doesn't look like nothing. I'm not letting this go. If something is bothering you, I want to discuss it. You wanted to know about my mom, and I told you everything. You don't think that was hard for me."

His words hurt. A punch to my gut and the butterflies fluttering there. Telling me about his mom and what they endured in his childhood is a million times more important than my sudden freakout. And I hate even comparing the two. It's so not fair to them.

"I know it was, T. I really appreciate you telling me." I turn to him, needing to touch him, and resting my fingers against his shirt. "I truly do, and this is so dumb compared to that. No, not compared to that because there's no comparison. But now, I definitely don't want to tell you. Like not at all."

I squeeze his hand, my eyes settling on his beard that he must have trimmed while I was getting ready. It seems slightly shorter now.

"If this is going to work, we have to be honest with each other. I've told you everything about me."

In actuality, he hasn't, but he's dropped enough truth bombs this week to last the rest of the month. The rest he can tell over the next few years to adequately space them out.

Maybe he's right. If I come clean and suck at sex with him, then he's fairly warned. Maybe he won't hold it against me or, worse, break up with me for it. I sigh, letting all the air out of my lungs and then some, hoping to convey how dumb and insecure I feel at the same time.

"I'm worried," I confess, as if those two words explain it all. And then I wait for his response. He leans forward, his eyes narrow and his mouth twists into a frown.

"Worried about what? Kylie? Pebble Beach? The garage, perhaps?"

He's going down all sorts of roads that I'm not on. I can't really blame him because I'm worried about the dumbest thing ever, yet these damn emotions of love and eagerness to make him happy and fulfilled are tripping me up, confusing the issue.

"Sex, T. I'm nervous," I blurt out, subtly never being my strong suit. "I'm nervous about it being our first time and that I'll suck ass with you."

His palm covers my hand, trapping it on his chest while his face fights between smiling and not smiling. It's the shittiest reaction in the history of reactions.

"Damn, man, why don't you outright laugh at me and get it over with?"

I'd throw up a hand if he didn't have them both trapped in

his. He doesn't do that at all. His hand releases mine instantly to grip the lapels of my robe and yank me to him. His lips descend with a fury, planting two dry ones before his tongue presses against the seam of my lips for a steamy hot plunge into my mouth.

I moan at how demanding he is, taking what he wants as I've always taken what I want. This is something I know. Something I can reciprocate. It's something that takes me out of my head and into my body, where desire and craving twist in a cylinder up my body and out through my nerve endings.

My hands find his ribcage, pulling his body against mine for that hard erection to lie against my stomach. I'm nearly breathless, giving as good as taking and absorbing his groans into my mouth. He ends it as abruptly as he starts it, never loosening the tight grip on my lapels to look me dead in the eye.

"That's one of the most real things you've ever said." I give him a look. That's not at all what I expect to hear, and my hands fall to my sides. "You don't get it, do you?"

I bite my lip and shake my head. I don't get half of his responses. Then he gives me an adoring smile that melts my heart.

"The day I saw your hair up on the sides of your head, you slapped my hand, telling me to keep my germs off your hair." Yes, he touched my pigtails. "When I ate your wings, you slapped me then. When I ate your donut, another slap."

Okay, so I slapped him a lot back in the day.

"If you could see what I see. Here's this shit-talking, hard-as-nail woman that everyone is scared to talk to, who took down two guys, propositioned a cop, racked me in the hallway, and shattered a window in anger, telling me she's nervous to be intimate with me? Well, isn't that the best damn gift you could give me?"

I'm missing something or Tomlin took too many hits to the head today. I'm not following, and my face must show it because his grip loosens on my lapels to hold my shoulders instead.

"You're vulnerable with me. This is you letting me in." Ah, yes. If he only knew how far in he was, he'd be laughing it up. "It's beautiful."

His lips descend to mine, softly and savoring this time. I match the sweetness of this moment, wanting to commit every detail to memory now that I understand where he's coming from. His tongue doesn't penetrate this time, only sliding to dust kisses over my cheek and against my temple before pulling away.

"And if we're sharing the truth, I'm a little nervous myself," he counters that with another bright smile, owning up to the words he's saying, and I have to clarify.

I have to confirm he's not lying because that would make us even or equal and relieve some of my performance anxiety.

"Really?"

I tilt my head, my hair falling across my face. His fingers dip to catch it and push it over my shoulder.

"Yes. You know I've wanted a long time for this, not just sex with you, but this. I was an idiot for denying it for so long. Now that I have you, I don't want to do or say anything to jeopardize it. So yes, I'm nervous too. When you ran out of the restaurant the other day, I thought I had blown it. It can be like walking a tightrope with you, push too much and I push you away. Back off too much and you back away. What I'm finally realizing is that you eventually come back in your own time and on your own terms, and I need to be patient."

Damn.

He's a tightrope walker. I'm making him a tightrope walker to be with me.

Double damn.

"I'm sorry, T. I don't want that. I didn't even know I was like that."

I didn't. I'd never want to put the man I love through all those mental gymnastics. It's got to be exhausting and something I'd never fucking tolerate if the roles were reversed. I say that, but I'd probably do it if it was the only way I get to be with Tomlin.

"It's okay. It's how you are. I've learned that now and I adjust accordingly."

His hands cup my face, his dark chocolate eyes full of sincerity. I vow right then and there to not put him through this anymore. I don't want it to be difficult to be with me. I want it to be so damn easy that he never thinks of leaving me.

"It's one of the things that attracts me to you. You said it yourself. You'll never be a yes woman, and I respect that about you. Do you keep me on my toes? Yes. Are you full of surprises? Yes. And I'm here for all of it. If you are nervous about being with me, know that I am too."

He couldn't have said a more perfect thing in the world to me. In that moment, my gut loosens, releasing those fluttering butterflies, and I launch myself at him.

Screw room service.

That shit can wait because the racing thoughts in my head are gone, the nervousness has dissipated and all I want to do is throw open this robe, get on my knees, and blow him.

23

I break the kiss to tug on the hem of his shirt. He's reluctant to let me remove it, his eyes traveling out to the living room beyond. It's selfish of me to stand between him and his first meal of the day, but I want my meal of the day and it's trapped behind his shorts.

"Off with it."

Demanding Dani has arrived. He complies, grabbing the back of it to drag over his head. While he's distracted with that, I yank down his shorts, kneel and come eye level with his cock as it bobs against his hard abdominals.

"Dani," he hisses when my hand clamps down on it. "Get off your knees."

I've heard that before for a very different reason. That time was justified in the middle of the airport. This time isn't and the hell if I'm going to listen to him now. I gaze up at him, having no intention of getting off my knees until he comes down my throat.

"I've been wanting to do this for the last two months. Ever since you pressed me up against those mirrors in that gym. And we both want to know how my piercing feels so . . ."

I intentionally don't finish my statement, too occupied licking my lips and eyeing my new favorite lollipop. The bulbous head is wide and perfectly shaped, with a pearl of pre-cum. His tight shaft is long and veiny, a roadmap for where my tongue should go. It's gorgeous.

A mischievous smile graces my face when he steps out of his shorts, scooting them over and widening his stance, giving me space to go to work. Who's in control now?

My eyes connect with his. The pupils eclipse the irises to full black and full of lust. I lay the flat pad of my tongue on the underside of his cock to flick the tiny vein connecting the head to the shaft. He groans deeply as if it's painful and it's the best damn sound in the world.

I work that little vein, showing no attention to any other part of him to drive him mad. It works when his hand threads into my hair, encouraging me to take more.

"No touching."

I shake his hand off my head. This isn't my first blowjob, and it certainly won't be my last. Giving head is one of my favorite things to do aside from having full-on sex.

I lift a taunting eyebrow at those lust filled eyes before licking him from the seam of his balls to the tip of cock. His smile falters as he releases a torturous grunt. Taking it slow is the best part. Guys want girls to blow them hard and fast, but slow and teasing are more my specialty.

With Tomlin getting me off all week long, I might make this especially long and drawn out to really get him going. Yeah, that's exactly what I'll do.

My hands drag up the front of his legs when I pull my tongue from his shaft to blow on the wetness left behind. It twitches, the vacancy causing him to push his hips forward in search of my mouth again.

"That's not allowed either."

My hand leaves the front of his thigh to dig my fingertip into his hip bone to push him back.

"I thought I treated you better than this," he grumbles, obviously not happy with my achingly slow pace. "I think you're intentionally torturing me."

I give him a quick lick, followed by an intense suck on the tip of his dick, before releasing it. It bops against his pelvis, and I blow on it again.

"Of course, I am. You rejected me three times in Colorado. Payback's a bitch, T."

I return to rubbing my palms up and down his thighs with my thumbs caressing closer and closer to his balls but never quite touching them. His stare bores into me with a different intensity, but he doesn't move, and he doesn't touch me. Look who's a good boy at obeying. I rather like this.

"You rejected me many more times, and I still got you off, quickly, I might add."

His body jolts back when my thumbnail scrapes his ball sac, garnering a half smile from me and a grunt from him. Someone is awfully squirmish.

"That's your problem. I'll blow you how I want."

I lean forward, take him wholly into my mouth, and nearly suck the skin off his shaft and tip. He groans long and hard, vibrating into my mouth as I let my piercing slide flatly against the velvety steel of his shaft before releasing him and blowing again.

"Now stop complaining and let me work," I tease, and his mouth parts watching me.

"Let you work?" he repeats, then shakes his head and says, "That's hot, Dani."

"I know."

I wink and I'm done with talking. I spit into my hands, rub them together, and aim to give him the best damn blowjob of his life. My fist grips his cock, twisting it up his shaft to make a tunnel to my mouth while my hand cups his balls. They are soft, with a light dusting of trimmed hair.

That little devious devil must have manscaped in anticipation of this, and I appreciate it. His pubic patch matches the length of his beard, and it's sexy as hell. I hate guys that shave. It makes it scrap in the worst way possible against my delicate skin.

His balls roll in a circle opposite to the twisting of my hand on his dick and the swirling of my tongue. The longer I suck him, the more slobbery it gets and drips past my wrist. He moans, his hand gently cupping the back of my head as if he can't keep his hands off anymore.

I really don't care. I'm locked into my pattern of sucking, swirling, and twirling over his manhood. When I feel his thighs clenching, I know he's getting close, and I pop off to trace his fat head over my lips. He grunts in protest, and I smile triumphantly at him, lazily licking that tiny vein again.

"Dani."

It comes out as a plea, a request, and a question.

My hand continues to roll his balls snugly against his body. He's so close and I love I can tell. Edging him now and in the future is going to be a hell of a good time. I reverse my hand on his cock, putting my thumb and index finger toward the top of his balls to ensure a nail scrap or two.

"Yes?"

He doesn't answer, his chest rising and falling as his fingertips press against my head. I know his orgasm is ebbing away, but it will come roaring back the second I suck him off. My hand keeps pumping his shaft when I duck my head to capture one of his balls into my mouth. He gasps. His legs tighten and his hips roll forward when I hum into the sensitive skin. I hold it in my mouth, licking and dragging the barbell across the ball, and he jolts away.

"Too much... too much."

He gasps, grabbing the base of his dick to pluck his balls out of my mouth.

Nice.

I love a guy with super sensitive balls. It's so much fun. Not to mention all this gets me going. I'm horny and wet and would be dripping on the floor if it wasn't for my new lingerie, plastering all my wetness against me.

The temperature in the room is about a thousand degrees and his skin is glistening with a thin sheet of sweat. I think I've tortured him enough when I slap his hand away and latch on for the last time. I set a super fast pace, my hand and mouth becoming a long, hard grip over his dick. His hand dives back into my hair.

His hips pump in the rhythm of my mouth and then the deepest growl rumbles through him as if warning me he's coming. I already know. His balls strain in my hand as I roll them around.

His release is hot and fast, filling my mouth with a mild, tangy sweet fluid. His thigh muscles clench, as do his abdominals, flexing into an eight-pack above me. I drop my tongue, letting my barbell scrap the last several strokes and the noises coming out of his lower a couple of octaves. It's sexy as hell.

The hand on my head lightens, massaging my scalp for a few seconds before sweeping my hair over my shoulders. With a few long, lazy licks, I rub his tip over my lips and gaze into his eyes. His expression is a mix of adoration and relaxation. I fucking love that I get to see him this way.

When he said everything stays between us, I know what he means, and I value his saying it. It gives me the comfort and assurance that I can be as sexually deviant as I want to be and it won't go beyond these walls, unlike others before. Tomlin would never tell anyone about our bedroom activities out of respect for me and us. He's too emotionally mature for that nonsense.

"How was it?" I ask, knowing it was good, but I always appreciate feedback for future times.

He cups my arm, helping me to stand, and dives into my mouth while squeezing my ass. The fact that he isn't grossed out by cum breath and making out with me after I blow him is manly as hell. So many won't do it and I hate it. Not Tomlin. His tongue is practically down my throat as if trying to eat me from the inside out.

I'm a moaning mess, more turned on than I can remember ever being. His hands are everywhere, clenching my ass, roaming up my back to clutch the nape of my neck, and squeezing my waist. It's when he tries to tug on my robe that I break the kiss to step back.

I want my unveiling to be like a present at Christmas. Not something rushed and ripped off in the heat of passion.

"No, no, no," I chide, pushing his hands away while that long cock stands straight up, watching me too. "No touching, remember?"

His eyes glint at the challenge, ready to continue our little game of who's in control.

"I remember," he says in an amused tone. "I also remember my fist in your hair. Therefore, who didn't enforce her own rules?"

He takes a step forward. I take one back, tightening the belt on my robe as his hands reach for it. Of course, that judo master would be a little rule follower. Control and discipline are practically his hobbies.

"I should punish you by pulling your ass hair," I scoff, knowing he doesn't have hair in his ass crack as some dudes have. He continues to descend on me, and when my back hits the dresser, he smirks.

"I'd *love* to see you try. You can be my challenger any time."

He leaps forward to grab me and I dart down the dresser because he's going to ruin his surprise.

"Stay right there," I command.

The floor-to-ceiling window is at my back and an image of him fucking me against it flashes through my mind. That would be hot as hell. Taken against it like I wanted him to take me against the mirrors. It makes me smile.

When he stops several feet away, my gaze slides over his handsome face, square jaw, and chiseled shoulders, to his sculpted stomach, hard dick, and muscular legs. He's utterly perfect and I can't believe he's mine.

"If you keep looking at me that way, I'll bend you over this dresser and take you right now," he rasps, his cock staring at me too.

Don't threaten me with a good time.

"Deal."

My fingers mess with the knot on my belt and when the robe opens to slide down my bare arms, I think his cock is going to burst.

"Christ."

His hand dives into his hair, pausing at the neck to squeeze it while he licks his lips. "That's . . . fuck."

Hearing him cuss is rare, but seeing how I affect him is priceless. This is exactly the reaction I want. I toss the robe away, stalking toward him. His eyes sweep from my face to my tits, pushed extremely high from the heavy underwire underneath, to the tiny triangle covering my tiny landing strip that he already saw earlier.

"You like?" I tease, planting my hands on my hips and doing a little twirl for him to see the bow nestle at the top of my bunny tail. I don't even get a full turn in when I'm seized around the waist and he's hauling me back against his chest.

"I fucking love it," he whispers against my ear before nipping the shell. "Normally I don't like candy, Dani. But I'll eat every bit of yours."

Damn.

Did he say I'm his version of candy? I'll take it. I push my ass against his body, feeling his erection against my back. His hand slides down my stomach, slipping a finger into the waistline and running it back and forth as I chant lower.

"Lower, T."

He pushes my hair away from my neck to drop kisses there and goosebumps break out over my skin. His other hand slips up to my breast, circling the outer edges of my areola without touching my nipple. I cave my chest inward, trying to slip away from his teasing fingers and squirming against his tight body.

"Somebody enjoys teasing, but doesn't enjoy being teased, huh? Demanding Dani?"

Ah, payback. Damn. I should've figured he wouldn't take me up against the window as I had hoped. He's going to draw this out, as I did him.

"I hate it. Now touch me, suck me, or fuck me. Your choice."

I'm twerking against him until he locks his arms, and I can't move. He bites my shoulder and slips his whole hand past my pubic bone to my soaking wet lips. The fabric is tight, cutting into my flesh, and it adds to my already buzzing skin.

"You're so wet already. Rest assured, I'm going to do all three."

Those long fingers rub a delicious circle around my clit, driving me nearly crazy with want. It won't take long to come. Not this time. I'm so damn close to blowing him, teasing him, and now him touching me. This first one will be easy. Nearly there if he keeps up this pace.

He slowly walks us to the edge of my bed, his hand leaving my breast to slip into the side of the thong. The fingers swirling my clit stop and drag my wetness up my pubic bone to hook the other side of the delicate waistband. I wiggle my ass as he pulls them down and startles me when he bites my ass cheek.

"Ouch, T." I try to whip around to punch him, but he's

already at my back again, so I glare at him over my shoulder. "Do that again and I punch you in the balls."

"You like it."

Not that I usually have a problem with biting, but damn man, that shit hurt. If he's one of those guys that are into freaky pain shit, then this isn't going to work. I seriously doubt that he is, but I need to clarify right now or else this isn't going any further.

"Biting, maybe. Pain, no. If that's what it takes to get your rocks off, then I'm not the girl for you."

His breath is light against my cheek as I glance over my shoulder. Those delicious lips graze my neck, teasing and nibbling while his hard cock digs into my back while we stand here negotiating sex.

"Wouldn't be my girl without a few threats first." The richness of his voice is sexy as hell, even if his words are lighthearted. "Now get on the bed, Dani."

Damn.

That command is hot, adding to the wetness that's already oozing out of me. My hand catches his thigh as he practically lifts me onto it. His warm chest leaves my back and I shiver from the loss of heat. I'm about to turn around to grab his neck and pull him on top of me when his hand catches my ankle, slides up my leg, and over my ass to push against the middle of my back.

"On your hands and knees."

"Ooo, you wanna watch your dick, huh? Okay."

Guys love that shit. Visual creatures that get off on watching their dick get off. I get it. I spread my legs and slowly slide forward, arching my back to prepare for that long shaft.

"Wait, did you bring condoms because—"

Holy fuck.

I nearly jump out of my skin when his tongue licks from the top of my clit to the end of my lips, burying his face in my folds.

His large hands push my inner thighs further apart and squeeze my flesh in time with his rhythmic sucking.

"Oh, damn," I murmur into my arm that shakes with want.

The orgasm that is so close is roaring forward at breakneck speed under his expert tongue. It's obvious that he's a master at oral sex with the way he flicks, licks, and nibbles all around my sensitive core.

Heat rushes through me, pumping all the blood from my body to that sensitive little bud at the end of his tongue. My palms slide forward, lowering my upper body to the comforter and tilting my face to the side, before closing my eyes.

Moans pour out of me as I wiggle and squirm against his face. When he adds a finger to the mix, I'm cursing and pumping against it, needing to get off and wanting way more than this.

"Fuck me, T," I whisper, opening my eyes to look between my legs.

I love his tongue and that he's taking it slow but if he doesn't ram that gorgeous cock in me right now, I'm going to die. That wonderful mouth and rough beard leave my aching flesh, adding another finger to pump in and out of me, which is good but not as great as a warm dick. His wet lips slide across the back of my thigh, depositing kisses as he goes.

"Come for me like this. I want to see you clench around my finger and then I'll give you what you want."

His teeth graze my skin, not a bite, not a kiss, something in between before returning to my core and vacuuming my clit. I'm trying to hold out, wanting my first orgasm to be him inside me, but damn if my resolve doesn't fall when he tells me he wants to see my pulsing pussy.

It's hot as fuck and now I'm racing to give him and me what we both want. My eyes fall close, my breathing shallows and my hips hinge into his face, receiving whatever he's giving and enjoying it the whole damn time.

I've held out too long, and once I allow myself to get lost in his licking, my orgasm tears through me, running from a steady hum to a full blast until I'm moaning into the comforter, fucking his face, and coming all over it. My lips clench over his fingers. His tongue slows down and moves away.

"Best damn view, Dani. So soft and pink, grabbing my fingers and sucking them in," he rasps.

The effect this is having on him makes me smile when my eyes flutter open. I shift to look back at him. His eyes are slits, drunk off lust, his lower face is glistening with my cum and his chest is rising and falling at the effort it took to not suffocate back there.

"Glad you like it. Now give me that dick." I shake my hips, wiggling my ass to entice him to fuck me when he withdraws his fingers and runs them along my slit.

"I need to get the condoms from my room," he says, stroking but not moving.

"Bring six or the whole box. Whichever." His knuckles caress over my clit, it's so sensitive and hard, and I twist away, waiting for him to leave to go get them. "What are you waiting for?"

His finger never wavers in smearing my cum all around and keeping me riled up. When I look over my shoulder at him, he's staring at my ass as is his dick and if he'd move his ass to his room to get them, we could be fucking. His eyes level mine, a half smile tugging at the corner of his lip.

"Don't move. Stay like this." It's not so much of a command, more a plea from him and I wiggle his finger away from my core. He's wasting precious time chatting when we could be fucking. "Damn, I love watching your pussy clench."

"What are you waiting for? Go."

I push my upper body off the bed, twisting my torso while remaining kneeling. It closes up shop down there and forces him to leave. A stifled groan escapes him before his hand brushes across my back, and he swiftly walks out of the room.

I can't help staring at the high and tight round globes of his ass that he's been taunting me with ever since I saw him all those months ago at his house in Denver. That seems like a lifetime ago and yet the banter between us and him not putting up with my bullshit has become the foundation of our new relationship.

24

It's probably ten seconds, but it feels like twenty minutes before he's back, dick bobbing as he walks in and tossing the box on the nightstand. He stands next to the bed, ripping one off the strip, his arm and chest muscles flexing as he works to get the clear ring out of the packaging.

"Play with yourself. I want to watch how you like it," he directs, while he rolls it on that perfect mushroom head.

My fingertips tease across my flat stomach, over the tight little landing strip of hair, and onto the delicate bud to stroke lazily over it. I'm slower, more deliberate in my motions, and he watches, mesmerized.

"You're so gentle. Like this?"

His finger pushes mine out of the way, mirroring my pace and lightening his touch a bunch compared to before. It's perfect with how sensitive I am after coming once.

"Like that."

I breathe, my eyes closing as he moves behind me, and I lean against his back. My head falls to his shoulder, tilting my face toward him for more tongue and kisses. My moans are trapped in his mouth, where he's aggressively sucking my tongue and holding my piercing opposite of his tender touch on my core.

That's one thing I love about him. The hard and soft, the hot and cold, the serious and playfulness. Everything is always in opposites and a real mind fuck that I enjoy. His teeth release my piercings, ending the kiss and whispering in my ear, "Bend over, babe."

Babe.

I racked him for it once. He tossed it at me when commenting on my confidence. Now, it's part of his instruction while one of his hands slips away from my clit to stroke past my belly button and cup my breast while the other grips my shoulder, helping to arrange me on the bed as he wants. It's all hot as hell. If he wants to call me babe and bend me over while doing it, well, then let's babe it up. I'm here for it.

When I'm back on my hands and knees, his hand slips from my breast and grips my hip, while the other brushes up my spine and between my shoulder blades to push my upper body down on the mattress. A thrill runs through me with my ass in the air and his dick pressing against my entrance.

"Ready?"

His fingers tighten over my hip, digging into the front of my hip bone as if trying to stop himself from ramming it into me. He can, I'd fucking love it. I exhale, my skin sizzling with desire, my heart beating faster and my brain chanting for him to shove it in.

"More than ready," I say, hearing the desire deepen my own words.

His calloused palm slides away from my shoulder blade, down the side of my body, and over my ass to pull my lips further apart as he pushes into me. That small action of working his long dick into my tight pussy is hot and caring at the same time.

I'd hoped he'd ram it in the first time, but this achingly slow and careful consideration is even better. Like drawing out the experience to make it even better for both of us.

"Damn," I moan. My eyes close, focusing on his delicious dick opening me up in the best damn delicious way. "That's fucking . . ."

Then his finger again, pulling at the outer lip even though I'm wet as hell and welcoming him home. No one has ever done that before, and I'll have to be sure to tell him it's one of my favorite things about him. One of many.

"You're so tight."

His words are hoarse as if my pussy is making him sound like that. I clenched my vagina, glad that I do those exercises when I hear him groan and his hand digs into my hip.

"Don't . . . I'm going to burst if you do that."

I fucking love that. He's as horny for me as I'm for him. Good.

His strokes are light, letting me adjust to his length even though he's not fully in. It takes several seconds for my pussy to finally release and when it does, he slides in the rest of the way and pauses, bending over to brush kisses up my spine. I will my body to relax, to enjoy how perfectly full I am, and a small sigh escape in the process.

"Are you okay?" he asks, his hands rubbing all over my body, up my back, down my sides, and even over my ass cheeks, to spread me a little wider. It's hot as hell and everything I have been waiting for.

"I'm fucking great, T."

I slowly start to move my hips, grinding against that powerful body and he takes that as a physical confirmation that I'm down to fuck. His cautiousness is sweet and unfounded. There's no way he'd hurt me, not with how slow and caring he's being.

The elite athlete that easily took down a two-hundred-pound competitor is as gentle as he can be with me. It's sexy as hell, to watch his aggression on the mat and feel his tenderness in bed with me.

His long cock stretches me divinely and when he picks up the pace, I push back against him. Fucking him back in time with his dick fucking me. It's the perfect pace that leaves me both horny and satisfied. I could do this forever.

"This is . . ." I sigh, a ton of words on the tip of my tongue.

"Perfect."

The fact that he finishes it is perfect. It's confirmation he's enjoying this as much as I am. His hands move to the front of my thighs as he rockets in and out of me. My cum squishes against his cock, his skin smacks against mine and the sounds of fucking fill the room when words don't.

I love the way our bodies sound, bringing pleasure to each other. I love the way he pants while putting in the work to fuck me right and the sounds escaping my throat to reward him for his fucking style. I didn't think we'd start off with doggie style, but damn if another orgasm isn't bursting out of me and all over his cock. He plunges even harder, riding out the wave with me as my fingers fist the comforter.

"That's it, babe, cum all over my cock," he hisses, catching some on his finger to rub against my folds. When his finger slides in next to his cock, it's super intense and opens me up more. "Too much?"

I don't know. It's a lot. More than I think I can handle, but damn if I don't want to try. It's new. Something that no one has ever done before. It borders on uncomfortable, but his finger moves opposite of his dick.

My brain can't decide if it's amazing or terrible. Then he slides it out, his hips piston against me hard as hell and damn if another orgasm is building right behind it. He took it out because I never answered him and must have thought it was too much.

"I like it. Put it back."

My breath fans my face against the mattress. My hamstrings cramp as I pump into him, and my shoulders seize, trying to hold on while he's ramming me so well. A half second later, it's back in, working next to his dick, and I figure it out. It's the burn, being taken too far and liking it, fearing that it will lead to more. It's exactly the mind fuck I need to push me over the edge, into the abyss, and free falling into the hardest climax yet.

"Oh, fuck. Oh, fuck. Oh, fuck," I whimper.

His sweat drips onto my back, proof of how hard he's fucking me as I lay here recovering. Then he stops, his finger and dick slide out, with a clap to my ass cheek.

"Turn over."

His words float through the haze of my pleasure while his hands are helping me move to my back. I'm about to sit up when he bends over to lick a trail from my slit up my stomach to one breast.

"Do you know how long I've waited for this? Do you know all the ways I fantasized about taking you?"

The rest of his words are lost in the nipple he's sucking before sending a teasing wisp of air across the skin to tighten the nipple into a hard bud. It's delicious and torturous at the same time.

"I don't."

My hand is in his hair, clutching the sweaty strands to guide him back to my tit. My back arches, my hips grind against his pelvis, and my pussy is weepy from the vacancy. His eyes raise to mine, black as night and full of lust.

"You're not leaving this bed tonight. I'm going to take you every way I've dreamed about."

Damn.

I couldn't get wetter than I already am. My horniness is making me a little cocky because I say, "Fucking ruin me."

His eyes glitter, challenge accepted, and he bites my nipple but not painful, heeding my warning. It's a declaration that he'll do just that when he jerks up, yanks my butt to the edge of the bed, shoves my knees to my chest, and pushes back inside me. His long groan matches mine.

When his eyes close for a moment and his mouth slackens, I finally get to see the effect my body has on his and I'm going to drive him as crazy as he's driving me. He's not the only one with a collection of fantasies to fulfill. I, too, have envisioned every way possible with him, played them all out on my head as my fingers twirled my clit almost every night. Let's fucking go. Like I said before to him, I'll fuck the skin off his dick. I'm so ready.

When his eyes open, they bore into me, and he's pounding me so hard, the bed squeaks in protest underneath me.

"Tell me if I hurt you, otherwise . . . "

He won't. He watches me way too much. Way too intentional and calculated with his actions. Pays too much attention to my body and its reactions to hurt me. But I appreciate it.

My moan is my answer. My fingertips trail down his chiseled chest, plucking each nipple before leaving to trace those sculpted abdominals contracting as he pumps into me. His hand slips on the slickness of my skin, clasping my ankle to set it on his shoulder and depositing a kiss on the inside of my calf.

I'm moving to put my other foot on his shoulder when his hand slides up the back of my leg to plant my foot on his chest, right where his heart is pumping hard in his ribcage.

"Push against me."

I do what he says, and with the way he leans in, and I push out, the angle changes.

"Holy fuck," I murmur, reaching for his hand to intertwine with mine. He gives me a taunting little eyebrow, knowing full well that move. Damn, if I don't love his cockiness mixed with plowing me.

A sweaty sheen covers both of us as we push and pull to and from each other. His eyes dart between watching his dick and watching me as his hips pump in and out, bringing me closer and closer to another orgasm. My pussy is tight, wetness pouring out of me and making a slicker channel for him.

"You feel incredible."

His dick punctuates each word and my hand slides over my stomach to swirl my clit. His eyes devour the sight of it while he licks his lips. I want this to go on forever.

Want to hear the grunts and groans of pleasure escaping his body. Want to watch the face of concentration and the occasional wave of pleasure that crosses it as he ensures I'm loving it. Want to feel his body behind me, over me, and in me. I swear, he could live in my pussy and I'd fucking love it.

"Damn."

My eyes close, concentration on his dick fucking me at a perfectly steady pace.

"Right there, T."

Thank fuck, he doesn't change a thing. He knows. He knows to keep that pace, that hardness hitting my G-spot, that hand squeezing mine, the other gripping my thigh while he playfully bites my calf.

This is perfection and it has me racing toward my orgasm. I hold my breath, clench my pussy, tighten my body, and push off his chest as we barrel toward the big one. The one that has me closing my eyes, cussing a string of profanities, and calling out his name.

Mid way through me coming, he throws my ankle over his shoulder, clutches my thighs to his chest, and fucks the shit out of me, barking out harsh Japanese as he comes equally hard. My eyes fly open, memorizing the view of him falling apart and us making it happen.

Our hips continue moving in a joined rhythm, wanting to ride out each other's climax to squeeze every bit out of it. This is the beginning of tonight and I'm already ready to go another round with him.

"That was . . ."

His eyes glitter when they catch mine, releasing my hand to cup the back of my head as he leans forward to make out. My legs slide off his shoulders, falling to the side as his torso covers mine to get closer to me. Our tongues tangle together, our breath intertwines as we pant into each other.

My body is buzzing, my veins are vibrating from such a powerful orgasm and my mind is quiet, no longer analyzing us. When his lips slide to my cheek to drop kisses across it until he rests in my hair, I finish his sentence.

"Fucking awesome."

I sigh, my hands roaming all over his back, collecting sweat as one settles on the top of his ass and the other in his hair. His face raises, his chocolate eyes inches from mine to stare for a few long seconds before he gives me a few pecks.

"Fucking awesome doesn't do it justice," he mutters, his head descending in one quick kiss before his body lifts off mine to grip his dick as he slides out of me to handle the used condom. I'm content to watch that fine ass specimen disappear into the bathroom while I slide out of the huge wet spot at the edge of the bed.

He strides into the room. His dick is still hard as he watches me peel my hair from my clammy skin and arrange it on the pillow above my head. He collapses onto the bed, scooping me in his arms and arranging for me to lie on his chest.

His hand grips my thigh, dragging it below his dick and settling it between his legs. He takes my hand, puts it on his chest, and covers it with his own. I'm draped over him and trapped against him. I've never felt so secure in my life. The world beyond those doors, tucked away in this penthouse and cocooned in us is a feeling beyond words.

I burrow deeper into him and am rewarded with a kiss on the top of my head before his chin rests against it. The silence stretches out before us, allowing me to enjoy the calm aftermath of our first time. My eyes flutter close, playing a movie of his face and body fucking the shit out of me. It's the hottest porn love story combined, and I smile that it's mine.

"What are you smiling about?" His voice rumbles into my ear resting against his pectoral.

"How did you know I'm smiling?"

"I can feel it."

I don't know why, but those little words twist something in me in the best way. He can feel my smile against his skin. It's sweet and innocent after such a raunchy act.

"Tell me."

"We should make a porno."

He laughs, catching me by surprise, and I shift my head to gaze up at him. His hand leaves mine to push his hair back, his fingers glistening with perspiration as he tucks it behind his head.

"You want to make a sex tape?" The chuckle still in his voice. "Now that would damage my career."

"Shoot, you could get a shit ton of new fans. Hot chicks that would eat it up. Or want to eat you up," I tease, knowing full well his super private nature and utter respect for the sport would never allow it to happen.

"And you'd be fine with that? Fine with sharing me?" His arm tightens possessively as if I asked him to share me with the world.

"Aren't I already sharing you with the judo world? Plus, you're not mine to decide whether to share or not. You're your own man."

It's true. The world he resides in is old, over two decades. Whereas we are super new, and I have no right to make any demands like that on him. He frowns for a moment, then it slides away as if changing his thought.

"You share me with that world as I share you with the

restoration world. But I'm yours, Dani. The same as you are mine."

My heart doesn't even have a chance to warm to those words as he rolls on top of me and buries me underneath him. This is my new favorite position.

"Round two?" I ask, clicking my piercing against my teeth and he growls, shoving his hard cock against my core.

"Definitely round two."

25

"Good morning, Dani," he says, sounding awfully cheerful at this god-awful time of the morning. Round two turned it into several more rounds until we were both starving and picking over the hours cold food room service brought in.

His fingertips tap down my spine, dipping into my butt crack long crusted with dried cum. It's gross as hell but I was too damn tired and worn out to shower after his dick woke me up in the middle of the night to play again.

"Do it again and I break your finger off," I grumble, scooting my butt away from him.

"That's not what you said last night."

A warm hand splays across my lower stomach, dragging me back to the warmth of his body. His leg hikes over my hips, that dick poking my ass cheek as his scratchy beard scrapes my exposed neck.

"If I recall, you were begging for my finger."

It was true. I did. He slipped one in with his dick while fucking me and I suddenly became a-dick-ed to it. Terrible joke, but one I kept saying last night. Wanting it every time. It's why my poor pussy is so sore lying here.

Hell, my whole body feels like it went through a week of pounding out the metal frame of an old car. Except, this time I received the pounding, having done little myself.

He surprises me, though, in all the best ways. Gentle with his caresses and rough with his fucking. Making love to my ears with his appreciative words while stretching me with an extra finger or two. Even slipping one in the back door while riding his dick. Damn. Both surprising and hot, rocketing my orgasm to the front of the line when it penetrated that tight ring.

"Yeah, well."

I crack open my eyes, and the light from the drapes blinds my ass to the point I turn into his body to avoid it. He deposits little kisses on my nose and face until I tuck my chin in and bury it against his muscles.

"You're awfully grumpy for being so well taken care of," he chides, gathering me in his arms to roll to his back, placing me on top of him.

I hate it because I want more sleep. I love it because I've dreamed of this so many times that my heart is doing flips laying on him. I tuck my arms into his side, pecking his chest before smashing my cheek to it and closing my eyes again. His hand rest at the bend of my hips as I straddle him, pushing me down so his hard cock smashes my sore pelvic bone. I hiss and wiggle further down so his erection is on my stomach instead.

"Are you sore?"

His hand swipes my hair to the side, massaging the tight muscles of my neck while his other hand rubs away a knot in my back.

"Hell yeah. I think you were trying to kill me with your dick." My eyes flip open when I hear my phone ringing somewhere in the room. There's no way in hell I'm getting up to answer it. "You made me choke on it."

He chuckles, the sound both heard in my ear and felt in my body.

"You said to ruin you. Whose idea was it to lie her head off the side of the bed and grab my ass while blowing me?"

Ah, yes, my signature move.

"Yeah, well. My throat hurts because of it."

Not entirely a lie. It also hurts from moaning, screaming his name, and begging.

"Babe, I'm sorry you're sore and maybe next time, we'll take it easier," he says in his sincere voice, causing me to turn my face to look at him.

His finger touches my temple, then slides down my cheekbone to trace my lips. The swollen ones that covered nearly every inch of his body and dragged my piercing across his most sensitive parts.

"Normally, I'd start a bath for you, but we need to pack up and leave if we're going to make our flight."

"Fuck me," I groan, dropping my forehead to his lower ribcage in protest.

He chuckles again, his hands stroking my sides, trying to infuse his morning motivation into me.

"I already did and will gladly do again when we get to Pebble Beach. But for now, you need to get this juicy ass into the shower." He pauses and then says, "If you want, I can pack your stuff for you so long as you pull out the clothes you are wearing."

"Deal," I mumble against his skin, giving him two pecks in a row to show my appreciation.

If we had more time, I'd show my appreciation in another way, if my body could handle it, but I'm almost glad we don't have time. I need a shower and to brush my teeth.

"And coffee. Make me some of that bland hotel coffee."

"Demanding Dani is back."

I look up at him, his eyes carrying the same humor his

words do. My heart does even more flip-flops at how well he knows me and still likes me anyway. If I were so lucky that one day he could love me, well, damn, game over. I'd be done for and utterly shattered if we ended.

Not Kylie shatter, way more than that. It's why I fought so hard not to fall for him because it meant losing myself in someone else so wholly that I could break. He could shatter me in a way that only Dad's death did, and I vowed I never wanted to feel that way ever again.

"Demanding Dani is tired as fuck."

I scoot up his body to stick my tongue in his mouth. It surprises him, but his reaction is instant. His arm is around my back, his hand cups the back of my head to change the angle, and his tongue swirls with mine.

He groans. The tip of his erection comes dangerously close to that traitorous pussy that's getting wet and horny for him again. Damn her.

As I eat his face off, I debate about having a quickie with him. Obviously, he's willing, but am I? Tomlin will do whatever I want, which I found out for sure last night. The man may hold the reins to his world tightly, but in the sack, he easily releases them to me, but only if I want them.

When I wanted to be dominated, he did, thoroughly and righteously, and made me come harder than I ever have. When I was dominating, it was sexy and my orgasms were cute, like little flutters. Nothing compared to the powerful ones he gave me. Dammit. I need to fuck him one last time with the amount of heat building in my core.

I break the kiss to glance at the nightstand, covered in empty wrappers, to find an unopened one. His eyes follow mine and his hands stop roaming my skin.

"Uh, what are you doing?"

He knows damn well what I'm doing and what I'm about to

do. I stretch to reach one on the far side, my tit smashing against his hard ribcage and tweaking the skin in the worst way.

"Ouch! Help a girl out and use those long arms to get that condom."

The last one sits on the edge of the nightstand, out of reach of my T-Rex arms. He continues to hold me while I strain and stretch my way over to it.

"Dani."

I know that tone and I stop, hanging almost halfway off his body to look at him while he keeps me from falling off the bed.

"Don't 'Dani' me. You know you want to. Hell, your dick is practically crawling up my pussy right now."

It isn't but it was a second ago before I tweaked my boob. His chocolate eyes stare into mine and even though I know he wants to, his expression is more concerned than desire.

"Of course, I want to. I've always wanted to, and I always will, but that doesn't mean we need to." I open my mouth and he continues, "Or should, in this case. We have another busy day ahead and you said you're already sore, so maybe tonight, depending on how you feel."

I stare at him. Are we seriously negotiating sex like an old married couple? Oh, hell no, that will not work.

"T, I know you're not turning me down. Like I've never . . ." Yeah, I don't need to talk about my past sex life and never being turned down with him. That's weird and borderline disrespectful. I'll take it down a notch. "Okay, I hear what you're saying, but I really want to."

Wow, that came out super whiney but begging for dick is hot in all voices, right? His long fingers fan out, gently lifting me on top of him and away from the last condom. I sigh, airing my grievances to his soft smile.

"I know you do, but we're already running behind and I'm sure you want to wash this off." His hand slides down my ass crack to the crusty stuff and I wiggle his finger away. "If we do this again, you're stuck wearing it in order to make our flight."

I wrinkle my nose. It's one thing to be covered in it during sex. That's hot. It's also fine-ish to wear because I was too lazy to go pee and clean up last night. It's completely different to look and smell like sex beyond the bedroom door, let alone security and a plane ride.

"Fine, but don't say, 'maybe tonight'. Because we're fucking tonight. You can bet your bottom dollar that we are." I don't know where that weird ass phrase came from.

Oh yeah, I remember, when I was waiting on the airplane to vomit and the dude by the toilet said it to the flight attendant when talking about how smelly the bathrooms were. Little did he know I was gonna add to that stench, but anyway.

"Pack that last condom when you pack my stuff."

I'd jam a finger in his face if I could, but they are currently occupied with his flesh in both palms. He cranes his neck forward, seeking my lips, and that's the easiest thing in the world to do.

I could make out with him all damn day. His scruff is rough against my skin and even more sinful on my pussy. I never loved those tiny barbs at the end of beard hair more than I did last night.

"Dammit, T. Stop making out with me if we can't have sex."

I exhale when I lift my head to his cheeky smile. He pinches my ass lightly, and this is the playful version I love so much.

"Get used to it because we'll be making out a lot when we can't have sex. Now up you go."

His stupid muscular arms easily lift me off him to place me in the middle of the bed while he swings to his feet. That beautiful body shines in the early morning light as he stretches this way and that, sending popping sounds into the air from his tight joints. It is only after he's done popping and stretching that he extends a hand to help me out of bed. It's sweet and gentlemanly.

"Oh, damn." My legs falter for a fast second and his hands cup my waist to keep me upright. "I'm sore everywhere," I whine.

This is worse. It's like I pounded out the body damage on two old cars, not just one.

"I have some stuff you can rub on your muscles. Let me go get it for you," he says, his hands falling away as I hobble around the bed to work out the cramping in my muscles.

I swear, my leg wasn't numb before this but suddenly, there's a bunch of pins and needles causing it to not work properly. Dang it if he isn't walking next to me, prowling like a cat, and looking all fluid like, as if we didn't go about eighteen rounds in a nine-hour shirt.

"Why aren't you all sore and stuff? Why am I the only one walking like an old person?"

"I'm used to getting my ass kicked by men. You're not used to getting your ass kicked by this man."

He points a fat thumb at himself and chuckles at his lame joke. Stupid elite athletes and their recovery rates.

"Hardy-har-har." I twist my arm and fake hit my knee like a slapstick comedian as I hobble toward the bathroom. "Even my back hurts."

If this dude isn't even sore from sex and I'm achy everywhere, I wonder about his general health. I mean, he looks like a muscle chart on the outside, but how about the inside?

"Wait. What is your heart rate?"

"Resting is usually mid 30s. Occasionally 40."

"Beats per minute?" I stop, my eyes almost bugging out of my head as I clutch the doorframe. "Are you even alive in there?"

He laughs so easily, and it warms my insides. Not to mention that perfect body and hard dick heat my core. His hands trail through his hair, but it's a lost cause with how long we've been rolling around that bed.

"Very much alive and willing to prove it again to you later. But for now, I'll get demanding Dani her coffee and grab a shower myself."

Him not pressing me on showering together is great because I need time under the hot water to relive every detail of last night.

26

The driver is busy loading our bags into the Rolls Royce Cullinan, another ridiculously priced car that I could never afford but not as expensive as the metallic Roadster. Another awesome surprise from Tomlin that had me stopping short when I saw him walking toward it and shaking hands with the valet.

"Do you like it?"

His smile is wide in the bright sunny weather. His dark hair glistens in the rays while he holds open the passenger door for me. I think surprises are his favorite things and if they keep coming in the form of amazing vehicles, I'm here for it.

"Hell yeah."

The interior is stunning. White buttery leather, Tomlin's favorite. I try not to roll my eyes when I slip inside. He must've specially requested this interior. It has bright blue stitching with the RR logo in the same color with tiger eye cross-grain wood accents. The instrument panel wraps around him like an airline cockpit when he slides behind the wheel. I wonder if he'd trade in his low-slung Porsche for something like this.

"Wait, what about the dude?"

I twist in my seat, looking beyond the back seats with chilled bottled water in the cup holders to search for the driver.

"He drops the car and leaves," Tomlin says, drawing my eyes back to him with the wide console between us. He leans an elbow on it to steal a quick kiss while I'm still confused about how this works. Reading my face, he says, "It's part of the service. They come in pairs, drop it off, and leave."

"I swear, being rich is everything."

I shift away from him, running a hand along that buttery leather covering the interior door, itching for me to touch it.

"Definitely not everything," he disagrees.

I ignore it for several reasons, one being I don't believe him at all, and another being I don't want to get into a debate about it right now. I want to keep staring at the sliding glass doors of the airport, waiting for Lars to get his ass out here.

"Anyway, thanks for getting this for us. Lars's going to flip his wig when he sees this."

I can't keep my hand off the leather. It's so damn soft and smooth, almost sensual under my fingertips.

"Stop caressing the car like that."

The way he says it sounds as if I'm hurting him. When I gaze at him, his eyes are dark brown with a distinct tent in his pants. A mischievous smile pulls up on my face as I lean across the console to stroke that hard shaft beneath his tan dress pants.

"That's not helping the situation," he says, manspreading in his seat to give me greater access to his dick.

If we were in a more secluded spot, I'd have him whip it out and blow him right here in this fancy car. But with people constantly streaming past our windows, we're both having to settle for a little over-the-pants teasing.

My phone chimes in my lap, tearing my attention away from him, and I start to slide my hand off his crotch when he grabs my wrist and holds it there. It's sexy as hell knowing two things. I have that effect on him, and he wants me to continue.

If you would've asked me six months ago if I'd be sitting in another state on vacation with the guy formerly known as the asshole, I would've said you're crazy as can be. Yet here I am, madly in love with this fine-ass specimen with his dick in my hand, in a Rolls Royce, and waiting for my coworker.

My attention divides between rubbing his dick and reading Lars's text message that he's in baggage claim. I flash the screen at Tomlin to read since cars are honking behind us, not necessarily at us, in case he wants to loop around the airport when a text message comes through from Eli.

It takes some maneuvering to open his text message while still rubbing on Tomlin, but when I do, there's the most beautiful picture in the world. Isla and Anna are reunited, smiling, and smashed between Eli and Ronnie in the front yard with their house behind them.

Shaking my head and rolling my lips together, I remove my hand from his pants to cover my mouth. I can't help the burning in my nose. I'm usually not emotional, but seeing this girl finally move out of that facility and into a loving home does it. The transformation over the last two months has been remarkable, aside from the brutal attack and hospitalization.

Isla's blossomed under Eli's motherly ways. He fawns all over her, making a big deal about everything, which pulls a smile out of this introverted girl. Ronald's reserved nature is a strength that hovers over both as a protector of those he loves.

He's not a man of many words, but when he says something, it's usually well thought out and profound. It's the perfect nurturing mix to raise this girl that's been through so much in the last several years.

"Look!"

My voice is raspy, a clear indication that there's a lump in my throat when I shove the phone in his face a second time. I remove my hand from his crotch, and he stops shifting in his seat to study the picture.

"She's home?" he says, taking my phone to mess with the settings, change the exposure and resize it to make it perfect before saving it to my camera roll.

"Yeah, I guess that attorney you had called helped the boys get her released from the hospital directly into their care. From the little I understand about the process, she'll stay with them while going through the court proceedings."

Tomlin's wrong about being rich and not being great. This day wouldn't have come this quickly if he hadn't gotten an old friend in family law to take on their case pro bono. I couldn't have rewarded him properly then because he had run off to Denver, but I sure can reward him now that he's mine and I am his. A phrase of his that I absolutely love.

The soft smile that lingers on his face when he hands me back my phone lets me know he's invested in her journey as well, even if from afar. Despite neither of us being big on having a family of our own, we understand the importance of her having her own family. Something that both Tomlin and I lost a long time ago and still affects us today.

"That's wonderful news, Dani. I'm thrilled for her and the guys. But I have to say, if it wasn't for you saving her, none of this would've been possible. I know you're not big on receiving praise. However, you should be proud of yourself for what you did and had to sacrifice for her to have a new life in a safe environment with people that love her."

His hand slides across the console to find mine, interlocking our fingers and giving me a reassuring squeeze. My eyes fill with tears, and I clear my throat, uncomfortable being praised for doing what every decent person would do. He once told me that not everybody would've done what I did.

I find that extremely hard to believe because the world can't be full of that many motherfuckers that would look the other way and not help a girl like Isla out.

"I don't—"

Suddenly, the rear passenger side door opens and Lars's voice booms through the car when he dumps his duffel bag on the floorboard.

"Sorry guys, it took longer than I thought. Can you open the back?"

I glance over my shoulder while Tomlin hits the button to raise the lift gate. Lars is dragging his suitcase to the back of the SUV and arranging it before I have a chance to properly respond to Tomlin. My hand swipes over my eyes to catch the tears in them while Tomlin watches. I know he won't say anything in front of Lars, but he might bring it up later.

The liftgate lowers while Lars climbs into the back seat before letting out a long whistle of appreciation for the car's interior.

"This is some car you got, Tomlin. I wonder how much a car like this goes for?" he says, shifting around in his seat and the SUV moves too. Neither one of us answers him immediately, causing him to say, "Is everything okay? Am I interrupting something because if I am—"

I didn't mean to put Lars in an awkward position, rather my mind is still on her and trying to get my emotions under control.

"Sorry Lars, I got this picture from Eli. She got beat up this week, but she's now living with them. Can you believe it?"

I show him the picture, my eyes capturing Tomlin's while doing it, and he smiles softly.

"What happened and is she okay now?"

Lars grips my seat, using it to lean forward for a closer look at my phone. Worry wrinkles his face. With all those sisters he's helping raise, his concern is expected.

"Mostly, she has a broken arm, but the important thing is

that she's finally with them and out of that place. It's sweet. They look like a little family already."

His deep blue eyes stare into mine for a couple of seconds before they flicker down to our intertwined fingers. His expression doesn't change from the concern he had for Isla as he sits back and buckles up his seat belt. That's one thing I appreciate about Lars. He doesn't gossip or dig around in other people's business. He takes things for how they are and who they are and lets it go at that.

"Yeah, they do. I'm glad she's safe. Now let's go see our car."

His hands roll together like they did when he first saw Tomlin's car that sunny afternoon at the top of the mountain. To also share this journey with Lars is very special and has me turning around to gaze out the windshield with the lump still in my throat.

Our car.

27

The weather in Pebble Beach is amazing. The sky is cobalt blue without a cloud in it. The sun is radiant, casting bright rays into the open sunroof and sending a crisp breeze through the SUV as Tomlin drives.

The guys chat back and forth about Tomlin's car arriving and transportation confirming delivery with a picture they sent to Lars. It shows that beautiful Gran Torino on the back lawn with the rocky cliffside ocean behind her.

I don't say much, instead watching a series of emotions flicker across Tomlin's face until those deep brown eyes fall on mine. I give him a reassuring smile and a quick squeeze of our hands before resuming looking out my window at the beautiful coastline.

The temperature is cooler, and I'm glad I packed more jeans and sweatshirts for the second half of this trip. I initially thought I wouldn't have fancy enough clothes, but after watching several videos of past events, I knew that I'd be fine in more casual clothing.

Tomlin looks more like a golfer playing in a winter tournament with his casual slacks and cashmere sweater. The blazer he had draped over his arm through the airport is laid across the luggage in the back. I remind him of that time I thought he was interviewing back at the garage, and he chuckles, shaking his head as if remembering something else that he doesn't want to share. I make a mental note to ask him about it later since Lars is in the car.

Nervous excitement builds within me as the navigation chimes. We are a couple of miles away. Even Lars rustles in his seat, reaching for his things as if we're going to come to a stop at any minute and leave him behind. My knee bobs against the passenger side door and I remove my hand from Tomlin's to flip down the visor and check my hair and makeup one last time.

I was tempted to wear my pigtails for old times' sake and to see what Tomlin would say, but this event is way too nice for all that. Maybe when we get to the bedroom tonight, I'll let him use them as those handles like he said in the stairwell when I racked him.

"I was able to secure our lodging on the Concours grounds out of convenience and to put us in the middle of the events," Tomlin says, mostly to me and I turn my head to gaze at him.

"Okay."

I don't really care where we stay. I'm wanting to get there as fast as possible because I'm both excited to be here and nervous to see how his car looks against these other fine machines.

Lars and I did a spectacular restoration. I'm not worried about that. This event feels like getting my paper graded by the teacher, and I want to hang out by the car to see who else appreciates our work. Maybe it's a little self serving, but after what we went through to get her ready for this show, I think it's a reasonable reward.

"Right," Tomlin mutters, appearing to want to say more when his eyes flash to the back seat where Lars is spouting off featured cars on his phone that he wants us to check out.

I nod at Tomlin, knowing that I'll ask him what's up when

we park. He's more reserved in the car with Lars present. It's something I'll have to get used to since I've been enjoying open and playful Tomlin the last several days when I've had him all to myself.

"Wow." Lars's sudden exclamation has me turning my head and I gasp as well.

The traffic is heavy when Tomlin brakes coming into the village. There are hundreds of people streaming all over the place. A snail could travel faster than us. I'm lucky that he's driving or else I would've hit a few by now.

I plaster my nose to the window, staring at various vintage and classic cars parked along the curb or driven through the crowded streets. I slide my window down, the cool breeze hitting my skin and sending both a chill over my skin and down my spine.

"Thanks, T."

I toss over my shoulder to him without ever looking away from the amazing chaos. This is a once-in-a-lifetime experience. There's no doubt about this. I could never afford this in a million years, and yet here I am. Who knew getting fired would be the best thing that ever happened to me?

Well, getting fired, meeting Hamilton, saving Isla, making friends with Eli, hiring Lars, and taking on Tomlin's restoration. That moment changed my life for the better and I had no idea the man I blamed for it all would be the man that saved me from it all. If this isn't karma whopping me upside my stubborn head, I don't know what is.

Super expensive houses are mixed in with the event. Tomlin tells us that he tried to secure one since most residents rent them out for this event, but he was too late. Maybe next year. Heck, I'd love to come next year, but people like me don't get to live this fantasy twice. I'm not dumb enough to believe that.

Tomlin's busy chatting away facts about the area, the schedule of events already underway, the festivities, the parade held today, and basically everything about this place while Lars and I simply ooh and aah at everything around us.

Apparently, this isn't Tomlin's first time coming here. I don't know why I thought it would be, but in a way, it makes sense to travel with someone who has experience because this is far more chaotic than his judo charity event.

As we crawl closer to the lodging, my heart rate increases, and I find myself smiling at people that are waving to me as if I'm in a parade or something. Granted, this car is badass and sort of fits in, price wise with some of these cars.

But it's glimpses of the finely crafted automobiles that keep my nose in the window and my eyes looking for another. Lars's window is down as well, pointing at different things for me to see and we probably look ridiculous as I take out my phone to take pictures.

"This is amazing," I say to no one in particular.

When I feel a hand on my thigh, I look at Tomlin, who's smiling as well. A few moments pass before he softly says, "Thank you for making this possible."

I didn't for a moment consider what he must be feeling right now. Being too absorbed in taking in the organized chaos, I fail to think about how he'll react to seeing his mom's car parked on the lawn and what that means to him. Dang. I really need to be more considerate. It's remarkable that he wanted it restored at all.

Lars's comments about finishing it off if it were his car float through my head. Yeah, I would've taken a match to it. The same thing I told Lars when he hunched over the garage diner counter, trying to make me understand. I can't say that I really do, but Tomlin does, and that's all that matters.

The crowd thickens as the shadow of the lodging facilities eclipses the sun and blocks our view of the cars and ocean beyond it. Lars raises his window and grabs his bags, ready to bolt from the car the second it rolls to its eventual stop. I can't blame him when my hand is curled around the door and my phone is in my purse on the floor.

The only one who's not like a kid in a candy store is Tomlin. His usual calm and cool levelheadedness prevail, which I appreciate more and more since it might allow me to run off with Lars while we leave him to handle the bags and stuff. New leaf, Dani. Stay here, offer to help, and then run around with Lars.

"You two look as though you're trying to race each other to see who can get out of the car first," Tomlin remarks, his eyes lingering on my bouncing knee and my hand on the door handle right next to it. I glance back at Lars, his face is sheepish with his rosacea burning red on his cheeks.

"Maybe we are."

I shrug my shoulder and unbuckle my seatbelt, sending the monitor beeping on the dashboard as the two valets dash toward the car. One gently opens my door to assist me out of the car as the other does with Tomlin while both toss greetings and well wishes all over the place. A third valet is at the back of the vehicle, carefully removing our bags and placing them on a rolling cart.

The speed at which they have us out of the car, suitcases stacked, and the driver rolling it forward, is impressive. When I see the long line of cars behind us waiting to get in, it all makes sense. The valet guides us to the curb with the bellman in tow, awaiting further instructions when Tomlin catches my elbow to hold me back from joining Lars.

"Dani, I hope you don't mind, but I took the liberty of canceling your adjoining room. I had wanted us to share, considering . . ."

He doesn't finish, intentionally lowering his voice when his eyes drift to Lars making small talk with the guys waiting for us. I cast Tomlin a bright smile, gently tugging on the front of his sweater to draw him close. He doesn't hesitate to wrap his arms around my waist, smashing us together while we look at each other.

"I'd love that," I say simply. It's true. I'm not letting nothing or anyone hold me back from enjoying this and us. "And who knows, I might even shower with you."

"I've been meaning to ask about that. Why—"

I grab his neck and plant one on him, not wanting to get into all that, especially right here on the curb. It seems unnecessary to unpack all that psycho garbage when I'm in such a beautiful place. Right when I try to deepen the kiss, he bails on him, standing straight and ghosting his hand down my arm to lead me by the elbow.

"Not here."

True and fair. The bellman sweeps his hand forward when he sees us approach. Lars and the guys wrap up their conversation before the dude jogs away to help another car.

"What was that all about?"

Curiosity gets the better of me when Lars stuff some green tickets in his pocket.

"Passes to the forums with different speakers like Leno and the McDreamy guy my mom watches on television."

He shrugs as if he doesn't know what to do with them. It's not really my thing to sit in a lecture hall listening to dudes yammering on about car stuff, but I'll go with him if he wants me to. I prefer to be part of the action or at least see the cars in action.

"That's nice of him."

Tomlin releases my hand once we are in the lobby and waiting in the check-in line. The place is swarming with people, some in old timey dresses and suits to match the old Duesenbergs and Lincolns, some looking like Tomlin in slacks and a sweater, but most are in comfy clothes like Lars and me.

I thought it would be a bunch of money bags walking around and there are certainly a lot of them, but seeing more normal people makes me feel less out of place than I thought I might be.

"That reminds me. Here are your passes," Tomlin says, retrieving his blazer from where it hangs on the dolly to dig inside the coat pocket for thick pads of paper tucked inside bright green plastic jackets. He hands one to both Lars and me while he stuffs his back inside his coat. It's embossed with VIP in gold lettering on the outer flap before I unclasp it to find a map, exhibit tickets, and a program of cars vying for awards.

"Why does this say VIP? Lars and I don't need that."

I trade a look with Lars, whose eyebrows are high before he looks away, as uncomfortable on the outside as I feel on the inside. We're definitely not VIPs here. Maybe Tomlin is, but not us.

"It's your first time here. I wanted to ensure you both can go wherever you want to go and see what you want to see. To get ideas and such," he says it coolly, but the way his eyes bore into mine, that's not the reason at all.

I tilt my head to the side, my hair slipping by my cheek when it dawns on me that this is another example of how long he's been wanting me. He had said longer than I wanted him and that may have been true, but as I look closer, I'm seeing it more and more. I narrow my eyes at him and then the line moves forward, breaking the moment.

"Right, ideas and such," I repeat, biting my lip to gaze at him a little longer.

"Tell you what, why don't you two get started? I've been here several times. I can handle the rooms and meet up with you in a little while?"

Either he knows he'll have to explain this later or he wants us out of his hair. I can't decide, but heck if I want to wait in line when we could be out there, mixing with the best of them and drooling over cars I've only seen online or in magazines.

"Best thing you've said all day." I adjust my purse's strap to make it cross-body.

"Pretty sure it's not the best thing."

He flashes me a sexy little eyebrow and I smile brightly when I think back to the teasing version of him back at the penthouse. Lars is super uncomfortable with our banter and is quietly inching away to give us more privacy. Poor guy, I need to bring him up to speed and then never tell him anything else again about us.

"True and thanks, T. I, no, we, appreciate it." I tap Lars on the shoulder with my tickets. "Let's go."

Lars nods at Tomlin and waits for me to lead the way through the crowd until we're a safe enough distance away that he lets out the biggest exhalation ever.

"How long you've been holding that in?" I joke, shoving an elbow into his ribcage.

His mop of hair shakes for a moment before answering.

"Since I saw you holding hands in the car. Are you two a thing?"

It surprises me that he's asking outright. It's very forthright and not in his nature at all.

"Yeah, why?" It comes out harsher than I intend, and he touches my elbow to stop me from walking.

"Don't take this the wrong way, but I was worried it could end badly for you, which might mean badly for me, which is terrible for my family."

Ah, yes, I can run down that road with him. Being poor like us, you're always worrying about money. I think Kylie called it poverty consciousness one time. I straight up call it poverty.

"Yeah, I get it, man. But he and I are all good. Better than before."

I do a terrible job trying to assure him because I barely want to dish on my relationship with Kylie. In fact, I haven't and have found answers with Eli, whom I still need to call back and congratulate and talk to Isla. But that will have to wait till later tonight. Talking about Tomlin and me with Lars feels weird, and he seems to be as uncomfortable talking about it as I do.

"Obviously better than before. You're hugging and kissing." A teasing smile spreads over his face as he elbows me right back. "Making googly eyes at each other."

I walk again, Lars falls in step beside me when I elbow him back and say, "We're not making googly eyes, bro."

He bumps me back. "Of course you are, that's okay though because we're here and I have you and him to think for it."

His cheeks burn brighter when I look up at him, his nose getting in on the action by turning a little pink and I can tell he's getting overcome with emotion by this overwhelmingly generous trip.

We're not the hugging type. At least I'm not with anyone, except Tomlin, and he's not with me, so I bump into his side again.

"Nah, just thank him. Me and you, well, you've helped me out more than you know, and we'll leave it at that."

I look away from those cerulean blue eyes, feeling wisps of feelings catching in my throat as well. He's the closest thing I'll ever have to a brother, and it's damn nice.

He clears his throat and says, "How about we look at some cars? It's why we're here."

I blink a couple of extra times, tap my VIP papers against his bicep and reply, "It's exactly why we're here."

28

Stunning works of art cover every inch of the place. The grass they sit on is the brightest shade of green reminding me of Tomlin's Denver house. I swear, they must cut it with scissors to ensure a blade isn't out of place.

My eyeballs don't know where to look and continue bouncing around from the breathtaking views of the breezy Pacific Ocean to the finely restored machines and everything in between. It's sensory overload in the best way possible.

"This is unbelievable."

Lars's whistle breaks the silence as we stand outside the back of the hotel, surveying the land before us. Thankfully, his large size acts as a human boulder, forcing people to move around us as we figure out where to go first.

"Yeah."

Between the beautiful weather, the beautiful cars, and the semi beautiful people, my game plan has gone out the window.

"Do you want to find our car first or start right here?"

Lars points to a huge golf fairway stuffed between the hotel and the cliffs, with beautifully restored and one-of-a-kind vintage cars from the 1920s and 1930s.

"Or the exotics to the right?" He points to another fairway, separated by the sand trap.

"Probably a good idea to find Tomlin's car first. Make sure it's how we want it."

Even though they sent us a picture, I want to ensure she's polished and gleaming in the bright sunshine. Lars rifles through his packet, pulling out the map and program to see which class Tomlin's car would be in, while I people watch. He thumbs through the book, then compares it to the map and points a thick digit on it to show me.

"Right here, to the left of these cars."

"Cool. Let's go."

Being around all these car enthusiasts and with the excitement coursing through me, it takes everything to skip down the sidewalk. With Lars's long legs and stride, I'm practically jogging beside him. Both of us are excited because this is our version of the Olympics.

Not that we're here to win any awards. Nor is his car eligible for awards, but delivering this high caliber of work and for other people to appreciate it is better than any plaque or trophy they could give us.

I linger a half step behind Lars, allowing his frame to guide us through the people. When it gets thick in parts, I clutch the back of his polo to avoid getting separated from him. He glances over his shoulder to make sure I'm still behind him but otherwise leads the way until the crowd thins and we're walking toward the circular grass with muscle cars trimming the outer edges.

Little white poles with chains looped through them keep me from darting between the cars to hunt for ours. Lars calmly continues up the path as butterflies flutter in my stomach. I stuff the VIP packet in my back pocket and wipe the sweat from my hands on the front of my jeans.

"Man, I've never been so nervous," I mutter as we climb

onto the green and make our way to the center to find his Gran Torino. Luckily, the bright color he picked stands out from the muted greens, browns, and blues of the other muscle cars.

"Over there."

I barely hear Lars say it when he speed walks across the lawn toward it. The picture is exactly like what they sent. She's stunning sitting cliffside, with the endless blue Pacific Ocean meeting the blue sky. There appears to be no horizon, and I immediately grabbed my purse to whip my phone out to video her right where she's parked.

There are clumps of people looking at her, a group at the front pointing and talking about different details, and another at the back, with a guy squatting at her tires. A small kid is standing on his tiptoes to see the interior of the car while his dad is holding another one in his arms, bent over, and peering inside.

It takes my breath away. I blink away the bright sun, mash my lips together, and that lump of feeling that keeps haunting me this whole damn trip is choking me. Even Lars is silent. Thunderstruck at her beauty and knowing we're the ones that achieved this. My chest swells with pride for both him and me, the amazing team that we've become, and the bright future ahead of us.

He's the first one to break the silence, rubbing that mob of hair and saying, "There she is."

The way his voice catches has me glancing up at him for a second, and he looks away to watch the family taking pictures in front of it. Something about him being here, providing for his family, and watching a family document this car in their memories, twists a knife in my gut.

Maybe that's what Tomlin and I will be for each other. Maybe when I sit in the booth hiring the next guy, I can say the business is family-owned, and smile, thinking of Tomlin and me living in that mountain resort together after his retirement.

The wind catches my hair, blowing it across my face, and I use it as an opportunity to wipe away the welling tears before Lars catches on. Not that he'd say anything about it, but it's a private moment between me and myself that no one needs to witness.

"Yup. You did a remarkable job with her. That bodywork and upholstery are all you Lars. You should be proud of yourself. That's where the real artistry is at," I say, as the family and another cluster of people move on, giving us room to see her up close.

"*We* did a remarkable job with her. The exterior and interior won't be anything without her engine and that was all you finding parts and digging through stuff to get them. Almost getting your hand bit by that snake at that one junkyard."

"Yeah, I never told Tomlin about that, so let's keep that between you and me."

I've never been especially fond of snakes, but they are popular in Colorado with all the rock formations. Dad used to tell me about the different kinds when we go up to the Royal Gorge for picnics. He thought it was important I know their patterns and which ones were venomous or not. I thought it was a waste of time until I came across an old Torino buried under brush and sitting at the back of the property.

With the sun beating down and sweat running off my back, I jammed my hand straight into the engine without really looking. If it wasn't for Lars literally grabbing me by the waist and sweeping me off my feet as fast as he did, I would've been bitten by the venomous snake.

It certainly gave us both a heart attack that day. After getting a shovel from the guy at the front shack to kill the damn thing, we finally got the last part we needed to rebuild the cylinder block.

"Anyway . . ." I mumble, about to say more when I notice the little white sign with fancy script writing sitting on the grass at the base of the front tire. Not only does it have the make and model of the car and Tomlin's full name as the owner. It also has my name and Lars's as the preservationists.

I gasp, my hand covering my mouth. Right there in black and white is credit being given to us as his team. When I glance around at the other cars, it doesn't have the restoration team listed. The owners of the other cars have taken all the credit without divulging who did the work. And yet here it sits in a fancy script for thousands of people to see our names sharing in the credit of this beautifully restored car.

Damn if those tears don't start racing forward, trying to make it across the finish line of my lower lids to trail down my face. Lars looks at me, and I point to the sign. His hand shoves into his curls to scratch his head and then he does the same thing that I do. He looks at the other white cards to see what they say before turning back to me with those cheeks redder than Tomlin's car.

"Well, I'll be damned."

He's as taken aback as I am. It's honestly the best damn gift Tomlin could've given both of us.

"Yeah."

I honestly don't know what else to say. I'm stunned and crying and sniffing my boogers because that wonderful man did it again. He gave credit where credit is due instead of hogging it like Carl would've done.

"I guess you didn't know anything about this."

His question comes out more as a statement when his fingers drop to his side. He shakes his head, staring from the car to the sign and back to the car. I don't bother wiping the tears from my cheeks this time. I let them fall because at this moment Lars and I are feeling the exact same thing. Gratitude, shock, and pride.

"No," I whisper, tucking my hair behind my ears to take a shaky picture of the sign and then the sign with the car when a guy behind us assumes Lars and I are a couple and offers to take a picture of us with the car.

Lars answers for us, understanding that I can't speak because I'm too busy crying. We shuffle to the passenger door about to take a picture when Lars grabs my shoulder and smashes me into his body with the biggest smile I've ever seen. The guy takes a few with my stunned face before saying cheese to garner a smile out of me.

When he hands back the phone to me, Lars grabs it, flips through the pictures, and takes a few more selfies of us at different angles. Trapped in my own little emotional bubble world and completely overwhelmed, I didn't realize how much this would mean to me.

All those times I asked Tomlin if I did the right thing that day punching Judd and he kept confirming I did are now validated as I stand on this California coast by the sea with his car.

It's only when I turn away from *our car* that I see it.

"What the hell?" I mutter, making a beeline across the green grass to the opposite side where there's a golden-brown Buick parked on the curve. A confused Lars catches up with me when I stand in front of another sign. The lump of overwhelming gratitude is burning into anger when I read the cursive writing.

Raul Hernandez

Carl Menkey, Carl's Timeless Classics.

Sure as shit.

That fucker took credit for my work.

Sitting right before my eyes is the last car I did. The one I killed myself over trying to get done in the two weeks while Tomlin was gone. When he returned, I called him Satan and ate donuts in front of him. He asked who was poetic now after hearing me beg Mr. Hernandez not to drive her in the coming rain.

"Dani, what's wrong?" Lars's hand on my sleeve is gentle

and I gaze up at him, not really seeing him as I process what is happening.

"Did I know?" I whisper to myself.

Lars's hand falls away when I walk down the side of the car, my fingertips tracing the stubborn back fender that gave me so much trouble to fix. To the brake light that kept shorting out until I chased down the electrical malfunction.

I look at the original hubcaps that I soaked in fluids to remove the corrosion. He told me, or maybe I told Kylie it was going into a show here in California. I never paid that much attention to where they went after they left my shop.

I was too backlogged, too overworked, and too exhausted to pay much attention. My job was to get them done, on budget, and on time. I never made the last one, but the first two I always did.

"He's taking my credit, Lars. Don't you see?"

He doesn't though. How could he see when he wasn't there? He didn't know. I told him the story about that day, but I didn't get into it about this car because I was working on the Shelby, the car after the Buick.

When I got fired, it didn't matter anymore. I was working on Tomlin's car, and we talked about that. Somehow, I cut Lars out of one of the most important periods of my life and I didn't even realize it. The only person who can understand this betrayal is Tomlin, and he's nowhere around right now.

"Dani, are you okay?"

Lars is both confused and worried when he sees my hands trembling with rage. Blood is pumping so fast through my body that I can hear my heart in my ears drowning out the sounds of the seagulls above.

"I . . . I . . ."

I can't explain it. Not here. Not now. I'll not ruin the beautiful moment we just had when I realized Tomlin did the exact opposite of what Carl's doing now. I can't let the old Dani prevail and eclipse the goodness of the new Dani's gratitude for Tomlin's benevolence. I have to keep what Tomlin did for us front and center in my mind to avoid giving myself a fucking heart attack and booking a flight to Colorado to beat Carl's old ass.

"Dani, you're making me worry."

There's a pleading in Lars's voice as if needing and begging to know at the same time. I take a few breaths in and out to calm down before I explain it in the shortest version possible.

"I worked on this car. It's mine."

I point to the two-toned brown leather exterior that caps the back half of the car's roof. Something Mr. Hernandez and I didn't think could be restored from excessive heat and elements damage, but I pulled off the impossible feat of bringing it back to life.

Lars's eyebrow hikes into his loose curls when he says, "You did the work on this car? Besides Tomlin's over there?"

"Yeah, this was the car that I killed myself to complete. I worked fourteen days straight night and day only stopping to eat, drink coffee and pass out upstairs, but I had no idea it would be in this show." As I spit out the words, it makes me angrier and my hands tremble even more.

"It's the same time I . . . holy shit. That motherfucker."

I spot that pornstache beyond the throngs of people walking the sidewalk leading up the turf. I push past Lars, bolting for that asshole as fast as I can tear through the clumps of meandering event goers.

"You motherfucker."

I shove my trembling index finger in Judd's face. The shock on his ugly mug is fucking priceless and I'm all up in his grill, ready to knock his ass out.

"Dani? You're here?" The surprised words move that nut brush in the most disgusting way.

I could ask the same of him because that cheapskate Carl

never paid me more than twenty-nine thousand a year and he would've never paid my way for a treat like this. Even if I deserved it a hundred times over.

"That's not your car to take credit for. Where is that fat bastard, huh?"

My raised voice garners curious looks and I couldn't care less. They'll be witnesses to his murder in about two seconds. The shock clears from his face and that fucking pornstache I vowed to rip off once before has grown wider and bushier. Good. More to grab when I yank it from his skin.

"I guess you saw our Buick, huh?" he smirks, pushing my finger away. I'm so close that I feel his nasty breath on my skin, and I want to gag. My insides are boiling, sending a heated flush over my body.

"Our Buick?" My voice shrills while my mouth falls open in astonishment. "You mean, my Buick."

"No one cares that you did it, Dani. You're a nobody here. Hell, Carl's a nobody here. At least his name is on that placard, which will bring in the business we need now that we're expanding and turning your old rat hole into our parts closet."

Expanding?

Dad's apartment and my only home are going to be used for filthy parts.

Judd's eyes widen and his shoulders roll back, trying to appear larger than he is when Lars's arm brushes against mine. That fucker's entire demeanor changes, by inching taller and shoving his chest out as he sizes up his competition.

"Dani?"

I glimpse Lars, his eyes darting from me to Judd and back, accessing the situation and probably seeing the waves of anger radiating off me. This is the side I've kept hidden from him. This is old Dani wanting to scorch the Earth in revenge and evil laugh while doing it.

I raise my finger in the air to Lars. "Just a second."

Judd's eyes are steady staring at Lars, and I know exactly why. That pin dick is sizing up the situation between us and probably wondering if he could take him in a street fight. Not that he would, but Lars could beat him into the ground the same as pounding a railroad spike into molded steel.

"First your ass gets me fired, then kicked out of my home and now you two assholes think you can take credit for my work? Oh hell no."

My blood boils, surging at a rate I can't control until my fist is rocketing through the air and smashing into his cheekbone. His head slams backward, the surprise in his eyes feeds my fury and I lunge toward him, only to be caught at the waist by Lars's thick arm.

"Fuck."

Pain rings around my knuckles. It's been a long time since I've done that, and my hand isn't used to it even though it feels damn good doing it.

"Dani," Lars warns, adjusting his hold on my waist while wresting my hand away from clawing Judd's nut brush. My fingernails scrape down his skin, missing their target. "You can't do that."

The crowd forms a curious circle around us, watching how uncivilized I'm being at this civilized event. I'm screaming obscenities at him, Judd's holding his swollen cheek and Lars's dragging me out of punching range from Judd.

"Some bitches never fucking learn," he taunts, stepping closer and closer with his hands by his sides, practically begging me to hit him again.

If my back wasn't already pressed to Lars's chest, carrying me out of the circle and away from Judd, I'd go MMA fighter on his ass.

"Calm down," Lars mumbles in my ear, my feet not touching the ground while he lugs me down the turf and onto the cart path opposite the direction of the muscle cars. "He's not worth it."

"I'll debate worth or not."

Judd is left explaining to some official that runs past Lars and me what exactly happened. My knuckles are blazing with red-hot heat, the pain radiating around the biggest one that took the brunt of the impact of his hard cheekbone. Only when Lars carries me far enough away with a grouping of trees blocking my view, does he set me down and rests his hands on my shoulders.

"Your face is red as can be. Let's get a drink and you tell me what that's all about."

Lars's patience is remarkable, even if he's using the same voice he uses on his little sisters when they're fighting. My eyes drift in the car's direction, trying to see if Judd's standing next to the Buick, taking my credit.

"What we're not going to do is get kicked out of here and ruin your boyfriend's mom's car's first show."

The way he says it brings my temper down a notch to first degree manslaughter instead of premeditated murder.

"Boyfriend's mom's car's first show? That doesn't sound right," I say, my gaze returning to Lars even though I'm on high alert for Judd's lucky ass to walk by so I can pounce on him.

The karma gods must hate my ass because of all the thousands of people, swarming around here, my ass has to see him immediately after I find out they stole my credit.

"I don't know if it's right or not, but it got you to stop casting daggers at every man walking by." True and fair. "Come on, let's put these passes to work. I heard they have shrimp cocktail in the VIP hospitality tent."

I snort and roll my eyes. Lars doesn't take offense in the slightest, too excited over free food to bother with being offended by my actions.

"Fine, but I'm having a beer after seeing that motherfucker."

I toss a thumb in his general direction and Lars removes his hands from my shoulders.

"Don't get drunk. I really don't want to get thrown out of here. This is my first vacation ever."

The eagerness in his voice is unmistakable, and it's one of the things that makes him so endearingly him.

"Deal and same."

29

The hospitality tent is basically a wedding without the bride and groom. They have fancy chandeliers hanging from the middle of a tent which I didn't know is possible. A four-piece band playing some soft jazz that I recognize from one of Tomlin's playlists.

There is more free food and booze than should be allowed at an event like this, and even a couple of obnoxious drunks for people to whisper about.

Lars is two overflowing plates in on the shrimp cocktail before I finish my story about the Buick. Not one to gossip, and not one to interrupt my rant either, he watches me guzzle down my beer before he says anything.

"You've already won."

A dab of cocktail sauce remains on his cheek, and I point to it saying,

"You got sauce right here. Now, you're going to have to explain how I'm winning in this scenario. I got fired, Carl made me homeless and now he steals credit for my hard work. That's three strikes in a row, and that, kid, in baseball, is what we call three strikes, and you're out." I even make the umpire call at the plate while he wipes his face.

"Yes, Dani, I know baseball. I played it," he says flatly.

"For real? I assumed football or wrestling."

"The way I see it, you've won. You've moved on in every way possible in your life and who's still at the old place out on Highway 123?" He ignores my sports comment. "You don't need to threaten to rip the guy's 'nut brush' off his face at a classy event like this. You're lowering yourself to their level."

Lars repeating the obscenities I screamed at Judd sounds weird and I look at his pile of food.

"You've got to see that you're doing so much better than them."

He picks up another prawn and swipes it through the sauce before inhaling the whole thing and pulling out the tail to dump it on his discard pile. I shake my head because I'm not better off than them.

They are both still working at my old place like nothing ever happened other than getting rid of me and probably congratulating each other for their effective backstabbing and betrayal.

"I don't."

He finishes eating his shrimp, leans forward, and looks me dead in the face.

"You don't see it because you don't want to see it. You want to hold on to your anger. You want to hold on to being right and them being wrong. It's understandable. What those men did to you isn't right and hasn't been right for a long time. You called it a boy's club a moment ago, but it's not that at all. It's sexist and misogynistic and not at all how real men behave in the workplace. What happened to you is both unfair and illegal and Tomlin was correct. You could've pursued a lawsuit and probably would've won, but you choose not to. And that's fine too. It's ultimately up to you anyway."

"Okay. All things I know already," I say, falling back in my chair.

"Those guys, that place, it's all they'll ever have. It's all they'll ever be. When our garage grows and you take on more clients, your name will be falling from the lips of your enemies. So, who's really winning? You're going to go onto bigger and better things. Never looking back at what you were. It'll be so far in your rearview mirror that you can't even see it anymore. Therefore, it won't exist. You'll never mention their names again. It won't even occur to you to think of them. But they'll always remember you. They'll talk about how you were when you worked there because that's all they have. Eventually, that business will die out, and so will they, and you'll live on, going to greater heights that you can't even imagine."

I look away, out at the drunks swaying arm and arm in front of the band as some official tries to shuffle them away from the tables of seated guests. Lars's hopes for the future are so dreamy that I don't know if it's true or not.

Am I winning and I didn't even know it?

My future is uncertain, but being chained to a shitty place of work is way worst. My attitude has gotten better and I'm far happier than I ever was there. I can breathe and think, rather than fly off the handle like I did today. I don't get into fistfights at the drop of the hat like I used to because of unresolved anger derived from unhappiness. Hell, I turned over a new leaf and like the direction my life is going.

My name falling from my enemies' lips is golden. Something I need to remember.

"Do you know the difference between a duck and an eagle?" Lars asks, taking my silence as a sign to continue cheering me up or calming down. I can't decide which. "Beyond the physical differences."

I shrug.

"One's badass and the symbol of our country. The other people kill and plaster the carcass to their wall?"

"Sure, but ducks waddle around quacking in their own shit. Eagles live in the treetops. They build their nests over a hundred feet off the ground. What do you want to be? A duck covered in feces or an eagle soaring across the sky?"

He did it again, blowing my mind with that analogy. I acted like a low-class idiot making a scene at this high-class event. Definitely duck behavior. Not only that but if Lars's right about my trajectory going up and theirs remaining the same until someone buys them out and fires their asses, why even think twice about them? Let my name fall from their lips. I hope it does.

"One last thing, Dani, and this is far more subtle."

He pauses, taking a drink of his lemonade before grabbing the underside of my folding chair and dragging it even closer to him. His face is inches from mine, so close that I can see his blue eyes have white strips that go out from his pupils across his irises.

"You got two cars into this show. They got none."

He sits back in his chair, mimicking a mic drop with his hand and a little explosion out from his head. I laugh but damn if he isn't right.

"Damn."

It is astonishing. Preservationists go their entire careers without getting any cars into a show like this and here I have two. Lars's dropping so many gems on me, I wish I had recorded this conversation on my phone.

I'm winning. Far more than they could or ever will. A deep satisfaction settles into the place where my furnace of hate and revenge lives and extinguishes the flame long enough to see them for what they are. Sexist and misogynistic bastards are unworthy of any more of my time, energy, or thoughts. May they eternally burn in hell.

"Now, are you going to finish your shrimp, or can I have them?" Lars asks, shooing away a fly that is trying to claim my uneaten shrimp for itself. I shove the plate toward him, having gotten my fill when I reach for my purse to dig out my phone.

"Have at it."

The second I pull out my purse, dread climbs up my windpipe. It's a vicious text from Kylie with a picture of Tomlin and me at the hotel. The one from the parking lot where he got me off against the gorgeous roadster. That was hot as hell, but afterward, yeah, that was a terrible idea on both our parts. This is bad.

"Shit," I curse a little too loud, getting a scowl from a lady passing by with a cocktail in her hand.

"What's wrong?"

Concern has Lars stopping mid chew to look at me and I bite my lip. It's normal for him to ask, especially after my outburst and potentially causing him to get kicked out of this place with my destructive behavior. This is different. He doesn't know about Kylie and me being on the outs right now. I don't think I even told him about Kylie and Tomlin's dating.

This is probably one can I shouldn't wait till Colorado to resolve like I originally thought. I need to woman up and handle this because I am Tomlin's, and he is mine and nothing is going to change that.

"It's an argument I had with Kylie this week. Do you mind if I step out to call her?" I ask when he's already shaking his head. Lars doesn't like conflict.

I learned that way up front when I was yelling at a supplier one time, and he calmly took the phone out of my hand to handle it. When I asked him about it later, he said he didn't like yelling. Had heard enough to last him a lifetime. I figured it was partly the reason he's helping raise his sisters instead of his dad or theirs.

Relief blankets his face. I feel bad for putting him on edge again. I completely understand because he acts like me, always waiting for the other shoe to drop and I hate being the cause of it.

"I can tell it's important so good. I'll be fine. Plus, I want to go back to the muscles cars, which is probably where you shouldn't go. Will you text me the pictures that the guy took? I want to send them to my mom."

"Of course, and thanks. I'll catch up with you later for that forum stuff," I say, standing and selecting the pictures to send to him. When I hear his phone ping in his pocket, I assume that's me and switch to calling Tomlin.

"Thanks, and I hope everything turns out all right," Lars says as I put the phone to my ear and start edging past groups of laughing people.

When I get to the end of the tent, I push open the flap, my eyes adjusting to the brightness when Tomlin answers. His end is quiet, mine is loud, and I can't hear him at all. I hang up, walk through the crowd, past the front of the hotel, and down the sidewalk before his call pops up on my phone.

"Hey, T. Where are you?"

I cup my hand over my eyes to protect them from the glare coming off several of the cars' windshields lining the road, waiting to get into valet.

"In our room. Do you want to come up here? I have something we need to discuss." His voice is void of emotion, which can mean a lot of things with him. This time, I know exactly what it means.

A car horn blares, the impatient driver rolling down his window to holler at someone ahead of him. One horn turns into many waiting in the valet line. I turn around, ducking my head to hear him, but I can't. It's far too chaotic on my end.

"I can't hear you, so text me the room number and I'll head that way in a second. I got a call to make."

Still unable to hear him, I end the call and jog away from

the noise, taking a left to duck into the neighborhood. The houses are of various sizes and styles.

All larger than I've ever seen, including Tomlin's mountain resort, and making me wonder what these people do for a living. A guy is pulling out of his driveway and waves at me when he passes. It's super friendly, but I don't wave back, as I'm preoccupied with calling Kylie.

My grip tightens on my phone, and I gaze at the sky to find the right words to start the conversation. If I had an ex and my best friend fell in love with him and he made her happy, I wouldn't stand in her way. I'd chalk it up to he wasn't the right fit for me but is a perfect fit for her. Maybe that's the angle I need to take right now.

As my finger hovers over the button, a weight settles on my chest, making it difficult to breathe. And take a few deep breaths in and out, blowing harshly through my mouth before I place the call. She doesn't answer immediately, but when she does a surge of adrenaline courses over me.

"Hey Kyles," I mumble, the uncertainty evident in my tone.

"Dani," she clips, with less bite than the other day, but still pissed. "I assume you're calling because of that picture?"

It comes out more of a statement than a question and I let out a sigh travel through the phone. She said she was done with me. That she couldn't deal with me. I hope that's not the case as I don't want to lose my lifelong friend.

"I'm calling to talk about us. You're my best friend and I don't want to fight with you. Not over this."

She scoffs, but I stand my ground. I want to resolve this even though I shouldn't have to choose between my best friend and the man I love.

"Best friend, my ass. You're having sex on that car?" Her voice shrills at the accusation. I opened my mouth to respond when she continues, "Not only are you dating the guy I like but you're throwing it in my face. Everyone's face. It's all over social media."

Well, damn.

"Wait, that's what this is about. You still like him?" I scratch my head, gazing at the palm trees swaying in the breeze without a care while I have a million worries. "But you're with Ryan and have been for a long time now."

"Of course, I still like him. I'm in love with him, Dani!" she screams into the phone, and I stop walking, immediately freezing at her confession.

She still loves him? But it's been months and months. Well, over half a year already.

"Love?" I whisper into the phone, still trying to wrap my head around how she can love someone that she hasn't seen in months.

"Yes. Love. I don't have to defend how I feel to you."

"But you saw him at the bar and patted his back like a grandma. I mean, it was painful to watch how awkward you were, but you said Ryan was the one or that you were eating healthy to have sex with him." I'm word vomiting to her, speaking out my thoughts as I try to process what she's saying versus everything that's happened. "You didn't seem to love him when you told me to take the job. I think I asked, and you said you were fine. Where is all this coming from, Kyles?"

I'm so confused. She's been a ghost with the amount of time she's spent with Ryan. I was a ghost spending all my time fixing up the car. Did something happen in between, and I didn't realize it? How can she be in love with him and date another?

"I saw your pictures, Dani. He takes you to LA, and that hotel is one of the most expensive in town. Then Pebble Beach. You don't even like that kind of stuff. You scoff at the rich people you work for and now you're hanging out with them? That's not you. It's not fair."

I clutch the trunk of a palm tree. The adrenaline coursing

through my body is converting to anger at a rate I can't slow down my next accusation when it flies out of my mouth.

"You're not in love with him. You love who he is and what he is." Like Tomlin's dad. "What he can do for you and where he could take you."

"Of course, I do. What woman wouldn't want to be with him and live that lifestyle? You said his place on the mountain was lovely and you know his place in Denver is expensive."

I release the tree, moving to sit on the curb with my head cradled in my hand because her confession continues to shock me. This is why Tomlin said that to me on the back deck.

He had come off that break-up with her, looking for something real or maybe it was looking for *someone* real after what I'm hearing. He said she molded into whatever he was interested in, that she became a chameleon to his wants in his life instead of having her own.

"This is why you two broke up," I say, hearing both sides now.

When she came to the garage bawling about the break-up, I told her to pack his shit in a box and burn it. She wanted me to drop it off instead and made me swear that I would when we lay on my bed that night. She said the classic guy's break-up excuse, was that he was busy with work and didn't have enough time to date.

At the time, I called bullshit, but now as I raise my head to look at the multi-million-dollar house across the street from me. He let her down in the nicest way possible.

"He knew you liked him for his money."

"Don't you dare call me a gold digger when you're doing the same thing yourself."

When I think I can't get more surprised, she lobs another insulting bomb at me.

"Gold digger? Me?" I laugh. Not the carefree kind that I love so much when Tomlin does it. But the grotesque one of every evil villain movie.

"I'm lots of things in this world, Kylie and gold digger has never been one of them. Ya know, I thought we could work this out. That's why I called because I wanted to clear the air. Didn't want any more pictures coming out that would surprise you. Now I'm thinking it doesn't matter what I say because you already made up your mind." Not even two seconds go by before I say the scariest thing in the world. "I think we need time apart."

I've never said that. Never had to say that. Never could handle saying that before as she has been my only support system. But now, it's crumbling. My actions are somehow misconstrued as me sabotaging her for my gain. Something I'd never do, and yet the exact thing I'm being accused of doing.

"I couldn't agree more, Dani. Don't call or text me. I'll reach out when I'm ready." Her voice is heavy with accusation and betrayal, even if it's misguided before she ends the call. I hunch over my legs, my cheek resting against my knee, with my phone draped in my hand.

I don't know what to think. My brain keeps replaying both conversations from this week. Unable to believe that in order to gain Tomlin, I lose Kylie. It's surreal. We've been best friends for longer than I can remember, sharing absolutely everything, and just like that, it's gone.

For once in my miserable life, I loved another, not Dad and it's costing me the sister I've had all along. I want to pick up the phone, call her back and demand it not be over like this. But I said the words first.

I spoke out of anger and pride when she called me a gold digger and I asked for a break. It seems right. I didn't want to go round after round if she wasn't going to listen. If she had her mind already made, then what could I do?

It doesn't make sense. Another change that doesn't make

sense at all. My chest hurts and I mash my lips together, willing myself not to cry even though I already am. I bury my face in my sweatshirt sleeve and bawl. I cry for losing her, losing us, and another loss in general. So many losses of late.

Too many. Another round of chest stabbing cries escapes my shaking body causing snot to leak from my nose and onto the fabric.

The crisp breeze tugs at my hair, the hum of the festivities buzz behind me and a light honk from a passing car pulls me back to reality. I wipe my face with my clean sleeve and watch a couple of seagulls hang in the air before flying toward the coast.

What do you want to be?

A duck or an eagle?

Lars never said how hard it is to be an eagle.

30

My phone rings. Tomlin's name is on the screen and a sigh loosens from my chest. I plaster the phone to my ear, look at the smooth asphalt road and try not to cry.

"Dani? Are you on your way? I don't mean to ruin your fun, but I really need to speak with you." He sounds hurried and maybe I should be concerned, but I can't muster up anything other than sadness and disappointment.

"I'm not."

I'm useless holding back the tears that flood my eyes and fall over the edge again.

"What's wrong? Are you hurt? Stay there and I'll come to you." Panic fills his voice and there's shuffling on this end. He doesn't need to bolt all the way over. I'll walk back. "Where exactly are you? What exhibit?"

"I'm not at any of them. I'm in the neighborhood but don't come. I'll make my way back. Will you stay on the phone with me?"

I sniff, dabbing my nose on my sleeve and knowing I'll need

to change out of this sweatshirt as soon as I get back to our room.

"Of course. Are you hurt?" Something clicks on his end, and I think it must be a dining cart or our luggage because Tomlin's suddenly addressing someone else. "Sorry, babe. Please tell me why you are crying."

"There's another photo. Worse this time."

My words come out shaky between worrying about the photo and losing my best friend. I rest my cheek against my arm, despair adding to the disappointment.

"Yes, I know. It's what I wanted to talk to you about."

"I'm sorry, T," I murmur. That one spontaneous moment of pleasure is causing all sorts of problems for both of us. "We shouldn't have done it."

He sighs this time, and I can envision him pinching his neck.

"Baby, don't say that. We got a little carried away. Who hasn't? Please don't regret it. Rex is handling it and would prefer we come out officially as a couple. It would make it easier for him, but he's not my number one concern. You are. Is this what has you so upset?"

That old familiar sincerity is in his voice, and it tugs at my heartstrings. It's one of many things I love about him. He's gentle and kind with me at all the right times.

"Yes. Kylie saw it." My chest feels heavier than before when I was arguing with her. "She said she's in love with you. Did you know that?"

A brief silence before he answers, "No."

Another pause and I really wish he was in front of me so I can see his face. I don't know if the silence is him thinking or if he's as shocked as I am. Needing to get to him, I push myself off the curb and head to the path leading back to the hotel.

"I don't even see how that is possible. It's been months since I have seen her. Many more since we were together, possibly almost a year." The bewilderment in his voice matches mine. "Dani, I hate having this discussion over the phone. Tell me where you are at, and I'll come to you."

I'm jogging past the houses to get to the main road, huffing and puffing into the phone, and almost certain he hears me.

"I'm on the main street now, but it's chaos out here and loud as hell. Are you still in our room?" I'm not jogging anymore. I'm flat out running up the sidewalk until I get to the crowds and cars again, knowing I won't hear him in about two seconds. "Tell me you don't love her back, T. Tell me that we're okay despite this crap."

"I don't. I never did and I never will, Dani," he says with a raised voice and a small bit of relief coats my conscious. "How far away are you?"

"Not far. I'm sorry about Rex. He must be flipping out."

We're really giving that man a run for his money on all this damage control.

"Don't worry about him. Rex will do what he always does. What he's paid to do."

I wish I were as confident as Tomlin is. All these gossip sites don't seem to bother him. I open my mouth to ask him how he can be so cavalier about Rex when the call drops and a curse falls with my breath.

I dodge and dart in between people and cars, only stopping for a stray kid that sprints across the sidewalk with his dad running after him. My purse smacks the side of my hip as I run past open car doors and valet staff in the parking lot and luggage carts and bellmen inside the lobby. I'm almost at the elevator bank when a portly man steps in front of me and I barrel into the back of him.

He tumbles forward, using the wall to catch himself while I'm trying to grab him.

"I'm so sorry. I . . ."

My words stop, as does my heart. His eyes bug out and his

mouth falls open. Surprise doesn't even cover what I'm feeling or how he's looking.

I thought I was prepared for this moment, having rehearsed it a million times before now. But standing with his hand plastered to the wall and mine to his arm, I'm not.

"Dani?" His recovery is faster than mine, and I snatch my hand away. My breath comes fast and harsh, as anger brew from the pit of my stomach. "I didn't expect to see you here."

His voice is shaky and uneven. It could be the hit he took. It could be the near fall he avoided. Or it could be me standing in front of him. Possibly all three.

"Carl."

Whispered like a curse.

I clear my throat, my mind racing back to all those days and nights of questioning what he did to me. Why he did do it to me? And why he did do that to Dad's stuff?

Days of hammering on Tomlin's car until Lars would take the hammer away after too many noise complaints from the neighbors. Nights of lying in the lonely cabin getting used to the resounding quiet reflecting off the mountains as I stared at the night sky. Too many wasted hours looking for answers that never came.

Now is my chance.

"You fired me. How could you have done that? I know I broke your window, and that was my fault, but you never did anything about Judd, no matter how many times I complained. The fact that you always took his side is disgusting and makes you a terrible boss." I vomit the first half of what I want to say, taking a breath to say the other half when a family interrupts, trying to get to the elevators.

I shuffle toward the long windows that cover the front of the hotel. Carl moves as well. His face is red, probably from his blood pressure skyrocketing at my accusations. Honestly, it's straight facts.

"Now Dani, I know things could've been handled differently, but—"

He plants his stubby fingers on his thick waist. The Dani from months ago would've let him finish out of respect for him, but not no more. He lost all my respect the second he told Tomlin to tell me not to bother to come back.

"Yeah, you could've fired Judd or stopped the harassment, or believed me every time I complained about him to you. Something, anything for Pete's sake. The shittiest thing is that you didn't have the decency to fire me to my face, or hell, on the phone, but to tell your client that I was fired. Who does that? I don't even know if that's legal?"

I step back, needing space because I can smell the stench of betrayal as his beady little eyes question me. The look on his face is a mix of surprise and confusion, and I immediately hate it. Own up to your shit, at least. I have, and so must he.

"You stole my customer. I took a loss on that job, all because you couldn't control your temper and then got the police involved," he defends, lowering his voice.

"Hamilton wasn't there for you or Judd. It was about Isla, the girl I saved, and you know that." My voice shakes with rage and my hands tremble at my sides as fire shoots through my veins. Never have I wanted to hit someone more than him right now. Far more than Judd.

"And I didn't steal your customer. Tomlin pulled the car because Judd was cheating him right under your nose. In fact, you were overcharging Tomlin too. One hundred grand? What were you thinking? Have you been ripping off all our clients over the years? How did you take a loss? I restored that car at a quarter of the price."

He tugs on the front of his pants, acting all blowhard and blistery with me. That might have worked once upon a time, but it doesn't work anymore.

"Now you listen here. I never cheated anyone. That's how

much it costs, and Judd was supplying receipts to that effect. Not that I have to justify it to some snot-nose kid. If your dad was here, he would be so disappointed in you."

My blood roars into my ear, eclipsing the racing heartbeat that was there a second ago. My entire body shakes with a murderous rage that I almost and I mean almost wrap my trembling hands around his neck to choke him to death. Murdering him is just fine with me and I wouldn't regret a day in jail because of it.

My jaws lock and through clenched teeth, I warn, "Don't you say nothing about Dad. You don't get the right. He was your friend for years and you screwed him over." My chest heaves as I throw the words of his ultimate betrayal at him. "You threw his stuff out like it was trash. His entire life sat next to the dumpster in the rain. You've got to be the saddest piece of shit to do that. Betray me, fine. But betray Dad?"

I can't help but scream at him. He deserves it. He deserves everything horrible thing that can ever happen to him. His face is overheating, a deep red on his cheeks, darker than his alcoholic nose. A guttural roar escapes from his stout body as his hand clutches the wall again.

"Don't you dare raise your voice at me. I tried to call you. Tried to work this out, but you didn't want to. You didn't return my calls and when Mr. Takahashi pulled the car, saying you're going to finish it, I thought how could she do this to me? I thought of you as a daughter after your dad died. I was there that night—"

My ears either clog from the murderous rage I'm holding back or I hear him wrong.

"Did you say Tomlin told you I was working on his car? That's why he was pulling it?"

I don't need him to go down memory lane about that night with my father. I've resolved that already and for him to say I was like his daughter is absurd. He wouldn't have let me get harassed and felt up for years if that were true.

Carl seems taken aback by my interruption, getting out his handkerchief to wipe his forehead before responding.

"Yeah, he called later that day, after you left with him."

"He was taking me to get my truck," I defend, thinking back to that day, so clearly etched in my brain.

Tomlin said he didn't tell Carl that. I asked him, about the morning on the back deck and he said Carl assumed I was working on it. I hadn't even decided to take his project until after Carl cleared out my place and I struggled to get Dad's chair in my truck. That was after Tomlin pulled the car. I turned him down a half dozen times before I agreed.

"No, he said you called and told me good riddance. It was after you threw away Dad's belongings."

He continues dabbing his sweaty face, only stopping to level my stare.

"I cleaned out your apartment when you didn't call me back. I left you a message on your phone. I wasn't going to let you live at my place and steal more customers."

My blood runs cold and I step back. The anger dissipates from my body as does my desire to argue with him. He left a message, but that little bubble like so many on my phone lingered for weeks and weeks.

What's one more bubble when I have thousands of them? His message sat there with dozens of other unopened voice mails. Now that bubble dances in my vision like the black dots floating around Carl's face. He's saying my name, I hear it and I don't. The hotel heats to a million degrees. I feel lightheaded, fanning my face because I feel nauseated as if I could vomit on Carl and not care.

"I gotta go."

I clutch the wall, needing it to not faint when I knock shoulders with him as I pass. He continues calling after me, but I can't. I can't remain there listening to his lies. Lies about Tomlin, about what happened, and how everything went down.

My feet pick up the pace, running into the bathroom at the end of the hallway and locking myself in the last stall. I pant and pace, looking down at the tile floor and piecing together his story with Tomlin's and mine.

What I know versus what I think I know. It's a mess, trying to remember all the conversations from then until now.

With shaky hands, I pull my phone from my purse. The bubble in question glows bigger and brighter as if pulsing on the screen when my thumb hovers over the icon.

I shuffle to the voicemail tab and scroll past dozens of unopened messages until I find that old number long ago deleted from my phone. I take in a few breaths, trying to calm my racing heart before tapping on the notification and then the speaker icon.

His voice rings loud and clear in the empty bathroom, throwing out venomous accusations as he did out there. I can barely breathe when the message ends and I listen to it two more times, trying to not believe it.

Carl lies.

Tomlin doesn't.

I want to believe Tomlin. Believe that he wouldn't betray me for his own selfish gains.

Carl is a filthy liar.

My hand clutches my sweatshirt, fanning the fabric to get some air inside it. I look at the ceiling, trying to get the tears to recede to wherever they came from, when my phone rings. It's Tomlin.

I need to answer it, but I don't. I'm scared. Scared that there's a sliver of truth in Carl's words. An inkling in the back of my mind keeps spreading like cancer through my thoughts, twisting them against Tomlin.

The look he gave me on the back deck when he clasped my

wrist and asked me if I was lonely. He couldn't have lied to me then. Nor the night before when he made me pizza while I napped on the couch.

No, he couldn't have lied to me then nor all the days and nights since. My phone rings again and I silence it. He couldn't have lied to me. Wouldn't have lied to me. Not after everything I told him and everything we've been through.

He would never do that to me. Never betray me as Carl betrayed me. No. I can't believe it. I won't believe it.

It rings a third time and I answer it.

31

The hotel room door flies open, his strained face lifts when he reaches for me, immediately tucking me into his chest and shutting the door.

As much as I want to stay in his arms, where everything feels right and makes sense, I can't. I need answers. Only ones he can give and the longer I delay the sicker I feel.

"Did you lie?"

The arms I love so much are now a trap that I must escape as I pull away. I want to vomit. My stomach is sautéing the shrimp prawns I ate with Lars and threatening to spew them all over the floor while Tomlin's calloused hands caress up and down the sides of my arms.

His face cuts with concern. His dark eyebrows pulled tight over his eyes that are boring into me. My heart is beating a thousand times a minute, needing to know, yet not wanting to know.

Sometimes the truth is a motherfucker like that. It demands to be known and let out in the light of day after hiding in the dark for months. But once it's out, there's no putting it back, leaving pieces to decay where they are spewed. It's why I have a love-hate relationship with the truth. I demand it from everyone else, even if it would be so much easier if I didn't.

"Baby."

He said it on the phone and he's saying it again, trying to pull me against his chiseled chest, but I resist, forcing them to fall away as I back up several steps.

"Did something else happen, aside from Kylie?"

His dark eyes never leave mine even as his head tilts in the balcony's direction, above the vintage car collection on the main fairway.

I held it together through the lobby of the hotel and the elevator. I held it together as patrons shuffled in and out as it finally climbed to this floor. I held it together when he ushered me in and kissed the side of my head. But the way he's looking at me now, reaching a hand to touch me and speaking in that soft, sweet tone, breaks the dam of tears flowing down my cheeks.

"You said you'd never lie to me. You swore it, but you did. You lied about your car. You told me on the back deck that you didn't tell Carl that I was doing your car, but you did. You lied to my face. My world was imploding, and you didn't care. You wanted to get your precious car restored. In fact, you fired me too. You told me that you would take it from here when I shared the news with Lars."

I wrap my hands around my waist, holding myself, like I've had to do so many times before when people disappointed me. But this is so much worse, far worse than anyone else. I've never been more afraid of hearing the truth.

"I don't understand. Where is all this coming from? We've been through it all. I'm truly sorry for that night. I overreacted, and you forgave me."

He steps closer, reaching for me. I want to reach for him too, but the truth has to prevail. I trusted him. He's never lied to me. Now I'm wondering if it's all been a lie. I'm so confused my head shakes both at his actions and my thoughts, trying to comprehend all this.

"Tell me," I whisper.

Maybe a part of me suspects, or a greater part already knows. These things have a way of happening to me. This feels exactly like the proverbial shoe that I have been waiting to drop. It's sort of like what Lars said a while back, that good things like this don't always happen to people like us.

Maybe somewhere deep down inside in places I don't want to acknowledge, I knew. Or maybe like Dad and his undying love for my mom, I swept it under the rug and looked the other way, somehow convincing myself that it was never true at all.

My fingertips clench the edge of my cuff to swipe it across my face. My nose stings and the lump at my windpipe burns.

"But did you lie? Please, T." The vision of him blurs through my watery gaze as I hug myself even tighter. "I have to know."

He sighs. His hand ruffles through his hair to stop at his neck and pinch it. It's his truth telling sign and a sob catches in my throat.

"Dani."

One word.

A beg or a plea.

I don't know which, but it confirms what Carl said and what I feared the most. This was all too good to be true. My hand covers my mouth and I curl into myself to sob even harder.

He's on me in a flash. His entire body is a shield over mine to protect me from the painful truth and intentional deception. The harder I cry, the more my body shakes against his.

The dream of him and us is fading fast behind my closed eyes. All the cans we kicked down the road stopped clanking and now sit silently at my feet with no desire to kick them ever again. This is what I was afraid of. I went all chips in on him and now it's a bust. Where do broken gamblers go when they are broke?

"I'm so sorry," he rasps, emotion catching in his throat. "I never meant for it to go this far. I wanted to tell you and then I didn't know how to tell you."

His grip tightens as if conveying the desire to confess all these months and didn't.

"And now?" I mumble against his soft sweater, my tears soaking the luxurious cashmere.

"Now I deeply regret not telling you." I hear it in his voice, the rise and fall of his chest, the suffocating hug he has me in, and his head resting against mine. "I can't apologize enough."

His betrayal burns in my chest so much that it steals my breath away. The sudden closeness of him on me with his quiet apologies and much loved cologne filling my senses is killing me slowly. I want to hate him. I want to rage and scorch the Earth like I always do, but I can't. This isn't like that.

A betrayal this deep breaks a person. Slicing them right through their soul to where they don't know how to be complete again. Scorched Earth would be so much easier than this. Dealing with the hot fires of revenge brings pleasure. Betrayal brings devastation and despair with no desire to live.

"Why? Why didn't you tell me? If what you're saying is true, why not tell me?"

My hands flitter to his ribcage, the muscles encasing his wide expanse flexing in response when I push against him. He's reluctant to let me go, but when I lift my head, his arms loosen in response. Pink rings his lower lids and tears of his own are on his cheeks. Sadness mars his handsome face before his eyes gaze into mine.

"I'm past the point of no return."

The corners of his lips pull into a deep frown when he says it. I pull out of his arms entirely, taking in a shaky breath and setting my purse down on the table.

"I don't know what that means," I admit.

He sighs, following me to the couch as I drop to the edge.

My head collapses into my hands while my elbows rest on my knees. He squats, his hands holding my forearms beckoning for me to look at him and pulling my hands away when I don't.

"It means I didn't want this to happen. I know I should've told you and I'll always regret that I didn't, but I couldn't. At some point, I had way more to lose telling you than I had to gain."

He inches closer, planting his hands on either side of my lap. Two lonely tears slide down his cheek at different rates, meeting at the bottom of his face as those beautiful brown irises eclipse with sorrow.

Anguish coats his words and with the way his lips press together, I feel it too. I search every part of his face, needing to know more as if that will somehow make-up for what he did.

"Would you have ever told me?" I muster up the courage to ask, clasping my hands together. My lip trembles, my throat burns, and my breath is shallow. The gaiety of the events outside float inward to the tragedy unfolding before us, and I'm barely hanging on.

"And risk losing you?"

"Yes."

His large hands cover mine and he looks down at them for a second before looking back up and saying, "No."

My gaze lifts from his to the ceiling, sending tears across my temples and into my hair as a ragged sigh escapes my clenched lungs. I feel buried alive. Buried under the truth I don't want to hear, the deception I don't want to feel, and the weight of his presence looming over me.

"I made a mistake, baby. I promise I'll keep nothing from you again. And I hope that one day you'll be able to forgive me. Just as you forgave me that night I acted like an idiot and asked you to leave."

His hands never leave mine. His thumb strokes my knuckles

as he moves to sit beside me on the couch. I bite my lip, trying to get ahold of myself and see him in a new light.

"Your lie changed everything. Upturned my whole life. I had to start over. I lost my home and most of Dad's stuff because of you. Because of your selfishness."

My default anger, buried amidst the rubble of heartbreak and disappointment is pushing through. It's forcing itself forward with every word I say until I'm standing and pacing the floor.

"You caused all of this. Was it an ego thing? Some twisted game where you win, and I lose. You said it yourself. You hate losing. Was I beating you? Did you have to take me down like I'm your opponent, by lying and cheating to get your way? I know I brought out the worst in you and hell, you brought out the worst in me. But never, and I mean never in a million years would I drive up to your training camp in Denver and lie to your boss to win."

My brain is flying down revelation road faster than my mouth can keep up and my piercing clacks against my teeth.

Tomlin slowly rises to his feet, his shoulders slumping as his hands stuff into his pockets. I know he hates being scolded. His entire demeanor says it, but this is so much different from knowing he did wrong. This is an intentional betrayal at someone else's gain and heartbreak. Mine.

"Dani, it wasn't like that at all. It was—"

I stop right in front of him, stretching my spine a little taller, knowing that I hit on something here.

"It wasn't?" I eye him for a split second before I start again. "Where does it end, Tomlin? When does one lie become another and then another to the point, until you're lying to me all the time out of convenience or winning or whatever sick reason you justify in your head? Where's the line between lying and being a liar? And to think, I believed you. Good 'ole gullible Dani and her po-dunk ways. She's too young and dumb. She'll believe anything I say because I'm all worldly and cultured. Is that it? Is that what you thought of me? Just some dumb girl that doesn't even have her GED. Yeah, I can pull a fast one on her. Hell, you're probably doing it right now. Probably have other lies that will pop up down the road."

My voice shakes from my whole body igniting with so much rage, I clench and unclench my hands. I'd never punch him, but the restraint I'm showing is extremely hard when all I want to do is pummel the hell out of him right now.

"I've never thought those things about you. I never would."

"You called me juvenile and immature on more than one occasion. Not to mention all that shit insults you threw at me in the beginning."

His eyes cast down, his expression falling with it because he knows I'm spilling some hurtful truths of my own.

"The thing is, I'd never lie to you, and I could have countless times. I could've let him finish your car with crap parts or I could've walked away entirely when you burned my life down, but I supported you and this dream of yours to be here. Well, congrat-u-fucking-lations because here you are with a beautifully restored car out there on that lawn. How does that make you feel? You got your way. All the way around, Tomlin. Look who keeps winning and look who keeps losing. I guess your record of only two losses, if you consider silver medals losses, still stands. You won again."

I lick my lips, and my head pounds in my skull as my heart pounds in my chest. He looks a wreck. His guilt eats him up as my words pour mounds of salt into those wounds. Moving around him to grab my purse, he tries to touch me, and I recoil.

"Don't you dare," I threaten giving him the same dagger look I was doing with Lars earlier today.

He retracts his hand immediately, running it through his hair as leans toward me.

"Dani, please don't. I want to talk this out."

"I'm done talking, and I'm not staying to listen to anything you say. Who knows if it will be the truth or another lie?"

It's a low blow. One he deserves after lying to me every damn day in a row and breaking my heart while doing it. I look around the room for my suitcase and when I don't see it, I stomp into the bedroom with him hot on my heels.

"Please stay, Dani. Don't do this. Please stay and talk this out. You promised no more running away." His voice teeters on the edge of frustration, and I whirl around to glare at him.

"The irony of that coming from you. The breaker of all promises."

I shove my hair out of my hot face. I'm sweating in my sweater and need to get out of here. Need to get away from him and figure out what the hell I'm going to do now.

A defeated noise, almost a groan, comes out as his hand rises and then falls in defeat, as if giving up.

"I'll go."

He doesn't wait for me to respond when he crosses the room, picks up his wallet and phone from the nightstand, and grabs the handle of his suitcase. For too many long seconds, we simply stare at each other, and I shake my head. This doesn't feel like he's winning either.

Something ripples across his face that I can't make out before he walks to stand directly in front of me.

"Say this isn't the end, Dani. Tell me we are not over." His voice cracks, the pink around his eyes redden and his chest rises and falls. He's right for asking. It feels like we are over, and we should be over. Where is the line when you're a liar? I learned there's none. Liars beget lying. It's who and what they are.

I mash my lips together, my eyes sting with more tears and I shake my head. I can't say that. It feels like the end because it is, and I sob into my hands. His arm is around my shoulders, pulling me into his chest where I press my forehead against the soft fabric while he kisses my head.

"Then I'll say it."

He holds me tighter, his tears collecting in my hair and dampening my scalp.

"We're not over, Dani. I know I fucked up and I'll make it up to you. If you believe anything at all, please believe that."

32

Another sob catches in my throat as I lift my head off his chest and shrug out of his hands, needing him not to look at me that way and not to hold me that way. I may be a relationship virgin, but even I know that some things can't be overcome, and this is one of them.

"I think you should go," I mutter, looking down at his hand tightening over the suitcase handle.

Those sad chocolate eyes hold mine before nodding and reluctantly leaving the bedroom. I don't follow him. There's no need to. Maybe he'll come back, wanna talk this out some more, but I know it won't be tonight. His manners and respect for privacy will assure me of the time and space alone to figure some things out.

I wait for the soft click of the hotel door before sinking to the edge of the bed. Numbness drains the energy in my limbs and grief clouds my mind to the point that I crawl to the pillows and collapse against them, crying like I did so many nights after I lost Dad. Weeping turns into wailing, my heart completely shattering as losing what we had.

I was a fool to have fallen so easily for him. Somewhere in

all the bickering and bantering, I had found a guy that would go toe-to-toe with me, wouldn't back down, wouldn't avoid me, and would stand his ground to argue it out if that's what it took. The constant push and pull, battling and yielding control, became both emotional and physical aphrodisiacs.

His commanding demeanor, quiet confidence, and elitist arrogance snared me into his trap. Never did I think he'd add liar to those traits in order to beat me. I never thought myself a worthy adversary, rather we're equals, but somehow in the battle and journey that was us becoming us, I turned out to be the one operating with more integrity.

Who would've thought that?

I keep on blubbering into the crisp cotton pillow until my lungs seize, my eyeballs swell, and my nose stings. My brain keeps going in a constant loop, piecing together everyone's story and trying to understand their motivation and actions.

In going through it all, I hope there's something I don't know or something I haven't considered, or just something to change reality, to change my mind, to change his betrayal, or to change us being over. It's exhaustive but there are no new conclusions or revelations, just an endless void of me in my sadness worrying about the future.

No Tomlin, no garage of my own, no Lars and I are working together, no place to live and no place to work. It's overwhelming. I had these exact thoughts before. Having come full circle as I roll to my back and stare at the ceiling. I worried about placing all my eggs in one basket, debated this exact thing two months ago when I took his project and I'm back here again, having lost it all. It's devastating.

The brutal reality of what has happened and where I'm at now slows my tears into a stupor. I honestly don't know what I'm going to do. Granted, I have most of the money left after getting that killer paint job for the El Camino and splurging on some stuff for this trip. Beyond that, I could float myself for a few months if I move into a cheap apartment and start looking for regular mechanic work.

What does that do for Lars? Thinking about him, his mom and his sisters hardens my stomach into a rock. He was terrified today that I'd ruin it for him out on the golf course. Little does he know Tomlin ruined it for us all. How do I tell him that? How do I tell him that he goes to the end of the unemployment line with me?

I chew my lip, mulling over ways to get us both out of this situation. Paul might still want me, especially after doing Tomlin's job and Mr. Hernandez's Buick. After all, Lars is right in that I did work on two cars that are at this show.

Even though I didn't get any pictures of the Buick, and the sign with Carl's name on it, maybe Lars did, and I could send those to Paul when I contact them. None of that, though, helps Lars and his family and that's what makes me feel worst of all.

My phone rings, cutting through the silence that surrounds me. When I dig the phone out of my purse, I'm relieved that it isn't Tomlin but Eli. Even though my life is falling apart, his and Isla's are coming together, and I can't avoid his call because of that reason.

"Hey Eli," I say, trying to lighten my voice so he can't tell I've been crying.

"Wrong, it's me." Isla's soft voice shrills through the phone to the point I hold it away from my ear. "Guess where I'm at?"

A small smile tugs at my sad face. I'd never tell her that Eli sent me that beautiful picture of them together. I don't want to burst her bubble and ruin her surprise.

"I assume at that facility?" I say flatly, playing into what I know she wants to tell me herself.

"Noo. Ugh, didn't Dad tell you what happened?" She groans and then giggles, sounding younger than her age and certainly younger than her life experiences.

Dad.

Eli is probably hyperventilating with happiness being called that.

"Of course he did, and I'm so sorry that happened to you, Isla. You know, if I was there, I'd burst into that place and start kicking asses. I swear I teenage girls are the meanest bitches ever."

My piercing clacks against my teeth and the struggle to stop cursing has been real but significantly reduced except for infractions against people I love.

"I thought you were going to stop cussing. Don't you see that this was the best thing that could've happened?" She doesn't even let me respond before rattling on.

"I got out of that place. I got out of there and now I get to live with my new dads. Oh my god, Anna is so feisty now, you wouldn't even recognize her. I almost don't. She runs this place and her cute purple feathered sweater. It's everything."

I love everything about this moment. I love the hope in her voice, the happiness in her words, and the forgiveness in her heart for those wretched girls. Here I am crying over what happened with Tomlin, and it is absolutely nothing compared to what this girl has gone through and her outlook.

She's grateful for a broken arm to move her life forward. Maybe my broken heart is supposed to move me forward in a way I absolutely can't comprehend.

"Are you still there?"

"I am. I was thinking how happy I am for you and little Anna."

And how I'm learning life lessons from you. I don't say that even if it's true.

She sighs, long and happy as if getting her dream life. This probably is. A safe home with loving parents and a chance at a normal life.

"Dani, I don't know how to ever thank you. If you hadn't seen me that day with Rick . . ." Her voice trails off and I jump in, not waiting for anything to take away from her happiness.

I know her *Dads* will protect her at all costs, but so will Hamilton and me. She got more of a family than she ever had before.

"Don't ever tell me thank you. You didn't deserve all that, and it's not your fault. And don't even give me that bullshit about running away and bringing it on yourself, because we've talked about that too. I want you to learn that not all men are motherfuckers. Take your two dads, for example. They would never do those things in a million years and, like me, they only want the best for you. And Hamilton, don't forget that dude, because he'll always be in your corner."

Her sniffles fill the phone as I wait for her to speak.

"You're like my big sister."

My hand clutches my chest, stealing the air from it when I hear her words.

Sister.

The word ricochets through my brain as I stare at the phone. As an only child, I never even considered the possibility of being someone's sister. Kylie came the closest as my best friend, and now that's in jeopardy. But being Isla's sister, and feeling as strongly as I do for her, even after a few months, leaves me speechless.

I'm terrible with labels and even worse about voicing my own emotions. Hell, I used the word emotions instead of describing which ones they are. And then this kid, younger than me, has lived more life than I ever have, is so in tune with her feelings and emotions that she can name them and easily attach them to people around her. I'm in awe.

"You don't have to say it back. But I want you to know that I love you."

A one, two sucker punch to the gut is what she does.

Sister and she loves me.

I mashed my lips together before concluding that I can label what I feel for this sweet kid, even if I really hadn't known it until now.

"I love you too, Isla and that little dog too," I choke, the lump in my throat and the tears running down my face, making it hard to speak.

The dogs bark in the background, making a bunch of ruckus, and the phone rustles a bit. She says something so quickly that I don't catch and when I ask her to repeat it, her voice comes through loud over all that background noise.

"Hurry back so you can sign my cast."

She must have passed the phone to Eli and all the commotion because I recognize his choked up voice anywhere. I hear him clearing his throat and I use the time to wipe my face on my sweatshirt and dry my eyes.

"Oh sweetie, did you hear her?" Eli's voice is thick. The barking fades, the door slams, and then it's quiet.

"I did."

I move to my side, put the phone on speaker, and lay it on the pillow next to me.

"And she calls me Dad, well, both of us Dad. It's confusing, but I love it." He chuckles, the happiness in his voice is unmistakable.

"Well, have to figure something out because she called Dad, and we both came running into her room. And her room . . . oh my god, it's the prettiest shade of pink that she picked out and she asked me to decorate it. Maybe it's not matching Halloween costumes, but this is so much better. Do you know she loves fashion? And you know how much I love it, too."

I didn't, but hearing the excitement spilling out of him is temporarily chasing away my sorrows.

"Get this. She has dreams of going to fashion school in New York. Can you imagine? I could be the parent of a famous fashion designer. What if she was so good that she had her own shows? Oh, and Anna Wintour came. Well, I could just die. Me sitting next to the queen, watching my daughter's designs on the runway and her coming out at the end. It's . . ." He chokes up again.

I'd probably die too if I sat next to a queen. I've never heard of this one, so no telling what country she's the monarch of. It's great to hear that Isla has big dreams and Eli is already dying over them.

"That's really sweet, Eli. I honestly am amazed at you. How you can love so openly and freely? It's . . ." Something I could never do.

I sigh, not begrudging him of his newfound love and family, but in the fleeting moment, I thought I had it too, and it makes me swallow another sob.

"What's the alternative? Sure, I've had my heart broken and boy, have I been through a doozy of them to find my Ronald and now my Isla. But you can't not want to fall in love again, it's the best feeling in the world," he says all airy and dreamy, causing me to lean into the phone as if I could borrow some of the euphoria he feels right now. "Wait a minute. Did something happen? Did you separate it as we talked about? I feel like something happened and you're not telling me."

Either Eli is super intuitive, or I have the worst poker voice in the world.

"Nothing. This call is about you and Isla. I'm so happy that she called and even happier that she's home. Does Hamilton know?"

I intentionally change my tone to throw him off my trail. Like I said, this call isn't about me and I'm not about to be selfish enough to spill my guts to him when he's the happiest I've ever heard.

"Way to deflect. I'll allow it for now, but we're coming back to it," he says with an edge that lets me know he's not messing around.

That's one thing I can guarantee about Eli, is that he doesn't let things go. He's definitely one to clear the air and make sure everyone is fine. Probably the best communicator I know and certainly one whom I can learn from.

"Alexander knows. He was the one that called us and met us at the hospital. I don't know what I'd do without him. I know you give him one heck of a hard time, but he really is an outstanding officer and a good guy."

Hearing him refer to Hamilton by his first name still catches me off guard, something I have to get used to. That's another thing Eli's right about. I tend to keep Hamilton at an arm's distance, especially when he asked me about California. I didn't think we were like that, but hearing this from Eli lets me know that's another relationship I need to work on.

"Yeah, well. Maybe I'll take the guy to lunch and back off his ass. It's that I get frustrated at how slow this process is and when he uses his patronizing voice on me, it pisses me off. I also feel like he's not doing enough for her."

I prop myself up, my elbow digging into the mattress as I grab the phone from the pillow and move it closer.

"Sweetie, I assure you that he's done everything possible and then some. And I've heard the way you talk to him at times. I appreciate the place in your heart where all that energy comes from, but he might not be so understanding," Eli warns, which has me scratching my head.

"Why? Has he said something to you? He's a police officer. He sees the worst side of humanity and deals with thugs and criminals all the time. Surely what I say can't hurt his feelings or bother him in any way." I hear what Eli is trying to say, but dang, he's going to have to break this one down further. "There's no way I'm hurting Hamilton's feelings by being so direct and upfront with him. If anything, he should appreciate it."

Eli makes a tiny groan. "All I'm saying is you could be a little nicer and not so direct. Softer thoughts equal softer words."

I'm not about to tell Eli that's the dumbest thing I've ever heard.

"Did you get that out of a parenting book?" I blurt out because that sounds like some of the hippie dippy stuff Tomlin says, and my chest burns when I think of him.

"Yes, and don't judge. I love it. I'm using it more and more and it works."

I honestly don't know how Eli can have any softer thoughts. He's already the most understanding, accepting, and loving guy I've ever met. He has to be taking care of all those animals at home and the pet store.

"Not judging, thinking."

"Now that you know my world is basically perfect and you'll be nicer to Hamilton, tell me what's going on with you. Everything from when we last spoke. And I have plenty of time because they are inside making homemade dog treats in the kitchen."

That makes me smile. Of course, they are making homemade dog treats. It's so wholesome and sweet. It's exactly the kind of calm life Isla deserves.

I let out a long breath before bringing him up to speed, all the way to how Tomlin held me before he left, except for the sex because that's private. By the time I finish, I'm a blubbering mess again and going into the bathroom to blow my nose before returning to bed.

The dust sky is pink and purple dipping into the blue ocean beyond the fairway and there couldn't be a more beautiful view. Picture worthy if I weren't bawling my eyes out.

"Oh sweetie, I'm so sorry. I don't know what to say," he says while I pluck at the comforter.

"There's nothing to say. He lied all this time. Every damn

day to my face. Who does that?" My voice sharpens. "And to tell me he never would've told me? Damn."

"Yes, none of that is good. He certainly should've told you. And you have every reason to be upset."

I love that he's agreeing with me, not patronizing, or judging, just being his usual supportive self. Maybe this is what he means by softer words.

"I-I just . . ." I exhale my gut cramping from all the emotional pain.

My mind is a closed loop again, thinking, analyzing, and contemplating everything before I ended it with him. Or tried to, even though he said it wasn't the end. And dammit if I didn't love that he said that.

"Breathe, sweetie. I know it's a lot to take in. My gosh, you literally just landed and all this. Here I thought you'd be having a grand old time standing by your car and showing it off to whoever passed by."

"That couldn't be further from the truth."

I'm actually locked away in my room, hiding from Tomlin and the show's festivities.

"What are you going to do?" he murmurs, and I scratch my head. That is one question that races around the closed loop of my thoughts.

I exhale the longest sigh of my life, catching the tears on my sleeve before they trail down my cheeks.

"I was a fool to rely on him as much as I have. Look where it got me, worse than Carl's—"

His response is quick. "You're not a fool. We do things out of love. We move in with people, we open our hearts to them, and we give up parts of our independence to be in a relationship. It's how it goes. You can't be in love without being vulnerable."

"Yeah, well."

I worried this would end in disaster. But what I didn't expect is how it would end. I assumed it would be the differences in our two worlds, or that one of the cans that we kicked down the road couldn't be resolved. Yet, we didn't even get to those problems.

"Can I ask you something?"

I'm almost certain he'll say yes, but this probes a little deeper than he may like. His answer may help me deal with what I'm feeling.

"Of course, sweetie, you can ask me anything."

Naturally, he would say that because he's an open book.

"Have you ever been betrayed? By someone you love?"

Like all the other decisions I didn't want to make with Tomlin seems so silly and frivolous compared to the ending of us.

"Of course, I have. I'd like to think that people don't intentionally set out to betray me, but it happens more often than I'd like. Well, it happened with Ronald. When we first moved in together, he would disappear in the middle of the night after we had gone to bed. I'd wake up to go to the bathroom, and he'd flat be gone. It was bewildering and very very hurtful. On top of that, he would lie about it, which was so surprising because I was literally right next to him in bed. There's no way to hide it. He'd deny it and gaslight me to the point where I thought I was crazy and went to see a therapist who recommended couples therapy. After working through his triggers, we're so much better now. And it's been years."

"Wow, why was he doing it?"

I play with my piercing, wondering if I could look past this and be years down the road with Tomlin talking about it as casually as Eli is now.

"Well, some of that I won't get into, but long story short, he wasn't ready to share a bed with another person. Things happened prior from his childhood that was triggering," he practically whispers, and I shake my head, reading between the lines.

It's sickening how common this all is. Too damn common and it breaks my heart for all these children, hurting at the hands of their abusers.

"I guess what I'm trying to impart to you, Dani, is what if I gave up and walked away? I wouldn't have this. And . . ." He stops. "Give me a minute."

I give him several minutes as his panicking thoughts call to mine and I'm tearing up too. The thought of not feeling this again, not having Tomlin hold me and love me, is ripping my heart in two.

"Are you in love with him?" he finally says.

"Yes."

It comes out as a tiny whisper, almost lighter than Isla's voice.

"Can you forgive him?"

His questions get shorter and harder.

"Forgive him? I don't think I've ever forgiven anyone in my life. I'm sure I forgave my father for something, but nothing big like this. How would I start now? How do I even do it?"

I shake my head, my gaze trailing back out to the ocean beyond the window, trying to figure out how forgiveness even works. I'm a scorch the Earth kind of gal.

Forgiveness doesn't enter my brain. I'm sure there are some super forgiving people in this world. I'm not one of them. Forgiveness is a foreign language. It's not something I do. Not something I've ever considered doing. And that's what it would take. That's what it would take for me and Tomlin to stay together.

"It's something you and him would have to figure out. What do you need from him to feel secure in moving forward with him? You asked earlier where is the line between being a liar and lying. When do they ever stop? But what about the reverse? What constitutes a liar in the first place? Does one lie make you a liar? Or is it the size of the lie? Or is it how big the emotion is?

Betrayal in your case, does that make the lie unforgivable? Where is the line, Dani? Have you never lied to someone you loved out of fear that telling them the truth will hurt them? Maybe one small lie will prevent them from a lifetime of hurt?"

Eli is asking too many questions I simply can't answer. The more he asks, the more confused I get and the longer I search the horizon for answers that don't immediately come to my mind.

"Haven't you been lying to your best friend? You said earlier that you hadn't told her, and didn't know the right way to tell her until those pictures came out, forcing you to tell her the truth. So, is that lie acceptable because you were protecting her from the pain? Did you lie to avoid this whole situation blowing up in your face, how Tomlin's lie is blowing up in his face? Did you intentionally not tell her the truth because you didn't want to lose her friendship? The same as Tomlin doesn't want to lose you."

Well, damn. I never thought about it like that.

"Sweetie, trust me when I say I'm on your side in all this. He should not have done it, but he also doesn't want to lose you, and he's fighting for you. It's not as clear-cut as you're making it. I know you love your right and wrong, your black and white, and your yes and no, but relationships are complicated and messy, and they take compromise. If you're so quick to shut him down and not consider his side and why he did it, you might not be ready for a relationship. Again, I'm not condoning what he did, but after what I've been through, I understand people need a bit more grace and mercy than we normally give."

My mind is a scattered mess. I was able to keep up with him sort of and trying to figure out the line and the size of the lie, but then when he compared my lie to Kylie similarly to Tomlin's lied to me, it messed it all up. He shook up all my thoughts and sent them flying around my head and they have yet to settle in any kind of pattern.

"And I'll leave you with this last piece because you know I love you. But you need to think long and hard about what you want out of your life. Not Denver or Cañon City or his garage or working for someone else. Put all that aside and think about what you really want from this man. If you decide to stay with him, you can't resent him, and you must forgive him to move forward. But forgiveness doesn't happen overnight, and it doesn't happen in a matter of weeks. It takes as long as it takes until you realize the forgiveness has already happened and you're living your best life. Once you decide what you want from Tomlin, you can figure out where you want to go with Kylie. But for now, put that one on the back burner and figure out you first. And maybe one day you'll get to be like my Ronald and me and laugh about it. Again, I'm not telling you what to do. I'll support you whatever you decide. I want all my girls to be happy and living their dream, whatever it is, and with whomever it is."

I'm full on sobbing right now. The tears stream so fast down my face, that they drip onto the comforter. My head throbs from crying so much.

My eyes are so puffy and painful, and my stomach hurts so badly that I want to vomit. But the beautiful discovery I've made from this phone call is not only do I have a little sister, but I have a big brother.

I may have lost my first family over three years ago, but now I have a new family and it makes me cry even harder.

33

I hurry off the phone, making excuses that Eli knows are just that to finish bawling my eyes out in private. This day has been emotionally draining and taking its toll. I haven't cried this much since Dad died.

I don't know if it's the phoenix rising from the ashes or turning over a new leaf or wanting to soar like an eagle, but all those analogies are all for shit right now. What I need is clarity through the fog rolling through my mind. I want to escape what I'm feeling in my head and in my heart.

Desperately needing to blow my nose, I crawl off the bed and walk into the bathroom. I look a mess when I glimpse myself in the mirror. Mascara streaks down my cheeks, my eyes are red as hell and my skin is blotchy and pale. The tissues pop out of a container in the corner of the counter, and I pull several to clean my face. Not that I truly care how I look because my heart is broken and my life is over.

Forgiveness.

Sure, I've heard others yammer on about it. Kylie said it when I blamed my mom for Dad's death. But I have never forgiven anyone, and that list is so long, I wouldn't even know where to begin.

How do you forgive when that means they've won? Doesn't Eli know that forgiveness is giving up and giving in to my enemy?

Not that Tomlin is my enemy, far from it. He's my first love and something everyone says is special. I'm not sure if special is the right word. It seems too weightless as to how I really feel about him. I didn't mean for all this to happen and now here I am, wanting to slide down this wall, collapse onto the floor and never get back up. Is that what first love feels like when it's over?

Is it meant to turn me into a lifeless lump that doesn't want to do anything or think anything beyond what I now know to be the truth? How am I supposed to get past this? How am I supposed to move on?

Thinking of life without him makes me want to curl up and die. Which is so not like me. I could've given up a thousand times before this. I had every reason to and never did. Now, all bets are off when Tomlin walked out that door.

Sheer muscle memory gets me through my shower and bedtime routine. As I crawl under the sheets, my phone chimes with a text message.

Hey, everything okay? Didn't want to bother you but let me know you're all right.

Damn. I bailed on Lars. I know he doesn't need a babysitter here. But I should've attended the forums with him.

I'm sorry for bailing on you. A lot of shit happened.

The three little dots circle as I click off the bedside light.

Oh no! Is everything okay?

Guilt surges through me. I can't tell him yet. I don't want to ruin his only vacation. I don't want him to worry until I have a clear plan for us. With my mind a jumbled, foggy mess, I can't tell him that the garage isn't happening.

I ran into Carl.

My fingertips hover over the keyboard, typing and deleting various sentences, when I finally hit the send button. I don't know what else to say that won't lead back to Tomlin and me breaking up.

Tell me you didn't attack him and you're sitting in jail. Is that why you missed today's forums?

I sigh. I got to do better by Lars. Even if my life is crumbling apart, he deserves better than this.

I didn't. I did accidentally bump into him and when he turned around, I realized it was him. Could've knocked me over with a feather. And I'm sorry I missed the forums.

Okay, that's at least the truth without getting into all the rest.

No worries. You missed a cool one about trends and developments in the classic car market and the direction it's going. I can tell you all about it over a late breakfast tomorrow.

As much as I want to hide out in this room figuring out my life. I owe it to him to go.

Sounds good.

Okay. I'm catching a beer with these guys I met. One's a collector. Let's hope I can get us another project!

That exclamation point is a knife to my heart, slaying me with his excitement to continue what we started. I sigh in the dark, searching for words that don't come.

Have fun. I'll text ya in the morning.

Will do.

I leave him on read. A glimmer of relief slides through my despair that Lars's enjoying himself tonight. When the chips fall tomorrow, it will be another story entirely. Guilt cuts my relief short. Pulling the covers over my head, I slide down the mattress, the blue light from the phone shining in my face. I text Hamilton.

Hey Hamilton, I heard the good news and wanted to say thanks.

I keep it brief, even though Eli's words flutter through my mind about being nicer. Surprisingly, the three dots circle, which must mean he's not working right now.

Just doing my job.

That doesn't sit right. He's done more than his job. Eli said as much when he bragged about him being a great officer and a good person.

Bruh, it's okay to admit you went above and beyond with her. Take the credit.

My fingers are flying across the screen and hitting send

before I remember softer thoughts equal softer words. I try again.

I know I give you a hard time all the time and I'm sorry. I appreciate what you do for her.

He sends a question mark around my last sentence, and I wait for his grandma texting skills to catch up. I watch the time on my phone and when a full minute passes, his response finally appears.

Who is this and what have you done to Dani? 😂

He did not seriously send a laughing emoji. How old is this dude?

I'm trying to be nicer to you, but you're ruining it.

Probably shouldn't have texted that but meh. I'm not unsending. He's faster to respond this time, which I prefer.

Nicer? Why?

Bruh, if I have to explain being nicer to you, then maybe I'm not going to be. Damn, can't a girl show you a little appreciation now and then?

A girl can and she does. 😉 Don't go being nice now. It's too late. I have you saved in my phone as Dani the Demon.

I almost and I mean almost send him the vomit emoji because I certainly don't want to know about Hamilton's sex life. I assume he's getting some looking like that and all, but I don't need confirmation.

Before I can respond, he sends me a screenshot of my name in his contacts, and sure enough, he has it saved that exact way. It makes me smile that he thinks I'm that tough. I'm about to reply when the banner drops from the top of my screen with the message from Tomlin.

My pulse spikes. Before I read it, I want to end my text exchange with Hamilton.

> Hilarious. I'm going to hit the hay. Early day tomorrow. Stay safe.

I don't bother waiting for him to respond. It could be another several minutes or several hours, depending on what he's doing.

Nervousness floods my stomach when I tap on Tomlin's message.

> I've written this so many times and the words aren't flowing the way I'd prefer. But if I were there, and you're willing to listen, I'd tell you that I'm immensely sorry. You had said my words don't mean anything and perhaps they don't, but I'd give anything to have those baby blue eyes flash at me in anger, have your finger pointed in my face, and thank every profanity you throw at me. I never meant to hurt you and even saying it now doesn't do justice to how regretful I am for what I did to you.

I throw back the covers, the cool air conditioning refreshing against my hot skin while my pulse continues to throb. For not knowing what to say, he has a good start.

I read it repeatedly until tears slide down my temples into my hair and I lock the phone to place it on my chest and think.

Regretful.

A fancy word for sorry. He said that before and apologizes again. I believe both things. What I can't figure out is why. His statement of being too far gone or whatever he said doesn't make sense.

His words didn't flow very well then when he tried to explain that to me, and maybe I should've let him stick around to explain it. But the betrayal is overwhelming, cutting so fresh and new into me that he had to go. I needed time alone with my thoughts, away from anything that he could say to justify his actions.

Damn, this day and the dominos falling one after another. Judd, Carl, Kylie, and Tomlin happening in a row. My world is collapsing in every way all at once. Tomlin doesn't know that. I didn't even have a chance to tell him about Judd or the Buick being here or ask why our names are on the sign.

My phone pings and when I pick it up to look at the screen, his message is brief.

I miss you.

More tears and that familiar sting settles into the back of my throat. I unlock my phone, hoping he sends more. How can it hurt me to my core, while I still yearn to talk to him? It doesn't make sense. Yet, I can't help it. In a way, I wish he could hold me against his chest and say nothing at all.

I want to close my eyes, turn off my damn brain and just breathe him in. Lay with our legs intertwined, my body cradled against his and his lips kissing the crown of my head as we drift into a peaceful slumber where problems, lies, and betrayal don't exist. Like the hopeless fool, I am, I text back.

I miss you too.

His response is swift, and it makes me feel a smidge better. Some small part of me wants to work this out. No, now I'm lying to myself. A bigger than I want to acknowledge part of me wants to erase all this crap, go back to not knowing, and live in our cocoon where nothing bad happens.

Christ. I wasn't sure if you would respond or even want to talk to me.

I reread those lines, biting my lip and at a loss for words. Like him, I say what I know.

I don't know what to say.

You don't have to say anything. I'm immensely relieved that you are letting me text you.

I release my lip. Anticipation of what he'll text next hangs in the dark room.

I shouldn't have lied to you. I knew it then and I know it now and every second in between.

I wipe the tears from my temples, take in a deep breath and slowly let it out.

Then why did you do it? I'm still not clear.

A second passes, then another, and another until too many pass that the nervousness converts to dread. Dread that he won't tell me anything more than he did tonight. That I'll never know the whole truth and probably my biggest fear is that I'll have to walk away.

Will you meet me tomorrow? Of course, you don't have to and if you don't want to, I understand, but I really want to explain everything in person and not over text. I owe you that much.

I move my phone away from my face to gaze at the cloudless sky blanketed with stars outside my window. Its beauty is lost on me with my world turned upside down.

He does owe me that. But do I want to see him? I still haven't figured out what to do with everything I discovered today. Will more answers help or harm? Answers only he can provide. I don't know what to think or what to do. Eli's words come back to me. What do I want?

My phone pings again and I turn the phone over to read it.

> I don't want to pressure you, Dani. That's the last thing I want. But if you are willing, I'll be on the fairway at our car at 7 am. Dress warmly, it will be chilly. If you don't want to come, I understand.

Our car.

He said it before, and I didn't agree. He's saying it now and I don't know what to think. He put our names on it, right by his. Even though he didn't have to and knowing him, he probably insisted to the organizers.

Our three names sit on that small white card, meaning nothing to the world and everything to me. Tomlin didn't exclude Lars. He gave him credit for his work and just like that we're a team, a company if I want it.

All his actions speak to that kind of integrity except this one piece. This huge lie hangs between us, taking me down a road I don't want to go down. Lies, betrayal, hurt, and pain. Opposite of the future I had hoped to have with him.

I mash my lips together, exhaling slowly. Maybe it's time I put all my cards on the table too. If this could truly be the end of us, then maybe I have a few truths I need to tell him. Give us both my truth before we part. Through watery tears, I text him back.

34

I slept like shit. I read our text exchange countless times. As if staring at his words would somehow let me stare into his mind to understand why he did it. No great revelations, no insights, and no new answers came, just an enormous pressure behind my eyes.

By the time my alarm goes off, it feels as if I've slept for a few minutes. When I drag my ass out of bed and into the bathroom, I look like death. My throat is raw from crying myself to sleep. My eyeballs are bloodshot and tightly compressed behind my swollen eyelids. My skin is pale, with dark circles hanging under my eyes. Even those baby blues he commented about last night are vacant and lifeless.

It takes all the strength I can muster to get ready, even though I desperately want to see him. The longer the night wore on, the more I wavered to staying, figuring out forgiveness and a path forward. Then the anger roared forward in a blaze of glory that had me thinking, "Fuck it and fuck him too."

When I locked my phone for the last time last night, I decided to walk away, rebuild the fortress around my heart and throw myself into work. The work of finding Lars and me new jobs. This morning, I don't know what to do.

Fatigue, grief, and sadness are clouding any logic or reasoning. Even my firestorm of anger extinguishes into a deep sadness.

When Dad died, I threw myself into work, long hours in the garage to avoid climbing the steps to that empty apartment and crying myself to sleep. This feels the same as that. The death of my first love. My only love.

My hair is a mess, having gone to bed with it wet, it's beyond saving, and I shove it into those old pigtails I only wear when working. It's not like I need to impress Tomlin. He'll take one look at my corpse and think, what the hell did I ever see in her?

With one last look in the mirror to apply lip gloss, I exit the bathroom and pick up my phone to a text from Tomlin. I'm already here but please don't hurry on my account. I'll wait as long as you need me to.

I couldn't hurry if I wanted to. I'm exhausted. Completely drained of all physical, mental, and emotional energy, and without coffee to pump life into me, I'm walking dead out to that fairway.

What should be a brisk five-minute walk turns into a snail's pace twelve-minute stroll. The anxiety builds with each step I take. What do I want? I still don't know. No, that's not true. I want to erase all this.

It's still not possible, but that's what I want. I want to go back to our last night at the penthouse, where we stayed in bed for countless hours, learning and exploring each other. Where I expressed my love for him physically since I couldn't say it directly.

The morning is crisp, cooler than I imagined, and I hug my arms tighter around my body, thankful I wore another sweatshirt. A gentle breeze tugs at my pigtails, and I run my palms over my hair. The ocean is quiet. Yesterday's roaring waves are replaced with a soft trickle and no seagulls are in sight. The morning sky is the lightest of blue with edges of gold as day breaks.

When the pathway curves, Tomlin's pacing the green with a little bistro table and two chairs nestled by *our car.* Atop the table sits a pitcher with a couple of coffee cups and a basket of pastries. The moment he sees me, his long legs cross the fairway until he's jogging down the path toward me.

When he's a few feet away, his arms open as if to hug me and then they immediately fall to his sides as if remembering where we stand with each other.

"Can I hug you?" he rasps, his voice hoarse and deep. This isn't his usual morning voice. No, this is him crying last night, just as I did, and I frown.

"Yes."

He closes the distance, gently folding me into his thick caramel cable knit sweater that looks great on him and smells divine with his usual cologne. My arms slide around his narrow waist while he holds me suffocatingly close. I tuck my chin, rest my cheek against his chest, and close my eyes. His head drops to mine for several long minutes we just are being.

Heart to heart, head-to-head, intertwined and one. This is what it should be. What I wanted all along. What I had for a few fleeting moments. If I say goodbye, this is what I'll miss. This and a million more memories with him.

I mash my lips together, trying to hold back my sobs until it becomes impossible, and I begin to cry. He doesn't say anything. He holds me, kisses my head, and leans into me. My forehead rests against his large bicep. His sweater absorbs my tears as his chest rises and falls, a sign that he's getting emotional too.

"I'm sorry."

His voice is low and thick. Words that have fallen repeatedly from his lips and probably would a million more times if that's what would fix us.

I clear my throat, sniff in my boogers, and get a hold of myself. When I pull back, he's reluctant to release me but does when our eyes meet. His eyes are bloodshot like mine, with purple rings around them and a permanent line between his eyebrows. He looks as rough as I do.

"Did you sleep at all?" I ask.

His finger ghosts down my pigtail and his lips twitch, but other than that, it's the only response I get.

"I have coffee. I know how much you need it."

He gestures for me to lead the way, but I shake my head. I don't want to lead. I don't want to follow. I want to walk side by side. It takes a second, but he gets it. We walk wordlessly up the path and onto the fairway, where he holds out my chair.

Only after he gets settled and pours the black motor oil into my white cup, do I ask him about the car sign. This is an easy question, allowing me to ease into the harder ones.

"Why did you put our names on the sign?"

It's not the burning question I need to know, but one that lingers from yesterday. He pours himself a cup, sets down the pitcher, and then offers me the pastries basket.

Knowing I should eat since I didn't have anything last night and to be courteous to him, I select a smaller muffin. My stomach is twisted in knots, cramping from heartbreak and not hunger.

"None of this would have been possible without both of you. This has been a dream of mine for several years. Not that we need to get into all of that, but if you and Lars hadn't done the work, it would not be here."

He sets a muffin on his little plate before putting the basket down. His eyes settle on the small cluster of red roses sitting on the edge of the table before poking a finger at one. I've never been a flower person, but these are stunning. This whole setup is lovely, and I briefly wonder how he got it set up on such short notice.

"This doesn't feel like winning, Dani."

Those deep brown eyes meet mine, full of sadness, and I nod. This isn't winning. I said it out of anger, my default emotion to mask my profound hurt. Today, I'm not angry. I'm broken open. Too far gone with him to protect myself. It's a horrible feeling to be this vulnerable.

I take a sip of my coffee. It tastes like nothing in my mouth and even my joy for the stuff is nonexistent in my sadness. He mirrors my actions, surprising me by not mixing a fussy little cup like he normally does.

"Why Tomlin? I keep coming back to that. I can't . . ."

I shake my head, glad I tied my hair back as the wind picks up. I cross my arms around myself, trying to save my body heat from being stolen by the breeze. Tomlin is up and out of his seat in a flash, pulling a thick blanket from the interior of the car to drape over my shoulders. It's in the colors of the Concours, with their emblem on it. I glimpsed it in the window of the gift shop before running into Carl.

"Thank you," I murmur, adjusting the blanket between my back and the chair. He sits, his eyes flickering from mine, down to his coffee as if looking for answers in the black liquid.

"Of course."

I pull the paper off my muffin, giving him the time he needs. Isn't that what Eli said about giving people grace and mercy? Is this included?

"I did not want to lose you. I still don't. You asked yesterday if I would have ever told you and I said no. I've replayed everything you said and my responses as well. And perhaps I could have phrased it better." His eyes lift, searching my face and edging over this little table. "I'd like to explain myself."

I blink away from that painful moment and say, "I think you need to."

"I meant no, but differently. I would not have told you like this. I would have never wanted you to find out this way. I have gone over it a million different ways and I should have told you yes, but I was fearful of this. If I never told you, then I could control that this would never happen. That you would never leave me. I thought if I controlled the narrative, it would be all right and that you'd understand."

Control.

He said he controlled so little in his life. I didn't believe it until I lived this week with him. I understand his need to control. We're alike in that regard. But controlling things in his life and controlling me are vastly different, and I refuse to be controlled by any man, let alone the one I love.

"I knew you'd be mad when I eventually told you that part. I can bank on that, but I never thought it would be the end. Perhaps if we were together longer, you could overlook it." I open my mouth when his hand raises from his coffee cup.

"I'm not asking that now. I understand it is impossible at this point. I want you to know my thought process. At a minimum, you should have heard it from me and not him."

Impossible at this point.

Last night he said we're not over and today he's unsure. He's wavering too and I hate it. I want his resolve and now that it's gone, I'm left wondering what I want again.

Is this the end? Do I want it to be the end? I'm justified if I want to end it. He just said so. The thought of us being over is about to send me into heart palpitations and my knee bobs.

"Yeah, that would've helped," I murmur, keeping my voice light and understanding so he can continue and so keep my heart attack at bay.

"I didn't handle it well yesterday. It flabbergasted me that he was here. I don't quite understand what occurred yesterday, but that's neither here nor there. I should have told you and I didn't, and again I apologize."

His heart bleeds into his words, staring at me so earnestly that I have to blink back my emotions. My bobbing knee catches his watchful eye and I immediately stop to pick at the top of my muffin. I'm making a mess of crumbs, but I need something to do with all the anxiety coursing through my body.

"All that time, T."

An indiscernible nod until his gaze wanders past me and out to the ocean.

"I needed that time, Dani. I needed you to like me."

When they return to mine, they burn through me, and he leans his elbows on the tiny table.

"Like you? What are you talking about? You didn't like me. You left. Hell, you rejected me three times and then ran off for six weeks."

An edge of frustration comes out as I tuck the corner of the blanket against my leg to stop it from flapping in the wind.

"Even in LA, you didn't do anything until you said you gave in or something."

I will myself to remember exactly what he said, but I can't. It was when I was sick, sunburned, and feeling violated by that traitorous boardwalk food.

"Don't you see?" The corner of his lip pulls up into a broken smile. "You hated me. You were so closed off and I was gone for you. I didn't want to be like that guy to you."

Like that guy?

Oh. Zach. He didn't want to be Zach. Damn. The mere thought of him being another Zach is repulsive. More than repulsive because Tomlin is leagues away from being a fuck boy.

"Oh." I lick my lips, trying to catch up to what he's saying. "Why?"

His finger moves slightly between us.

"I wanted this."

The way the wind curls the edge of his hair, the thick roll of his collar against his bobbing Adam's apple, and the desperate look on his face for understanding are something I'll never forget. He's broken and vulnerable like me, and it makes my heart swell.

"Then why leave?"

The more he tells me, the more I don't get.

"Why did you need that time? To train?"

I get that. He told me that straight up. No more hiding out from his recent loss in Tokyo. It's also what his dad accused him of doing. He gives me a full smile. A flash of humor comes and goes in the blink of an eye when it slides from his face.

"I needed time for you to stop hating me for what happened between Kylie and me. To stop hating me every time I came around. The way you looked at me and spoke to me, I knew it would never change if I was always around. You actually said it many times. When I came back from Tokyo, I wanted to try again, but then everything went to shit."

Hearing him cuss is rare and true in this case. My life did go to shit, and he was there every step of the way, helping me pick up the pieces.

Only now do I see it. Don't they say hindsight is twenty-twenty? I wish that weren't the case. I wish I knew at the moment when I was in that hindsight, so I made different choices and took different actions.

I take a drink of my coffee, the liquid chilling to a cooler temperature.

"You can say that again."

His finger slides across the table to trace my knuckle when I set my cup down. It doesn't linger, just a quick touch to stay connected.

"I was terrified when you walked into the shop. I wanted to take a page out of your book and beat whoever's ass did that to you. Little did I know my girl already handled it," he says with pride in his voice and a soft smile on his face.

My girl.

I love it, but it stabs my heart because I'm not his girl. One lie changed that.

"Carl never told you what happened?" I know, but I want to hear it again.

"Never. I suspect he knew I would do what I did if he told me outright."

Yeah, I can see where that part was unavoidable now, but back then I certainly didn't.

"When you showed up in the rain that night, I was elated. I thought you picked me."

His smile fades fast, and I know why. I didn't pick him. He was my last choice, and I was angry as hell about that. I was doing his car out of revenge and staying at his place because I had nowhere else to go. That must've been very hurtful for him. I know it would be to me.

Even though I want to hold his hand and stroke his knuckles to show I understand, I don't. There is more to tell, and I don't want to hijack his explanation.

"When I found out that wasn't the case, I lied. I was hurt and egotistical. Christ, Dani. I can't say sorry enough."

He leans back, sending a hand through his hair and down to that neck muscle, but his eyes never leave mine, begging for my forgiveness. Then it dawns on me.

"That's why you asked me about being lonely on the back deck that day."

"I did. I wanted to see if you felt anything at all for me," he confesses, taking a sip of coffee without making a face since it's not how he usually drinks it.

"But how? It was all chance meetings and . . . I rarely saw you."

Now it's my turn to look away, look at the Buick across the

green that consumed me night and day with Tomlin popping into the shop sporadically.

"Man, I worked like a fucking dog to get that car done."

I point at the Buick, innocently parked with the taunting sign at its wheel. Tomlin twists in his chair to look at it, his face awash in astonishment.

"That's yours too?" His eyebrows are sky high until his eyes narrow to read the sign.

"Yeah, well. Carl's name is on it."

He turns around and gazes at me in wonder.

"You got two cars into this show."

Then that beautiful smile slowly spreads across his face as if truly happy for me, whereas none of it matters. I'm still needing to know the rest of his story to figure this all out.

"Yeah. That's the car that you accuse me of getting all poetic about."

I tuck my hand underneath the blanket to block the chill slowly seeping into my sweater.

"The guy hugged you and you hated it." His smile grows wider. "You should be proud of yourself, Dani. No one gets two cars into this show. Or at least, not two restorations back-to-back."

His eyes flicker to his mom's car, a glimmer of pride in them before they return to stare at me.

"Yeah, well." I shrug. Pride is the last thing I feel. None of that matters now. "You left after the back deck."

I nibble at my lip, my teeth catching on the chapped skin and tearing it off. It doesn't matter how many cars of mine are in this show. It only matters what he says. He adjusts his chair, inching closer to mine as if disliking the table dividing us.

"The back deck let me know your guard was higher than ever, impenetrable. The gym confirmed it. If I would've taken you against that wall and Christ, I was so damn close to. You were dripping onto my fingers and fuck, I wanted to," he says with a primal groan, as if was painful for him not to fuck me against the wall when we both want it.

"I knew it would never give us this chance. I couldn't risk it, so I turned you down. You were angry, but that was your norm, so I knew I hadn't ruined my chance. I couldn't sleep that night. I stayed up trying to figure out how to convince you that I wasn't the asshole you accused me of being for months."

Like the sun clearing away the ocean fog, the haze around my circular thoughts is clearing. The more he talks, the clearer the picture is becoming.

"I came up with leaving. I figured if I wasn't there, in your way, as you put it, you would not get angrier or more annoyed with me. It would stop the progression. Then I had to work on regressing it back from there."

I take another drink. The liquid is cold and somewhat gross, but the caffeine helps me process what he is saying. Well, damn. I thought he left because of his dad's brief visit. That and needing to train. I never in a million years thought he wanted to be with me and was giving me time to get used to the idea. Hell, he was firmly my nemesis back then, or in the beginning, before the phone calls started.

"The nightly talks."

His smile is quick, the light firing in his eyes again.

"I could be close without upsetting you. The car was an easy segue into getting to know you more. You slowly opened up, and let me in. This one time you laughed so hard you snorted, and it sent me. I wanted to make you laugh every time. I did miss not being there for my mom's restoration, but you were more important. I had to sacrifice one thing for another. The mom from my past or the girl for my future."

"Don't say that. Your mom is number one. Always will be."

I'm quick to defend because Dad will always be my number one. The fact that he thought this all out blows my mind. Carefully calculated and very Tomlin-like.

"No Dani. It might bother you to hear this, but she's not my number one and I'm fine with that. You are my number one."

His palm opens on the table, an offer for mine, and I stare at it, willing the tears to go back to where they came from while I roll my lips together. I can't look at him, it's too much.

He's breaking down my resolve. Breaking through all the hurt he caused to heal it again. I don't know how he does that. It's the way I love his sincere voice when he uses it. When he moves his hand to cup my shoulder and leans in to kiss the side of my head, I'm a goner.

I love this man with every fiber of my being, and I'm justified in scorching the Earth between us for what he did. Although that's the last thing I want. I'm tired of being right all the time. It's a heavy burden to bear. I want to be loved. His lips leave my head and his hand falls away, giving me the space I need to think.

"I didn't mean to stay away the entire time. I meant what I said in the kitchen that day, that I'd only be away for a few days. I had planned to be back by the weekend. The more we talked, the longer we talked, to the point where some nights you'd fall asleep on me, and I got to hear you snoring from exhaustion. I got scared. I knew with the distance apart and our nightly phone calls you could handle that, but I didn't know if I went back to the cabin if it all goes away. I didn't want to ruin it. I couldn't jeopardize it so soon. Thus, I stayed away, as hard as it was, and it seemed to work."

His eyes squint as if recalling something bad from those long days apart.

"Christ, the weeks were so damn long. I got on that road several times to come back to you. Only to turn back around in fear. Fearful that I hadn't made enough inroads with you. By the time my mom's car was done, I couldn't take it anymore. I had to see you and hoped enough time had passed for the possibility of us getting together to have entered your mind. It is the biggest risk I've ever taken and the most restraint I have ever exercised, but it's been worth it. You are worth it. When you ask me yesterday if I would have ever told you the truth, and I said no, I probably should have told you this instead."

Tears drip down my face, only to be caught by his knuckle and wiped away.

This is what planning gets you.

He said he was a planner that day on the winding road, right before he showed me his mountain resort. I grossly underestimated the amount of planning and forethought he put into approaching me. Giving me the time and space to be alone with my thoughts to decide what I wanted from him.

Not controlling, or manipulative, just him practicing patience, waiting, and hoping that all of it would lead me to like him, eventually. I know I could never reciprocate this in a million years. I'm not patient or practical or a planner. I couldn't take six weeks to hope and wish for a desired outcome. No, I would have taken it by force or walked away.

His explanation takes the sting out of his betrayal to where I'm taking in every little detail of his story and trying to poke holes in it to make sure it stands the truth test.

"That day you came back, you looked at me. I had said your mom's car was a vision of beauty or something like that and you stared at me and agreed."

I remember that day clear as can be. The tires crunching on the gravel, his door being thrown open and him swinging that long body out of the low-slung car. His smile was stunning as he ripped the sunglasses from his face to slowly look me up and down. I need him to explain that look and those words.

"When I left, I said something about being business partners only and not life partners. I think I said that to challenge you because you were so stubborn that day. If I came right out and asked, you wouldn't be open like you are now."

He's not wrong. I had my guard way up, feeling so alone and wanting to rage against humanity.

"The day I came back, you had walked out of the garage wearing those little shorts, your tan legs went on forever and you gave me the most welcoming smile I've ever seen from you. It did something to me. I thought I can easily get used to coming home to this beautiful woman every damn day."

My throat closes around the lump, and my hand slips out of the blanket to reach for his. He's quick to engulf it, the heat from his palm warming my chilled fingers.

"Life partners?" I gasp, the words that plagued me all this time escaping my lips in a plea for them to be true.

He leans in, his lips inches from mine when he says, "If you'll have me."

"But even here in California, when we landed, you seemed closed off and pulled away again. What was that?"

Those chocolate pools look from my lips to my eyes, as if staring into the depths of my soul wanting understanding and acceptance.

"I wasn't sure. We were both upset the night you agreed to come with me. I acted poorly and you let me explain. You stayed and didn't run off that time. It was progress. When you said yes, I wanted to carry you to my room and make love to you right then and there, but I hadn't covered enough ground. I still had more work to do, and I hung back, tried to give you more space, and hope you'd choose me. Even though I knew what I wanted, I wasn't sure if you wanted it too."

"You said it was giving in, but you didn't know what you were feeling."

That night after he got me off for the first time. His actions confused me.

"Always a delicate balance with you, Dani. I push too hard, and you bolt. I'm too lax and you close up."

Both are true. He said that before. I made him a tightrope

walker, and I hated hearing it. I still do. Something I need to change.

"And now?"

My pulse quickens and I can scarcely breathe. It's my choice, I know it. For the man that loves control, has so little of it, and has planned all this time for me to come around in my own way, he's relinquishing control and patiently waiting for me to decide.

"Before I say anything more, I need to tell you something else."

My heart skips a beat. This is what I am most fearful of. Lies coming up down the road and we aren't even on the road yet.

"What?"

I can't hide the dread in my gut, in my words, in my mind.

"In full transparency, last night when I left your room, I did something that you might not like and before you make your decision, I need you to know this upfront. You asked where is the line between lying and being a liar. Well, I lied, but I'm not a liar, nor will I ever lie to you again."

"You slept with someone else, didn't you? I mean, that what's guys do, right? They lie and cheat and—"

I try to yank my hand away, but he doesn't let go. Instead, he digs around in his pocket and puts a set of keys in the palm of my hand.

"I didn't sleep with anyone else. You can ask Lars. I bummed a shower and bed from him last night," he confesses, and wondering where he slept didn't cross my mind until he says it.

"Don't worry, he doesn't know anything. I said my snoring was keeping you awake, and you kicked me out."

He flashes me a cheeky grin, and I partially smile.

"I hope you don't mind that little white lie, as I'd think what happens between us continues to stay between us."

I love he's using the same words from the penthouse that

assured me I could remain vulnerable with him after having sex and not clamming back up.

"You'll have to cover for that at breakfast today if he makes it. He got pretty torn up last night, mumbling something about a new client when I left this morning."

I should care about Lars, and I do, but not now. The weight of these keys is getting heavy with each passing moment, and Tomlin knows I hate surprises. His lie is another example of me continuing to hate them, even if he's giving me some really great surprises on this trip.

"That's great. But what are these?" My hand trembles in his. "You need to tell me what you did, Tomlin. I'm barely hanging on here."

I clack my piercing over and over my teeth and my knee bounces, needing to know what new lie haunts us.

He plants a hand on my knee, stilling it to gaze into my eyes.

"When I left our room last night. I went in search of Carl. Apparently, you had a confrontation with Judd and attacked him."

He flips my hand over, swiping his thumb over my knuckles and continuing when he doesn't see any damage.

"I wish I was there for you when that happened or even afterward. I never want you to have to fight like that again, Dani. I don't know what caused it, but you have changed these past couple of months and it hasn't gone unnoticed. I want you to know that I'll do everything I can to protect you."

I can't figure out the inflection in his voice. It's somewhere between regretful and proud. Possibly a mix of both, but I let it go to answer.

"I punched him."

I don't respond to the rest. I don't know what to say. I want him to protect me, but he hurt me. Granted, it's all making sense now. To wholly depend on a man, that day will never come, but to have someone to rely upon and that will have my back when I am down.

Well, damn, that would be nice. Something I've wanted ever since he asked me about it on that back deck.

"After a very long and frank discussion, those are yours," he says, in a completely neutral voice as I flip my hand over. "Do you recognize them?"

I pluck them up by the ring and hold them in the air between us. They dangle in the wind, eliciting a tiny tinkling that reminds me of Anna's collar. The longer I stare at them, the more the realization sets in. A chill runs down my spine, not from the weather, but from knowing these are my keys.

The keys to the garage and my old apartment.

My old life.

The one that his lie took away and the one that he's restoring. I look at the warm chocolate irises beyond the silver keys and lower them, my fingers curling around the edges to ensure they are even real.

My lungs seize, forcing my breath into quick bursts as my pulse pumps against the silver metal burning in my palm. What did he say to get my keys from that old man? I thought he'd have to pry them from his cold dead hands from what Judd said yesterday. They are expanding and turning my apartment into a parts closet. Did Carl change his mind?

"I . . . he-he's giving me my job back? My old apartment?"

This is everything I want. I won, vindicated. He's choosing me over Judd. Righting a wrong and letting me move back in. Everything I want is coming back to me and yet, this doesn't feel like winning. I'm getting what I want, but I no longer want it.

Suddenly, panic snatches at my clear thoughts, muddying them into brown slush as I try to figure out what to do. How to give them back to Tomlin and say, thank you but no thank you?

I search every inch of Tomlin's stoic face until it cracks and a knowing smile peeks through.

"No. He can't give you what he doesn't own."

My heart is thundering a thousand miles a minute in my chest, my knee is back to bobbing, and I'm not following. I need him to spell it out. Just say it because I can't keep playing dot-to-dot with his truth bombs. I had some of my own, but hell if I can remember them now.

"What are you trying to say, T? Spill it already."

His hand sweeps down my pigtail, holding the end and giving it a playful tug while his expression is so loving I can barely breathe.

"I bought the garage. Your garage last night."

Blood rushes to my head, clogging my ears. His mouth continues moving as I stare at him.

He bought the garage.

He bought Carl out.

Carl's Timeless Classics is no more.

Gone. Over. The old man will finally hang it up in retirement, where he deserves to be, and Tomlin is the new owner.

"I must've hallucinated. I think you said you bought Carl out."

I scratch my head, my fingers tightening over the keys to where it hurts my hand. I know Tomlin would never lie about this. This is big. Almost as big as the one he confessed to and apologized for a dozen times already.

"I did. My lawyers are working on it as we speak, and the deed will be in your name."

His smile is beyond dazzling, and I'm stunned.

My name.

The place where I grew up. The place where Dad worked his whole life and sacrificed to raise me is mine. The very place I learned how to restore cars, the years of working like a dog, putting up with all the sexual harassment, the hostile work environment, Judd, Carl, and every memory of that place is now solely owned by me.

It's surreal. I can't even fathom what he's trying to say right now. I can't wrap my brain around it. Maybe it's too many truth bombs. Maybe it's the emotions from the last day or so. Maybe it's a lack of caffeine, but I can't believe what he's telling me. I stare at him in utter disbelief.

"I . . . uh . . ."

My hand reaches for his sweater to clutch the softness. If I wasn't already sitting, I would've fainted by now.

"How? Wait, is this part of the deal? Like take you back and then I get the garage or —"

"No, this is righting a wrong that I did to you. I don't want you to take me back because of the garage. The garage is yours either way."

His warm palm covers mine, both resting on his chest as he stares at me in earnest.

"I don't want you to want me for these types of things. And I know you never would. That's one of the things I love about you. You don't have an angle. You don't care who I am or what I do. It's unimportant to you. I want you to want me because of me and nothing else."

Love about you.

He said it before and he's saying it again. I don't know how much my heart and soul can take, but damn if this man isn't killing me slowly on this cliffside.

"You're right. I don't care about those things. I just care about you and that espresso machine," I croak, trying to get ahold of myself before I burst into tears.

"We can put one in at the garage if you'd like. But Dani, the garage is yours. Do with it what you like. Keep it and start your own garage like we discussed, sell it, or burn it to the ground. I'll help you spread the gasoline if that's what you decide."

The garage is scorched Earth, and maybe it should burn to the ground, leaving only ashes.

Those traitorous tears fall. How could they not with how he's looking at me with so much love? My heart is going to burst, but that dreaded shadow falls over his beautiful actions.

"But you lied. I don't know how . . ." I hate I keep coming back to it, but I do. Garage or no garage, I need to know what happens next. "How do I get past it?"

I know what I want. I want Tomlin. And I remember Eli saying that we would figure it out and eventually move past it somehow. But I don't even know the first step and I'm hoping he does.

"I earn it back, Dani. I will spend every day of my life earning back the trust that I destroyed. And I hope from today forward you will see it in everything I do. You before me, always."

The keys are smashed over his heart, with our hands covering it as a silent vow that he will uphold the truth in every way and every day.

"I've never forgiven someone before," I confess, wanting from the depth of my being to forgive him now. He gives me a reassuring smile and a bop on my nose.

"Then I'll be your first."

Another first. So many with him. Just like that, he's stealing my forgiveness virginity. I smile at him. Hope and love shove fear and sadness aside. This feels like winning.

"Do you really mean it about the garage? I can set up shop in Cañon City? Not Denver?" I ask, holding my breath. "What about retirement and all those offers?"

All those cans we kicked to get to this point. They seemed too big at the time to make any decisions, but they are still in play. His hand releases mine to cup my face.

"We figure it out together, life partner."

Life partner.

The words haunted me for weeks and now I know why. His answer quiets the demons of doubt and worry, releasing a new excitement and love within me for him. I don't want to lose myself in this man, nor do I want him to follow me into my world.

I want to meet in the middle and continue building on the life we started. A life that started with a lie and is ending with the truth. I smile, the rush of air from my lungs caressing his hands before I pull them from my face to move onto his lap.

"Did I ever tell you that's the hippiest dippiest term I've ever heard?"

The chair squeals under our combined weight while his warm hands cup my ribcage. I drape the blanket around us both, mimicking our cocoon where only our two souls exist.

"No, but you love it. Just as I love you, Danielle Louise Winters."

His eyes sparkle when he says the words I've waited to hear. With the sun peaking over the roof life of the hotel and glittering off his black hair, I say it too.

"I love you too, Tomlin. Now kiss me."

The End

BONUS SCENE #1

TOMLIN TAKAHASHI POV

She doesn't go to the garage right away. Not that I expect her to. One thing I know about Dani is she takes her time with major decisions since they are no longer forced upon her. Being a planner myself, I understand.

Considering everything that she has been through in such a short amount of time, I want to ensure I'm here for her and can provide a soft landing at the end of the day. The last thing I want is to rush her decision about the building that houses both her memories and nightmares.

I take the liberty of emptying the place of anything that can trigger her, especially Carl's office. Not that there is much left to salvage, there isn't. I have the moving company pack and index everything before they haul it to storage. I want everything off-site that reminds her of those despicable men.

That night at Pebble Beach, her world crumbled and her heart was destroyed by what I did. I knew I had to do this for her. Whether she stayed and forgave me wasn't a factor in giving her this building. It was the right thing to do. To right a wrong. It's not only my wrong to right but those two men as well. I don't know if she understands that, but I think she will when she sets foot in that place today.

Thankfully, she has forgiven me. It honestly scares the shit out of me to think I could lose her before I barely have her. It's right up there with losing my mom. Dani doesn't know how far gone I am for her.

If that girl walks out the door and never comes back, I'll be over. Worthless and destroyed. No amount of therapy can bring me back from that. I've been looking for her longer than she knows. I didn't fully acknowledge it until Tokyo.

What a shit show. It was an omen when they lost my luggage, causing me to be late to practice rounds. From there, everything slipped away, out of control, until I slept with my colleague.

Fortunately, Dani doesn't hold it against me. I have many regrets in my life. That night is one ranking high on my list of them. Lying to Dani is up there with failing to protect my mom.

She scared me many times on that trip. Running away, shutting me out, and staying in that head of hers. I've always treaded carefully with her. In LA, I pushed her out of her comfort zone and then waited to see if she would come back to me. She did, even though my heart raced every time I gambled on that tactic.

It seemed to be the only one that worked with her. Even when I thought I had her, having fucked and made love to her countless times that night, she was gone the next evening.

Hearing my lie, forcing me to face the truth, and laying it all at her feet for her to decide, is the end of this tactic. No more pushing and yielding. This is exposing myself and hoping she accepts me, lies, flaws, and all. And loving me.

Fuck.

That is a precious gift for her to give. I'll never fuck this up again. I'll walk the tightrope, have a racing heart, and hope she always comes back to me when she turns away to contemplate things.

I love that girl more than life.

"Can you go faster?" She scowls at the speedometer, conveying her desire to get this whole thing over with.

"Of course."

I kiss the top of her hand before releasing it to place on the steering wheel and speed up as requested. I invited Lars to attend today. She relies on him more than she admits. His exuberance and excitement may chase away the ghosts that still haunt that place in her mind.

Last night after I took her from behind and she lay sprawled on my chest, she told me it was time. Worry ruled those deep blue eyes as they stared at me for permission, acceptance, and understanding. I held her close, murmured how proud I was of her for being so strong, and reminded her if she wanted to set a match to the place, I had plenty in the outdoor kitchen.

She laughed. The sound caught in my chest and gripped my heart as no one had before. She murmured on the beach that my mom was number one. If she only knew, she'll always be my number one. She admitted I was her first love.

She doesn't know she's mine. I'll never keep a secret from her again. However, something about being each other's first love is so rare that I want to treasure it a bit more before I share it with her.

"Lars is already here," she whispers over the music she selects.

I park the Porsche in the same spot I used to when I came to visit her. She's not the only one dealing with flashbacks of how it all began, even if mine differs vastly from hers and are mostly cherished as the precious memories they are.

"That's good." I keep my voice neutral.

I am here, how ever she needs me, but it's her that needs to walk through that door first. I called Lars last night when she was beating the hell out of the punching bag in the gym. A recent development of her taking up working out to deal with some of the unresolved anger from her past. We discussed a general game plan for how this should go.

We both agreed that Dani needed to be the first one to enter that place and meander about to chase away some of her demons. Lars asked if he should attend at all, and I assured him it would be better for Dani if he was there.

"I guess it's now or never, huh?" She chuckles. The sound is as lifeless and vacant as the building before us.

That wall she kept up when I first met her and, for several months after, is sky-high right now. If that's what it takes to get through this initial step and on to the rest, then so be it. I'll kiss away the hurt every time this comes up and take great pleasure doing it.

“Whenever you're ready, baby,” I assure her, reaching for the keys that sit in the cup holder next to her and pressing them into her open palm. It's the second time she has held them and stared the way she is right now.

The morning on the beach she handed them back to me and hasn't wanted to see them since. I stowed them away with the other house keys until she said she was ready. On the ride over here from the cabin, she glanced at them more times than I could count, and I almost turned the car around preemptively trying to save her from this.

“Okay.”

She exhales, throws open the door, and gets out in a hurry as if wanting to get this over with as soon as possible. Whatever way she wants to handle it, I’ll be right behind her.

I climb out of the car and quietly close my door as she stands with her hand over her eyes, blocking the sun. It takes me back to that day when she threw out her hip and explained car restoration in so much detail, I might have fallen in love with her then.

The way those baby blues angrily flashed at me, the way she threw it back at Carl so easily, and the way she dragged her feet when she didn't agree, were some things that instantly drew me to her.

Nothing about her was proper. Nothing about her reminded me of the world I came from and grew up in. It's what enthralled me right from the beginning. She didn't give a damn who I was and made that known repeatedly. It's what made me realize she could survive my hectic world.

She surveys the place, noticing everything is clean, and the trash is gone. The grassy lot next door where my 'hunk of junk' was unloaded is mowed and trimmed ready for a fresh batch of cars. I had taken down the Carl's Timeless Classics sign, an empty shell awaiting her name, and installed a new black wrought-iron fence surrounding the property, including the new entry gate.

The thin glass windows that framed the storefront and the one that Dani broke have now been replaced by thick bullet-proof glass, one of many upgraded security features for this not-so-great area. Her safety is my utmost priority.

Having decided that she's seen enough, she slams the car door and walks past me to throw a hand up at Lars climbing out of his truck. He takes his time walking toward the front door as do I. His eyes move from me to her as she unlocks the door and throws it open.

It's not a split second later that she spins around to me with her hands planted on her hips and the fire in her eyes that I love so much.

"Where's the bell?"

I tilt my head, leveling her glare with my gaze and fighting a smile. Whenever this garage has come up in the last four weeks, she gets a ghostly, almost absent look on her face. This little show of anger is miles apart from that, and I welcome it.

"Bell?"

"Yeah, there was a bell above the door. Remember?" The front door silently closes, and she glares even harder. The edge in her voice is full of accusations. "Where is it?"

"It could be in storage, or they could have thrown it away when I had the place cleaned. But if you want a bell mounted on the door, we can get you a bell."

"Fine."

I stifle my amusement as she huffs and spins around to throw open the silent door. This is good. Very good. Lars joins me on the sidewalk.

"What's the big deal about a bell?" he asks, completely bewildered.

His long hair has been trimmed back, a suggestion I heard Dani tell him when discussing uniforms or something about setting an example for employees.

"It has nothing to do with a bell and everything to do with her embracing the pieces of her past that bring her fondness that she wants to replicate. It'll be interesting to see what she wants to keep and change."

"Ah," Lars mutters while opening the front door more carefully than Dani did.

I follow, taking the keys out of the lock before it closes behind me. Dani disappears to who knows where, and Lars pushes through the swinging glass door to the garage bays loaded with heavy equipment.

Gone are the stations that Judd pressed her up against. I made it a point to have those thrown out. The place needs a fresh coat of paint and new flooring, but I don't want to overstep beyond the clean-up and security measures. The bank of chairs sits along the wall where she held Anna against her boobs with blood splattered on her shirt, in her hair, and on her shoes while sporting a black eye.

I nearly had a heart attack when I saw her. Never did I expect to come home to a hurt Dani, and it took everything in me not to beat that guy to death. I should have done more that day when I saw Judd harassing her. I should have protected her that day, and I didn't. Another regret I harbor and another thing that will never happen again.

She appears in the darkened hall, having left Carl's office when she stops at the counter where we bickered over donuts and coffee.

"What do you think?" she asks, uncertainty crossing her perfect features.

"I think I should bend you over the counter for not sharing your donuts with me."

I flash her a mischievous look.

"What?"

Her nose wrinkles and then she realizes.

"Oh, you got all hoity-toity with the brown napkins. I'm surprised you didn't have those ripped out of the bathrooms when you cleaned this place," she says, leaning a hip against the very counter I'd like to christen.

The way she throws it back, makes me want to christen every surface, wall, and countertop of this place.

"Consider the brown paper towels, my bell, if you will."

She laughs, with a little more life in her, and I think it helps to have all three of us here.

"Maybe we could upgrade them to paper napkins, especially since you promised me that nice espresso machine."

Her eyes glint with determination as though I forget about her machine. Little does she know, I'd buy her so much more than an espresso machine.

"Sounds like an upgrade to this place already."

I walk to her, pulling at her wrist and placing it around my waist. She flashes a quick look to Lars, who's dipping his hands in and out of the machinery and too consumed to pay attention to us.

"He's preoccupied," I assure her.

"Good."

A little breath leaves her body as she relaxes into my embrace. She may think I'm trying to make out with her, and I always will, but this hug is to reassure her. Her pulse throbs against my hand at the back of her neck as she chews on that bottom lip.

"Have you been upstairs yet?"

Those endless blue eyes stare into mine. The instant panic is evident, and I give her another comforting smile.

"We don't have to go up there today. Maybe next time," I say, folding her into me. Her other arm snakes around my waist, clutching onto me as her lifeline. That feeling will never get old. "And if you never want to go up there again, that's okay too. It's all up to you, baby."

She adjusts her head, moving her forehead off my chest and replacing it with her cheek. Her finger tugs on my belt loop, the only sign she hears me as her breath fans my shirt. I kiss the top of her head and lie my cheek against it to be present in the moment with her.

This is a big step and a lot to take in. Something she won't get over today or anytime soon. What I learned in therapy is trauma unfolds slowly, doling out little pieces when we are strong enough to handle them and never really stopping.

Temporarily losing Dani brought up the same feelings as losing my mom, only worse. It's the continuation of my trauma from the past overlaid onto my new lover, making it twice as difficult to deal with. I'm faster at recognizing when it's happening and can correct my actions quicker. However, Dani is still in the process, and I'll help her every step of the way.

"This place is awesome." Lars comes barreling through the

door, brimming with excitement, and breaking us apart. I keep my hand on Dani's shoulder as she pulls away to talk to him.

"Ya think so?"

Her voice is light again, looking from him to me and back. She is haunted by what it used to be. Lars sees it how it could be. I just see her in all the ways she scoffed, scolded, and dismissed me. This place will always be precious to me. I hope one day it will be for her.

"Yeah. All those bays and equipment are ready to go. We could start on that guy's car tomorrow if it were here." Lars doesn't register the discomfort on her face. That's a good thing because, in his way, he's moving her forward. "When do you think we could open?"

She opens her mouth, closes it, and then both look at me.

"It's up to you. The occupancy permit has already been transferred, and we have insurance on the place. Perhaps interior and exterior paint and new flooring might be worthwhile. The sign company needs to come out and measure, but beyond that, a few weeks?" I answer when Dani doesn't.

Dani already knows this, having discussed all the things she'd like to do to the place when we flew back from California.

"That's no time at all," Lars says, looking around the lobby with a smile on his face. "What do you say, Dani? Ready to get back to it?"

"I don't want to use that office," Dani says, the vacant look returning.

Maybe we should have taken a match to this place after all. Let it burn down and rebuild it from the ground up.

"We could turn it into a break room. Put a small sofa in there, mount a television on the wall, and put your beloved espresso machine in there."

She nibbles on that lip, then switches to playing with the piercing I love so damn much.

"Put the computer out here on the counter. That way, you

could show clients the rendering of what their completed cars will look like. Possibly help them decide and such," I continue, hoping to chase away more of her ghosts when she stops toying with her piercing and nods her head.

"I like that idea," she finally says.

I let my hand slide down her back as she steps toward the entrance, cutting short the visit. When she pushes through the front door, she looks at the top of it and frowns. The missing bell still bothers her as she walks outside.

"Think she'll be okay?" Lars asks when he joins me, watching her gaze up at the missing sign.

"She racked me once, on the back stairs. I lost my footing and tumbled down a few of them before catching myself."

I turn to Lars. His eyes are wide, and his mouth is agape.

"Why?"

His face is expressive and a mask of confusion. He only had a glimpse of violent Dani, from what I heard of her punching Judd on the fairway. He never knew the girl that fought against male privilege her whole life.

"I called her babe."

I chuckle, the memory sharp in my mind.

BONUS SCENE #2

TOMLIN TAKAHASHI POV

Her knee bobs the entire way here after she peels her nails down to the nub and throws them out the car window. It took a lot of convincing, but she finally agreed to stay in the Denver house overnight. As long as I made her some of my famous spaghetti from the night I left her 'high and dry.' Her words, not mine. It's the easiest deal I've ever brokered with her.

"Do you want to talk?" I offer, casting a long look in her direction, hoping to draw her out of that introspective shell she's been trapped in ever since she got the call at the garage. The little memory box sits atop her lap the entire car ride from Cañon City to Denver and now to Fort Collins.

When I offered to place it on the floorboard behind her seat, her arms tighten over it as if I were about to snatch it from her. I merely leaned over and asked for a kiss. She gave me a peck and resumed gazing out the window. I tried to run as much interference as I could with her mother's husband, before finally agreeing to relay the information back to Dani.

He's an officer in the military, having grown tired of his wife's closed-off attitude when it came to a stepdaughter he never met resulting in the call to the garage. I wasn't there that day to intercept it, having commuted back to Denver to spend the week training for the upcoming Olympics.

Lars was there and calmed her down long enough to get her on the phone with me. I raced back to her side. Forced her to stay on the phone most of the time I was on the road from Denver, even when she wanted to get off and take care of a client's car. Thankfully, Lars blocked the doorway to the garage after his gentle encouragement failed to get her into the break room to talk with me.

Lars and I shared the same fear of her hurting herself by doing repairs while trying to burn off her rage. About thirty minutes outside of Cañon City, she hung up on me and I immediately called Lars. He confirmed she was upstairs boxing the punching bag she insisted we hang from the rafters of her old place.

That girl loves punching things, having gotten addicted to the bag I had in the gym at the cabin and insisted on having one at the garage too. It was but a week later that Lars was walking into the garage with a heavy bag over his shoulder, climbing the stairs to hang it. Lars and she are good friends. His laid-back personality and calm voice bring her temper back to par, faster than I can sometimes. Her temper and her toughness are two of the many things I love about her.

I've learned how to convert that temper into some explosive sex and that's how she prefers I calm her down nowadays. She calls it 'hate me sex', which makes me chuckle. Telling me to fuck her like I hate her and not to let up until she tells me to. I remind her that I could never hate her and oblige her, nonetheless.

"How much longer?"

There is uncertainty in her voice as she nibbles on her bottom lip, chewing it mercilessly for the last several days in anticipation of this meeting. She overpacks, unpacks, and then repacks twice for this weekend trip. It was her idea to grab a hotel room up here, even after I told her I would be more than happy to drive back home to Denver. She would not hear of it. I want to make this as easy on her as possible, considering this phone call out of the blue has shaken her to the core.

"About ten minutes."

She releases that lip to roll them together, a common thing she does when lost in thought.

"How are you holding up?"

I offer my hand across the console, and she wipes her palm on the front of her jeans before slipping the hot and clammy skin against mine. I click the air conditioning up a notch to make it cooler in the cab and watch as the vents blow her golden honey hair away from her heated face.

"I don't know, T. How should I feel?"

Her big eyes are deep blue water wells, so expressive and quick to show emotion. Another thing I love about her as they are both stunning and reflective of what is running through her mind. The fire she had in them the day she gave me a nipple burn with Kylie's memento box is something I had not seen before. Little does she know, she had my interest then.

"Well?"

She's asked me this question a half dozen times, sometimes truly puzzled, other times furious and resentful. The question that hangs between us now is looking for a consoling answer I am more than eager to provide.

"Hurt, betrayed, disappointed, confused, a plethora of emotions, baby. And it's okay if they switch in a matter of seconds. There's no right or wrong way to feel in this situation and if you run through a myriad of emotions trying to sort through all this, that's okay."

I have been through enough therapy to know I can help her with this. Having spent thousands over the years, I'm well prepared to be her therapist, her rock, or anything else she wants and needs me to be. Her hand loosens from mine as if needing it free to wave around while the words spill out of her.

"I feel all those things and more. Like how can she do this to me? How can she just . . . I don't know. Show up after almost seventeen years and decide that she's going to have some dude, I don't even know . . . says he's my stepdad, call me. Bro just says, 'Hey, your mom wants to meet'? Like who does that, T? And how is that fair to me? Like she's been gone. She hasn't been part of my life. Why show up now? And how incredibly selfish of her to say that she wants to see me now. Like she's the queen and just commands that we drive up here to her throne and see her. And what is so urgent now? And the thing that burns me the most, the thing I just wanna bitch her out to her face, is how could you do this to my dad? How could you have my dad get on that road to come to see her, and then he dies, taking him away from me when she was already remarried to another man?"

She's asked these questions before. Her mind runs a loop looking for new answers that only one woman has. The one who is sitting in a house with her military husband, hopefully as nervous about seeing her daughter as her daughter is about seeing her.

"And another thing, how am I even supposed to act? Am I supposed to be all nicey nice and just sweep all this under the rug or like water under the bridge? Hell no, that bridge broke, the logs washed away, and took the soil with it. There's no bridge left. Or do I go in there and be exactly who I am today and let her see what walking out on me and my dad did? Let her see the kind of person that I turned into because she couldn't stick around to be a mom to her daughter."

Everything she's feeling is fully justified. Her reservoir of anguish and pain is endless. I wait until those angry eyes flash at me, expecting an answer before I speak.

"There is no right way to handle this situation. It's a lose-

lose from the start. I agree the phone call is jarring. Her request to see you in person is even more so." I reach for her hand, dropping a kiss on her knuckles before intertwining it with mine again. "But I think you have a lot of questions that need to be answered, and that is the point of today. This might not be the only time you will need to see her. As you work through everything she has to say, you might find more questions and with that, I'd leave the door open."

I swipe my thumb across the back of her hand to let her know everything will be okay. Even if this all goes south, then she still has me and I'll more than make up for what she has lost.

"No, I'm never seeing her again after today. I'm going to make her feel guilty as shit, show her my dad's old love letters and then we're leaving, maybe burn her house down before going back to the hotel."

That is what I expect her to say, apart from the burning of her house.

"If that's what you want, then that's what will be. However, before burning anything down, decide what answers you truly need to know, as you may not get them all. Prioritize them if you will."

I give her a reassuring squeeze when I really want to turn this car around, race back to Denver and show her how much I love her in our bed.

"Yeah, well."

Those baby blues turn away from me again, lost in thought as she returns to looking out the window. Her knee never stops bouncing, only increasing in speed as the car slows to make the last turns into the neighborhood. When the navigation announces our destination is on the right, she looks as miserable as possible. Downright sickly, as if she's going to vomit right here and now. Once the car is in park, I gently tug on our hands, which gets her to look at me.

"Dani, whatever happens in there, I want you to know that you are my family, and I am yours."

I press my lips to the back of her hand, keeping them there as to infuse so much love into my gaze. She rolls her lips together and quickly nods, holding back the tears at the bottom of her eyes. She leans forward and tucks her chin for me to kiss her forehead while the tears fall on the console between us.

"I love you, T."

Seeing her so broken like this makes me despise her mother. I had tried to talk to the stepfather to see if he and I could meet, but he, or rather, she, wouldn't hear of it. That added to my anger. If she cared for her daughter and felt any emotion at all for her, she wouldn't be so selfish.

"I love you too, demanding Dani," I murmur against her forehead.

That silly nickname that started in jest in the penthouse gets her to raise her head. Salty tears track down her cheeks and a small smile appears on her lips.

"Promise me that you'll fuck the shit out of me when this is over with. Because all you've been doing is that cheesy making love stuff and sometimes a girl needs to be rammed from behind."

With our faces inches apart, I return her smile while wiping the stale tears from her blotchy skin. She's not wrong, though. Ever since the call, I have been very careful with her both in and out of the bedroom. The last thing I wanted to do was be demanding in any way, and that included sex. She may be truthful about wanting to get rammed, but I also know she's enjoying all the babying I've been doing.

"Let's see what happens and go from there."

"Fine. Let's get this family reunion over with."

Just like that, the badass girl I know, and love, is front and center. Ready to face the challenge even if she's still a scared little girl on the inside. She unravels from me at lightning speed to throw open her door and get out before I even have the car turned off.

While I'm busy collecting my keys and wallet, she's pacing the sidewalk, the box shoved into her side as a security blanket she's guarded for the last four years.

When I round the car, she's two steps ahead on the pathway leading up to the modest, government-issued housing. The house matches all the others in the neighborhood with a tidy yard, an American flag flying on the front porch, and a planter box under the front window. The door opens before she knocks, causing her to falter for a moment before she straightens her shoulders and glares at the man standing on the porch.

"Danielle, it's very nice to meet you. My name is William, but people call me Bill," he says with a calm smile while extending a hand to her.

His gray hair is thinning on top. His face is weathered from the sun, with deep lines around his mouth. His demeanor is more easygoing than I expected on the phone, but that could be for her benefit and her mother's.

"No one calls me Danielle. It's Dani," she clips, ignoring his hand. Yes, this is the girl that carved the D in my front door that I never fixed.

"Tomlin Takahashi." I accept his hand for a firm shake. "We spoke on the phone."

We discussed some ground rules, moreover my ground rules, the most important being, if Dani wanted to leave, we would, and all further communication would go through me. Lars agreed to monitor the phone at the garage since we've hired two more preservationists to free him up for more administrative responsibilities in advance of Dani accompanying me to the Olympics in a few months.

"Oh yes, come in. Come in."

He releases my hand to sweep it toward the open door and

empty foyer. If Dani's mom is here, there's no indication from the outside. My hand touches her lower back, wanting to reassure her that she can still turn and leave if she wants to. Her eyes bore into that dark foyer, even though her feet don't move.

It's a few long seconds before they shift to mine and with the smallest nod to me, she forces herself to follow Bill. The moment she crosses the threshold, she stops, turning in my direction, and I give her a reassuring smile.

"Say the word and we're gone," I repeat.

The same phrase I have said repeatedly as she wavered with her decision to meet her mother.

"No. I prioritize my questions," she says.

The hardness in her voice matches the same steely determination in her gaze. I'm proud of her for facing her fears and confronting the darkness of her past.

"That's my girl," I whisper, winking at her before she turns to head into the living room, leaving me to follow.

Bill stands in the center of the room while an older version of Dani slowly rises from an armchair by the window, awaiting our arrival. She's short like Dani, not as curvy, and much more demure, like a shell of her former self. She doesn't look at Dani, choosing to glance at her husband.

I clear my throat, the sound echoing in the otherwise silent room. Bill jumps into action by holding a hand out to his wife to guide her over as if the action is too difficult on her own. My chest brushes against Dani's back, a sign of solidarity and comfort. Dani grips the little memento box so tight that her fingertips are red, and her knuckles are white.

"Uh, Dani, this is your mom, Jessica," Bill says, making introductions. Her mother offers her hand, the polite thing to do, even if this is not a social call. Once again, Dani ignores it.

"Tomlin Takahashi," I say, shaking her hand. It's fragile and lifeless in mine. "I'm Dani's partner and spoke with your husband on the phone."

Not that I have any expectations of how this would go, but this is an odd start. It's painfully uncomfortable, making me wonder whose idea this meeting really was. Bill's or Jessica's.

"Danielle."

Jessica's voice is light and timid. Her eyes bounce from mine to Dani's before settling on Bill's.

"It's Dani. Not Danielle," Dani says, that steel edge in her voice hardening as if not seeing what I am seeing.

The life has gone out of this woman. With no idea what has happened, even the casual observer can see the loss of will here. It scares me, reminding me of my mother in the last year or so of her life. Dani's fiery temper is the opposite of this zombie-like void, and I'm so thankful she's my little spitfire.

"Why don't we all have a seat? It's been a long drive," I suggest, leaving the assumption out there that we drove straight from Cañon City.

"Yes, please," Bill says, moving from the center of the room to motion us over to a brown couch set against the far wall with a perfect view out the front window. "We also have lemonade and cookies, if you'd like some."

As Dani stomps to the edge of the couch, I skirt around the coffee table loaded with refreshments. Once we are all situated, Bill leans forward in his recliner, his forearms pressing into his knees with his hands clasped in the air between his legs. Her mother drifts back to the armchair that faces more outward than inward and seems to withdraw herself from the situation.

"We, Jessica and I, thought it would be nice if you—" Bill starts.

"Why did you leave, Jessica?" Dani demands, with so much venom that it shocks Bill and surprises me.

Years of heartache pour into that question. The room falls silent as her mother's hands shake, the only indication she heard her daughter as those empty eyes drift outside to gaze at the sunny weather.

"You're not going to answer me? We drove all this way for this?"

Those accusatory eyes turn to me first. When I open my mouth to answer, they turn to Bill, who looks from her to her mother and slowly shakes his head.

"Fuck this. I'm outta here."

Dani jumps off the couch in a second, two more and she tosses open the front door to slam it so hard, the picture window shakes. Yet, that still doesn't get a reaction out of her mother.

I rise to my feet, disappointment settling in, for I want my girl to get the answers she so desperately needs to finally deal with the tragedy that happened all those years ago. Answers to bring her to a conclusion, not closure. I learned long ago that closure is impossible.

"Bill," I say with finality, as I will never let them contact her again. "Jessica."

His shoulders slump and with a curt nod of his head, he agrees. Her eyes are unmoved from the glazed-over look while her trembling hands cup together in her lap. I walk toward the foyer and am eager to drive Dani far away from this place.

"Mr. Takahashi, can we talk in the other room?" Bill is on his feet and beside me before I reach the foyer. "I promise, I'll be brief."

I nod. An explanation of this situation is warranted, as I can share it with Dani on the drive back to the hotel. I follow him to a back bedroom off the center hallway and out of ear range of his wife.

"I want to start by saying thank you for bringing Danielle. I mean, Dani." His hand runs over his buzz cut, obviously not the outcome he had hoped for, either. "I thought maybe seeing her would bring Jessica out more, but that was selfish of me."

It is selfish. Selfish motives always hurt others far more than the selfish party. My temper climbs having lived decades with a selfish parent and enduring it. I sure as hell won't stand for him to do this to my girl.

"Why did you? What do you hope to gain that couldn't be achieved with a phone call beforehand?"

I let the same venom flow into my words as Dani did hers. These people intentionally gave her hope and ripped it away, in the cruelest fucking way imaginable.

"You insisted. No. Downright demanded she comes here, and for what? For this? Dani is not in the wrong. That woman in there destroyed her when she walked out years ago and again today. Your being an accomplice to it is repugnant and unforgivable. It's no wonder Dani burns with unresolved hurt and anger. It's justified in every way."

"I understand how you and she must feel, and I am sorry about that."

"No, you don't. You don't get to take the easy way out. Dani deserves far more than a zombie staring out a window. She deserves an answer to every question she has. She deserves an apology, at the very least. She deserves a mom that loves her, that doesn't abandon her with no explanation only to show up years later demanding to see her. Dani's right. Fuck this."

I can't imagine how Dani feels right now, but if it's one-tenth of the murderous rage vibrating my muscles, then I understand the desire to burn the house down. My hands clench at my side. The hatred I'm feeling now is worse than what I feel for my father since it's happening to the woman I love and adore.

"She had a stroke. Jessica did. It's been about four years now. It's why I called Dani's dad. We didn't know if Jessica was going to make it, and I wanted him to know. Wanted him to maybe tell Dani if she wanted to come to say goodbye."

Bill collapses on the bed, resuming the position he had in the living room but looking at his hands this time.

My pulse is still pumping at a feverish rate through my

veins, but I unclench my fists as I try to put together the timeline.

"Dani thought her mother was trying to get back together with her father," I start, the words coming as I sort through the events that Dani laid out for me the lonely night where I held her soft body on mine. I move further into the room, catching the door to close it because I have a few truths I need to tell myself on behalf of Dani.

"She doesn't say much about it now, but when she first told me about her dad passing away, she assumed it was for them to reunite. Apparently, her father was still very much in love with your wife at the time of his passing."

His head rises. A single tear runs down his face, dropping to the floor as his hands grip each other tighter. He looks down, nodding to himself as he puts the information I'm sharing with his own.

"I didn't know that he loved her," he rasps, glancing up. "I didn't know he passed away. I figured he backed out and didn't want to see her."

"I'm certain you didn't. That box out there that Dani is holding. It contains all the love letters he wanted to send her but didn't know where she went."

Lose-lose.

That's what I told Dani this situation was in the car and it's much worse than that.

"He died in a car accident outside of Denver. He had told Dani it was to run an errand for his employer so she wouldn't worry."

As I speak, it becomes harder and harder to tell him. Tears continue to fall onto the shag carpet, and the devastation on his face is clear. I stick to the absolute facts and do not disclose Dani's feelings of guilt or blame toward her mother for her dad's death.

My beautiful Dani is an innocent bystander to the hurt

caused by two people years before, just as this guy is now. He's picking up the pieces of Jessica's mess, and it shows. I roll my shoulders, trying to relieve the tension as I let out a long breath.

Bill grabs a rag from his pocket to clean his face and nose, before saying, "Her father said that he'd have to see Jessica for himself. That once he did, he'd decide on telling Danielle. I knew little about the guy. Hell, I knew little about Jessica before she got pregnant. We got married when we found out. She talked very little about her past, only that she was pretty wild back in the day, smoking and drinking and not ready to be a mother to a daughter down in Cañon City."

I stop squeezing the back of my neck and stare at him.

"Pregnant? As in . . . Dani has a half-sibling? That you and Jessica are raising a child?"

My skin heats as my mind races down roads I never thought we'd have to go down. She's an only child. I'm an only child. We have that in common. Now to hear she has a half-sibling living with the mother she never had.

"Christ."

I pace the room as he stands up to swipe a picture frame of a little boy from the dresser. The child has the same blonde hair and blue eyes as Dani. The likeness is remarkable, and my hand clenches to the point of hurting.

"That's Dylan. He's almost four. She had a stroke after giving birth. Doctors said it's not common but can happen. It's why I called her dad. If Jessica died, I wanted Danielle, sorry, Dani to know about Dylan."

His hand trembles as he looks at his son's chubby cheeks, smiling back at him.

"Now that I know about her dad, well . . . I guess she's run out of family other than us."

My glare levels him as his eyes raise from the picture.

"Rest assured, Dani has a family." She has me. To a lesser

extent, Lars, Isla, Eli, Ronnie, and Alex. That's enough family that cares more about her than this so-called family.

"I apologize. I didn't mean it like that. This is just . . ." His voice trails off, filled with sorrow and disappointment, as he puts the frame back on his dresser.

Like Dani, I don't know what to think about this situation other than here's a guy raising a kid alone while caring for his sick wife. The responsibilities on his shoulders are evident, as is the stress weighing heavily on him.

For once, I'm at a loss for words.

"I'm sorry. I don't know what I was expecting out of this," he concedes, having given up on his original objective that I can no longer find myself.

This is a damn mess.

I pinch the bridge of my nose, taking a moment to figure out the best place to tell Dani all this. I left the car unlocked, assuming she is waiting for me and expecting to hear a car horn at any moment.

"I've got to go, Bill."

I open the bedroom door, the silence of the house hitting me. I'd assume it would be louder with a child living here.

"I've got your number. I'll be in touch."

He doesn't respond. I walk down the hallway, past the living room where her mother hasn't moved a muscle toward the open front door. Puzzled that Dani slammed it shut, I cross the foyer to look outside when I see her sitting on the front porch holding a toy car in her palm and her brother is right beside her.

In the highest voice I've ever heard her use, she's pointing to the parts of the car and telling him the names. His stubby finger follows hers, trying to remember the words. When he gets one wrong, she points to the place on the car that matches his word and waits for him to say it again.

He says something I can't understand, and she laughs. Her

head falls back, and her eyes look to the sky as her carefree voice floats between them, eliciting giggles from him as well. Bill joins me in the doorway, a flash of surprise crosses his face as he watches them together.

Their laughing settles down when his finger points to her dad's box. Her face falls, the unabashed joy wiped away when she slowly places it on her lap and opens the lid. Her brother leans into the side of her body, his blonde hair matching hers when he rests his head against her shoulder.

She pulls out a dream catcher.

It's woven with browns and creams with feathers dangling at the bottom. She holds it toward the sunlight. The feathers blow in the gentle breeze as his chubby hands try to catch them. Her sun-kissed skin glistens in the light. Her smile is bright and easy, and her hair caresses her shoulders as the wind moves it. When those baby blues lift to mine, there is peace within them.

Turn the page to read Chapter One of Officer Hamilton's story in *Hamilton*.

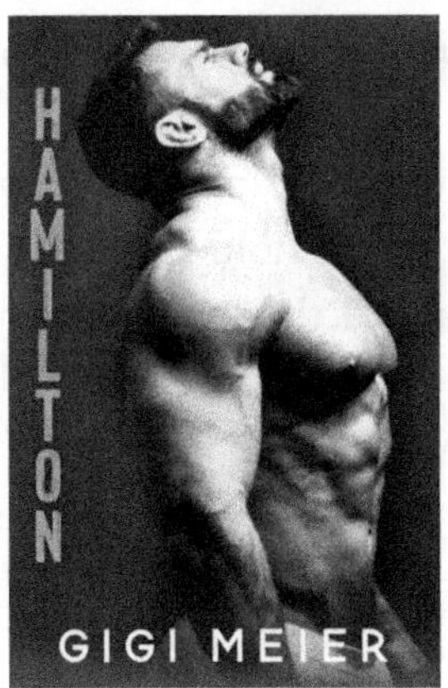

HAMILTON: CHAPTER 1

OFFICER HAMILTON'S STORY

"Dispatch to all units. We have a report of a robbery in progress at the 24-hour convenience store on 5th and Main. The suspects are armed and dangerous, requesting immediate back-up."

The radio crackles to life, jolting me from my thoughts on this cold and clear night. My heart rate spikes as I reach for the radio, pressing the button on the side for my transmission.

"This is Unit Three. I'm en route to the location. ETA five minutes."

"Copy that," the female dispatcher confirms.

I drop the radio into its holder before reaching for my seatbelt. Once it's fastened, I throw the car in drive, hit the siren and lights, and take off full speed down the highway, weaving past a few eighteen-wheelers.

Adrenaline pumps through my veins while I grip the steering wheel. Calls fly over the radio as other units race across the vast territory to get to the scene. Matt's unit took the initial call. Requesting backup is both a precaution and a precursor, the former I hope when dispatch tries Matt's radio and there is no response. No one on the force wants to hear the dreaded 10-999.

Racing off the exit ramp, I slam on my brakes and narrowly avoid a car changing lanes. Swerving into the right lane, I hook the corner and speed up. The engine revs under my foot, and the buildings whiz by on both sides as I barrel down the steep road. Glimpsing his squad car in the distance, I radio my arrival to dispatch. My blood runs cold when I see him crouched behind his open car door, taking on heavy fire. I angle my unit diagonal to his and duck for cover as the bullets tear into my car.

Matt is returning fire, giving me seconds to grab my weapon and open my door to join him in the melee. Peering over the window frame, there are two assailants inside the convenience store. One man is waving a gun and shouting at the cashier. The other is firing at Matt, who continues taking cover and shouting into his shoulder mic.

The noise is deafening, the wailing from customers trapped inside the store mixes with the sirens and gunfire. Sweat pours down my back as I survey the parking lot lights, how bright the inside of the store is, and the advantage we have. While Matt reloads I return fire, drawing the assailant's gunfire toward me. Shattering glass rains over me as he shoots out the driver's side window and I duck down behind the door, waiting for a chance to fire again. Blood surges into my head, my heart's beating outside my chest and my body is overdosing on adrenaline.

When the second assailant fires on us, I press my back into the car and aim for the parking lot light directly above me. Carefully squeezing the trigger, I shoot directly into the lightbulb, sending orange sparks through the night sky and drowning me in darkness.

I do the same to the light above Matt and hear him curse and then scream, "I'm hit. I'm hit. I'm hit."

"Fuck!" I grab my mic, hit the button, and yell that dreaded 10-999. "Hang on, Matt."

With us shrouded in darkness and the store lit up like a stage, I creep to the back of my unit. Rounding the trunk, I keep my gun ready as I sprint to Matt's side. He's rolling around on the ground, blood pooling from the top of his chest.

"Shit! I need an ambulance! Now!" I yell into my mic and tug on the top of his vest to pull him out of the line of fire. "Stay with me, man."

I kneel over him, checking the side of his neck and, thank fuck, his pulse is strong. I feel around for the top of his chest, searching in the dark for the wound when his blood squirts through my fingers.

"I got-got a . . ." Matt gurgles on his blood and this is fucking bad.

"I know, man. They are coming."

The hole is warm. The bullet is lodged at the top of his chest and the edge of his vest. I flatten my palm across the wound, applying as much pressure as he can take and feeling his fucking breath against my fingers.

"You're doing good, Matt."

He moans. His body wiggles and his legs flail back and forth. All good signs. I straighten as much as I can while keeping the same pressure on his chest to return fire until my gun clicks. Out of bullets.

"Fuck!"

More sirens scream into the night air as another unit speeds into the parking lot, followed by an ambulance. I holster my gun, reaching for Matt's weapon laying a few inches away when Rico flanks my hip, dumping his medic bag on the ground behind him.

"Where's he hit?" Rico asks, his voice tense.

"Upper clavicle."

He hovers over Matt's legs, searching up his vest to find my hand. When he grips my wrist and follows it down to the wound, we change positions.

"Matt, it's Rico. We're going to get you out of here," he yells, straddling Matt's waist and applying far more pressure than I was. Knowing that he's in good hands, I army crawl past them and keep my frame low as I get to the front of Matt's car.

Peering over the edge of the hood, one suspect is using the cashier as a body shield, yelling at the other officers who just arrived on the scene. The other fires through the broken window, taking cover between the aisles.

"Police! Drop your weapon!" the Police Chief yells over the bullhorn, his voice echoing through the bullet-riddled store.

The man holding the cashier startles, pointing the gun at the woman's head instead of at the police outside. For a moment, it seems like he is going to fire but must have thought better of it, realizing he is outnumbered.

"Hell no. You guys are gonna shoot me," he hollers, wrestling with the crying woman as she struggles against him.

I keep my eye on the other assailant nervously striding up and down the aisles without the same body protection as his friend. This guy knows he's trapped and is looking for a way out.

"Put your weapon on the counter and let her go," the Chief continues, his voice booming over the horn.

The first assailant hesitates, his gaze shuffling between his partner yelling at him and the officers' guns trained on him. Panic covers his face as he debates what to do. The Chief continues pressing him over the horn. His friend gets edgier, and I ease forward, crouching against the brick wall of the convenience store.

The first assailant slowly raises his hands, the gun clattering to the floor as the cashier runs to my colleague, waving her toward him. The suspect drops to his knees, his hands on his head while his friend yells a string of expletives and dashes toward the back of the store. I advance on him, jumping through the shot-out window and over snacks strewn across the floor to glimpse him barreling through the back door. His hoodie and ball cap block his face, but I make out a large snake tattoo on the top of his hand as his arms pump faster to get away from me.

"In pursuit of the assailant heading West on Main behind the shopping center," I shout into my mic, the radio crackling with shouted commands.

My hot breath comes out in white puffs, visible in the night sky while the cold air rips the sweat from my forehead. The assailant is fast for his size, putting more distance between us with each echoing step through the dark alley behind the center. My gun belt rattles as I run full tilt after him, the moon shining a path as he darts into the adjoining neighborhood, hoping to lose me.

The assailant's footsteps pound against the pavement, growing fainter and fainter as he runs away. I refuse to give up, willing myself to sprint faster and forcing my legs to burn with exertion. This isn't enough. I lose him on the deserted streets, jogging to a stop and surveying the row of houses to my right and the open clearing to my left. As I reach for my mic to call it in, a dog barks in the distance, garbage cans crash, and running footsteps signal his location. I take off again, rounding a corner, and the assailant disappears into the shadows.

"Stop! Police!" I yell.

He doesn't stop, breaking into a full sprint to scramble over a fence and disappear on the other side. As fast as I am running, I'm halfway up the wood planks and throwing myself over it to catch up to him. We hit the pavement with a hard thud, knocking the gun out of my hand to skid several feet away and sending a spray of dirt into the air.

"Get off me, pig."

The man reeks of weed. If he's high, it might account for his actions back at the convenience store. He twists, kicks, and wrestles in my hold, delivering blow after blow— fighting being subdued. The junk he's on gives him more strength than it should.

"You're under arrest," I start on his Miranda rights, knowing I'll repeat them when he's cuffed.

I use my weight advantage on him as we fight over the gun in his hand. He stretches it out of my reach, long enough for him to sink his teeth into my forearm and latch on.

"Fuck," I groan, punching the side of his head and trying to dislodge his jaw from my flesh. My legs clench over his in a wrestling maneuver I learned in high school. Neither of us is willing to give up.

"You have the right to remain silent."

He locks his jaw and I grunt, landing an even harder punch to his ears, eliciting a shriek and his teeth loosen from my flesh.

"I can't fucking hear," he screams into my ear, and I almost can't hear.

I turn him over, grabbing for his gun when a glint of silver catches the dim streetlight before his blade sinks into the side where my vest twisted.

"Shit."

I grind my teeth, the blade lodging in between my ribs and sending a radiating pain over my torso. My breath is harsh as I bear down, gripping the end of the knife and pulling it out. My head falls back as I shout obscenities at the star-lit sky and ram his face into the pavement.

"Anything you can say."

I pant through my clenched jaws, putting him in a chokehold while I try to get his hand tucked underneath us.

"Will be used against you in a court of law."

He throttles his head back, connecting with my jaw and rattling my teeth as my blood seeps under my vest and drenches my clothes. My temporary lapse causes a gap in my hold as he tries to break free.

He thrusts his back into my chest, forcing me onto my back long enough for that arm I am trying to get to brandish his gun. His eyes are crazy. Wide and wild as he spits on my face.

"You're gonna die, pig."

He fires the gun, the click loud in my ear as I roll us forward, changing the trajectory of the bullet. It tears into my leg.

"Fuck!"

I collapse, my hold loosening enough for him to slip away. Searing pain separates the flesh of my upper thigh. The gunshot is on the same side of my body where he stabbed me. The assailant aims his gun at me but then takes off, hearing footsteps pounding on the concrete near to us. I hold my breath, bearing down as I roll to my stomach and use my forearms to drag myself toward my gun.

"Freeze!" Rico yells, his gun drawn, running past me and ducking for cover as he exchanges gunfire with the suspect.

Bullets speed by as I cover my head. Rico ducks behind a car, firing back and then weaving up the street to get closer. The suspect is quick, but Rico is quicker. After getting a couple of hits in, the suspect goes down, cries out, and hits the pavement with a thump. His weapon discharges one last time as Rico and another officer approach, their guns trained on him.

I ease onto my arms, my gun still a foot away and the assailant isn't moving. Fuck. Rico's rushing to my side, shouting for an ambulance when my head falls to the concrete.

"It's going to be okay," Rico says, shoving a hand against my side that has me surging back to life. The pain is indescribable as the pressure threatens to tear into my internal organs. "Just hang in there. Help is on the way."

"Matt?" It's all I can muster past his fucking hand digging into my wound, trying to see how bad it is. My breath is labored as he applies pressure to my wounds in an attempt to stem the bleeding.

"Transported."

That can mean a lot of things.

I grit my teeth, my heart pounding in my chest and the adrenaline is wearing off as exhaustion and pain take over. As the minutes tick by, I feel my strength vacating my body. I pant, white puffs exiting my chest to dissipate in the cold air. A chill seeps into my bones, and I tremble on the pavement. My body is going into shock.

As I stare at the twinkling stars in the dark night sky, I think about one star. Not part of the constellation above, but in a world all her own. I never knew if she made it. I stopped looking long ago when her number was disconnected and I had no other way of contacting her.

Another ambulance races through the streets, the sirens wailing loudly as it draws closer. As the haze of excruciating pain and confusion takes over, I fight to stay conscious to enjoy the fantasy of her bending over me with concern instead of Rico.

As the paramedics rush toward me, falling to their knees on either side to administer help, I slip into unconsciousness, hearing a voice in my head that sounds like her.

"You're a hero, Alex. Never forget that."

Read the rest of Officer Hamilton's story in *Hamilton*.
(The Cañon Series, Book 3)

Alexander Hamilton, a second-generation law enforcement officer is deeply ingrained in the fabric of the law. Raised beneath the enduring shadow of his father, a steadfast small-town police chief, Hamilton's life has been molded by relentless scrutiny, exacting standards, and towering expectations. However, an unforeseen injury sustained in the line of duty thrusts him into a realm far darker and more illicit than his father ever confronted.

Amidst the outskirts of town, Molli Sitara finds herself entangled in the gritty world of illegal and illicit activities. The allure of quick money and easy access to drugs draws her into a life of loveless transactions. Yet, her reality takes a perilous turn when an ill-fated night brings her face-to-face with a formidable figure—Officer Hamilton. With his piercing green eyes and a tangled history, Hamilton's presence stirs up memories of their shared past, where love and passion were once shared.

As their worlds collide once more, Hamilton discovers that Molli is not only caught in the crosshairs of her own precarious choices but also targeted by a ruthless cartel captain and former lover. Fueled by a desire to safeguard Molli and driven by an unwavering commitment to justice, Hamilton must navigate the treacherous line between his duty as an officer and the growing passion he feels for his first love. Racing against time, he's forced to confront the shadows of his town, unraveling a web of corruption that threatens to consume everything he holds dear, all while protecting the one woman who has ignited his heart again.

Hamilton is a single POV, second chance, small town, forced proximity, cop/hero romance containing dark themes. Content warnings are available on the author's website.

Looking for steamy, naughty fun? Turn the page to read *Paolo*, the first book in my Cougars and Cubs Series.

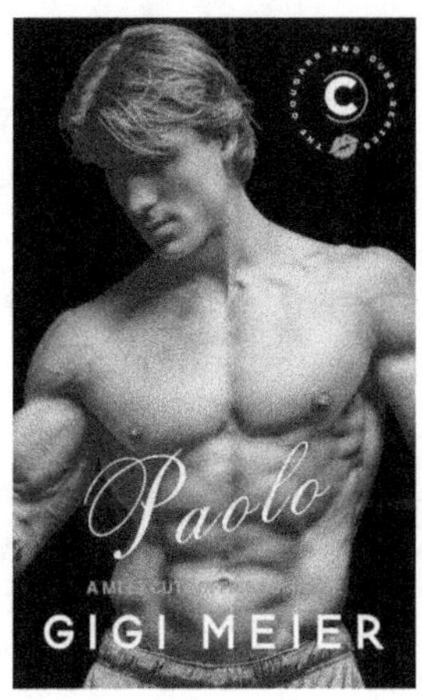

PAOLO: CHAPTER 1

PAOLO AND TAYLOR'S STORY

My fingers dance across the keyboard, basking in the afternoon glow that floods my corner office every Friday. The skyscrapers outside my window stand tall, silent sentinels guarding the bustling financial district below. This view used to fill me with pride, but now it's a constant reminder of the lifestyle that holds me captive. Golden handcuffs are what they call it. Making too much money to walk away and with too much work to feel accomplished at anything.

The clock on my computer marches toward 5 pm. The echoes of colleagues granting well wishes for a joyous weekend fill the halls as they escape out the door to their family and home lives, leaving the corporate grind behind. It's another weekend, another trio of lonely nights in my high-rise apartment, a routine that's become all too familiar since my divorce a year ago.

The moment I opened that bedroom door and saw them entangled on our bed, my world tipped on its axis. My heart shattered into a million pieces, and the pain was excruciating. In the aftermath, I became a different person. I threw myself into my career with an intensity I had never known before, hoping my success would fill the void the betrayal left behind.

There are days when the questions still haunt me. How did I miss the signs? How could I have been so blind in the first place? The painful days are few and far between, but the loneliness is almost daily.

My phone buzzes, interrupting my thoughts. Glancing at the caller ID, I see it's Chloe, my best friend and colleague. I chuckle because she's probably still in the office too.

"Hey, Chloe."

"Taylor, I just heard Williamson's charging down the hall like a dark storm cloud," she whispers through the receiver. "He's looking for you."

By Williamson, she means Theodore R. Williamson III. Firstborn son and current Chairman of the Board of the expansive investment house that bears the moniker of his grandfather. Rarely is he on this floor. Even more rare is that he's looking for me.

My heart rate spikes as I furrow my brow.

"What for? He never talks to me, not directly, anyhow."

He goes through my boss, the Chief Executive Officer, who's a stickler for following the chain of command and never stepping outside of it. When I glance across the glass offices, the CEO is already gone for the day, and his secretary is packing her bags to leave.

"I'm buried with the quarterly filing due in two weeks."

Before I can continue complaining to her, Mr. Williamson bursts into my office. His usually impeccable gray hair is in disarray, and his face is a roadmap of bulging veins and angry red splotches.

"Taylor, just the person I wanted to see," he barks with an open collar and his tie hanging askew. "We've got a mess on our hands."

I replace the receiver in its cradle and gesture toward the guest chair on the other side of my desk.

"Please, have a seat."

Mr. Williamson remains standing, slamming a thick folder onto my desk. It hits with a resounding thud, startling me.

"This is Mr. Jacobsen's file, our most lucrative client. He's been with us for over a decade and is threatening to leave."

I blink at the name on the folder. Jacobsen & Associates has been a loyal client for years. They have an extensive real estate holdings company in addition to their oil drilling and mineral rights leases. I can't fathom why they'd want to cut ties now.

"What happened?"

"He's furious about some miscommunication regarding his portfolio. He's been trying to reach Jim all week about some recent trades he took the liberty of making into volatile international stocks, which directly conflicts with Mr. Jacobsen's risk tolerance. And now Jim isn't returning his calls." Mr. Williamson's voice drips with fury.

Fucking Jimothy.

Jimothy is what I call him. It's a disparaging nickname since he doesn't deserve the respect of being called by his proper name, Jim. The man is nearly twenty-five years older than me. He is a narcissistic egomaniac who regularly cheats on his wife with the country club beer cart girls. He broods about the office like he owns the place and treats me as if we are not equals when, in fact, we are. Something I remind my male chauvinistic boss of all the time since he continues to let Jimothy run amuck.

"I'm sorry to hear that, sir."

I'm not. I hope this is the straw that breaks the camel's back in getting him fired since the last three hostile work environment complaints against Jimothy haven't done the trick.

"I knew you would be. Since you're the only one of my senior executives still here, I will need you to get right on it.

Familiarize yourself with his portfolio and trades, then be prepared to present your recommendations on Monday on how we save this relationship."

My stomach churns. My inbox is overflowing with emails, and my calendar is a cluster of back-to-back meetings. I don't have the time nor the inclination to handle this just because I'm still here on a Friday afternoon or to save Jimothy's ass yet again.

"Mr. Williamson. With all due respect, I'd love to help. As you know, I'll do anything for the good of the company. However, I have my accounts to handle, and I'm double booked with the quarterly filings due in two weeks. Perhaps another executive . . ." I crane my head to look back to the row of empty glass offices, knowing full well I'm the only one here. "Or perhaps Jim could come in this weekend and work on it. Since he's responsible—"

"Taylor, he's in Mexico on vacation with his wife."

"Oh."

I haven't had a vacation all year, prioritizing work over everything, even my well-being. Now I have to clean up the mess made by this rotten, scheming, and lazy bastard.

"It's settled then." He doesn't look pleased by my objection. That makes two of us. I'm not pleased either. "You'll present first so we can open it up to questions before proceeding with the regular agenda."

I hate Jimothy for this. And right now, I hate Mr. Williamson too. Mostly, I hate my loyalty to this company that goes unacknowledged and unrewarded.

"I'll get right on it and reach out to Mr. Jacobsen." I reach for my phone when his waving hand stops me.

"No need, I already did. Just see what you can find. Then we'll regroup before approaching the client."

He doesn't wait for my reply when he strides out of the office, leaving me alone to grapple with this situation. With an exasperated sigh, I pick up my phone and dial Chloe's number. She's always the one I turn to when work becomes unbearable, especially since I got her the job here.

She picks up on the first ring. "What happened?"

I lean back in my chair, feeling the weight of the world suddenly on my shoulders.

"You won't believe the mess I'm in right now. Mr. Williamson just dropped this colossal problem on my desk. Jacobsen & Associates is about to jump ship because of some disaster with their portfolio. And guess who's responsible for this disaster?"

"Who?"

"Jimothy."

Chloe lets out an empathetic groan. "Jimothy again? That guy is a menace. I don't know how he keeps getting away with things around here."

I shake my head, my frustration mounting.

"You and me both. I've had it with his antics. The guy must have glossy pictures on someone here because nothing ever happens to him."

As I sift through the mess on my desk, I sigh into the phone.

"I hope this colossal blunder will be the final straw that leads to Jimothy's long-overdue termination from the company. Maybe, just maybe, it's time for him to face the consequences of his actions once and for all."

She grunts in disbelief. "I doubt it. Nothing ever happens to him. Not even when the Head of Human Resources filed a complaint. You know she left because of him."

"I didn't know that," I murmur, flipping open the client folder. "But right now, I must figure out how to salvage this relationship. I am going to have to work late tonight and all weekend to sort through this mess."

"Taylor, you're overworking yourself." Chloe's voice softens with sympathy. "This isn't healthy. When was the last time you went out and had a little fun?"

I can't remember.

"I don't even know, Chloe. It feels like forever. But I can't afford to drop the ball on this."

There's a brief pause on the line before she speaks again.

"I get it. Just promise me you'll take some time for yourself soon. We can plan a weekend getaway or something. Maybe get laid. Oh, wouldn't that be nice? To find two hot guys to wine and dine us, then drill me into the mattress."

I manage a faint smile. I can't remember the last time I had sex either. At least no one since the ex. That's absolutely something that needs to be rectified once I get past these deadlines.

"Yeah, a wild and carefree weekend is long overdue. I'd like that, but after this and after my quarterly filings." I sigh for the third time as if the exhalation will somehow change my reality. "Anyway, I need to order my dinner since security won't let anyone up after 6 pm."

"Okay, call me if you need me."

I put the receiver down, pull the folder closer, and begin poring over the documents.

Fucking Jimothy.

Read the rest of Paolo and Taylor's story in *Paolo.*
(The Cougars and Cubs Series, Book 1)

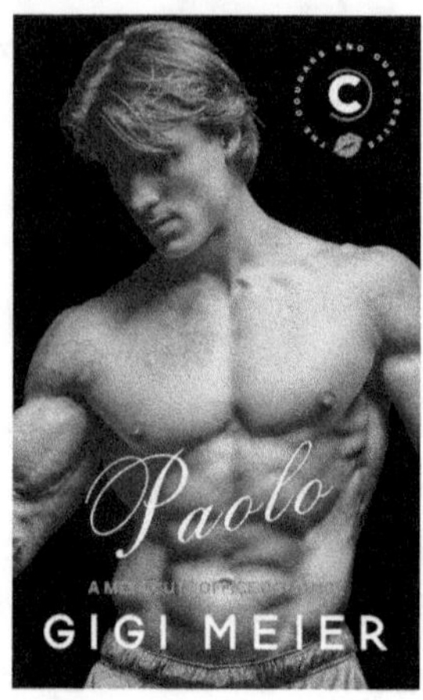

When a weekend fling turns into more . . .

In the heart of the bustling city, Taylor Woods, a seasoned executive, finds herself engrossed in an impromptu work project at an enchanting bakery, and her life takes an unexpected turn. There, she meets Paolo Cavallaro, a younger man whose magnetic charm draws her in. With a boldness that takes her by surprise, Paolo asks her to dinner that very night. Intrigued by the novelty of being pursued by a younger man, Taylor agrees, leading to a passionate one-night stand that neither can forget.

But when Paolo surprises her with a text inviting her for breakfast the next morning, their chemistry ignites a weekend fling that defies age and expectations. As their whirlwind romance unfolds, they find themselves caught in a corporate scandal that forces them into an unexpected partnership. Together, they set out to unmask the corrupt executives responsible for a possible company's downfall, all while navigating the complexities of their age-gap romance, meet-cute beginnings, and the irresistible pull of desire.

Embark on an exhilarating journey of forbidden romance, corporate scheming, and the unwavering strength of their connection. Follow Taylor and Paolo as their paths unexpectedly converge at a quaint bakery, setting the stage for a romance of undeniable chemistry and steamy encounters.

Can their blossoming love withstand the turmoil of the corporate world, or will the pressures of their demanding lives extinguish the flame of their fateful encounter?

Paolo is the first book in The Cougars and Cubs Series and is a connected standalone. It is a steamy, reverse age-gap, forced proximity, multicultural couple, office romance.

ACKNOWLEDGMENTS

To my beautiful Elle. Thank you for letting me bounce ideas off you when you probably preferred I didn't.

To my handsome Elkan. Thank you for understanding why I had to write in the car during long baseball tournaments to make my deadline.

To my sweet sisters. Thank you for talking up my books to everyone you know. I know you're proud of me.

To my old-fashioned mother. Yes, another shirtless man on the cover and I don't need to go to church to confess my sins. God already knows I'm a sinner.

To my furry colleague. Thank you for making me work pool-side on this book. I had to fight the cold, the heat, the humidity, the mosquitos, several wasps, and a startled opossum that played opossum when we locked eyes.

To my beta readers. THANK YOU to Emily Beath, Sally Williams, Sarah Cudlipp, and Sarah Hughes. You know this story wouldn't be what it is without your help! The more brutal, the better. That you to my lovely friend Sarah, in Vienna, for reading through my judo scenes to make sure they were accurate and for answering a bazillion questions about the sport. 🖤

To my readers. THANK YOU. Thank you for loving Dani and Tomlin as much as I do! Thank you for going on the journey as their stories unfolded slowly and methodically so you can see how deep their trauma runs and how it affects their lives. I love all the messages and comments I receive rooting them on and hoping that love wins. Spoiler alert, love always wins in my books. 🖤

To my editor. THANK YOU for catching and fixing all my errors to ensure the conclusion to their story is as special as intended. You're the best!

ABOUT THE AUTHOR

After retiring from a thirty-year career in corporate America, GiGi Meier is delighted to be writing romance novels about strong female characters and their complicated, swoon-worthy men.

She loves telling stories and figuring out why her characters do what they do. With heartbreaking angst, panty-dropping lust, and enviable love, her stories linger long after you close the book.

When GiGi is not eating over her laptop, she likes to spend time in the pool with her children, walk her furry babies, and film videos for Instagram and YouTube. Whether attending a book club or hosting a game night, she loves connecting with new people and making friends.

www.gigimeier.com

Books by GiGi Meier:

Standalone Book
Coyote
Sammie and Carlos's forced proximity
cartel, kidnapped, Military hero, dark romance

The Cañon Series
Tomlin
The start of Dani and Tomlin's
slow burn, enemies-to-almost-lovers
Tomlin Takahashi Duet #1
The Cañon Series, Book #1

Takahashi
The conclusion of Dani and Tomlin's
friends-to-lovers, happily ever after
Tomlin Takahashi Duet #2
The Cañon Series, Book #2

Hamilton
Hamilton and Molli's second chance,
small town, police officer romance
The Cañon Series, Book #3

Isla
Isla and Gabe's opposites attract,
age gap, forbidden love romance
The Cañon Series, Book #4

The Cougars and Cubs Series
Paolo
Taylor and Paolo's reverse age gap,
forced proximity, office romance

The Cougars and Cubs Series, Book #1

Sebastian

Sebastian and Chloe's reverse age gap

Opposites attract, Christmas romance

The Cougars and Cubs Series, Book #2

Giovanni

Giovanni and Kacie's reverse age gap

Protector, Alpha male romance

The Cougars and Cubs Series, Book #3

Kadus

Kadus and Bex's reverse age gap

Best friend's brother, rockstar romance

The Cougars and Cubs Series, Book #4

IF YOU ENJOYED THIS BOOK

Thank you for reading *Takahashi,* the second book, and the conclusion of Dani and Tomlin's love story. Stick around, you'll see more of them in the rest of the Cañon Series.

If you enjoyed it, please consider leaving a review on BookBub, Goodreads, or your favorite retailer to let others know about this cute and feisty couple.

Reviews are greatly appreciated!

They help independent authors, such as myself, get our books in front of more readers.

Check out my website for deleted or bonus scenes not found in the book.

https://www.gigimeier.com/freebies

HOTLINES FOR HELP

Help for Suicide Prevention and Crisis Lifeline:

- Call 988
- TTY: Dial 711 then 988.
- Visit: **https://988lifeline.org/**
- Live Chat: www.1800runaway.org

Free and confidential help to prevent suicide. The Lifeline provides 24/7, free and confidential support for people in distress, prevention and crisis resources for you or your loved ones, and best practices for professionals in the United States.

Help for Victims & Survivors of Domestic Violence

- National Domestic Violence Hotline
- Call 1-800-799-SAFE (1-800-799-7233)
- TTY: 1-800-787-3224
- Live Chat: www.thehotline.org

Free and confidential help is available for victims of domestic violence 24 hours a day. If you need help or just want someone to talk to, please call the National Domestic Violence Hotline at: 1-800-799-SAFE (7233) or TTY 1-800-787-3224. As a survivor of domestic violence, your safety is at high risk when you leave an abusive relationship and right after you make that decision. It is important to work with a domestic violence advocate to develop a safety plan. Advocates can help you develop a plan for emergencies, connect you to community resources and discuss your options. For additional information on accessing help and resources, read Getting Help with Family Violence.

- National Resource Center on Domestic Violence
  - Call 1 (800) 537-2238

- National Indigenous Women's Resource Center
  - Call 1 (855) 649-7299

- Battered Women's Justice Project Criminal and Civil Justice Center & National Clearinghouse for the Defense of Battered Women
  - Call 1 (800) 903-0111

- National Health Resource Center on Domestic Violence
  - Call 1 (888) 792-2873

- National Center on Domestic Violence, Trauma & Mental Health
  - Call 1 (312) 726-7020

- Resource Center on Domestic Violence: Child Protection and Custody
  - Call 1 (800) 527-3223

- Asian Pacific Institute on Gender-Based Violence
  - Call 1 (415) 568-3315

- National Latin@ Network of Healthy Families and Communities
  - Call 1 (651) 646-5553

- Ujima, Inc.: The National Center on Violence Against Women in the Black Community
  - Call 1 (844) 77-UJIMA (844-778-5462)

- Expanding Services for Children & Youth Exposed DV Technical Assistance Futures Without Violence Children's Program
  - Call 1 (617) 426-8667

- National LGBTQ Institute on Intimate Partner Violence
- Call 1 (206) 568-7777

www.ingramcontent.com/pod-product-compliance
Lightning Source LLC
Chambersburg PA
CBHW072254020726
47501CB00002B/264

* 9 7 9 8 9 8 7 7 3 3 6 3 9 *